SALISA K. GARRAND

The Weight We Carry

To anyone who has ever been told they're too much, or feared they're not enough... this one's for you.

"Owning our story and loving our-
selves through that process is the
bravest thing that we'll ever do."

- BRENÉ BROWN

Foreword

Author's Note

This story means so much to me. I wrote it for the younger version of myself who felt like she was too much and not enough all at once (until she found her Hunter). *The Weight We Carry* is about healing, vulnerability, and second chances. It's about finding love when you've convinced yourself it's not meant for you. It's messy and tender and full of the kind of hope that sneaks up on you when you least expect it.

Trigger Warning

This book touches on some heavy topics, including abandonment, family trauma, intimate partner violence (off-page), substance abuse (off-page), and mental health struggles. I've done my best to handle these themes with care and honesty, always through the lens of resilience, growth, and love.

Please take care of yourself while you read this and know that it's okay to pause, to skip, or to come back when you're ready.

If you are ever in crisis, please reach out for support or visit your nearest emergency room. The Crisis Text Line offers 24/7 support via text by texting "Home" to 741741.

Acknowledgments

To the readers who found this story: thank you for choosing it, for feeling it, and for staying through every hard-earned moment.

To my family and friend: thank you for standing beside me through my own journey with trauma and for supporting me as I found the courage to tell this story.

And to my beta readers: thank you for your time, your insight, and the care you poured into these pages.

Thank you for finding this book.
Thank you for staying.

Love, Salisa

Chapter One

Camille

I wasn't even supposed to be on the dating app.

Technically, sure, the app was on my phone. But that wasn't really on me. I was knee-deep in laundry, hands full of mismatched socks, while my best friend Dani perched on the counter, legs swinging, her grin all mischief and trouble.

"Your love life is pathetic," she declared, eyes glinting as she spoke.

I frowned, tossing another shirt into the basket. "Okay, girl. It's not that bad," I countered, half-heartedly.

"And what about those lovely 'u up?' texts from guys who should've lost your number months ago?" she teased, brandishing my phone as if it were a sword.

I rolled my eyes. "Point taken."

"Exactly. You deserve someone who isn't allergic to commitment." With a flourish, she swiped through the dating app she had just installed. "If you won't get out of the house and date, then the men can come to you. Swipe, woman."

I rolled my eyes, but I didn't delete it. Maybe I should have, but the ache of exhaustion was louder than resolve. Letting things linger felt less painful than mustering the energy to care. Even apathy came tinged with disappointment.

Two weeks later, and still, nothing had changed. The apartment felt claustrophobic. The week smothered me. My thumb, aching now, traced through endless profiles, each swipe a small resignation. Swiping was muted background noise: a quiet, repetitive no, not this one, not today.

Our apartment wasn't glamorous. Two bedrooms housed four people's lives. The worn couch, prone to squeaks, felt as familiar as my favorite slippers. The aroma of reheated coffee threaded through the air, grounding us in a comforting ritual. Despite its disarray, it was ours, a sanctuary where laughter offset the clutter. Laundry baskets overflowed, colors spilling into corners. Cartoon jingles looped in the background, relentless and tinny, broken up by squeals and the sharp, bright shriek of a child's delight. Cramped, messy, chaotic. But every sound, scent, and object was a thread in our story. It was home.

Zeke, my five-year-old, had already transformed the living room into a Lego battlefield. He hummed the Paw Patrol theme under his breath, curls bouncing as I tried to dodge the sharp plastic mines scattered across the carpet. Across the room, the twins, Avery and Chloe, held court in their high chairs. Avery was banging her spoon like she was auditioning for a heavy metal band, while Chloe smeared mashed banana across her tray with the flair of a modern artist.

They were the very beings that kept me going on weeks like this. Zeke's clever eyes sparkled every time he thought he was being sly, and the girls, identical with chubby cheeks and wide brown eyes, were impossible to tell apart unless you noticed the tiny freckle on Avery's cheek. They were still in the stage where every discovery: spoons, books, even their own hands, was a miracle. It was chaotic and loud, yet it was somehow still the one thing that filled my chest with aching gratitude. Maybe that's why swiping through strangers felt jagged, unfitting. Who would see the beauty in this wild circus? Who would stay?

Then.

Him.

The profile picture stopped me cold.

The first thing I noticed was his blue eyes, bright with a grayish undertone, staring back at me from the series of pictures I scrolled through on my phone screen. Each photo seemed to tell a different story, and I was sitting on my couch, trying to piece them together like a puzzle. His light brown hair was cropped short, neat in a way that said he cared without trying too hard.

One picture showed him in a Marine Corps uniform, jaw set, clean-shaven, posture sharp enough to cut. He looked like someone who knew how to hold himself together, who carried discipline in his very bones. Yet, beneath that stoic presence, there was a hint of warmth in his eyes, suggesting compassion and an underlying gentleness. Despite his polished appearance, I noticed the scuff marks on his boots in a group picture, a small reminder that even the most disciplined lives aren't immune to wear and tear.

The next photo was a contrast: T-shirt and jeans, laughter caught mid-breath. His muscles pulled at the sleeves, broad shoulders filling the space. Strong. Solid. I couldn't help picturing how it might feel to lean into those arms, to have that kind of strength wrapped around me. Heat crept up my neck at the thought, quick and uninvited.

Another photo: sand and sky stretching behind him, a landscape that could only belong to a desert far from here. He stood in full gear, helmet in place, grinning widely with his squad. The smile was different, edged with grit and a kind of camaraderie. My chest tightened because beneath that grin, I could almost see it, the shadows of where he'd been.

And then, a photo in a suit. Suit crisp, tie loosened, a reddish beard trimmed close along his jaw. His hand rested under his chin like he was half-bored, half-amused. That look hinted at trouble. Not the kind that ruins your life and maxes out your credit cards. The fun kind. The kind that makes your stomach flip and has you grinning into your pillow at night.

Each photo showed a piece of him. The Marine. The friend. The man who laughed easily. The one who looked like he'd keep your secrets but tease you mercilessly anyway. And through each image, a feeling fluttered in me, much like a butterfly softly landing, something I hadn't felt in years.

I stared at the pictures, breath caught somewhere between hope and disbelief. Men like him didn't date women like me, my mind whispered. I was twenty-five, five-foot-two, and wore whatever I could find that fit, which was usually a pair of leggings and a clean shirt. I had three kids under five. A job at a doctor's office that paid mostly in gratitude. Student loans stacked high, reminding me I was still trying to become someone who helps others carry pain. On paper, I was a noisy, adorable circus, with psychology exams looming. Not the kind of thing that stopped a man in his tracks.

But underneath, the fears ran deeper. A low hum of anxiety warned that my heart couldn't take another break. The echo left by old loves haunted the edges of my days. I worried my life, with spilled cereal, frantic school runs, tired glances in the mirror, couldn't fit the kind of romance that existed in movies or late-night novels. I was guarded. It wasn't about being worthy of love. It was about finding my way through self-doubt, balancing chaos, and daring to hope when everything in me said not to.

So, because I felt like taking a risk, and maybe because my heart had other plans, I swiped right. Half as a joke, half because something in me had started to thud, quiet and insistent.

"Oh no!" I told the empty room, dropping my phone. Then the app glowed: *Match! Send a message to Hunter*, and I remembered the rule: I had to send the first message. Why would Dani sign me up for this? For someone who'd survived everything I had, being expected to make the first move felt like a tiny battle.

My thumb hovered. I typed without thinking, the words embarrassingly simple, and immediately regretted it.

> *Me:* Hey handsome, how's your day going?

I hit send and immediately wanted to crawl under the couch, hide from my own boldness.

I tossed a toy off the couch and sank into the cushions, phone pressed to my ear, before the spiral could start. Dani always knew how to talk me down, how to make the world feel a little less heavy. We've been inseparable since high school, when we both joined the cheer team, finding trouble and laughter in equal measure. I can still see us crashing the school dance, Dani grinning as she sweet-talked the DJ into playing our song, the two of us spinning wild and free while the crowd clapped along. Our principal wasn't amused, but it was worth every second. When I found out I was pregnant with Zeke, Dani slipped into the role of fun aunt without missing a beat. She came to every ultrasound, held my hand, and made the waiting rooms feel less lonely. She still shows up for the kids and me. Her own life runs on caffeine and case files, late-night strategy calls, and early-morning hearings. She's built for the pace. She's sharp, vibrant, a person who can light up a room and still win an argument before 10 am.

After I embarrassed myself again by telling her about my message, she teased me about it, saying I should run all my wild ideas by her first. She makes everything lighter, easier. I love her for that. We hung up quickly, her laughter still echoing as she slipped off into whatever adventure was waiting for her next.

Five seconds later, the typing dots appeared. My stomach twisted, anticipation and dread tangled together. Of all the possible responses: boring, weird, creepy, what would he choose?

Hunter: Hey Camille. Day's been
   long but better now. How about
   yours, Beautiful?

The word landed softly and unexpectedly bright.

My mind went quiet, which seldom happens. For twenty minutes, I stared at the screen, overthinking my response. He was easy to talk to from the start, funny without trying, asking genuine questions about my classes, about my ridiculous late-night snack preferences (Twinkies, of course). He asked about my dreams, not my baggage. That felt like a foreign language.

But the walls were still there, thick and a little sore. Men had come and gone, promises stacked up like forgotten books. The man who left took more than his clothes. He took my trust, my quiet belief that anyone could stay. He left fingerprints on my map of the future, then folded it up and walked away. Still, I was learning to heal, one small step at a time. Some days were harder than others, but every new conversation, every tiny risk, chipped away at those walls. Folding a shirt, listening to Zeke's sleepy voice from the other room, I tried to smooth out the creases in both the fabric and my thoughts. The soft chatter, the warmth of cotton in my hands, anchored me. Tidying up, setting small things in order, was my way of taking back a little control.

So when we exchanged numbers and he asked me out after three days of messages, he didn't take my attempts at pushing it off as rejection. Nope. He didn't ask once and let it be. It was almost like he saw it for what it was, fear. He sent me a picture of his dinner attempt, captioned comically, "I might need a taste tester. Free tonight?" Another message arrived with a snapshot of a sunset, "Thought you might like this. My offer stands, by the way." It was the little jokes, the moments shared through pictures, the way he seemed genuinely interested in the details of my day that made it harder to keep saying no. I made up an excuse, easier to stay tucked inside the safety of my routine, wrapped in the familiar chaos of home, where no surprises were waiting for me. Each 'no' felt like another layer of protection. But it wasn't about a date to me; it was about dipping a toe into vulnerability, choosing the unknown over the comfort of safety. There was something in his persistence, his patience, a promise of laughter, a glimmer of hope, that made me want to try.

That night I watched my kids sleep: Zeke clutching a plastic dinosaur, the twins turned the same way, shared in their small-sibling ordinariness. I kissed each forehead, whispered my usual prayer, *Please let me get this right*, and sat in the kitchen with the light over the sink on and my phone warm in my hand.

Hunter: Goodnight, beautiful.
  Sweet dreams.

I grinned despite myself. *Careful*, my inner voice warned. He probably would, like most people, find the constant whirlwind of our lives a little too loud. The house was messy, my life louder than most, and yet there, at the table under the cheap lamplight, the hum of the refrigerator filling the quiet, I felt seen in a small, terrifying way. Maybe that was the point. Maybe I could be messy and tired and still be wanted. Or maybe I was setting myself up to be hurt again. Hope and fear, tangled together, both refusing to let go. I turned the phone face down, unwilling to watch the tiny hopeful flame flicker out in real time.

Chapter Two

Hunter

Since getting out of the Marine Corps a little over a year ago, I mostly kept to myself. Just a few dates here and there, nothing that stuck. I'd rather spend time with my buddies, grab a beer, work on my bike, than sit across from someone who spent half the night scrolling their phone and the other half pretending to care. The loneliness sneaks up sometimes, hitting harder than I'd like to admit. It brings back the weight of things I don't talk about, a silence that seeps in and stays. The reminder that people leave when you fail to hold it together.

Still, it's easier than the empty kind of company that reminds you what it feels like to be forgotten while someone's sitting right next to you. So while I found myself on a dating app, I knew I wasn't chasing anything serious. At least, that's what I told myself when I came across her profile a few days ago.

Her smile was unguarded, warm, and effortless. No filters, no angles practiced in the mirror. Just a smile that made me want to lean in and ask what was so funny. Her eyes were deep brown and kind, holding a quiet resilience I recognized from my own rough seasons. I was caught before I even knew it. Her curls tumbled around her shoulders, the California sun catching her in a way that made her glow. I studied the images, hope and nerves rising in my chest, not sure what it was about her that felt so different.

Another photo: her with a friend, arms thrown around each other, laughter spilling out, faces tipped to the sky. Her friend, a taller blonde, might've been the one who stood out first, but it was Camille who pulled me in. There was warmth in her olive brown skin, light in her eyes, something real that didn't try too hard. I wondered if I was getting ahead of myself, but the idea of swiping past her felt impossible.

The third photo was cropped close, showing a kid's birthday party in the background, with presents stacked behind her. Still, her smile was easy, unbothered, as if she wasn't trying to hide the raw parts of her life. Most people curated their stories in sunsets and brunches. She let it be there, like the mess was part of her story, and she wasn't ashamed of it. That alone told me more than words could.

Nervousness wasn't the usual concept for me, but I felt nervous at the thought of meeting someone so genuine. She was beautiful, sure, but it wasn't just that. It was the way her smile felt honest, the kind of thing you could chase for a long time and still not get tired of.

By the time I realized I was smiling back, my thumb was already moving. No hesitation. No way in hell I was letting her slip by.

A few minutes later, a message lit up my screen.

Camille: Hey handsome, how's your
    day going?

I stared at the message for a minute, grinning. She might've thought she sounded awkward, but to me? It was solid. No games. Straight to the point.

Me: Hey Camille. Day's been long
        but better now. How about
            yours, Beautiful?

The first time I asked her out, she said she was busy. The second time, she had school. The third time, she was stuck at work. "Maybe this weekend," she'd type, and I could almost hear the hesitation between the words.

Most guys would've stopped asking. Hell, I would've, if it were anyone else. I had my pride, and I wasn't in the business of begging anyone for their time. But this wasn't begging.

Late at night in the garage, the smell of oil and gas in the air, I worked on my bike. Every turn of the wrench helped clear my head. My phone sat on the bench, screen lighting up with her chat. She laughed at my jokes, actually seemed to care if I was alright. She sent pics from work, her textbooks laid out on a coffee table, her in scrubs, and it made me grin every time. There was something about Camille that made me want to keep pushing. Maybe she was worth taking another shot.

So I asked again, but this time I switched up my tactics.

Me: Alright, Camille. You keep dodging
        me. So here's the deal...FaceTime.
        Tonight. Ten minutes. No excuses.

Camille: What if it's a valid excuse?

> *Me:* Only valid excuse is death. Since
> you're texting back, you're very
> much alive. So no excuses.

I smirked at the screen, already hearing her laugh in my head, already picturing the way she'd roll her eyes but secretly smile.

For a minute, nothing came. Just the three blinking dots, her hesitation stretching long enough that I tapped the side of my phone as if I could will her answer out faster.

Finally, the message lit up the screen.

Camille: You're ridiculous. But fine.
  Ten minutes. If I look like death,
  it's on you.

I read that line five times, a grin spreading so wide my buddies gave me shit for it, but it didn't matter. I'd waited for firefights longer than this. I could handle a few 'I can'ts'. Because the second she said yes, I knew she'd be worth every single one.

Chapter Three

Camille

I prepared myself for the call, considering the advice Dani had given me as I ran around, scrambling to make myself presentable. *"When in doubt, smile, you'll distract him from whatever craziness comes out of your mouth."* It was relatively unhelpful advice, but that is what I planned to do.

The screen flickered, and there he was. Blue eyes, brighter than any photo could have captured. Ginger beard, fuller than the clean-shaven shots he'd posted. My first thought wasn't fair. No one should look better on FaceTime than in their carefully chosen profile pictures. My second thought was worse: *I can't keep my eyes off him.*

I tried to play it off, angling the phone so the lamplight wouldn't catch every tired line on my face. My reflection stared back, curls twisted into a loose bun, dark circles louder than anything I could say. I almost wished I hadn't answered. I decided to put my degree in psychology to work and redirected my anxiety. Deflection would suffice here. I found my voice, tilting my head. "You know, I think this technically counts as catfishing. You lured me in with Mr. Clean-Shaven Military Man, and now here you are, rugged mountain man with a ginger beard."

His laugh was low and easy, warmth settling somewhere deep within me. He leaned back, the light catching the copper in his beard. "Catfish, huh? Should I be offended?" His voice teased, soft and sure, washing over me.

I bit the inside of my cheek, fighting the smile that wanted to give me away. "Not really. Turns out I don't mind at all." My gaze lingered on the scruff, how it softened him, made him look less polished, more real. *Too real. Too good. Too close to dangerous.* "You wear scruffy well."

The grin he gave me should've been illegal. "Glad you approve, Beautiful." His voice dipped just enough on that last word to make my pulse skip. "And for the record, I wasn't lying. I don't take pictures often. Those were… older."

Beautiful. The word echoed in my mind, unexpectedly heavy. He didn't toss it out the way people do with pet names; he meant it, called me that like a fact. I felt exposed, uncertain how to receive it. Why does this word feel like a risk? I touched my hair, trying to steady the nervous flutter in my stomach, unsure of what to make of things.

"Older, like six months?" I teased.

He rubbed the back of his neck. "Try a couple years. From before I got out. I don't like pictures, never really did."

I remembered his texts from a few nights ago, the way he'd said it so simply. *I'm not active duty anymore. Did ten years before getting out a year and a half ago. I'm a government contractor on the same base now.* He hadn't offered more, and I hadn't asked. Still, the mention of his military past left me tangled in curiosity and caution. There was something dependable in that kind of service, a dedication that hinted at who he was beneath the surface. But I couldn't help wondering what a decade in the military did to a person, what it left behind. I wanted to ask what made him leave, if he missed it, or if the shift to civilian life still felt strange. The questions hovered, quiet and insistent, threads I wanted to pull until his story unraveled between us.

Instead, I gasped, letting the drama fill my voice. "So you admit it! You've been hiding behind retired military pictures. Definitely a scam." I pressed my lips together, fighting off a wave of childish giggles.

His grin widened, all boyish mischief. He leaned in, the camera catching the way his smile tugged sideways. "First off, a catfish is when someone pretends to be someone else completely. Fake name, fake pictures, different age, the whole scam. That's not me at all," He lifted a brow.

"Fine! You're right. I guess I'll give you a pass." I said, shaking my head, trying not to smile.

He laughed under his breath, low and rough. "A pass? Careful, Cami. You hand those out too easily, and I might start thinking you actually like talking to me."

I rolled my eyes, though the corners of my lips betrayed me. "Maybe I just feel sorry for you."

"Yeah?" he said, leaning in a little closer, voice warm and teasing. "Funny. Although it doesn't sound like pity when you say it."

"I'm at a loss for words," I said, half laughing, half breathless.

His grin turned lazy, eyes dark with amusement. "Didn't think that was possible. Should I be proud or worried?" The confidence in his voice wrapped around me. And the truth? I couldn't remember the last time I'd smiled this much with anyone.

I tucked my legs beneath me on the couch, chewing my lip, wishing I didn't feel so exposed through a glowing screen.

We talked until my cheeks ached from smiling. Our conversation drifted: the motorcycle he'd been working on before our call, his family, the Marine Corps, my dream of becoming a therapist, my craving for vanilla ice cream. Each piece slotted into place with a kind of ease I wasn't used to. The conversation made me forget everything else I had going on. Connection with him was a breath of fresh air: equal parts exhilarating and terrifying.

"So," he started, drawing the word out. "Since I've already survived your catfish accusations, when do I get to redeem myself in person?"

I blinked. "Redeem yourself?"

"Yeah," he said, nodding as if it were obvious. "I think mini golf should do it."

I raised a brow. "Mini golf?"

I should be careful. Careful protects me and the kids; being careless brings pain. Letting someone new in means risking more than my feelings. It was risking three little hearts, too. Last time, trusting someone cost pieces of myself I didn't get back whole, and I can't do that again. Am I ready for this? Still, as he looked at me, doubt tangled with hope. Why does his gaze make me feel seen and dangerous at once? My hand moved to my hair again, signaling nerves I swore I'd hide.

He smirked knowingly. "Am I making you nervous?"

I groaned, covering my face with my hand before dropping it just enough to peek at him through my fingers, and he winked. Heat crept up my neck, and I hated how fast my stomach flipped. *Ugh, I'm ridiculous. He's just a guy on a screen.*

Stop acting like a teenager.

I muttered. "I'm not nervous."

He leaned in closer, his eyes crinkling at the corners, the screen filled with that maddeningly confident face. "You are. And it's cute."

I rolled my eyes so hard I was sure he saw it. "Stop calling me cute. I'm a grown woman."

His brows lifted, tone dipping into something low and teasing. "Who says grown women can't be cute? "

I shook my head, biting down on a grin I couldn't stop. "You really don't quit, do you?"

"Not when it comes to you," he said, leaning in again, voice warm and smooth, "And you don't seem to mind. You're still on this call."

My stomach fluttered. My fingers tightened around the phone. Should I say no? Should I remind him how impossibly messy my life is? Everything feels tangled and relentless: last night, up past midnight finishing a report as the twins clambered out of bed, convinced monsters lurked in their closet. This morning, syrup from Zeke's breakfast cooled on my bare feet while I tripped over a forgotten toy, a plastic wheel pressed into my shin. Chaos reigns, every moment demanding, barely space to breathe. Yet underneath, I ache for a sliver of peace. Could someone fit into this whirlwind, bring laughter and warmth? All I managed was, "I'll… let you know… About mini golf. My schedule's crazy."

"Fair enough," he said easily, no pressure in his tone, just reassurance. "But I'll hold you to it. Mini golf. You and me."

And that's when my pulse skipped, because he didn't sound annoyed or disappointed. He sounded sure. Like he had all the time in the world.

"Okay, fine," I said, fumbling for composure. "Mini golf sounds fun."

"Good. Talk soon, Beautiful," he said, his voice low and warm.

When the screen went black, I just sat there for a moment, staring at my own flushed face in the dark reflection of my phone.

Mini golf. A date. The thought alone sent my stomach into knots.

Because it wasn't just mini golf. It was everything that came with saying yes. Letting someone see me outside the world I worked so hard to hold together. Letting myself be more than a mom or student. I was stepping onto an overgrown path. Each step revealed something new. Thrilling and a little daunting. Maybe, just maybe, that path could lead to laughter and warmth even chaos couldn't touch. Maybe, beneath all my hesitations, there was a spark of wanting. A breath of something new. A leap into the unknown. Hoping for something I hadn't dared to imagine.

My eyes drifted toward the hallway, where the soft glow of the nightlight spilled across the kid's door. The twins' little snores carried faintly through the apartment. They were my world. My first, last, and every choice in between. The thought of bringing someone into that world felt reckless. Dangerous.

And yet...

I couldn't deny how easy it had been to laugh with him. How natural it felt, even through a screen, to talk about everything and nothing all at once. I pulled the blanket tighter around me, sinking into the couch as if I could hide from the flutter in my chest.

I could tell him I was busy, push it off a little longer. Keep things safe. But the truth was, his teasing smile lingered in my thoughts. When he joked with me, it was as if he could sense the yes hidden beneath my excuses; it made my defenses weaken, even when I told myself I wasn't ready. Was being ready even important? What if, instead, it mattered more that I admitted I wanted this? With that thought, I let hope take root, daring to imagine something bright and new could grow from this cautious step.

Chapter Four

Hunter

When her text came in, I was mid-workout, sweating through push-ups on the living room floor. My phone buzzed against the hardwood, vibrating against a stack of unopened mail. I'd been staring at the same pile for a week: bills, VA paperwork, junk ads, as if I ignored it long enough, it would go away.

My one-bedroom apartment smelled faintly of laundry detergent and last night's takeout. Simple and functional, just how I liked it. A couch, a coffee table scarred from moving too many times, blinds half-closed against the morning sun. Not much else. No photos on the walls. No clutter.

I dropped onto my knees, breath catching, wiping sweat across my forehead with the back of my hand. Then I saw her name light up the screen.

Camille: So… I know that you know I am a mom.
  But before we go out, I should probably tell
  you that I have 3 kids. A 5 year old son

and twin 1 and a half year old girls.

I froze. Three. Kids.

I sat back on my heels, wiping sweat off my forehead, staring at the message, thinking the words might rearrange themselves if I blinked enough.

Part of me respected her for being upfront. Most people hide their baggage until the third date or never mention it at all. Another part of me was cautious. Three kids isn't something you ease into. That's a whole life and a true responsibility.

And then there was the part of me. The stupid, reckless, hopeful part, whispering: *You've always wanted this.* I pictured barefoot mornings, the sunlight creeping into the kitchen where laughter bounced off the walls. I imagined helping with homework spread out on the kitchen table, teaching my kids how to ride dirt bikes, the joy-filled chaos of pancake breakfasts, and showing them the peace of a day in the woods. The kind of family rhythm that wasn't perfect but felt like home.

My apartment often boasted a quiet atmosphere. I'd filled it with workouts, work, mindless TV, anything but family. Ten years in the Marine Corps had taught me how to survive in desert heat and sandstorms, how to clear rooms in seconds, how to keep my face blank when my chest was screaming. But it hadn't taught me how to come home to nothing.

My marriage hadn't survived it. Maybe it never had a chance; we were young when we married. She'd told me she couldn't handle the deployments, the distance, the version of me who came back quieter each time. She was right. I hadn't handled it well either. And when we split up, I'd told myself

I wasn't meant for family. Not anymore.

That was before she came storming in funny, smart, gorgeous, and honest as hell. She had kids. A whole world orbiting her. Yet, instead of fear, I felt that dangerous pull. I wanted it.

I typed slowly, careful not to overplay my hand:

> ***Me:*** I would like one of my own one day. If you didn't want to have any more kids, I would understand… but it may be a deal breaker for me.

My thumb hovered before hitting send. It felt too honest, too forward. But I'd promised myself I wasn't going to play games anymore. If I wanted real, I had to be real.

So I hit *Send*. Then I waited. And waited.

The typing dots came up. Disappeared. Came back again. I imagined her reading my words, frowning, maybe deciding this was the moment to ghost me.

Then, finally:

Camille: What's another car seat, right?

I stared at it for a long second, not sure if she was joking or testing the waters. Relief loosened the tight knot that had been sitting in my chest all night.

> ***Me:*** You say that like you're okay with it.

Camille: I don't know. I think…
  part of me could be. Maybe
  not now. But someday.

> *Me:* Someday sounds pretty
> good to me.

Underneath the jokes, my thoughts kept circling. Three kids. That wasn't just dating. This wasn't "grab a drink and maybe text tomorrow." But I wasn't afraid of it. I was afraid of screwing it up.

I set the phone down, leaned back against the couch, and let the truth sink in.

She thought this would scare me off. Maybe it should have. But her honesty made me want her more. If she could lay it all out, maybe I could be man enough to try again.

The next afternoon, I picked up my phone that sat at the coffee table beside a half-drunk energy drink. I thumbed a new message before I could overthink it.

> *Me: So, about this mini golf date…*
> *what's the prize for the winner?*

Camille: Pride. Bragging rights.
  Ice Cream.

> *Me: Sounds like you've thought*
> *this through.*

Camille: Only because I plan
  on winning.

Me: I admire the confidence.
Even if it's misplaced.

Camille: We'll see about that. And for
  the record, if you don't let me win,
  you're a monster.

I chuckled, shaking my head. I wasn't going to let her win. And I had a feeling she'd respect me more for it. I told myself it was just mini golf, nothing more. But as the day went on, I kept checking the time like a damn teenager.

Eventually, I found myself at the mini golf lot, ten minutes early. Old habits die hard. In the Marine Corps, you're taught that you're either early or late, nothing in between.

I leaned against the fence, watching families chase kids with ice cream cones, a couple arguing quietly near the ticket stand. It was all background noise until I saw her walking toward me.

She was shorter than I expected, her curves soft, her hair a wild swirl of brown curls framing her face. Her jeans fit like they were made just for her, hugging each curve of her body. She paired her jeans with a loose-fitting top that moved as she did. Her presence was genuine and warm, and it knocked the air out of me for a second.

"Camille?" I asked, even though I already knew it was her.

She gave me a small, almost shy smile, eyes flicking up and down, telling me she wasn't sure if I was real yet.

"Hunter." Her voice was soft. Reserved.

When I leaned in for a quick hug, her scent hit me first.

Vanilla, with a trace of rose and jasmine that lingered just long enough to mess with my head. She fit perfectly in my arms, like that's where she'd always been meant to be.

It was her. Completely, undeniably her.

When I pulled back, she was hesitant, as if she was still sizing me up. I offered a grin, trying to lighten the weight in the air. "Still disappointed that I catfished you?"

That earned me a surprised laugh, and I filed the sound away immediately. I needed to hear that again.

We grabbed our putters, hers neon pink, mine neon green, and headed to the first hole. I could tell she was nervous. She chewed on her lip when she thought I wasn't looking, kept her eyes down a little longer than most people do. But underneath all that, there was something steady in her. She might not have realized it, but I could tell she wasn't the type to break easily.

"Alright," I said, lining up my ball. "Before we start, ground rules: I don't let people win. You've got to earn it." I should have probably done the chivalrous thing and let her win. I've been told I can be too competitive sometimes, but something told me she could handle it.

She arched her brow. "Wow. Straight to intimidation. Bold."

"Not intimidation. Just being straight with you. You want fake? Wrong guy."

Her lips twitched. "Noted. But if I lose, I'm blaming the putter."

"Of course," I said, deadpan. "Always blame the gear." She laughed again, softer, and it left me with a feeling I couldn't name.

When she took her first shot, the ball ricocheted off the

windmill and bounced straight into the little fake stream running along the side. She froze, then groaned. "Oh my Gosh. That did not just happen."

I bit my cheek, trying not to laugh. And failed. "Don't worry, rookie mistake. Happens to the best."

"You're enjoying this way too much," she muttered as I fished the ball out for her.

"I'm a simple guy," I shrugged. "Good food, cold beer, and watching my date try to kill golf balls."

She shot me a look, equal parts glare and amusement. "Careful. I might take you down with this putter."

"Noted. Mental checklist: don't anger the five-two woman with a weaponized mini golf stick."

Her smile widened, spark in her eyes. That right there was worth every bad date and lonely night. As we played, she relaxed. Banter clicked into place. I teased, and she fired back. Quietly competitive; she pretended not to care, but the little fist pump when she sank a shot said otherwise.

The game went like that: her groaning at wild shots, me teasing, her firing back. Grass and flowers in the air, background noise from other players. Somewhere between the bad shots and the laughter, she loosened up. And me? I couldn't stop watching her. Not just her curves or her curls, but the way she carried herself. Like she'd built her walls high, but underneath, she wanted someone to try climbing them.

"So I guess we gotta lie and tell your kids you won?" I asked playfully.

She snorted. "Please. Like my kids would ever believe that."

"Smart kids," I said with a grin. Her laughter rang out again, and damn if something didn't shift in me. I found myself laughing alongside her. It's been a long time since I let myself think about forever. But watching her brush curls from her eyes and roll them at my bad jokes, I realized something I hadn't expected.

Forever didn't feel like a threat. It felt like a shot I might actually want to take.

Chapter Five

Camille

Hunter smiled at me as we walked back to the lot, and wow… pictures hadn't done him justice. He was taller than I expected, broad shoulders filling out a plain gray t-shirt that clung to him and hinted at muscle without trying too hard. His joggers looked lived-in but clean, displaying a casual confidence that didn't need effort to make an impression. And those Vans, crisp and spotless, said more about him than I expected. He noticed the little things and took pride in them.

Then there were his eyes. Blue. Not just light-blue-like-the-ocean cliche, but sharp, clear, and so direct it made my stomach flip. It was a warm day in California, but I don't think it was the outside heat that left me feeling flushed.

What really drew me in was the tattoo on his left arm, inked from shoulder to wrist in intricate lines, weaving together two koi fish circling each other. The detail was beautiful, scales shaded with care, water curling around them so the tattoo almost seemed to move. My eyes lingered longer than

I meant, and when I glanced up, his grin had deepened, just a little.

He carried his past on his skin; the places he'd been, the things he'd survived, all there in the ink and the way he stood. Confident and grounded, a man who'd seen too much and still smiled. And I couldn't look away.

I wasn't supposed to like him this much. That was the first thought running through my head as I pulled into my apartment complex, parked my car, and gripped the steering wheel as if it might tell me what to do next.

The second thought? Dang, he's cute.

Not just in the obvious ways: blue eyes, ginger beard, tall enough that I had to tilt my chin to meet his gaze. Cute in the way he laughed easily, in the way he didn't coddle me during mini golf, like he trusted I could handle the teasing.

And me? I was spiraling.

It should have been a warning sign; men who seemed too good to be true usually were. Still, I kept replaying the small things. The way he leaned on his putter, patient, like he had all the time in the world. The way his eyes crinkled when he smiled. The way he fished my golf ball out without making me feel small, and didn't show frustration when I accidentally slammed my putter into his shin.

I leaned my forehead against the steering wheel and groaned. "Oh no. I like him." That was dangerous. Liking him meant risk, and hope was an idea that had burned me before.

Inside my apartment, the kids slept tangled in blankets, their cheeks soft and warm beneath my fingertips as I tucked them in. My mom was dozing on the couch, glasses still perched on her nose, some crime show humming low in the background. Gratitude pinched my chest. Without her, I wouldn't even have the chance to date again.

I tried to busy myself with packing lunches, rinsing sippy cups, picking up Legos, but my mind was still on him. On the way, he looked at me like I wasn't *too much*.

Then my phone buzzed.

Hunter: Did you make it home, beautiful?
Thanks for not throwing the game.
I'm still proud of my win.

A laugh slipped out. He was right. I'd never forgive him if he let me win.

> **Me:** I'm home. And I guess I'll just
> have to train for the rematch.

Hunter: Oh, so we're already planning
a second date?

I pressed the phone to my chest, hating myself for how much I loved the way it felt.

Later, in bed, sleep didn't come. I replayed the way he leaned close, the way he didn't flinch at my chaos, the way he teased but never crossed the line. And still, the fear lingered. What if he's like the rest? What if he gets bored? What if three kids is three too many?

Hunter: So, honest question… if there was
a trophy for worst mini golfer, do you
think you'd win, or should I still enter

the competition?

> *Me:* Bold words for someone who almost tripped over his own putter.

Hunter: That was strategy. Distract the competition.

> *Me:* Right. Sure. Keep telling yourself that.

Hunter: Admit it. You had fun.

I hesitated, thumb hovering. Admitting I'd had fun felt risky since it meant wanting more, and wanting more always carried the chance of disappointment. But the truth was there. My cheeks still ached from laughing.

> *Me:* Fine. Maybe I did. Don't let it go to your head.

Hunter: Too late. It's already there.

I tossed the phone onto the couch, as if I could put some distance between myself and the giddiness bubbling up inside me. Twenty-five, single mom, bills, classes, laundry piling up. Yet here I was, feeling like a teenager with a crush.

Still, when the phone buzzed again, I reached for it like it was air.

Hunter: So… second date? Or are you too scared to lose again?

My heart stuttered. He wasn't running. He wanted more.

> *Me:* We'll see. Don't you know you're
> supposed to wait three business
> days before asking?

Hunter: Pretty sure that rule
was invented by people who
didn't have my charm

> *Me:* Wow. Modest too.

Hunter: You'll learn to appreciate it.

I curled up on the couch, warmth spreading through me even as the old voice whispered in my ear. The one that said I was too much, that no one stayed, that I came with too much baggage. The voice left behind by the man who walked away, who chose freedom and late nights while I pieced together a life for three babies under five.

Then one last buzz.

Hunter: Goodnight, Beautiful.
Sweet dreams. Don't practice
too hard without me.

> *Me:* Goodnight. Thanks for making
> me laugh tonight.

I turned off the lamp, curled onto my side, and let the thoughts slip into the dark.

The next morning, the apartment was in chaos. Cheerios spilled on the light laminate counter, my oldest insisting his favorite shirt was "lost" (it was in the hamper), my youngest crying because her sister stole her pacifier. Mom slipping out quietly with a hug and a "call me later."

By the time Dani showed up mid-afternoon, I was exhausted, barefoot, and already halfway convinced I had made the whole date up. She walked in like she owned the place, tossing her purse on the couch.

Dani had this presence you felt before you even saw her. She moved through the world with bold, unstoppable energy, the type of friend who barged through doors instead of knocking. Her straight blonde hair was usually left down, sleek and shiny, catching the light when she tilted her head in laughter. A pair of oversized sunglasses often rested on her head, even indoors or after sunset, because subtlety had never been her strong suit.

She was sharp-tongued, soft-hearted, the type of friend who could roast you one minute and show up with fries, a milkshake, and a hug the next. Dani filled every room, not just with her voice or her wit, but with a loyalty so fierce there was never any doubt. If she was in your corner, she was *all in*.

"Okay, spill. Was he a creep, or is that post-date glow I see?" Dani said.

I groaned, flopping onto the couch. "Do I really look like I'm glowing?"

"Like a light bulb, babe. Come on, don't hold out on me."

So I told her. About mini golf, about how he didn't let me win, about his laugh, and the way he called me Beautiful. About how he'd texted me goodnight.

Dani grinned like she had just won the lottery. "Oh my God, you *like* him. Like-like."

"I don't like-like anyone," I said too quickly. She raised an eyebrow. "Camille. You're smiling while you talk about him. When's the last time you did that?" I bit my lip. She wasn't wrong. "OMG, did you guys kiss?" Dani whisper yelled. But of course it was loud enough for listening ears.

"Kiss who, mommy?" Zeke said innocently, showing he was listening in even as he played with his sisters a few feet away.

"No one baby, Auntie Dani is just being silly." I said, glaring at her while mouthing "Seriously?"

But then the doubts spilled out too. My kids, my past, my ex, my fear of letting someone in. Dani listened, her hand squeezing mine. "Look," she said finally. "You've been carrying the weight of the world for years. Maybe it's okay if someone comes along who actually wants to help carry it with you. Just… give him a chance."

I wanted to. I really did. But giving chances was how I'd been hurt before. That night, as I tucked my kids into bed, her words echoed in my mind. *Give him a chance.* And lying awake, staring at the ceiling, I realized the scariest part: I already wanted to.

Unfortunately, Monday mornings at the doctor's office didn't care if you'd had a magical first date over the weekend. By eight a.m., I was in scrubs, hair pulled into a puff of curls that were already trying to escape, and answering phones that wouldn't stop ringing. Insurance questions, prescription refills, patients arriving late for appointments, it was the usual chaos.

"Camille, do you mind rooming Mr. Collins?" the lead medical assistant asked, handing me a chart.

"On it," I said, flashing a polite smile that was more muscle memory than sincerity.

The routine was familiar: check vitals, ask questions, type notes into the computer. All while pretending I wasn't running on three hours of sleep because my mind had refused to shut down the night before.

Every patient reminded me why I was in school. I wasn't just clocking hours for a paycheck. I was watching, listening, collecting stories of pain and resilience. The way I placed a gentle hand on a distraught patient's shoulder, offering a reassuring smile or a few comforting words, was a tiny step toward the role I aspired to play. One day, I wouldn't just be the one taking vitals or handing out clipboards. One day, I'd help people untangle their thoughts, help them feel seen. But for now, I was juggling: full-time mom, part-time student, full-time employee, and maybe, just maybe, someone with a dating life.

When my lunch break finally came, I sat in the break room with my sad Tupperware of leftovers, a smile tugging at my lips when my phone buzzed on the table.

Hunter: Hi Beautiful, how's your Monday going?

> **Me:** Boring. Do you know how many times I've had to explain copays today?

Hunter: That doesn't sound fun.
  Want me to come rescue you?

> *Me:* Pretty sure the front desk
> would call security.

Hunter: Worth it.

I laughed into my food, catching a look from my nosy coworker, but I didn't care. It had been a long time since anyone checked in on me in the middle of the day. Since anyone wanted to make me laugh when I was drowning in routine. My mom checked on me, sure. My little brother helped when he visited. Dani teased me into surviving. But a man? That was new.

As I leaned back in my chair, images of my past came uninvited. My ex, walking out the door without looking back. My son, asking why we packed up our things and never saw him again. I never admitted to most people the truth behind our relationship, like the nights where I had to swallow my screams and wait for the storm to pass. I can still hear the slamming of doors some night. And now, I faced it alone. The exhaustion of raising babies while working double shifts, scraping money together for diapers, and begging family for childcare. I was safer, happier, but alone.

That was my history. My normal. And yet, walking next to Hunter on that mini golf course, I had felt a lightness. Not the absence of weight, but the hope that maybe, just maybe, I wouldn't always have to carry it alone.

Hunter: What do you have going
  on after work?

> ***Me:*** Mom duty, class, then maybe
> pretending I'm going to study before
> falling asleep with my laptop
> still open.

Hunter: I don't know how you do
   it all. But you make it look easy,
   and I know it's not. Kinda blows
   my mind, honestly.

Heat crept into my cheeks. Compliments usually slid right off me; I never trusted them, but something about the way he said it felt different. He actually saw me. I locked my phone and stared at the pale gray wall, letting the feeling settle.

> ***Me:*** Enough about me, what have you
> been up to today?

That night, after my evening class, Dani came over with her usual flair: arms full of takeout bags, sunglasses still perched on her head, even though the sun was long gone.

"I brought fries!" she announced, kicking the door shut with her foot.

"God bless you," I said, dropping the Psychology of Social Change textbook on the couch and reaching for the bag.

She flopped dramatically onto the couch next to me. "Girl, you look dead. Like, cute dead. But dead."

I rolled my eyes, sinking down beside her. "Thanks. I feel it."

The kids were sprawled on the rug, coloring and fighting over crayons.

Dani greeted them with kisses, setting them up with sweets that it was far too late for them to have, then turned her full focus back to me like a spotlight.

"Okay," she said, grabbing a fry. "Tell me, how are you balancing all this? Job, school, mom life, and now Mr. Marine?"

"I'm not balancing it," I admitted. "I'm barely hanging on."

"You're hanging on," she said firmly. "That counts."

Part of me reached for her words, craving the hope in them, but the rest of me still remembered the fall. And in the quiet hours, when the house finally stilled and the hum of the day faded, I could still feel how close I was to breaking. Like I was always one bad day from it all coming undone.

So when Hunter texted me during my break, asking about class, it shouldn't have meant as much as it did. But it did. The idea that someone cared whether I made it through Monday felt bigger than I was ready to admit.

I told Dani about it, and she grinned like she'd been waiting for this moment. "That's it. That's how you know he's different. He's not just showing up when it's convenient; he's showing up in the cracks of your day."

I shook my head, laughing. "You're way too invested."

"Someone has to be," she teased. "You overthink everything. I'm here to point out the obvious: you like him, he likes you. Now stop trying to ruin it with your brain."

I hesitated, then admitted quietly, "He feels… different. Not bad-different. Scary-different."

Dani leaned forward, her teasing fading. "Camille. You deserve someone good. You've been through hell and back. It's okay to want more than just survival."

The fries blurred for a second before I blinked the tears

away. Because she was right. My whole life had been about survival; work, school, kids, bills, repeat. No room for anything else. At least, that's what I told myself. But now, with one evening and a handful of texts, Hunter was starting to carve out space I didn't know I still had.

Her words followed me into the night, through bedtime routines and the quiet at the kitchen table, textbooks open but my eyes drifting to my phone. It wasn't just that Hunter made me laugh. He checked in. He noticed. He made me feel like maybe this messy, overwhelming, exhausting life wasn't too much for him.

And that terrified me almost as much as it thrilled me.

Because the last time I let someone in, he walked away. And I had promised myself I'd never let anyone break me again.

That night as I finally crawled into bed and let the darkness wrap around me, the truth pressed in, quiet but insistent.

I wanted to hope again.

Chapter Six

Camille

Friday night found me sitting at my kitchen table, laptop propped open for a Zoom class while the kids quietly watched a movie on the couch. The girls munched on those Gerber star-shaped puffed snacks that stuck to everything. Zeke was curled up with a blanket, and for once the apartment wasn't a circus. My professor's voice droned through the screen about upcoming presentations, but my eyelids kept fluttering.

It wasn't that I didn't care; I cared too much. I wanted this degree more than anything. But after a full shift at the doctor's office, making the kids dinner, and wrangling the kids into clean clothes after a bath, my brain was fried.

How was I supposed to pour into clients when I felt stretched this thin? When my coping skills consisted of coffee and hope. And how could I even consider letting someone new, like Hunter, into this already overstuffed life?

I sat at the kitchen table after class, phone in hand. His message from earlier still waited: *Want to grab ice cream this weekend?* I started drafting a polite excuse, then deleted it. Typed another, deleted again. My thumb hovered over the screen, heart racing with doubt.

That's when Dani barged in, like she had radar for my self-sabotage.

She flung off her flip flops in a dramatic thud, plopped onto the couch across from me, greeting the kids with hugs and tickles, and held up a milkshake with a flourish. Mischief clung to her like perfume. She was loud, unignorable, and exactly what I needed, which fit her in her new position as an attorney in the public defender's office.

"Saved your life again," she announced, shoving the too-large cup in my direction.

I laughed despite myself. "You're ridiculous."

"Ridiculously loyal," she corrected, putting her hair up in a clip.

Dani helped with the kids most Friday nights, often staying over. She claimed it was because her place was too far, but I knew better. She stayed when I was burning out, when exhaustion was written across my face, when the weight of bills and homework and single motherhood pressed too heavily. More mornings than I could count, I'd woken to the smell of cinnamon rolls in the kitchen. Zeke would beam with pride, sticky fingers dusted in flour as he carried me a plate, bragging that he'd "helped." Food and sleep were her weapons of choice, and she wielded them like armor for me.

She glanced toward the kids on the rug, then leaned forward, zeroing in on me. "Okay, spill. Why do you look like you're about to break up with someone you haven't even dated yet?" she demanded.

I sighed, shoving my phone across the table. "I can't do this,

Dani. Work, school, kids. How do I add dating on top of it? It feels impossible."

She slurped her chocolate milkshake obnoxiously, then set it down. "Let me answer that with another question: when's the last time someone made you laugh so hard you forgot your stress for even a minute?"

My throat tightened. I knew exactly when. Mini golf. Hunter's grin. His teasing voice calling me Beautiful.

Dani leaned forward, her tone softening. " It's okay to let yourself have fun. Even if it's complicated. You don't have to cancel him out of fear." I sat in that moment as Avery climbed into my lap, rubbing sleepy eyes. I rubbed her back lightly as I processed the weight of Dani's words.

I blinked at her, tears pricking my eyes. "But what if he leaves? What if he decides I'm too much?"

"Then that's on him," she said firmly. "Not on you. You've survived worse."

The silence stretched. My heart pounded, thumb hovering over the keyboard as doubt started to creep in. Before I could spiral, Dani broke it with her trademark grin.

"Plus," she said, leaning back and sipping her milkshake casually, "you know if he hurts my bestie or my nieces and nephew, I'll just have to kill him." She laughed, the sound bright and ridiculous in the heavy air.

I couldn't help it,I smiled, shaking my head. "You're insane."

"Insanely loyal," she corrected, winking. And just like that, the knot in my chest loosened.

Finally, I typed: *Ice Cream sounds good. Sunday?*

The reply came almost instantly.

Hunter: Perfect. I'll pick the place. And I

promise not to make you play mini
golf again. Yet.

I smiled, setting the phone down. The exhaustion was still there, the fear still lingering at the edges, the past still a shadow I couldn't fully shake. But beneath all of it, something new stirred; a flicker of warmth somewhere between anticipation and quiet excitement

Chapter Seven

Hunter

I stared at her text again. *Ice cream sounds good. Sunday?* It had been a simple message, barely a handful of words. But to me, it felt like a green light I had not expected.

It was not that women never said yes to me. They did. I just had not let myself get emotionally invested in a long time. Not since my marriage ended. Not since I decided it was easier to keep people at arm's length than to risk letting them in again.

The divorce was only a year behind me, although the marriage was over, and the separation happened long before the ink was finalized. Regardless, it was still fresh enough to sting if I thought about it too long. Ten years in the Marine Corps had been hell on both of us, but the last few deployments were the nail in the coffin. She wanted stability, but I could not give it, and eventually, she walked away, finding warmth in another man's bed. I told myself I understood. I told myself it was for the best. But some nights, lying awake in an empty apartment, I still felt the weight of that failure.

Now, for the first time since then, I was dipping my toe into life outside the Corps. Civilian clothes. Civilian schedules. Working as a contractor on base. A foot still in the world I knew, but no longer part of the brotherhood that had defined me for a decade. It was a strange and unsettling feeling.

So why was this woman, the one who laughed too easily, the one who admitted her chaos up front, the one who had three kids and a full plate, suddenly make me want to risk it again? That was the question I could not shake.

Sunday came faster than I expected. I pulled out a shirt I had not worn in months, scrubbed my beard down, and checked myself in the mirror twice, hoping that would erase the parts of me that still felt flawed. I had not felt this nervous about a date in years. Not the "first-date butterflies" kind of nervous. I had already had that. This was different. These were the types of nerves that came when you realized you were in way over your head and did not hate the feeling. It had been a long time since I cared about how I looked for someone else, but tonight I needed to show up for her.

Camille. Even her name felt different in my mouth.

She was not what I expected when I downloaded that app. Truthfully, I was not expecting much at all, just a distraction, a little flirting, maybe something casual to fill the silence. But from the first message, she had been different. Witty. Guarded, but not bitter. Soft in ways I did not think existed anymore.

And then she told me she was a mom of three kids.

You'd think that would make me hesitate. The truth? Her being a mom did not scare me. What scared me was how much it did not scare me. The idea of sitting at her kitchen table, hearing little voices call her name, tucking kids into bed did not feel like baggage. This was a chance at the kind of life I thought I had lost. That was dangerous because it was way too soon.

I splashed water on my face, trying to wash away the heaviness that always lingered when I thought about my past. The nights overseas when sleep would not come because every sound might mean danger. The sandstorms. The firefights. The long flights home to an empty bed. The way I woke up, even now, sweating from dreams I did not talk about. Post-traumatic Stress Disorder, the doctors called it. I just called it normal. How could I hand that to her? To her kids?

But then I remembered her laugh at mini golf.

I grabbed my keys. A simple ice cream date, nothing big.

Driving over, I caught myself running through things like a pre-mission check on what to say, what to ask, how not to let too much slip. This was not combat. It was ice cream. Yet for some reason, my pulse did not seem to know the difference.

The shop was one you noticed more by smell than sight. Sweet cream, sugar cones, and the faint sizzle of waffle irons drifted into the parking lot before you even stepped inside. The neon sign above the door flickered just a little, buzzing in protest, but the window displays were cheerful: painted cones, rainbow sprinkles, little chalkboard doodles announcing the "flavor of the week."

Inside lay pastel walls, polished linoleum, tubs of ice cream behind foggy glass, flavors chalked out: Rocky Road, Cookie Dough, Pistachio, all of it buzzing with families and teenagers and background noise. I picked a table in the back near the window, facing the door. Habit. Always keep an eye on entrances. I told myself it was about safety, but if I was honest, it was more about nerves.

I watched the door until she walked in, curls bouncing, eyes scanning for me. That jolt in my chest is hitting me again. She wore jeans, a soft sweater, nothing flashy, just her, a little reserved but with warmth underneath. When she smiled, I knew I'd wait as long as it took to see all of her.

"Hi, Beautiful," I said, standing.

She smiled, shy but genuine, eyes on the floor. Quiet, "Hi, Hunter."

We ordered. She didn't hesitate, "Vanilla cone with rainbow sprinkles," like she'd been craving it all week. I went for mint chocolate chip, my usual, and caught the wrinkle of her nose when she heard it.

"That's toothpaste with chocolate chips," she teased.

"Wild," I said, deadpan. "This is top-tier ice cream." She laughed, and it hit me square in the chest.

Ice cream in hand, we returned to the table, except that she didn't take a bite of the vanilla. She went straight for the sprinkles, licking them off with deliberate focus, ignoring the melting scoop beneath. She had mentioned enjoying vanilla ice cream mainly for the sprinkles, but it was even funnier in person.

I stared, then shook my head with a laugh. "You weren't joking. You're seriously just eating the sprinkles?"

"Obviously," she said, eyes twinkling. "That's the best part. Everything else is just… there."

I leaned back, grinning. "Full disclosure? That's the quirkiest thing I've ever seen on a date."

"And?" she asked, daring me.

"And I kind of love it."

Her cheeks flushed, but her grin widened, and for a moment the noise of the shop faded out.

We talked, easy and light. She told me more about her kids: Zeke and his mismatched socks, the twins trying to outdo each other for attention. She described their little habits with so much affection, I caught myself imagining them sitting at this table, sprinkles smeared on their faces, chattering at her side.

When she asked about me, I kept it simple. "Contracting on base. Same base as my last duty station, different role. Fewer sandstorms, steadier hours."

So I smirked, shifting the spotlight back to her cone. "You've got about three sprinkles left. What's your strategy when they're gone?"

She laughed, caught mid-bite. "Panic, obviously."

"Good to know. I'll keep the refills coming," I said.

She rolled her eyes, but her laugh stuck with me. Her gaze lingered, like she knew I was holding back. She didn't push. That restraint, that grace, meant more than she knew.

I leaned forward, deciding to nudge the banter back. "Alright, your turn. Tell me something I don't know. No pressure."

Her brow arched. "That's how you start a second date? With an interrogation?"

"Not interrogation. Curiosity. Big difference."

She pretended to think, then smirked. "When I was ten, I broke my mom's favorite vase, blamed it on the dog, and never confessed. Fifteen years later, she still doesn't know."

I barked out a laugh. "Fifteen years? You know you just confessed on record."

"Good thing you're not a cop," she shot back.

Her eyes sparkled as the banter flowed easily. I sipped my cone. "Most people try to impress on a date. You came out swinging with childhood crimes."

"Better you know now," she said with a shrug. "Full disclosure."

That word, *disclosure*, hit me harder than it should have. Because she'd already given me more honesty than most people ever had. She told me about her kids up front. She didn't pretend her life was simple. And sitting across from her now, I realized how much I respected that.

The more honest she was, the harder it got to hide every fracture I'd learned to disguise. The nightmares, the triggers, the war that never fully left my head.

So instead, I forced a grin. "Well, in the spirit of disclosure, I should tell you something too."

Her eyebrows lifted. "Oh?"

"I'm terrible at mini golf rematches," I said solemnly.

She groaned, hiding her smile behind her cone. "That's the best you've got?"

Seeing her smile like that didn't leave me feeling like a broken man pretending to be whole. I just felt… alive.

"Okay, I'll go again," she said, half a laugh in her voice. "Full disclosure? My life's… complicated."

I leaned forward, elbows on the table. "Complicated how?"

"Work. School. Kids," she said, ticking each off on her fingers. "I work at a doctor's office, go to classes in the evenings, and then, you know, raising three tiny humans in between." She gave me a look, a little daring, as if I hadn't already been aware from the little glimpses she shared. "Still think ice cream with me was a good idea?"

I didn't flinch. "I think it's the best idea I've had in a while."

That earned me a surprised smile, small but genuine. She tilted her head. "You say that now. Wait until you see me trying to do homework while one kid's crying for snacks and another was asking me to explain why Johnny only has 5 apples. It's chaos."

"That doesn't scare me," I said without thinking. Her eyebrows shot up.

I smirked, softening it. "Different kind of battlefield, but hey…I've seen people survive worse. You're still here, aren't you?"

Her smile faded a little as she looked down at her hands, twisting her cup. "Yeah. Still here."

I caught myself then. I knew that tone. That weight. It was the same one I carried when people asked about deployments or the divorce, too much truth sitting just beneath the surface. My hand itched to close the space between us, to trace the line of her wrist, but I held back. Instead, I leaned back, kept my voice steady. "You don't have to impress me. The fact that you're holding all that together and still who you are? That's already impressive enough."

Her eyes lifted, locking onto mine. For a moment, the noise of the café around us faded out.

"Most guys don't think so," she said quietly. "Most guys hear 'single mom' and suddenly remember they left the oven on."

"Well, I'm not most guys." It came out sharper than I intended, but I meant it.

Silence stretched between us for a beat, heavy but not uncomfortable. She studied me, trying to decide whether to believe me.

So I softened it with a grin. "Besides, if I'm being honest, you juggling all that just makes me feel lazy. I only have one job, and I still complain about Mondays."

She laughed, the heaviness breaking. "You? Complain? Shocking." Rolling her eyes theatrically.

"Don't tell anyone. You'll ruin my reputation."

That laugh hit me. Made me want to keep stacking jokes just to hear them again. But under the banter, the truth was clear: she was strong. Stronger than she knew. And I was already in deeper than I'd planned. Closer than I meant to be.

A year out of marriage. A year as a civilian. And here I was, already picturing what it'd be like to sit at her kitchen table, help with homework, carry some of the weight she carried alone. Dangerous thoughts, too soon. But as she ate her ice cream and gave me that crooked smile, I wanted to see where this went. I wanted to try.

So I leaned into what I knew best, lightness. Keep things simple. Keep things easy. "So," I said, nodding at her cone, now free of sprinkles. "Looks like we got a crisis?"

Her eyes flicked up, warm and mischievous, before she rolled them dramatically. "Oh, please." A grin tugged at her lips, giving her away.

"Figures," I said, smirking as I leaned back, trying to look casual when my chest felt like it was buzzing. "Losing sprinkles is serious business."

Her mouth fell open in mock outrage. "Excuse me? That was not just sprinkles. That was the best part."

"Noted," I said, biting back a grin. "Next time, I'll order you a side of sprinkles. No ice cream required."

She laughed, shaking her head, the sound spilling into the air. "One day you're going to regret making fun of me."

"Highly doubt it." I let the corner of my mouth curve into a cocky grin, but inside? I was just relieved. Relieved, she was laughing with me, not at me, that she hadn't decided I was too much or too little.

And the way she leaned across the table, eyes sparking, told me she was enjoying it too. We let the moment linger, her laughter mixing with mine, until the weight between us eased again.

She told me a little more about her life while I listened, actually listened, because the way she told stories was magnetic. Animated hands, quick wit, a little self-deprecating humor. I could tell she had insecurities by the way she shared things and often kept her eyes everywhere but on mine.

When she flipped the question back at me, "So what about you? What's life like now that you're out?" I kept it vague.

Her eyes searched mine, waiting for more, but I didn't give it. Not yet. The rest, the late nights, the nightmares, the divorce, stayed locked down. She didn't push. Just nodded and smiled like she understood more than I'd said. We lingered until the place started closing down.

When I walked her out, the night air was sharp. I wanted to reach for her hand, tuck a curl behind her ear, anything to make the moment last. I didn't. Not yet.

"Thanks for meeting me," I said, leaning against my truck.

"Thanks for inviting me," she said, brushing her curls aside. The streetlight caught her smile, almost knocking the air out of me. We stood there a moment, silence heavy but good.

She laughed softly. "Guess this means you get a mini golf rematch after all."

"Looking forward to it," I said, grinning.

I walked her to her small white Ford hatchback. I wasn't sure how she fit three car seats inside, but when I opened the door, there they were.

One grey. Two bright pink. All crammed together in the back like puzzle pieces in a space too small for the lives they were holding. The sight stopped me for a second. They weren't just car seats. They were proof of the world she lived in, the world she carried everywhere with her. Sticky fingers, mismatched socks, little voices calling her name. Those three seats meant three lives depended on her every single day. And if I were being honest, they made the air shift. I'd seen a lot in my life: combat zones, endless desert, explosions that rattled the earth under my boots. But this? Three small seats in the back of a car hit me harder than I expected. It wasn't theoretical; it wasn't a story she told over ice cream. It was right there in front of me. Tangible. A reminder that dating her wasn't just dating *her*. It was stepping into all of this. Into them.

She noticed me looking and gave a little laugh, almost self-conscious. "Yeah. It's a tight fit. We make it work."

I forced a smile, but inside I wasn't laughing. Inside, I was taking in the gravity of it. Three kids who didn't know me yet. Three kids who didn't need another person walking in only to leave. The thought made me uneasy. Not because I didn't want it. But because I did. She deserved more. One day, I'd get her the car she deserved, which offered space for her and her kids. I respected that she worked hard and did her best; her kids' smiles showed that, but I hated that she felt she should be embarrassed. Responsibility had once been a weight that broke my back. But standing there, looking at those three seats? I realized maybe the door wasn't closed at all. Maybe I'd just been too afraid to try again.

"You've got a superhero car," I said, keeping it light. "Looks small, but it carries a whole world."

She smiled, brushed a curl behind her ear, and for a second, I wished I could tell her the truth. That I wasn't scared of the car seats, the noise, or the chaos. I was scared of wanting to belong there too much. "Thanks, Hunter," she said, voice low. I started to say "Anytime," but the words stuck.

For a second, we stood there too close, too aware. Then she leaned in and kissed my cheek. It shot through me like a live wire. "Goodnight," she whispered, cheeks flushed. I couldn't help but grin.

"Goodnight, Beautiful." She climbed into her car, and I shut the door behind her, still feeling the ghost of that kiss on my skin. That night, I drove home with a fierce and unfamiliar burning in my chest.

Chapter Eight

Hunter

The apartment was quiet when I walked in, keys hitting the counter with a dull clatter. That was the thing about living alone. The silence pressed in, heavier than any sandbag I'd ever carried. Tonight, after hours of her laughter and the hum of a parlor, it felt suffocating.

I kicked off my shoes, dropped onto the couch, and leaned back. Her face wouldn't leave my head. Those curls falling into her eyes, the way she smiled when she teased me, the way she looked right at me when she said most men ran from single moms. She didn't realize it, but I respected the hell out of that honesty.

And yet, underneath the warmth she left me with, the edges of something darker crept in. I should've been relaxed. Instead, my body was humming, still on high alert. My shoulders wouldn't unclench. My jaw ached from being locked. I closed my eyes, tried to breathe it out. But my mind didn't want to stay in that ice cream shop. It wanted to drag me back.

The hum of the ice cream machine became the whir of a helicopter. The laughter at the next table morphed into shouted orders. The smell from the coffee shop next door twisted into dust and sweat and cordite.

My eyes snapped open, chest tight.

"Not tonight," I muttered to myself, scrubbing my hands over my face.

I got up, paced the living room, and checked the locks on the door for the third time. Rationally, I knew I was safe. Civilians didn't think like that, didn't keep their backs to the wall, didn't catalog every sound in the night. But my body hadn't gotten the memo.

Sleep didn't come easily on nights like this. When it did, it wasn't peaceful.

Hours later, I jolted awake, breath caught somewhere between a gasp and a choke. My heart slammed hard enough to make my ribs ache, each beat too fast, too loud. The room tilted for a second before I realized I was sitting up, palms braced against the couch cushions, shirt clinging to my skin with sweat. My body didn't get the message that I was safe. Every muscle was still wired tight, waiting for the next hit.

My throat burned, the taste of metal lingering there. My ears rang, sharp and hollow, like the echo of something that wasn't really there anymore. I could smell it too—dust, smoke, the dry sting of gunpowder that my mind had dragged back from nowhere.

It took a moment for the room to come into focus: the couch, the soft glow of lamplight, the hum of the TV. Home. Not the desert. Not the noise. Just home.

I dropped my face into my hands and dragged in a breath

that trembled on the way out. My body still didn't believe it. My pulse was a drumbeat against my palms, the edges of my vision still buzzing.

This was the part of me she couldn't see. The part I didn't talk about. The part that scared me more than any firefight ever had: the thought of letting someone in, of letting *her* in, and her seeing that I wasn't just guarded. I was haunted. But sometimes, in the moments when the shadows pressed in and my chest felt tight, I tried to hold onto a memory. A small, comforting moment from when I was a kid, before life felt so heavy, like the sound of the engine starting on my first dirt bike, the smell of fall as the leaves changed back home, a simple memory of safety. I focused on my breath, holding myself in the present, and imagined myself standing in that warm kitchen, far from the chaos that now chased me. It didn't always work, but sometimes it was enough to pull me back from the edge.

That's the part they never teach you in boot camp: how the danger ends, but your body keeps fighting ghosts.

The red numbers on the clock glowed *2:14 a.m.*

I sat on the couch, hunched forward, elbows on my knees, staring at my phone intently.

Her contact name glowed back at me: *Camille.*

I thumbed the screen, opened our thread. The last message was from her earlier that evening: *Thanks for the ice cream. It was nice to just laugh.*

I reread it for the tenth time. "Just laugh." That's what she'd said. And, it was nice. The kind of nice I hadn't felt in years.

But here I was, sweating through another shirt, body wired like I was back in the desert, mind replaying sounds and sights I couldn't explain to anyone who hadn't been there.

My thumb hovered over the keyboard, but the words wouldn't settle. What was I supposed to say? "Hey, I really like you, but sometimes I wake up convinced I'm still overseas. Still in the fight. Still broken."

No. That wasn't fair to her. Not now. Not when things were still so new.

I locked the phone and tossed it onto the cushion beside me. My breathing came rough, uneven. I forced myself through breathing. Again. Again. Until my heart stopped trying to punch its way out of my chest.

Still, sleep didn't come.

I leaned back, eyes on the ceiling. I'd promised myself after the divorce that I wouldn't drag anyone else into this. Better to keep things surface-level, keep myself detached. And yet here she was, laughing at my stupid jokes, looking at me like I wasn't a disaster, telling me about her kids and her classes and, trusting me with pieces of her world.

Every instinct told me to text her. To tell her she made me feel alive again. To admit she scared me in all the right ways.

Instead, I stayed quiet because hope was dangerous, and I wasn't sure if I was ready to let her see all the shadows I carried.

Chapter Nine

Camille

Morning came like a slap.

"Mommy!"

"Mommy! Snack!"

"Mommy, I spilled the milk…"

I rolled out of bed to the chorus of my kids, half-dressed and half-ready, like a marching band of chaos. My curls stuck up in every direction, my eyes heavy with sleep I didn't get.

"Shoes are by the door!" I called, tying my youngest's hair into a ponytail. "Stop touching your sister! We don't have time for fighting, we're already late!"

I hustled them into clothes, filled sippy cups, and yelled reminders to brush their teeth like a drill sergeant. My mom popped in right on cue to lend a hand and laugh at the spectacle.

"You look tired," she said, pouring herself coffee.

I groaned, shoving one kid's arm into a jacket. "I *am* tired."

But it wasn't the kind of tiredness I usually carried, the bone-deep exhaustion of working, studying, and raising three kids alone. This was a different tiredness. A softer one, because under the chaos, under the spilled cereal and homework papers, I was still smiling.

Every time I thought about Hunter leaning back in the chair, smirking at me, calling me out on my sweet tooth, my stomach flipped. Every time I remembered the way he said, *Well, I'm not most guys,* when I mentioned single moms being left behind, something warm spread through my chest.

"Why are you smiling?" Mom asked, raising an eyebrow.

"Am I?" I asked too quickly.

She smirked. "Mmhm. I know that look. It's a boy."

I rolled my eyes. "It's not a boy. It's…coffee. Always coffee."

"Sure it is." She said slyly.

After I dropped off Zeke at school, I headed to work at the doctor's office, running on caffeine and adrenaline. Patients came and went, phones rang, my supervisor asked me to file paperwork. I did it all on autopilot, the edges of my mind still stuck in that café, still replaying his crooked smile.

"Earth to Camille," my coworker teased, waving a chart in front of me.

"Sorry," I muttered, cheeks burning. "Just tired."

But the truth? I wasn't just tired. I was distracted.

Distracted by the way his eyes crinkled when he smiled. Distracted by the way he gave just enough of himself to be authentic without dumping everything on me. Distracted by the desire to know more.

By the time I picked up the kids from my Mom's, the day had chewed me up and spit me out. Chloe whined, Avery cried the entire ride home because she dropped her toy, and

Zeke lectured me about the importance of buying more juice boxes.

But even in the middle of it, when my phone buzzed with a text, my heart skipped.

Hunter: *Hope your day wasn't too crazy. Did you survive?*

Me: *Barely. Lost a soldier to spilled milk, but we'll recover.*

Hunter: *Proud of your bravery, Beautiful.*

I grinned, shaking my head, enjoying the welcome distraction.

Dinner was mac and cheese night. Which meant one would declare it the "wrong kind" of cheese, another would attempt to drown theirs in ketchup, and Zeke would eat exactly three bites before insisting he was "full" and demanding cookies instead.

"Mommy, you said broccoli makes you strong," my son argued, pushing his green pile around. "But I don't even *want* to be strong. I want to be fast."

"Eat two bites," I bargained, pointing my fork at him. "Ninja Turtles are both strong and fast. You gotta be both buddy." He huffed but ate them, glaring at me as if I'd ruined his Olympic career.

By the time I got them bathed and into bed, my hair was frizzing, my shirt had three mysterious stains, and I was pretty sure I'd stepped on at least six Legos. Glamorous single-mom life, right?

But here's the thing: even in the chaos, even in the mess, I was smiling.

Because in the middle of pouring milk, stealing cuddles, and refereeing a fight over toys, my phone buzzed again.

Hunter: *Did the troops settle in*
for the night? Or are they staging
a rebellion?

I snorted, typing back one-handed while holding a toothbrush for my youngest.

Me: *Rebellion was crushed at 2100*
hours. Victory is mine.

Hunter: *Sounds brutal. Any casualties?*

Me: *A Lego car lost its wheels.*
We will rebuild.

I bit my lip, grinning down at the screen. He made it so easy. Effortless.

When the kids were finally asleep, I collapsed on the couch, blanket pulled up around me, textbooks glaring at me from the table. My brain screamed, *study*. My heart whispered, *text him again.*

I gave in.

Me: *Thanks for ice cream the other day. It*
was nice to just... be a person. Not "Mom"
or "student" or "employee." Just me.

Hunter: *You are pretty great as "just you."*
  But for the record, I think you being
  a mom and student is perfect too.

I covered my face with the blanket, groaning into it. Who even *says* stuff like that? Men were supposed to vanish at the word "kids," not compliment me for juggling them.

Still, my cheeks hurt from smiling and I let myself laugh at the ridiculousness of it all. I was running on fumes, my to-do list was never-ending, and somewhere in all the chaos there was this man.

This man who made me laugh in ice cream shops. This man who texted me about Lego casualties. This man who made me feel like maybe, just maybe, I wasn't too much. And that was both the funniest and scariest thing of all, because this little space told the story of who I was: a woman doing the best she could with what she had. A woman patching together stability from the scraps life had left her. A woman who'd been left behind more than once before, and who still feared she might be again.

I tucked my blanket tighter, letting myself imagine, just for a heartbeat, what it might feel like to hear his laugh echoing in this apartment. What it might feel like to watch him step over toys, sit at my table, sip coffee from one of my mismatched mugs.

It was a dangerous dream. But it made me smile anyway.

And as I finally turned off the lamp, sinking into the too-small couch with textbooks still scattered across the table, the last thought that carried me into sleep was simple, terrifying, and impossible to shake.

Chapter Ten

Hunter

I returned my phone to my pocket as I walked into the clinic. The VA waiting room always smelled the same, like stale coffee and hand sanitizer. The walls were a bland beige, the kind of color that made you want to disappear into them.

I sat in the hard chair, jaw tight, boot tapping against the floor. Across from me, a guy I half-recognized from base years ago stared into space, eyes glazed. Another rubbed his hands together so hard it sounded like sandpaper. None of us talked. That was the unspoken rule. When my name was called, I stood too fast, shoulders already squared.

The therapist's office wasn't much better. There were posters about breathing exercises on the wall, an outdated desk stacked with papers, and two chairs facing each other like a trap. I took the edge of the chair, hands clasped in my lap, posture stiff.

"So, Hunter," she began, voice calm, practiced. "How have things been since we last spoke?"

"Fine" was my default. But the truth wouldn't stay down, pounding against my ribs with the memory of crouching in that dark room, breath caught on a ghost.

Instead, I shrugged. "Busy. Work. Life."

She tilted her head. "Any trouble with triggers lately?"

The word made my skin crawl. Triggers. As if I were a malfunctioning weapon.

I clenched my jaw. "Nothing new."

She studied me quietly, waiting for me. And I hated it. Hated the way she was trying to read me like I was a file on her desk. Marines aren't supposed to talk about feelings. Marines push through. Handle it. The first thing drilled into us was don't show weakness. Don't show cracks, that's what gets you killed.

And I learned it long before boot camp. My dad had made sure of that. I could still hear his voice, sharp as a belt: *Stop crying. Toughen up. No son of mine is soft.*

So I didn't cry. Didn't talk. Didn't break. I locked it all down, carried it tight, because being a man meant control. Except I wasn't in control anymore. I could handle firefights, deployments, and missions. But I couldn't handle the sounds of the neighborhood kids accidentally throwing a ball against my window or a nightmare as I tried to sleep in the comfort of my own bed.

The therapist asked another question, but I barely heard it. My thoughts were already with Camille, the way her eyes were on me as we played mini golf. Or the small dimple she has when she allows herself to truly smile, thinking I wasn't watching. I'd rather sit with these thoughts; they were safer.

I hated this room, this chair, these questions. But more than that, I hated myself for thinking maybe she'd be better off if I just stayed away. Because if my own dad thought I was weak for feeling, how the hell was I supposed to believe she'd think otherwise?

The therapist prompted me again about "strategies" I'd been using when the nightmares hit. I shifted in the chair, staring at the diploma on her wall like it was supposed to mean she understood. Truth was, I'd been sitting in chairs like this since my last deployment to Afghanistan.

These sessions were mandatory. Something I've had to do since getting diagnosed with PTSD once I got out. They awarded me monthly checks to compensate me for the bruises on my body and mind, but it didn't make it better. Neither did these box-checking exercises dressed up as concern. We'd file in one by one, sit across from someone half the unit's age, and nod through the same questions: Any trouble sleeping? Any panic symptoms? Any thoughts of hurting yourself or others?

You learn quickly what they want to hear. Keep it light. Shrug. Joke. Let them tick the box and move on. Because if you tell the truth, if you say you wake up drenched in sweat, heart pounding like it's still under fire - suddenly you're "flagged."

That second deployment left marks. The kind I don't talk about. We lost guys. Good ones. And some nights I still see their faces when I close my eyes. I walked off that plane knowing I was never walking back into life the same. I carried more than just the physical scars of those four deployments.

And sitting here, across from this woman with her mono-toned voice and clipboard, I felt it all over again, the uselessness of it. Because she didn't know me. Didn't know what it meant to keep people alive under fire. Didn't know the weight of going home when others didn't. I glanced at her again, her polite patience, the way she leaned forward like she could coax me into spilling what I'd spent years locking down.

And damn if I didn't think, not for the first time, that Camille would be ten times the therapist this girl was. I was still getting to know her, but she spoke about becoming a therapist with such passion. Camille wouldn't press with clinical questions and head tilts. She wouldn't rush me. Wouldn't try to fix me with a worksheet.

She'd just…be there.

Chapter Eleven

Camille

The week blurred into the usual storm: school drop-offs, late shifts at the office, night classes that stretched my brain past exhaustion.

And yet, it all felt a little lighter because in between the chaos, my phone kept lighting up with his name.

Good luck on your exam today, Beautiful.

Did the milk survive breakfast this morning?

Sometimes, the messages came when I needed them most, like when I was fighting with the printer at work and wanted to cry, or when the twins refused to nap and I thought my sanity was on its last thread. He had this uncanny timing, like he knew when I needed a reason to laugh.

By Friday night, I was sprawled on the couch, hair a mess, kids finally asleep, when my phone buzzed with a FaceTime call.

Hunter.

My heart stopped. I almost didn't answer. My shirt had a juice stain, the lighting was awful, and I looked exactly like a mom who'd been through a war zone of toddlers and cheese puffs. But then I remembered the way he teased me for dodging his jokes, the way he'd said, *Well, I'm not most guys.*

So I answered.

"Hey," I said, shifting so the camera didn't catch the toy explosion in the background.

His face filled the screen. Bright blue eyes, scruffy ginger beard, that crooked grin that made my pulse trip. He was leaning back somewhere quiet, his voice low. "Hey. You look… comfortable."

I snorted. "That's polite code for 'you look like a hot mess.'"

"Not at all," he said easily. "I mean, I wouldn't call that a red-carpet look, but you still pull it off." A smile tugged at his lips.

I laughed, tucking my curls behind my ear. "You're lucky I like honesty."

"Good," his eyes softened. "Because that's all I've got."

We talked for an hour. About everything, and nothing at all.

His day at work, my latest class assignment, the kids' antics. He asked what they were like, and I found myself telling him more than I meant to: how Zeke wanted to be an astronaut, how Avery could throw a tantrum worthy of an Olympic medal, and how Chloe still found her way into my bed at night.

He listened. Truly listened. Nodding, asking little questions, smiling as he took in every messy detail.

His gaze was caught on mine. "What?" I asked, self-conscious.

"Nothing," he said softly. "I just like talking to you."

I didn't know what to say to that. So I just smiled, hoping he couldn't see how my chest ached. Because if I let myself believe him, if I let myself hope, I knew I was already deeper than I planned. I tilted the phone a little closer, narrowing my eyes at him. "You know, for someone who talks a lot, you don't actually *say* much."

He smirked. "That's my strategy. Keep you intrigued."

"Oh, so you're mysterious now?" I teased, propping my chin in my hand. "I tell you about my mismatched-sock kid and the doll rebellion, and you give me… what? That you work on base and eat toothpaste-flavored ice cream?"

"Hey," he said, holding up a hand. "Ice cream says a lot about a man."

"Mmhm. Says you're stubborn."

"Says I don't need fluff," he corrected, that grin tugging at his lips.

I laughed, shaking my head. "You realize this is the part where most girls would demand details, right? They'd want to know about your past, why you don't talk about it."

He went quiet, just for a beat too long. His eyes flicked down, then back up. "Maybe someday."

The way he said it, steady and not dismissive, made my chest ache. He wasn't shutting me out. He was just… protecting himself.

I softened my tone. "I wasn't prying. Just noticing. You keep things close."

He nodded once. "Habit, I guess."

I let it go, even though curiosity buzzed in my veins. I didn't push because I knew how it felt to have scars you weren't ready to peel back for anyone. It can be hard sometimes. I appreciated questions, exploring how people felt, and why they felt that way. But with him, I could try to be patient.

So instead, I leaned into the humor again. "Fine. Keep your secrets. But just so you know, I'm still winning this conversation. I've given you at least three embarrassing stories. You owe me one."

His grin returned. "Embarrassing story, huh? Alright. When I was in grade school, maybe first or second grade, the teacher had written 'island' on the board. No one raised their hand to read it out loud, so I did. " He was already laughing before he even reached the hook of the story.

"I was so confident that I knew it, made a big 'ol scene." He continued. "So when the teacher called my name, I said 'Is-land' all proud and she yelled 'WRONG!'… I was so embarrassed, I felt like a fool. Lost my street cred and everything."

I burst out laughing, the sound echoing through my quiet living room. "Is that a real story?"

"Unfortunately, yes," he admitted. "I don't think I ever recovered from that." He replied, dramatically shaking his head, his laugh booming through the phone.

I was still laughing when Zeke made his way into the living room. He blinked at the phone screen and whispered, "Who's that?"

"This is Mommy's… friend," I said carefully, heart thudding.

Hunter smiled warmly, not missing a beat. "Hey, buddy. Escaping bedtime?"

"I don't want to sleep," Zeke said with sass and sleepy eyes.

"Me either, it's a lot more fun giving your mom trouble." His response was witty, leaving Zeke with a giggle as he buried his face in my shoulder. And for a moment, the whole world tilted. It was just a call, just a face on a screen, but I could already picture him here. In this home, in this mess, in this life.

When he finally shuffled back to bed, I glanced at the screen again. His smile was softer now, quieter.

"You're pretty good at this," I said.

"At what?"

"Not running." He didn't answer right away. Just held my gaze through the screen, unspoken words sitting between us.

"I think it's time you get some rest. Goodnight, Beautiful," he said finally.

"Goodnight," I whispered, even though I wasn't ready to end the call.

When the screen went dark, I lay there in the quiet, blanket tucked under my chin, heart racing with equal parts giddiness and fear. This wasn't just a distraction. It was the start of something that might matter.

Chapter Twelve

Hunter

The faint scent of diesel hung in the air, mingling with the warm aroma of deli sandwiches as Camille and I sat in the bed of my truck, eating lunch during her break. The sun glared off the scattered cars, and the metallic clang of the tailgate echoed each time we shifted. I had been off work for the day to attend another tedious appointment for my VA disability, and I surprised her with lunch after she shared she had forgotten hers in the morning rush out the door.

She was leaning against my side, her curls brushing my arm, and tilting her head up at me with that look that I was beginning to learn meant the gears in her head were churning.

In that moment, there was a quiet clarity. Her simple presence seemed to ease the weight of the day, grounding me in a way I hadn't felt in a while. Her being here turned an ordinary day into something memorable, something that felt like home.

"So…" she started, dragging the word out.

I narrowed my eyes. "So what?"

"Have you ever dated someone like me before?"

I raised a brow. "Define *like you*."

She huffed, sitting up straighter, her hands gesturing wildly. "You know. A mom. With kids." Her voice dipped. Her gaze flickered down for a moment as she seemed to brace herself, her fingers fidgeting with the edge of her scrub top, a small but telling movement that spoke louder than words ever could. Her eyes met mine again, and in that brief connection, I sensed her hesitation, wondering if I could see beyond the roles she believed defined her.

I leaned back, studying her like she was the only thing in the room worth seeing. "Someone like you?" I said finally. "No. Never."

Her brows pulled together, like she wasn't sure if that was a compliment or a confession.

I ran a thumb along her hand, slow and sure. "Because there's no one like you, Cami. And if you're asking if I can handle it — yeah. I can."

She looked at me then, really looked. Like she was trying to see if I meant it. That soft uncertainty in her eyes hit harder than any deployment ever had. I wanted to take it from her, that doubt, make her believe that everything she'd been through hadn't made her too much, it made her more.

She went quiet. Her gaze dropped to our hands, then back up to my face. For a second, she looked like she was weighing every word, every risk.

"Hunter," she said finally, voice low. "What happens when it gets hard?"

This was the question she never quite asked, always circling, hoping maybe this time I'd say something that would settle the worry in her eyes. I knew that look. The way she apologized for things that didn't need apologies, as if being a mom was something she had to excuse.

In the quiet, I saw the way her doubt crept in, and each time, all I could think about was proving her wrong. Showing her that every flaw she named was something I loved.

So I told her the truth.

I didn't hesitate. "Then I stay," I said simply.

She searched my face like she was waiting for the catch, like she was testing if I really meant it. And when the silence stretched, I saw the flicker of every fear she still carried.

So I leaned back on my arms and let out a groan. "Woman, you ask more questions than a recruiter on enlistment day."

Her mouth dropped open, eyes narrowing in mock offense. "Excuse me for trying to get to know you."

"You *interrogate* me," I said, pointing a finger at her, but the corner of my mouth tugged into a grin.

She rolled her eyes. "C'mon. Don't you ever have questions for me?"

"Nope," I said, popping a chip in my mouth.

She gasped, smacking my arm. "You're lying."

"Not a lie," I smirked, enjoying the way her cheeks flushed, the color rising like the morning sun. I didn't need to ask. I saw the way she absentmindedly tucked a curl behind her ear when she was feeling nervous or the little crinkle by her eyes that appeared every time she was about to smile. These small things told me more than words ever could. "I don't need to ask. I just watch."

Her eyes narrowed. "That's creepy."

"Observant," I corrected, leaning closer, lowering my voice. "Besides, every time you open your mouth, you're already telling me a hundred things."

Her lips parted, preparing to argue back, but I didn't give her the chance. I grabbed her waist and hauled her closer, fingers digging just enough to tickle her sides. She squealed, twisting against me, laughter spilling out so loud that others walking by glanced over.

"Hunter! Stop!" she cried, kicking her legs.

"Not until you admit you're nosy." I teased, pinning her lightly against the bed of the truck, her laughter echoing in my chest.

"Fine!" she gasped between giggles. "I'm nosy!"

I let up, chuckling as she shoved at me, her cheeks pink and eyes shining.

"Ridiculous," she muttered, trying to fix her hair, but she was smiling too, even if she was pretending not to.

And damn, she was beautiful like that. Loose. Laughing. Walls are coming down without even recognizing it.

"Your laugh is everything. Worth every moment and every unnecessary question." I said without thinking.

The truth was, yeah, she frustrated me sometimes. She didn't see herself the way I saw her. She asked those questions as if she were bracing for me to say the wrong thing, to confirm her fears. But what she didn't get, what I wanted to shake into her, was that none of it mattered. Not the kids, not the past, not the so-called baggage.

Having grown up with siblings and a single mom who juggled work and family, I'd learned early on that life was never a straight path. Relationships came with a mix of chaos and clarity. It was something I understood, having experienced it personally. Perhaps that's why I felt I knew her struggle, the feeling of being caught between responsibilities and relationships.

My phone buzzed in my pocket, a reminder from the VA office lighting up the screen. I barely glanced at it before silencing the noise, turning back to her instead. In that small moment, as she laughed and rolled her eyes, I realized she was the reason for all of it. The point, clear and simple.

Our reflection shimmered in the truck window. She was laughing, loose and unguarded, her eyes bright, while I sat steady beside her, a quiet smile tugging at my mouth. I knew I'd keep teasing her, keep finding ways to make her laugh, if that's what it took to remind her. Even if she couldn't see it yet, I did. Clear as sunlight.

Chapter Thirteen

Camille

By the time the weekend circled back around, nerves had settled into my skin. They sat there humming beneath the surface as I got ready for our next date. Just days before, we sat on the tailgate of his truck, sharing lunch.

We've been texting every day, trading late-night FaceTime calls that stretched long past midnight, his jokes catching me off guard and making me laugh even as I folded laundry. Still, this felt different.

I was beginning to see there was truly no man like him.

He was the perfect blend of everywhere he had been and everything he had seen. There were the small-town mannerisms from his childhood in upstate New York, like the way he always held the door a second longer just to make sure it didn't close on anyone behind him. Or the way he loved the outdoors, the smell of fresh-cut grass after rain, and late drives down back roads with the windows down.

Then there was the edge of the west coast woven in with

the easy confidence, the way he styled his clothes, and the calm assurance in how he carried himself. Every piece of him told a story, and the more time I spent with him, the more I wanted to listen. Taking another step forward, the kind that made my heart trip over itself, afraid I'd find a way to ruin it.

I'd spent the last twenty minutes pacing my living room before finally giving in and heading outside. Now I was standing at the curb, waiting outside as Hunter's truck came into view.

He drove a massive F-450 in a muted blue-gray, the kind of color that looked different under every light. It gleamed like polished steel, clean but not overtly flashy, and purposeful in the way he was. The cab sat high, tall enough that I'd have to climb, a reminder of how small I'd feel beside it.

And him. It was so *him*. Solid. Grounded. Larger than life. A little intimidating at first glance, but the kind of intimidating that made you feel safe once you got close.

When he parked at the curb, the engine cut off with a growl, and the silence left behind seemed louder than before. For a moment, all I could do was stare at the shadow of his frame behind the wheel, my pulse already racing. I nearly tripped over my own feet getting to the door.

Before I could reach for the handle, Hunter was already out of the truck. The slam of his door broke the quiet as he rounded the front, moving with that easy confidence that always made my stomach dip.

"Hey, Beautiful," he said, that grin tugging at his lips before his hand extended toward me.

I hesitated for half a second before slipping my hand into his. His palm was warm, solid, and steady in a way that made my pulse trip over itself. He helped me up into the truck, his other hand brushing the small of my back as I slid into the passenger seat.

"Careful," he murmured, his voice low enough to vibrate through me.

I looked up, our eyes meeting in the soft glow of the streetlight. "You always this chivalrous?" I asked, aiming for casual, even as my heart pounded against my ribs.

His mouth curved, slow and deliberate. "Only when I'm trying to impress someone."

I bit back a smile. "And how's that working out for you?"

His thumb grazed my knuckles once, deliberate and easy. "Guess I'll find out."

I swallowed hard, gripping the edge of the seat as he closed the door. Through the glass, I caught the faintest trace of his grin before he circled back around to the driver's side, completely unaware of the mess he'd just made of my pulse.

He drove us to my favorite taco spot just outside town, the kind wedged between a pawn shop and a car repair place, with faded paint on the walls and iron bars over the windows. The type of place you'd drive past twice before knowing it was open. But in Southern California, you know the rule: the sketchier the spot, the better the tacos. And this place? Legendary.

The air smelled of grilled carne asada and sizzling onions, smoky and rich, the kind of scent that clung to your clothes long after you left. A stereo on the counter buzzed out old ranchera music, blending with the hiss of the fryer and the clatter of spatulas on the griddle. The picnic tables out front were sticky with years of hot sauce bottles and laughter.

"They have the best fries here!" The enthusiasm was clear in my voice.

Hunter raised a brow? "We're at a taco stand, and you're thinking about the fries."

I smirked, dipping one into the little paper cup of salsa. "Don't hate. Fries are universal." I leaned across the table, lowering my voice. "At least I don't pick tomatoes out of my food like a picky five-year-old."

That got him. He groaned, dragging a hand over his beard. "Tomatoes ruin everything."

"Oh my gosh!" I said, popping a fry into my mouth with exaggerated delight. "You're lucky you're cute."

He shook his head, chuckling, and the weight between us softened instantly. The conversation flowed easily, like we've been sitting at tables like this for years instead of weeks. And somewhere between the salty fries, his smirk, and the smoky air clinging to my sweater, I realized just how much I enjoyed this, him, us, the way it felt so natural to be here together.

When we left, we ended up walking by the water. It wasn't planned, just one of those things where the night felt too good to end, so we kept moving. The breeze lifted my curls, the moonlight softened everything, and for once, I wasn't thinking about bills or homework or who needed a packed lunch. I was just… me. We stopped by the railing, the water lapping quietly below us. He leaned against it, arms crossed, watching me with that look that made me feel seen all the way through.

"You know," I said, trying to lighten the weight of the moment, "you're not as mysterious as you think you are."

"Oh yeah?" he asked, one eyebrow raised.

"Yeah. You're stubborn, you drink an unhealthy amount of energy drinks, and you think you're funny."

He grinned. "Think?"

"Okay, fine. Sometimes you're funny. But I still want to know more. "

He leaned back, a smirk tugging at his lips. "You ask a hell of a lot of questions, you know that?"

I raised a brow. "Curiosity is a virtue."

"Oh, is it?" he countered, leaning in until I had to laugh.

"I'm a Therapist-in-training, duh," I shot back, poking his side. His mock gasp turned into a grin as he caught my hand before I could pull it away, brushing a teasing kiss across my knuckles.

He shook his head, chuckling softly, and then his smile faded into something more tender. His eyes locked on mine, firm and intent, he was peeling back every layer I'd tried to hide behind. My breath caught, the air suddenly thick between us.

The world around us seemed to hush. The distant splash of water against the shore dulled, and the cool night breeze brushed over my skin, carrying the faint scent of cypress and lime that clung to him. It was sharp, earthy, and clean, a contrast that made me feel grounded and lightheaded all at once.

Being this close to him felt like trouble, the kind of trouble I didn't mind leaning into. I shifted slightly, resting my hand against his chest, feeling the steady beat of his heart under my palm. His warmth bled through his shirt, grounding me in a way I hadn't felt in years.

My rules, my careful boundaries, they felt flimsy here, flimsy against the weight of his arm draped so easily around me.

For a while, neither of us spoke. The sound of waves crashed against the pier, the salty breeze tugging at my curls.

He reached out suddenly, brushing a stray strand of hair from my face. His knuckles grazed my cheek, light as a whisper, but enough to send my pulse racing.

"Cami," he said, voice low, rougher than usual. He said my name like he treasured it.

I looked up, and the way his blue eyes caught mine nearly stole my breath. Everything else disappeared. It was just him, staring at me as if I were the only thing in sight.

He leaned in slightly, close enough that I could smell the faint mix of leather, salt air, and the fresh woodsy scent that clung to him. Close enough that if I tilted my chin just an inch, our lips would meet.

My breath caught. My rules screamed *don't,* but my body betrayed me, leaning toward him before my brain could catch up. He hesitated, his forehead nearly brushing mine, giving me every chance to pull away. But I didn't.

Instead, I whispered, "You're trouble."

A slow smile curved his mouth. "Yeah. But maybe the kind you need."

And then, just before the moment tipped into something I wasn't sure I was ready for, he pressed a soft kiss to my temple instead. Gentle. Careful. Like he knew I needed space to want more before I asked for it. The restraint, the choice to hold back, lit a fire in me stronger than if he'd kissed me outright.

And then my mouth was on his.

It wasn't delicate. It was greedy, desperate, like he'd been holding back for too long. His hand slid to the small of my back, anchoring me, as I clutched at the fabric of his shirt. The kiss deepened, his beard rough against my skin, his breath warm, tasting faintly of. I felt it everywhere. Down my spine, at the tips of my toes, curling low in my stomach.

Being this close to him felt like fire. If we had not been sitting on the side of the road, looking over the pier, I may have been tempted to break more of the rules I created to protect myself. This was uncharted territory, and I did not mind. I leaned into the moment, enjoying his embrace and allowing my hand to feel the swell of his biceps.

When he finally pulled back, both of us breathing hard, his forehead rested against mine. His voice was rough, almost ragged. "Still trouble?"

My answer was a shaky laugh as I buried my face against his chest, giggling like a girl half my age. "Shh, no talking."

His chest rumbled with quiet laughter, and his arms tightened around me. In that moment, with him holding me with no intention of ever letting go, I knew I was already deeper than I planned to be.

I grinned, unable to help it, still clutching his shirt like I needed proof he was real. Before doubt could creep in, I pressed my face into his chest, breathing him in. A nervous laugh slipped out, bubbling up before I could stop it. His arms tightened, creating a sense of safety that I knew I could hold onto when everything else felt uncertain.

And in that small, imperfect moment, I realized just how much I wanted this. How much I wanted him.

Chapter Fourteen

Hunter

Her laugh was still caught in my shirt when I finally eased back, brushing one last kiss to her lips before we headed toward the truck. She slipped her hand into mine without question, her fingers small but certain, her warmth anchoring me with every step.

The whole walk to the truck, I kept sneaking glances at her. Memorizing the curve of her smile, soft and secret, like she was still replaying the kiss in her head. Hell, maybe I was, too.

When we reached the truck, I opened the passenger door with a mock formality, bowing slightly. "Your chariot awaits."

She arched a brow, clearly amused. "Pretty sure a chariot doesn't come with oversize tires and a lift."

"Only the best for you," I said, smirking, enjoying her laugh as she climbed in.

By the time we hit the road, she was already fiddling with the radio, scrolling through my presets until she found one of my playlists. The beat that filled the cab was hard and fast, bass thrumming through the seats. She gasped, clutching her chest in fake horror. "Is this... EDM?"

I side-eyed her, one hand steady on the wheel. "What's wrong with that?"

"Five minutes ago, you were humming along to Florida Georgia Line. Now it's...whatever this is. Explain yourself," she teased, grinning.

"It's called music, Cami." I deadpanned.

She laughed, the sound bubbling out in a way she couldn't stop. "Music? This is a war crime. One second, it's cowboy hats and heartbreak, the next, it's bass drops and club lights. Who are you?"

"The best of both worlds," I deadpanned.

She snorted, leaning back in her seat. "You're like if Spotify had an identity crisis."

"Jealous?" I muttered, tapping the wheel in time with the beat.

"Of what? Your chaotic playlists? Please." She crossed her arms, a smirk tugging at her lips. "This just confirms what I already suspected. There are so many layers to you, *Hunter Bennett*. What are you going to tell me next? You're secretly a cowboy who dreams of break dancing."

I barked out a laugh, shaking my head. "Don't tempt me, *Camille Brooks*. I've got some moves." Emphasizing her name in response to her using mine.

"Oh, I bet you do," she teased, eyes sparkling. "Do I get to see them?"

"Not a chance," I said quickly, though I couldn't help the grin spreading across my face. "The world isn't ready for all of that."

She leaned her head back against the window, still smiling.

"You're ridiculous."

"Ridiculously charming," I corrected.

"More like ridiculously confident."

"Same thing," I shot back, and her laugh filled the cab again, warm and bright in a way that made me want to keep her talking just to hear it. I shook my head, biting back a smile. Her laugh tumbled out, unguarded, the kind that made the heaviness I carried feel lighter for a moment. And as the miles slipped by, the banter slowed, making way for a more intimate moment. She stretched her legs, bare knees brushing the dashboard, her head leaning lightly against the window.

"You know," she said quietly, her fingers tracing invisible patterns on the purse in her lap, voice almost lost under the hum of tires on asphalt, "I feel… different with you." It was as if the quietness of the cab allowed her thoughts to surface, ones she'd been hesitant to voice. There was a warmth that flooded through me at her admission, a mixture of relief and vulnerability. Her fingers stilled for a moment, a subtle pause that seemed to carry words left unspoken. "Like I can breathe. Like, I don't have to be everything all at once."

For a moment, words wouldn't come. She had seen right through to the part of me I kept hidden, the part that had learned to survive on silence and solitude. I thought about telling her how much I needed this, needed her, even when fear had its hand around my throat. The ache wasn't just about comfort; it was the kind that made it clear I wasn't here to drift—I was here to stay.

So I just reached over, laying my hand over hers on the center console. Not pushing. Not holding her tight. Just letting her know I was there. She turned her palm up, threading her fingers through mine like it was the easiest choice in the world.

The rest of the drive, she alternated between roasting my playlist choices and humming along when I caught her knowing the words. Every time she laughed, the cab of the truck felt a little more like home.

By the time I pulled up to her place, I knew one thing for sure: I was already in too deep. She shifted in the seat, suddenly quiet, her fingers playing with the strap of her purse. I tried to find the right words, something clear enough to make her believe I wasn't leaving, but they wouldn't come.

So instead, I killed the engine and turned toward her.

"Thanks for tonight," she said, voice low but controlled as she smiled softly, eyes searching mine, telling me she wanted to ask what I wasn't saying. But she didn't push. She just leaned in and brushed her lips across my cheek, quick and light, a promise she wasn't ready to put into words.

I cleared my throat, forcing myself to let go of her hand. "Goodnight, Beautiful." Pressing a kiss to her lips, I felt her smile. As I pulled away, her smile widened, "Goodnight, Hunter."

Then I watched her walk up the path to her apartment, every part of me wanted to call her back, kiss her one more time, hold onto this night a little longer.

Chapter Fifteen

Camille

The butterflies hadn't stopped since that kiss and instead followed me as I made the short walk from his truck to my apartment. They were in my chest, my stomach, my fingertips tapping nervously against my jeans. It was ridiculous, really. I was a grown woman, a mother of three, someone who had lived through abandonment and bruises and years of struggle. I had once believed in love fiercely, letting it sweep me up. It was in these moments that made the heartbreak later feel so much sharper. And yet, one kiss had undone me. I thought about his laugh, his blended choice of music, the way he didn't pull away when I admitted my chaos. He'd kissed me anyway. Maybe even because of it.

By the time I kicked off my shoes and sank into the sagging couch, my cheeks still ached from smiling. And every time I replayed Hunter's ridiculous impersonation of me ordering fries at a taco stand, laughter bubbled up again. My stomach hurt in the good way that lets you forget, just for a moment, how heavy life can be. But as the laughter faded, joy gave way to a quiet thread of doubt. What if this feeling was as fleeting as the sunset we watched, shadows stretching long over the ache I'd barely stilled? I tried to shake it off, clinging to the happiness a little longer.

I wasn't ready to say it aloud, not even to myself, but I already missed him. Which was absurd. We'd just parted, his truck easing away as I stood there like a lovesick teenager watching taillights fade. The scent of him still clung to me, blending with the echo of laughter scraping against the hush. But beneath this aching hovered a fear I couldn't shake… a voice murmuring warnings about opening my heart too quickly. Trust, once broken, is delicate. Even with warmth in my chest, I wondered if exposing too much would leave me defenseless again. I didn't want to text *I miss you already;* it felt too raw, too soon. Still, I reached for the thought of her, aching to close the gap between yearning and caution.

My fingers drifted through my playlist until I found it. Taylor Swift's "Love Story." Too obvious? Maybe. Too cheesy? Definitely. But honest. That soft guitar intro had kept me company on lonely nights before, back when love was just a pipe dream. Tonight, though, it felt like more than a dream. It felt possible.

I hesitated, thumb hovering over send. My heart raced; my mind screamed too much, too soon. But the part of me that laughed with him over greasy tacos and sticky tables pressed anyway.

The link sent with a soft whoosh.

For a full minute, I stared at the screen, nerves crawling up my spine. Then my phone buzzed.

Hunter: You sending me Romeo and Juliet
  stuff now? That's dangerous.

A jolt of excitement shot up my spine. I couldn't stop the small, nervous grin tugging at my mouth, heart pounding harder as I tapped out my reply.

Me: OMG, Hush. Just listen.

Hunter: Fine…You're lucky I like you.

A few minutes later, another reply.

Hunter: Cheesy…but I may be grinning like an idiot.

I thought about how he'd smiled on FaceTime when Avery peeked into the screen, about how he hadn't flinched when I told him stories of Zeke's sass or Chloe's stubborn streak. Instead, he'd leaned in, curious. Like he wanted to know them, too.

That thought gave me butterflies all over again. Still, fear coiled in my chest. Because I knew how it felt when men decided this life was too much. I'd seen the back of the door close before.

Me: Don't get used to it. You'll start
  thinking I'm soft or something.

The dots appeared, disappeared, then came back.

Hunter: Beautiful, you sent me Taylor Swift.

You're already soft.

Heat flushed my neck and I laughed, burying my face in the pillow. He was relentless.

But when I closed my eyes and the chorus played in my head:

"Romeo, take me somewhere we can be alone..."

"You'll be the prince and I'll be the princess. It's a love story, baby, just say, Yes".

For a moment, I let myself believe that maybe this was my second (or third) chance. This feeling was more than hope. It was a quiet promise, echoing against the old scar I kept hidden. Years ago, when trust broke and love felt impossible, I promised myself I'd only open my heart again if it felt right, truly right. Maybe this thing with Hunter was the answer I'd been waiting for, the light that could finally reach the places I'd kept in shadow.

Chapter Sixteen

Hunter

The base thrummed with the same steady pulse as always. Boots striking pavement, radios murmuring, the quiet choreography of routine. Working as a government contractor never felt glamorous, but it kept me tethered to what I understood. Structure. Familiarity. The comfort of knowing what comes next.

At least, it was supposed to be.

By midmorning, I was on my third energy drink, and my focus was shot. The noise in the office: phones ringing, keyboards clacking, the low hum of conversation, blended into one long, dull blur. I rubbed the back of my neck, exhaustion pressing behind my eyes.

I'd been up half the night airing out my apartment. The place still smelled faintly of smoke and burnt chicken, a reminder of how badly I'd screwed up dinner.

Dinner had been my way of saying thanks. Camille had invited me into her world, given me time that I knew was valuable. It had meant more than I'd expected. I'd wanted to do something small, something normal, to show her that I didn't take any of it for granted.

But the second she walked through my door, all plans went out the window.

Every time she laughed, it hit me right in the gut. I'd told myself to concentrate, to act like I had a handle on things, but the truth was, I couldn't keep my hands off her. She made every rational thought scatter.

Music had been playing low from the speaker; some country playlist that was supposed to feel casual but now felt too intimate. The soft light from the window caught the edges of her hair as she leaned against the counter, barefoot, curls messy and falling out of some knot on top of her head.

She leaned against the counter, barefoot, curls wild and falling loose around her face. Oil popped in the pan, and behind me, she was humming. I didn't tell her I liked it. I just let it fill the space.

She'd changed out of her scrubs into one of my old T-shirts that hung off one shoulder, and I was doing my best to focus on dinner instead of her.

"You keep looking at me like that, and I'm gonna burn the chicken," I said, flipping the spatula in my hand to distract myself.

She tilted her head, smiling in that way that made my chest go tight. "You mean the chicken that's already smoking?"

I turned, smirking. "You volunteering to take over?"

"Maybe," she teased, stepping closer and peaking over my shoulder, her voice dipping just enough to make my pulse jump. "But, you seem pretty confident."

"Confident?" I grinned. "It's called skill, Beautiful."

"You mean, ego?" she shot back, crossing her arms.

"Maybe. Good thing you're here to keep me humble."

Her laugh filled the small space, bouncing off the walls.

I didn't mean to move closer, but I did. The air between us grew heavy. Rosemary and the faint sweetness of her perfume tangled together, grounding me and making me dizzy all at once.

She tilted her chin up, pretending to look unimpressed. "Are you gonna move, or are you waiting for the kitchen to catch fire?"

I smiled, slow and deliberate. "Depends. You planning to kiss me or keep talking?"

Her breath caught. That half-second, that hesitation, hit me harder than anything. And then, like gravity had its own plan, I stepped forward, bracing my hands on either side of her. The warmth of her body radiated through the space between us. I could feel her pulse where my thumb brushed her hip.

She'd looked up at me like she wasn't sure whether to roll her eyes or kiss me first. I didn't give her the chance to decide. I lifted her onto the counter, and she laughed, bright and unguarded, a sound that rewired something deep inside me.

"Hunter!" she said, half laughing, half breathless. "The food—"

"Can wait," I murmured, voice lower than I meant. "You were staring."

"Was not."

"Uh-huh," I said, leaning closer. "Is that why you're blushing?"

Her lips parted, and that was all the invitation I needed. I kissed her before she could say a word, and everything else fell away.

The kiss started softly. Then it deepened, slow and certain, the kind of kiss that felt like a promise you weren't ready to make but couldn't help believing in.

Her hands slid into my hair, fingers curling at the nape of my neck. The world narrowed. No noise, no fear, no past. Only her.

Then the smoke alarm went off.

We both jumped, laughter and chaos colliding as I swore under my breath, grabbed a towel, and started waving smoke like an idiot.

"You distracted me," I yelled over the shrieking.

"Oh, sure," she said, laughing so hard she nearly doubled over, "blame the woman!"

"I'm serious! You've got that…" I pointed between us, "…that look. It's dangerous."

"Dangerous?" she said, still grinning. "I was just standing here."

The alarm finally cut out, leaving a ringing silence in its wake. The only sound left was her laughter, now booming throughout the kitchen.

"Exactly my point." I tossed the towel aside, stepped in close again, and returned my hands to her waist. "You done making fun of me?"

"Not even close," she'd said, smiling up at me.

"Good." I'd kissed her again, just because I could.

We ended up ditching the food completely, ordering pizza instead. She sat cross-legged on the floor in one of my old hoodies, eating straight from the box while I grabbed us a couple of beers. The apartment smelled faintly of smoke, but it didn't matter.

Now, hours later at my desk, I could still hear her laugh.

After the divorce, I told myself I'd never have that kind of life again. It felt like walking through a minefield, never sure which step would set everything off. The end wasn't a single explosion, just a slow unraveling, a thousand small cracks until there was nothing left to hold.

I promised myself I wouldn't make the same mistakes. I told myself not to try again. I'd had enough of disappointment, of silence that hardens into walls. It felt safer not to want what I couldn't keep.

But then there was Camille. The wild curls. The loud laugh that turned heads for all the right reasons. The way she looked at me left me feeling like maybe I wasn't beyond repair.

I ran a hand over my beard, exhaling hard.

The guys at work would laugh if they knew what was in my head. Probably call me crazy for losing it over a woman I'd barely known for a few months. And maybe they'd be right.

But the truth was simple. I couldn't get her out of my head.

And no matter how much I told myself to slow down, to keep things simple, that spark she lit in me said otherwise.

Chapter Seventeen

Camille

The bench creaked beneath us, the sound sharp in the hush of night, almost startling. The air was thick with the scent of cut grass, spring pressing close. Dampness clung to my skin, and the constant hum of crickets filled the quiet. A rhythm that had become the soundtrack of these secret nights.

Things were good between us, better than I'd let myself imagine they could be, but I still wasn't ready for Hunter to meet the kids. Not yet.

So, he'd slip over after they were asleep. Sometimes we talked for hours. Other times, we didn't talk much at all. Just sat there, side by side on the porch, the soft glow of the porch light catching in the dust floating between us.

Tonight, we sat on the bench he'd brought over a couple of weeks ago, a thoughtful replacement for the old folding lawn chairs we used to perch on. The bench wasn't just a seat; it was a quiet gesture, something that told me he planned to be around to use it.

I curled my legs beneath me, a blanket draped around my shoulders, while Hunter leaned back, one arm stretched across the back of the bench like he'd always belonged there. His knee bounced before he caught himself and smiled sheepishly.

"You ever think about how much of us comes from back then?" I asked suddenly, not even sure why the words slipped out. Maybe it was the hour. Maybe it was the way the night felt softer with him in it.

He tilted his head. "Back when?"

"Childhood." I traced the rim of my mug, avoiding his gaze. "Who we are. What we carry."

He didn't answer right away. His jaw flexed, eyes narrowing just slightly in thought. So I went first.

"My parents divorced when I was four," I said. "It was just me, my mom, and my brother after that. She… she did her best, you know? Worked two jobs, stretched every dollar, kept a roof over our heads. But I watched her go through men who didn't deserve her. I saw her get her heart broken more than once."

Hunter's eyes stayed on me. He had a way of listening that made you feel both exposed and safe at once.

"I admired her, though," I continued. "Her resilience. The way she kept going, even when life kept knocking her down. She made survival look effortless, but I think… that's what did it. That's why I grew up believing that needing someone was dangerous. Because she always had to pick up the pieces alone."

I swallowed hard, staring into the dark yard. "And my dad…" The words caught for a second. Thinking about my dad always hit me in a special spot in my chest. "I remember being seven, standing at the window watching him pack his car to move across the country. He waved like it was no big deal. His visits after that were… fine. Fun, even. But they were quick, and didn't come often."

Hunter's gaze softened, but he didn't interrupt.

"He was in the Navy. So was my mom," I said quietly. "But where my mom was all emotion and softness, he was the opposite. They didn't really teach us how to handle things well when they got hard. Just how to get through."

Hunter leaned forward, forearms braced on his knees. "Yeah," he said, voice low. "I get that."

When he looked up, his expression had shifted, like a door he didn't open often had unlocked.

"My parents split when I was nine," he said. "My dad was a Marine right out of high school. Hard as hell. Emotions weren't really a thing for him either. If something hurt, you walked it off. Simple as that." He rubbed his thumb against his palm, the motion small, almost unconscious. "Mom was strong in her own way. She had to be. Dad was gone a lot, so she held it all together. But it meant nobody talked about how they felt."

His voice roughened, quieter now. "Truth is, I don't remember much from my childhood."

My heart squeezed. "Yeah, sometimes the brain forgets the things that are too heavy to deal with."

He gave a half-smile, more a twitch than a grin. "Guess I boxed it up like I was taught to do. Lock it down. Keep moving."

The silence that followed wasn't awkward, just heavy with shared understanding. The kind that only comes from two people who've both learned to live inside their armor.

"Tell me more?" I asked softly, falling into my old habit of asking questions.

He hesitated, then looked down at his hands. "By the time I was a teenager, I was a mess. We moved a lot, never long enough to feel rooted anywhere. I acted out: picked fights, raced cars I had no business driving. My mom tried to rein me in, but I wasn't exactly easy to parent. I didn't know who I was, so I chased anything that made me feel something. I was pretty reckless."

I didn't say anything, didn't fill the space with reassurance. I just listened.

"Eventually, I moved in with my dad, hoping it'd straighten me out. It didn't," he said with a wry laugh. "By eighteen, I was either going to end up in a ditch or a cell. Joining the Marines felt like my last chance to get it together."

He told me about the drill sergeant who'd barked until his voice was gone, the way the structure and discipline had both saved him and hardened him. "You don't process things there. You push through. You get strong. You survive." He looked at me then, his eyes steady in the dim porch light. "Guess I'm still trying to unlearn that."

My throat tightened. "That sounds... hard."

He shrugged, but there was no denial in it. "It was. But then I met you."

The words weren't loud or dramatic. Just simple and honest, landing in the space between us like truth.

I reached out without thinking, my fingers tracing the lines of the tattoo on his forearm. The ink rippled over muscle, the orange and black scales soft beneath my touch. "Maybe that's why we work," I whispered. "Because we both know what it's like to grow up without softness. And maybe now we get to build something different."

He turned his hand over, threading his fingers through mine. His skin was warm, calloused, and grounding in mine.

"Maybe," he said, voice low. "Or maybe it's just you. You make me want to try."

The night stretched quietly around us, the air thick and humming, the crickets still keeping time. I could feel the weight of his words settle deep inside me. And as I sat there in that moment, on the bench he had bought, I didn't feel like I was reaching for something that would disappear.

I just felt seen.

Chapter Eighteen

Hunter

The night air felt both cool and dense as I thought about her latest question, the hum of distant cars often fading into the background whenever I found myself lost in thought. It was the small moments like these that revealed the progress we'd made.

She asked questions, always. Not sharp or prying, but gentle, like she was tracing the outline of who I was, mapping out the places I kept hidden. Sometimes I pictured her inner monologue running wild, teasing herself for being so relentless, but it was never just a game. Beneath the jokes, there was a quiet, vulnerable shift that pulled us deeper.

I smirked, rubbing a hand over my beard as I shared more stories of my reckless teen years, too busy racing cars and skipping out on curfews to be worried about school or girls. The one…or two times I found myself in trouble after getting caught racing down quite backroads.

Her laugh bubbled out, bright, and I caught the sparkle in her eyes. "That actually makes so much sense."

But then her questions dug deeper.

"What was deployment really like?"

"Do you still talk to your ex-wife?"

"What was the hardest part of all of it?"

Silence pressed in, her eyes searching mine for answers I wasn't ready to give. My knee bounced, restless, the night air cool against my skin. I rubbed my hands together, chasing warmth, words heavy and unspoken between us. The quiet filled up with everything I couldn't say. Her gaze lingered, waiting, and my heart thudded with the weight of things I kept buried. Old scars flickered just beneath the surface.

Finally, I broke eye contact, staring down at my hands. "I know..." she said carefully, "some things are just hard to talk about."

"They are," I admitted, voice low. "And I'll tell you what I can. Just... not everything. Not right now."

The air felt thick, heavy with everything unsaid.

I forced a grin, trying to break it up. "What is this, anyway, twenty questions? You planning to write my biography or something?"

Her eyes narrowed with mock offense. "Oh, so now you're complaining?"

"I mean..." I leaned back, smirking. "You do ask a lot."

Before I could react, she lunged, laughing, and climbed onto my back like she was tackling me. "Fine! If you won't answer, I'll annoy it out of you!"

"Camille!" I barked, laughing hard now, trying to shake her off. Her curls tickled my face, her giggles filling the night air.

I bent forward, pretending to stumble, then spun, making her squeal as I scooped her legs tighter around me. "You think you can torture a Marine for information? Rookie mistake."

Her laughter turned breathless, forehead pressed against my shoulder.

She poked at places I usually kept locked up, but with her clinging to me, both of us laughing until our ribs hurt, it didn't feel risky. The tension in my shoulders eased, breath coming easier, laughter making room for a lighter feel. It felt like stepping out of shadow into sunlight, each laugh a gentle nudge toward safety. Her weight on my back wasn't heavy; it was comforting, a quiet reminder that letting someone in could feel like this.

I wasn't just surviving the questions. I was enjoying the fact that someone actually wanted to know the answers.

She clung to me until we both collapsed onto the bench in a heap, breathless from laughing. My chest hurt in the best way; her giggles still spilling into my shoulder as she tried to catch her breath. I couldn't remember the last time I laughed like that: full belly, no filter, the kind that left me lightheaded.

When the noise settled, it was just us. Her weight still against me, her curls brushing my jaw, both of us sinking into the quiet. I pulled her around until she straddled my lap. My arms slipped around her waist, holding her there without thinking.

She shifted slightly, her hand flattening against my chest, right over my heart. It thudded harder under her touch, and I knew she could feel it. Her laughter faded, replaced by that look, the one that always leveled me: soft, curious, too damn knowing.

"You know, you always joke when you don't want to answer," she murmured, not accusing, just observing, her fingers fidgeting slightly with a loose thread on her sleeve as if trying to rein in her nerves.

"Maybe," I admitted, my thumb brushing absently over her hip. "Some answers aren't easy to give."

Her eyes softened, and for a second I thought she might push again, but she didn't. She just nodded, her lips curving in the faintest smile. "That's okay. I'll wait until you're ready."

Her words landed heavier than she probably intended. No one had ever said that to me before. Not my mom, not my ex, not anyone. Most people either pushed or walked away when I went quiet. But she stayed. Her steady gaze told me she wasn't going anywhere, forcing my jaw to unclench just a little. Her presence was a kind of quiet bravery I wasn't used to.

A memory flashed up, sharp and raw: the day I signed divorce papers, signing away promises left behind with the emptiness. But now, with her beside me, that loneliness didn't stand a chance. She stayed. That changed everything, and I felt myself come undone, just a little.

I bent, pressing my forehead to hers, breathing her in. She smelt of warmth and sweetness, like coconut lotion and a hint of vanilla from whatever candle she burned in her apartment. My chest tightened, and before I could stop myself, I whispered, "You make it harder to keep the walls up."

Her breath hitched, her smile soft but certain. "Good," she whispered back.

The bench creaked beneath us, familiar now, a quiet reminder of where we started and how far we'd come. It didn't startle us anymore. Instead, it echoed the comfort and trust we'd built, holding the weight of authenticity between us.

We stayed there breathing each other in, the world around

us fading to nothing. My fingers slid into her curls, hers curled tighter against my chest, and when her lips finally found mine, it wasn't playful anymore. The distant sound of cars thickened the quiet, a gentle hum beneath the night. But even amidst that fear, I couldn't pull away; the moment held us suspended, both tender and terrifying in its intimacy. I wasn't afraid of being seen. Not with her.

The laughter slowly ebbed, replaced by the soft hum of the porch light flickering above us. She tucked her legs under her and looked at me again with that same curiosity.

"Do you ever get tired of me asking questions?" she asked.

I tipped my head back, pretending to groan. "C'mon, don't you ever run out?"

She smirked. "Nope. It's kind of my thing."

I shrugged. "Guess I'd rather just… be here. With you."

Her face softened, voice threaded with care. "My questions aren't just small talk. It's how I understand, how I connect." She picked at a loose thread on the blanket, eyes drifting somewhere far away. "Maybe that's why I want to be a therapist. I spent years wishing someone would ask the right questions. Not to fix me, just to see me. So now I keep searching, trying to give what I always needed."

Her words settled inside me, stirring something I hadn't let myself feel in a long time. I just watched her, the porch light painting soft gold across her skin.

"You do that," I said finally. "You make people feel seen."

Color bloomed across her cheeks. "I just… want to understand you."

I brushed my knuckles against her knee. "Careful, Beautiful. Keep asking like that, and you might actually get past my walls."

Her laugh was quiet, caught between teasing and tenderness. "That's the point." I grinned, leaning closer until our shoulders touched. "Good luck, then."

We sat together in the hush of night, porch light flickering, shadows shifting across her face. My breath slowed, and I noticed how my shoulders seemed to drop, releasing a tension I hadn't realized I was holding. For once, I didn't feel the urge to fill the silence. Maybe the questions didn't need answers yet. Maybe it was enough that she kept asking, and that I wanted her to.

Chapter Nineteen

Camille

We've been on several dates now. Spent late nights laughing on my porch, and today, Hunter decided it was time to test my limits and take me out on his motorcycle. If anyone else had suggested it, I would have flat-out refused. My anxiety never allowed for things that felt reckless. I liked seat belts, four doors, and safety ratings. But with him? Somehow, the word "no" never made it past my lips. He'd already earned a kind of trust I didn't give easily.

So here I was listening to the rumble of his Harley, its sound deep and commanding as it rolled down my street. My stomach churned with a mix of anticipation and fear.

He pulled up with easy confidence, the kind that comes from being one with the machine. My heart raced as I eyed the bike sitting at the curb like a beast, all black steel and sharp chrome. This thing looked like it ate miles for breakfast and spat them back out in smoke. Small pops of purple flashed against the black, showing a glimmer of his personality.

I swallowed hard. Every instinct screamed I should be afraid, but it wasn't the kind of fear that held you back. It was the kind that pulled you forward, reckless and intoxicating. With him at the controls and me wrapped around him, this danger also held a bit of freedom. The kind that makes your pulse race, your breath catch, and your body crave the ride anyway.

Hunter turned off the engine, swung his leg over, and tugged off his helmet. My breath caught. Broad shoulders, scruffy ginger beard, that lopsided grin. He was every bit the danger I kept promising myself I would avoid. And yet, here I was.

"Hey, Beautiful," he said, voice warm with humor.

"Hey," I answered, though my voice sounded thinner than I wanted.

He gave me the rundown, each rule spoken with patience and a quiet seriousness as he leaned against the motorcycle, tossing me a playful grin. "Okay, you ready? Rule number one: lean when I lean," he said, tapping the side of the bike. "You up for that?"

I bit my lip, eyes darting to the bike. "I think I can manage that."

"Good," Hunter nodded, the humor evident in his voice. "Rule two: hold on tight. I don't want to lose you back there. Deal?"

I laughed softly, the sound easing the tension. "Deal."

Hunter took a small step closer, eyes serious but still light. "Rule three: always, and I mean always, get off on the left side."

"Why's that?" I asked, brow raised.

"Exhaust's on the right, burn your leg, and then I'll have to explain to your kids why there's a burnt spot on mommy's jeans."

That made me chuckle as I gave him a mock-shiver. "Noted."

He watched me for a moment longer, a quiet assurance in his gaze. "And don't panic." My grip tightening slightly. "Got it. No panicking."

Our eyes met, and there was a moment's pause, where seriousness mingled with excitement, his light smile putting me more at ease. I swallowed, nodding.

"Good girl." His voice softened as he held out a helmet. He didn't just hand it to me; he gently placed it over my head, adjusted the strap, and clipped it under my chin. His fingers brushed my skin, careful, deliberate. The simple intimacy of the gesture rattled me more than the thought of getting on the bike.

Climbing on was clumsy and awkward. My sneakers scraped against the peg, and I wobbled before managing to swing my leg over. I could feel his shoulders shake as he suppressed a laugh.

"Not a word," I muttered.

He chuckled anyway, and the sound was so rich I almost forgot how terrified I was. He twisted back slightly, meeting my eyes through the visor. "You ready?" No. Absolutely not. But my hand found his, squeezed once, and I said, "Yeah."

And then we were off.

The first rush stole my breath. Wind whipped against my sweater, the world blurring past in streaks of neon and shadow. My instinct was to stiffen, to fight every lean, every tilt of the bike. My arms locked around him, my helmet knocking against the back of his when he braked or accelerated.

At a red light, he turned his head to allow me to hear him. "You've got to lean with me, Cami. Don't fight it. If you don't trust me, we both go down."

I wanted to argue. But his voice was patient, steady, and unshakable, like he had all the time in the world for me to get it right. So I tried. I let myself go with the motion, pressed tighter against him, and slowly the fear loosened its grip. He must have felt it too, because every so often, his hand left the handlebars long enough to squeeze mine where it rested against his stomach. Those little squeezes grounded me, reminded me I wasn't doing this alone, safe with him.

By the time we stopped by the water, my body felt different. Lighter, alive in ways I hadn't been in years. I pulled the helmet off and shook out my curls, trying to catch my breath. My cheeks hurt from smiling, my heart still racing from the mix of fear and freedom. Hunter swung his leg off the bike, moving with an ease that made me jealous. He pulled off his helmet and ran a hand through his hair. His eyes found mine, and that small, knowing smile tugged at the corner of his mouth.

"Still mad I took that turn fast?"

I smirked, trying to sound braver than I felt. "You did it on purpose."

He shrugged, stepping closer. "Maybe. You were holding on pretty tight."

"Because I like being alive."

He laughed softly, the sound rough and low in his chest. "Yeah? 'Cause it felt like more than that." He set the helmets down and pulled two bottles of water from his saddlebags. We walked just a few feet away from the curb and sat side by side on a bench overlooking the water. I admired his bike as it sat there gleaming under the pier lights, as he told me more about growing up in upstate New York. How he'd spend days out in the woods hunting and riding dirt bikes before he was old enough to drive. And eventually choosing the Marine Corps because he thought it might give him the same sense of direction his father had found.

The more he spoke, the more his walls slipped. His humor was still there, but now with a raw edge. And I soaked it in like sunlight, watching the way the shadows caught in his jawline, the way the streetlights danced in his eyes. I was seeing pieces of him that no one else had been allowed to touch.

At some point, I realized I wasn't just listening. I was staring. His hand rested loosely on my thigh, the veins in his forearm visible under the ink of his tattoo, the koi fish seeming almost alive in the dim glow. My fingers itched to trace it, to learn every line of him the way he was trusting me with every word.

When his gaze flicked to mine, I froze. But he didn't look away. He just held me there, steady and searching, and it was suddenly impossible to pretend that this was just another date. The air between us had shifted: charged, expectant.

Hours went by of us talking and sharing stories until the warm colors of the sky started to shift with the later hours. We began to make our way back to his bike to return home. As I reached his bike, I turned to where he stood beside me.

The crashing of the waves, the salt in the air, the faint warmth radiating off his body; it all pressed in a way that felt both too much and not enough. I moved closer without meaning to, his height forcing me to tilt my chin up. The warmth of his skin against mine spread through me like fire, and suddenly the world shrank to the inches between us. My back brushed the bike, the metal still warm from the ride. The vibration seemed to hum through me, grounding and electric all at once. He took a half step forward, close enough that his shadow spilled over mine, close enough that I could feel the heat radiating off him. His eyes flicked from my mouth to my eyes and back again, waiting for permission he didn't need to ask for.

He let out a shaky, uneven breath, then cupped my jaw in one calloused hand. His thumb brushed the corner of my mouth, and my breath hitched. The first touch of his lips was soft, almost hesitant, as he tested the weight of the moment. I felt it everywhere: in the back of my knees, in the quick flutter under my ribs.

When I leaned in, everything changed. He kissed me like he'd been holding back for too long. His other hand slid to my waist, fingers splaying against my hip, drawing me in until my body pressed against the solid heat of his. The bike behind me steadied us, but everything else tilted. The air, the ground, and my heart.

He tasted of salt and wind. His beard grazed my chin, a soft scrape that made my skin shiver. I felt the faint tremor in his hand when it traced up my side, resting at the small of my back as if he was memorizing me.

When we finally broke apart, neither of us moved. His forehead rested against mine, his breath mingling with mine, both of us unsteady. The fabric of his shirt was warm beneath my fingers.

Hunter's voice came out low, rough. "You make it real hard to keep my head straight."

I smiled, still breathless. "Maybe that's the point."

He chuckled, the sound deep and lazy in his chest. "You're dangerous, you know that?"

"Pretty sure you were the one going ninety down the coast." I teased, tracing the line of his collarbone with my fingertip.

His lips quirked. "Yeah, but you didn't exactly tell me to slow down."

"Maybe I liked it," I said softly, meeting his eyes.

"Careful saying things like that, Cami."

His voice dropped lower, rough enough to scrape against my pulse. The warning should've made me nervous, but it didn't. It only pulled me closer. His hand slid to the back of my neck, thumb tracing lazy circles against my skin.

"Why?" I whispered, breath catching.

His gaze darkened, heat and restraint tangled together. "Because I'm already fighting every instinct not to take you right here."

The air between us went still, thick with something that felt both dangerous and inevitable. My heart raced, the edges of everything else blurring until it was just him—his breath, his voice, his touch.

"Who says I want you to fight it?" I murmured, my fingers curling into his shirt.

His jaw flexed, the muscle twitching as if he was barely holding himself back. "You're playing with fire."

"Maybe I like that too," I said softly.

He exhaled through his nose, that small, crooked grin returning—half hunger, half surrender. "Yeah," he muttered, pulling me closer until our foreheads touched. "That's what I was afraid of."

And then he kissed me again—slower this time, deeper, like

he'd given up pretending he didn't want to. The kind of kiss that didn't ask for permission, but still felt like an answer to every question we hadn't dared to speak.

When it was time to get back on, I climbed clumsily again. He looked over his shoulder, a grin tugging at his mouth. "So, quick question before we head back, were you trying to knock me out back there, or is headbutting just your way of flirting?"

My jaw dropped, heat rushing to my cheeks. "I did not headbutt you!"

"You did. At least three times. I was starting to worry you were going to give yourself a concussion."

I smacked his shoulder lightly, laughing despite myself. "I can't even with you."

He only grinned wider as he settled his helmet back on. "And yet, you keep getting back on."

As we rode back, I leaned without hesitation. Letting go, letting him guide. It had been so long since I'd trusted anyone enough to just… follow. No plan, no control. Just me, pressed against him, the night roaring around us.

It wasn't just the freedom that shook me. It was him. The solid feel of his body between my thighs, the steady strength of his hands, the warmth radiating through his shirt, the ache curling low in my stomach was undeniable. I craved him. Craved the weight of his touch, the heat of his mouth. Craved him in a way I wasn't sure I'd ever allowed myself to crave anyone before.

Chapter Twenty

Camille

It was strange how quickly months could slip by when someone new made the days brighter. Hunter and I had built something secure, almost without realizing it. Dates that turned into late-night drives. Coffee runs that turned into lazy afternoons by the water. Texts that turned into calls, calls that turned into FaceTimes, FaceTimes that turned into I miss yous.

And somehow, against every wall I'd put up, he kept showing up. He hadn't run. Not when I had meltdowns about exams. Not when I canceled at the last minute because the twins spiked fevers. Not when Zeke barged into one of our calls and demanded to know who I was talking to.

Instead, he'd stayed. With patience, with humor, and with that steady look in his eyes that said he wasn't going anywhere. He'd spent time building my trust since the day I decided to allow him a chance that day on the bike.

Which left me here. Sitting at the kitchen table, staring at my phone, heart pounding at the thought of the next step.

The true make-it-or-break-it moment was meeting my kids.

It wasn't casual anymore. Once he stepped into their world, it wouldn't just be my heart on the line; it would be theirs, too. Zeke was five now. He was sharp, curious, and already asking questions I wasn't sure how to answer. He remembered things no child should have to. And he'd been hurt before, even if he couldn't put it into words. Avery and Chloe were toddlers now, identical chaos machines with curls and big brown eyes. They were clingy, in the best way, and full of love. At this age, they wouldn't remember every detail, maybe, but they'd know his presence. They'd feel if he was temporary.

I chewed the inside of my cheek, stomach tight.

What if he decided this was too much? What if he saw the sticky fingers, the tantrums, the exhaustion, and realized he didn't actually want this? But then I remembered the way he'd listened when I told him stories about them. The way he laughed when I recounted Zeke's "ketchup phase." The way his eyes softened when one of the twins made their way into our FaceTime calls and shouted, "Hi!" at him. He wasn't flinching. He was leaning closer.

Still, the weight of it pressed in on me. Because letting him into this part of my life wasn't just about me trusting him. It was about trusting that he could be a safe place for them, too. I imagined Zeke watching Hunter, cautiously, sizing him up as he often did with new experiences. Avery and Chloe would likely be giggling, entranced by the novelty of having another adult willing to share their world. Their reactions would be a test of sorts, not just for Hunter, but for me as well, to see if this puzzle piece could fit into our complex, chaotic picture.

I talked through this moment with Dani and my mom a few

days ago. Their gentle reassurance that it was long overdue rang in my ears as I picked up my phone and typed out the message.

> *Me:* So… how would you feel about coming over for dinner this weekend? Just us and the kids.

My thumb hovered over "send" so long my phone screen dimmed twice. Finally, I squeezed my eyes shut and tapped it. Message sent.

And then… instant regret and panic. My stomach twisted. What if this was the point where he bailed? What if months of constant texts and late-night calls and stolen kisses didn't matter the second he saw the reality? My kids, my chaos, my life in its loudest, truest form? Maybe he was just enjoying our time and hoping to keep only the part of me that didn't come fully loaded.

I dropped the phone on the table, heart thudding in my ears.

Then it buzzed.

> *Hunter:* Dinner with you and the kids? That sounds perfect.

I froze, staring at the screen. Perfect? He thought this sounded perfect?

> *Hunter:* Do I need to bring backup mac and cheese, or should I trust the head chef?

> **Me:** Absolutely not. Probably best you stay out of the kitchen after your last cooking disaster.

Hunter: It wasn't that bad…

> **Me:** Oh, it was. But I'll allow you to bring dessert. Troop morale is usually higher with cookies.

Hunter: Copy that, commander. Cookies incoming.

I bit my lip, grinning like an idiot at the screen. Butterflies exploded, wild and insistent. He wasn't hesitating or stalling. He was saying yes, eagerly. I leaned back in my chair, the weight of what this meant pressing in. This wasn't just another date. This was me opening the door to the most sacred part of my world, and he was walking through it like he was intent on being there.

Chapter Twenty One

Hunter

I read her text three times just to make sure I wasn't imagining it.

Camille: How would you feel about coming over for dinner this weekend? Just us and the kids?

My heart kicked as if I'd just been dropped into a cold ocean. Not terror, something sharper, cleaner. The feeling you get right before a plane lifts off and your stomach forgets its job. I'd been wanting this and bracing for it in equal measure for months. Now it was here.

I typed back, "That sounds perfect," and immediately started second-guessing the wording. Too eager? Not eager enough? Should I have added an emoji? I deleted a salute emoji because that felt… wrong.

Meeting the kids wasn't a date; it was a test you don't get to retake. I could feel old training whispering unhelpful procedures: recon the terrain, plan, worst-case scenarios. But this wasn't that, this was spaghetti night with three tiny humans who might decide I was a good idea… or a bad one.

I grabbed my phone and texted Nate. My buddy from the Corps has 2 kids. I've spent enough time with him and his family over the years that his kids now call me Uncle Hunt. His advice wasn't always dependable; all the guy did was crack jokes. But it was the best I had right now.

Me: You around?

Nate: I'm always around. What's the emergency?

Me: I'm meeting her kids Saturday.

Nate: LOL send the address. I need to watch this go down.

Me: Unhelpful

Nate: I'm kidding. Kind of. Proud of you, man. You good?

Me: Yeah. Just don't want to screw it up.

Nate: Then don't. Rule 1: don't try too hard. Rule 2: if you break Rule 1, bring snacks. Kids love snacks.

Me: She said cookies.

Nate: Perfect. Also, bring something small
   for them. Low-stakes. Nothing that
   makes noise. Don't be that guy.

Me: Noted.

Nate: Also don't call her "ma'am" in
   front of them. You did that to Jen
   once and she almost threw a fork at you.

Me: I'm never going to live that
down am I?

Nate: Never

I tossed the phone on the counter and looked around my apartment, as if there might be answers lying under the mail I hadn't sorted. There weren't. There was just me, the old couch, and the sense that the gravity of my life had shifted three degrees to the left.

So I grabbed my keys and did something I had never done before: I went to the toy aisle.

The store smelled of plastic and cinnamon pretzels, the kind of scent that makes you overspend and forget your list. I didn't have a list, just panic and a mental image of three small judges banging gavels. I hit the toy section and froze. Shelves glittered like a rainbow had exploded. Action figures posed mid-punch next to dolls whose eyes followed me like tiny security cameras. There were puzzles, blocks, art kits, plushies the size of armchairs, and an entire wall of things that made noise.

Nothing that makes noise, I repeated, stepping away from a drum set.

A store associate in a vest appeared at my elbow. "You look lost," she said kindly. "New uncle? Birthday party? First rodeo?"

"Third option," I said. "Meeting my girlfriend's kids. I need something that says 'I am fun but also safe and won't ruin your house.'"

She nodded like she'd been waiting her whole day for this. "Ages?"

"One's five, Zeke. The other two are twins, one year old. Avery and Chloe."

"Adorable," she said, already walking me toward a shelf. "For the five-year-old, try this." She handed me a small building set labeled *STEM Starter*. "Ninety pieces, which is a lot, but they're chunky blocks. No tiny choking hazards. And look, no batteries. Quiet."

"Quiet is good." I exhaled.

"For the twins," she continued, moving through the aisles, "you want tactile. Soft stackers, board books, or these little crinkly animals. Here, a fox and a bunny. They're machine-washable."

I held the fox and bunny up. "They feel like they make noise."

"They crinkle," she admitted. "But it's a *polite* noise."

"Polite noise I can live with," I replied.

She smiled. "You're going to do fine."

I added a small pack of sticker sheets at the end of the aisle on impulse: stars, dinosaurs, and something sparkly that said *Queen of Everything.*

On the way out, I called Nate.

"Report," he said, like he was going to log it.

CHAPTER TWENTY ONE

"STEM blocks for Zeke. Crinkle animals for the twins. Stickers as backup."

"Strong load out. Don't forget cookies."

"I remembered cookies," I said, turning into the bakery parking lot. "Question, do I get the cheap sugar cookies with the neon frosting or go full fancy?"

"Fancy says, 'I'm insecure and think sugar can buy love.' Neon says 'I'm fun, but I might not respect nap time," he said. "Chocolate chip. Universal currency."

"Got it."

I hung up and stared at the bakery case for ten minutes like it was a high-stakes draft. I settled on a box of snicker doodles and two dozen chocolate chips. Half soft, half crispy. Back home, I lined everything up on the counter: cookies, toys, stickers. *Don't try too hard,* Nate had said.

Right. That was the trick, wasn't it? Show up. Don't knock anything over. Don't make this about me. Just be the guy who makes the kids laugh, and knows when to step back and let a mom be the expert.

I opened our message thread.

> **Me:** Any allergies I should know about?

Camille: No allergies. Zeke will try to convince you he's allergic to broccoli. He isn't.

> **Me:** Noted. I'm bringing dessert. May have gone overboard.

Camille: Overboard dessert sounds like my love language.

> **Me:** Thinking of bringing
> something small for the kids.
> Is that okay?

I waited, aware of all the ways this could go. Too much, too soon. Or maybe it landed the way I hoped: not a bribe, just a gesture.

> **Camille:** That's sweet. Nothing big, please.
> We're drowning in toys as it is.

> **Me:** Small. I promise

> **Camille:** Thank you. And… thank
> you for asking.

The warmth in that last line went straight through me. Asking mattered. Not assuming mattered. I wanted to keep getting these things right.

I paced the apartment, the old floorboards creaking under my steps. Every now and then, my brain spits out a what-if: *What if Zeke hates you? What if one twin cries every time you speak? What if you stand in the doorway with your hands full of cookies and suddenly forget how to smile like a human being?*

I picked up the fox and squeezed it. It crinkled obligingly. "Polite noise," I remembered. The fox made no promises.

My phone buzzed. Nate again.

> **Nate:** Last tip: learn a kid joke.

> **Me:** Like what?

> **Nate:** Why did the cookie go to

the doctor?

Me: Why?

Nate: Because it felt crumby.

Me: I'm blocking you.

Nate: You're welcome. Also, don't
linger in the doorway like a weirdo.
Knock, smile, shoes off if she's
a shoes-off house.

Me: I hate that you're useful.

Nate: It's a burden.

I set the phone down, exhaled, and looked at the clock. Two days to overthink myself into a knot or get comfortable with the idea that this is real. That I want it to be real.

Saturday came with the kind of vivid blue sky that makes you suspicious. I checked the toy bags twice, the cookie boxes three times. I left early, because I always leave early, and then sat two blocks away for ten awkward minutes so I wouldn't be *too* early. I texted Nate a picture of the steering wheel as I waited.

Nate: Loosen up. You got this.

Me: If the five-year-old challenges me
to a duel, I'm calling you.

Nate: Just lose with dignity.

I laughed under my breath, shook out my hands, and drove the last two blocks.

Her building looked the same as the first night I picked her up. Modest, clean, a row of porches where kids' scooters leaned against the exterior walls. I balanced the cookie boxes in one hand, the small toy bag in the other, and tucked a simple bouquet under my arm as I walked up the steps.

I'd settled on the flowers on my way to her apartment. Nothing fancy, just a handful of bright daisies and sunflowers from the corner shop. They felt cheerful, something simple. Something that felt like her.

Before I could knock, the door swung open. Camille stood there barefoot in jeans and a soft T-shirt, curls pinned up, eyes bright.

"These are for you," I said, holding out the flowers before I lost my nerve.

She blinked, then smiled. That small, startled thing that didn't quite hide the sadness underneath. "Thank you," she whispered, cradling the words close to her chest.

My chest tightened, a dozen words catching behind my teeth. But then…

"Mommy, who's that?" A small head peeked around her leg. Zeke. Curly brown hair, solemn brown eyes, studying me like a tiny judge.

Camille smoothed his hair back gently. "Zeke, this is Hunter. He's Mommy's friend." She looked up at me quickly, as if to check that the word didn't sting. It didn't. If anything, it steadied me.

I crouched down a little, careful not to crowd him. "Hey,

buddy. I brought cookies. Two kinds."

Zeke's eyes flicked to the boxes in my hand. "Did you get chocolate chip?"

I grinned. "I did." He gave a single solemn nod, like I'd passed the first round of questioning. Then from the hallway, twin squeals erupted. Avery and Chloe ran forward, curls in little pigtails bouncing, wide brown eyes locked on me.

Camille bent down, gathering them close. "Girls, this is Hunter. Can you say hi?"

"Hi!" one shouted. The other followed with a shy little wave as she hugged Camille's leg.

"Shoes off?" I asked, my voice a little rough.

She nodded. "Yeah. Shoes off."

I took off my boots, stepped over the threshold, and let the smell of sauce and garlic and crayons pull me into their world.

For once, my brain didn't reach for exit routes or worst-case scenarios. It cataloged different things: sippy cups on the counter; a coloring page taped slightly crooked to the fridge; tiny socks in a woven basket by the door; a small, mismatched kingdom that felt, somehow, like the center of the map.

I set the cookies down, handed Zeke the STEM box, and crouched to the twins' level with the fox and bunny. "Brought some friends who make polite noise," I said seriously, giving them a little crinkle. I lifted the fox and bunny from the toy bag, their ears sticking up like silly antennae. Both girls gasped. One snatched the fox, the other the bunny. They squeezed, giggled, and I swear the temperature in the room shifted with their smiles.

Avery (or Chloe) squeezed the bunny and gasped at the

crinkle. Chloe (or Avery) tested the fox, eyes going huge. They looked up at me as if I'd performed a small, excellent magic trick.

When I looked back up, Camille was watching me, flowers still pressed to her chest. Her eyes were soft, shining in a way that made my throat tighten. The smile she gave me brought my pulse down two notches. I hadn't won anything, not yet. But I'd shown up with quiet toys, chocolate chip cookies, and a willingness to sit on the floor.

"Dinner in ten," she said, a little breathless.

"Copy," I said, then caught myself and grinned. "I mean, sounds good."

She rolled her eyes, amused, and I thought: Remember this. Remember the way it starts, so if it gets hard later, you'll know what you're fighting for.

Zeke climbed onto the rug with his new toy and looked at me expectantly. "Can you build a rocket?" I sat cross-legged on the floor, accepted my assignment, and tried not to overthink the answer.

"Yeah, buddy," I said, fitting the first two pieces together. "Let's build something that goes far." His little voice was full of enthusiasm.

The twins squealed when the fox and bunny crinkled in their hands, and Zeke was already sprawled on the rug, eagerly tearing open the STEM block box. He looked up, grinning, and I could tell I'd passed another unspoken test.

And then, with the kids happily distracted, I turned back to Camille. "You didn't have to get us anything." She said softly as she arranged the flowers in a vase she pulled out from the off-white cabinets, for a flicker of a moment, her smile wavered, touched with something sad. Like she couldn't remember the last time anyone had handed her flowers, let alone just because. That ache hit me hard.

"I wanted to. You deserve them," I said simply.

Her eyes met mine, shining in a way that made my throat tighten. She didn't answer. She just gave me a small, grateful smile before turning to set the flowers gently in a vase on the counter.

Zeke held up the few blocks he had snapped together. "Look, Mommy! It's a rocket!"

She laughed, wiping at her eyes before turning back. "That's wonderful, buddy." Then her gaze flicked back to me, softer now. "Come on. Dinner's almost ready."

I felt the weight and the possibility in my chest again. Not just her smile, not just the kids' laughter, but the way she held those flowers like no one had thought to remind her she deserved beauty, too.

I thought I was nervous about cookies and toys. But what scared me more was realizing how much I wanted to be the man who kept handing her flowers and showing up.

Dinner smelled of garlic and tomatoes, the sauce simmering low on the stove. Camille moved easily in the kitchen, stirring with one hand while balancing Chloe on her hip, the little girl still squeaking the crinkly bunny like it was the best thing she'd ever owned. Avery sat next to me on the floor. I knew it was her because Camille gave me the secret to telling them apart, a single freckle on her cheek. She looked like she wanted to crawl into my lap, but was also uncertain of the stranger sitting in the middle of the living room.

"Let's go to the table," Zeke said, taking his new role as guide very seriously. He marched me over to the small wooden table, where a stack of coloring pages and a lone sippy cup had been pushed aside to make room. "You sit here."

"Yes, sir," I said, sliding into the chair he'd chosen. He gave me a look like he wasn't sure if I was making fun of him or not, then nodded, apparently satisfied with my compliance.

By the time plates were on the table, the twins were in their highchairs, Zeke bouncing in his seat, and Camille finally sitting down across from me. She looked tired, curls frizzing a little, but when she smiled, it lit the whole table. "Okay," she said, clapping her hands lightly. "Who's hungry?"

Three little hands shot up instantly. Mine followed half a beat later, earning me a surprised laugh from her. The twins dug into their pasta with both fists, sauce painting their cheeks like war paint. Zeke twirled his noodles carefully, clearly proud to show me he knew the "grown-up way."

He looked at me with narrowed eyes between bites before his next line of questioning. "Do you like Ninja Turtles?"

I swallowed my pasta, then leaned in conspiratorially. "Absolutely."

His eyes narrowed further. "Who's your favorite?"

"The red one... Raphael?"

That earned me a smile of approval. I'd passed round two.

The twins babbled at me next, proudly holding up spaghetti strands. I clapped each time politely, and they giggled like I was the funniest man alive. Camille watched all of it, quietly studying every move, every reaction.

Halfway through dinner, Zeke tilted his head. "Do you live far away?"

"Not too far," I said. "About twenty minutes."

He frowned, like he was working through an equation. "So... you can still come back if you forget something."

"Exactly," I said, biting back a smile. "I'll never be too far away."

Camille's fork stilled, her gaze lifting to mine. For a second, something unspoken hung between us. Heavy. Important.

Then Chloe threw her fork on the floor with a triumphant squeal, and the moment broke.

"Oh no," Camille muttered, scooping it up and setting it on the counter.

"I'll get it next time," I said quickly.

She shot me a look. One that was half amused, half grateful. "Careful. You'll get stuck on fork duty."

I grinned. "I've survived worse assignments."

By the end of dinner, Zeke was chattering to me about rockets and ketchup again, the twins were covered in sauce but happy, and Camille was leaning back in her chair, watching all of us with a look that made my chest ache.

When I helped clear the table, she brushed past me at the sink, her shoulder grazing mine. "Thank you," she murmured.

"For what?"

"For showing up," she said simply. "For not making it weird."

The corner of my mouth lifted, but the ache in my throat stayed. I wanted to tell her it wasn't weird at all. That it felt... right. But the words caught in my throat, too big for the moment. So instead, I just nodded, dried a plate, and thought to myself: *You can't afford to screw this up.*

Chapter Twenty Two

Camille

Dinner ended the way every dinner did: dirty hands, sauce stains, and one fork mysteriously missing under the table. Only tonight, there was Hunter at the end of the table, laughing with Zeke and clapping politely at the twins' spaghetti "performances."

It was… surreal.

I hadn't realized how much space another person could take up in this house until he was here. His laugh mixed with theirs. His calm filled the edges of the noise. He didn't flinch when sauce splattered or when Zeke asked about the physics of spaghetti noodles. He just smiled, listening like it was the most natural thing in the world.

It did something to me.

When I first invited him over, I'd braced for awkward. Polite smiles. Quick exits. That familiar look adults get when they realize dinner with three kids under eight means chaos. But Hunter didn't seem overwhelmed by the noise or the mess. He belonged in it. He met the kids where they were, without trying to take over or tune out.

I kept stealing glances at him, wondering if he saw through me. Through the practiced composure, and the way I tried to make everything look fine. I'd spent years making it look fine. Tonight, I didn't feel like I had to.

When Chloe dropped her fork for the third time, he simply handed her his.

And Zeke asked. "Are you coming back?" Hunter hesitated only a beat before saying, "If it's okay with your mom."

Three little heads turned toward me.

I smiled, pretending my pulse wasn't thudding in my throat. "We'll see."

"Cool." Zeke had said, satisfied before finishing his food. I didn't know whether to laugh or melt right there at the table.

After dinner, I stood to start the bedtime chaos. "Bath time," I announced, already bracing for the chorus of groans.

Zeke groaned on cue. The twins clapped because they didn't know any better yet.

"Need help?" Hunter asked, pushing his chair back. The scrape of the legs across the floor snapped me out of the daze I'd been in all evening.

I shook my head quickly, maybe too quickly. "No, I've got it. Just… make yourself comfortable on the couch. There's the remote."

He studied me for a second, then nodded. "Okay."

I left him there, sitting on my worn couch with cartoons queued up on mute, and led the kids down the hall.

Bath time was the usual circus. Zeke tried to sink action figures. Chloe tried to drink the water. Avery splashed until half of it was on the floor. I kept my voice steady, my hands busy, but my mind kept drifting back to the living room where

Hunter was waiting.

What was he thinking out there? Did he feel out of place? Did he see the peeling paint on the bathroom door, the cheap towels, the clutter I never seemed to catch up on? Did he regret saying yes to all of this?

By the time the kids were clean, pajama-clad, and smelling like bubblegum soap, I was half-exhausted and half buzzing. When I came out of the bathroom after brushing Chloe's teeth, I found Hunter sitting on the couch, an arrangement of princess band-aids thrown across the coffee table as he patched a stuffed bunny's missing ear.

He looked up and smiled, soft and sheepish. "Emergency surgery. She insisted."

Avery's little face lit up. "All better!"

"Good work, Doc," he said, saluting her.

Something in me twisted, because I'd seen men try to fake this before. The patience. The kindness. But this wasn't that. He wasn't pretending.

"Alright," I said, my voice gentler now, "time to say goodnight."

Zeke frowned. "Already?"

"Already," I said, trying not to laugh. "You can say goodnight to Hunter before bed."

Zeke hesitated, but the twins ran right up to him.

Hunter crouched down to their level, his hands braced on his knees. "Thanks for having me for dinner, ladies. Best spaghetti I've had in years." ??Chloe giggled and launched herself at him, arms wrapping around his neck. Avery followed without hesitation.

For a second, he froze, unsure of what to do with the tiny arms around him, but then he smiled. Really smiled. He hugged them back carefully, gently, understanding just how fragile trust could be.

Zeke lingered near my leg, watching. Hunter turned to him next. "You too, buddy. Thanks for letting me crash dinner."

Zeke shrugged, a flicker of approval there, before disappearing down the hall. Hunter stood, still watching after them. "They're good kids," he said, voice low.

"They are," I said, almost whispering. "Thank you for… handling it so well. I'm just going to lay them down. Do you want to leave? I don't want you to have to wait around for me."

"I can wait," Hunter said.

Heat crept up my neck before I could stop it. "You don't have to—"

"I know," he said softly, eyes fixed on mine. "But I want to."

I didn't know what to do with the way he looked at me like he wasn't seeing the mess or the exhaustion, but the person under it all. I nodded, not trusting my voice, and turned toward the hallway, my pulse still unstable.

I tucked the kids into bed as three little bodies wriggled and resisted, before finally giving in. It was the same routine I'd done a thousand times, only tonight, every step felt heavier. More loaded. ??I tucked Zeke in first. Eyelids drooped as he managed to whisper, "Mommy, Hunter's funny. Is he nice?"

I kissed his curls. "Yeah. He's nice."

"Good," Zeke said, drifting off.

The twins babbled their own version of "night-night." I leaned down, kissed each of their foreheads, and whispered the same words I always did: "I love you. Always." Then I pulled the door closed softly behind me, the click echoing louder than it should have.

And in the silence that followed, I felt every ounce of nervousness, excitement, and fear pressing into my chest and reminding me exactly how much I stood to lose, and just how much I wanted to believe this could be different. I lingered a moment. The weight I carried. The reason I'd built walls so high around myself. And the reason tonight felt like such a risk.

Chapter Twenty Three

Hunter

The house was still after she disappeared down the hall, though "still" felt like the wrong word. It was the kind of quiet filled with small noises. I listened to the faintest echo of giggles and bedtime protests.

I sat on the couch, staring at the cookie box, remembering the excitement on their faces when Cami told them I'd brought them cookies. And the way she pretended not to notice when I snuck Zeke another cookie when she had turned her back.

My instincts screamed to stay put. Don't interfere. Don't overstep. Let her handle her world. But another part of me, the part that had been watching her juggle three kids, dinner, and conversation without ever letting herself rest, wanted to move.

I thought about the flowers in the vase on her counter, the way she'd held them to her chest like they were fragile, like she hadn't been appreciated in too long. The way she'd whispered *thank you* with that flicker of sadness behind her smile. I found myself needing to ease that weight, because she carried it with a strength that humbled me. So I stood there restlessly as I scanned the room for something to make her night a little lighter.

The table was still cluttered with dishes, sauce smeared where Chloe had clearly missed her mouth. Avery's sippy cup lay dripping in her high chair while Zeke's rocket sat proudly in the center like a flag planted on new territory. The twins' toys were abandoned on the floor.

Without a second thought, I rolled up my sleeves and started clearing.

Plates stacked, cups rinsed, forks gathered from under the table. I moved stealthily, the way you do when you don't want to spook anyone. It wasn't about making it perfect. It was about her not coming back to more work than she'd already done. Halfway through loading the dishwasher, I caught myself smiling because it felt… good. Simple, but good. Just the quiet satisfaction of helping in a home that wasn't mine, with people who weren't mine… at least not yet.

Wiping my hands on a towel, I glanced toward the hall where she was tucking them in. I could hear her voice, low and soft, promising safety without saying the words. I thought about how much trust it took to let me sit in her living room while she whispered those promises to her kids.

By the time she'd return, I'd be back on the couch, trying to look casual, as if I hadn't just had an epiphany in front of a dishwasher.

But in that moment, standing there in the quiet with my hands smelling of dish soap, I knew one thing for certain: This wasn't just about her anymore. It was about all of them.

I'd just set the last fork in the dishwasher when I heard her footsteps carefully padding down the hall.

I quickly sat back on the couch, pretending I hadn't just been waging war on marinara stains. When she walked in, her eyes immediately flicked to the table, now clear of dishes. The counters, wiped down. The sink, empty.

She stopped mid-step. "You…" Her voice trailed off, eyes darting from the kitchen to me. "You picked it all up?"

I shrugged, forcing my tone light. "Figured I'd do my part since you wouldn't let me help you cook."

Her lips parted like she wanted to say more, but all that came out was a soft, almost breathless, "Hunter…"

Her face showed a mix of surprise, gratitude, and underneath it all, a solemness I didn't think she meant to show.

"I didn't want you to come back to more work," I said simply.

Her eyes softened, and for a second, she just stood there, looking at me, not quite knowing what to do with what she was feeling. And in that silence, I felt the truth press in heavily. This wasn't about grand gestures or perfect lines. It was about showing up. Picking up forks. Washing plates. Sitting on the couch while she tucked her kids in, and being here when she came back out because sometimes, that was everything.

She finally crossed the room, settling onto the couch beside me with a soft sigh. Close enough that I caught the faint floral scent of her shampoo. But not so close that we were touching. A careful middle ground.

"You didn't have to do all that," she said, nodding toward the kitchen.

"Maybe not," I admitted. "But I wanted to."

She glanced at me then, and I saw the wall she always kept up slipped just a little. Her lips parted as if forming words, but it was as if they got caught, wrapped in a breath she didn't quite release. "You're going to make it hard for me, you know," she said finally, each word layered with an unspoken question, a pause hanging in the air that demanded gentle courage.

I raised an eyebrow. "Hard, how?"

She gave a small laugh, shaking her head like she couldn't believe she'd said it out loud. "Hard not to get used to this. To you being here."

That hit deeper than I expected. For a second, all I could do was stare at her, the steady, brave woman who carried so much on her shoulders and still smiled at me like I meant something.

So I went with humor, because humor felt safer. "Well, you've got three tiny humans who seem to think I'm pretty cool. Might be too late to *not* get used to me."

Her lips curved, but her eyes stayed serious. "That's what scares me."

The air between us shifted, heavier, but not uncomfortable. I didn't press. I didn't need to. She'd given me more than she probably meant to, and I knew better than to push her past what she was ready to share.

Instead, I leaned back into the couch, keeping my voice light. "Then I guess I'll just have to keep showing up until it's not scary anymore. I want to be here, Cami."

Her shoulders loosened, and she let out a breath she'd been holding. She leaned against me before her hand entwined with mine.

We sat like that for a while, in the quiet hum of her living room, the sound of the kids' gentle snores down the hall, the flowers on the counter catching the glow of the lamp. And in that moment, I didn't need to say anything else because just being there felt like enough.

Chapter Twenty Four

Chapter Twenty Four

Hunter

The drive home felt shorter than it should've, probably because my head was still back in her living room. I dropped my keys in the bowl, kicked off my boots, and sat on the couch. I leaned forward, elbows on my knees, trying to catch up to the way my chest still felt too full.

I hadn't expected to feel that…at ease. Camille's place was small, but it was alive. The sound of little feet running down the hall, the smell of spaghetti still lingering in the air, the soft laughter that came from somewhere deep in her. It all stuck to me.

Zeke had grilled me about Ninja Turtles and space, the twins had me making up various voices for their stuffed animals, and somehow, between the chaos and the mess and her trying to wrangle bedtime, it felt like I fit there. Like I wasn't just visiting.

I rubbed a hand over my jaw, shaking my head at the thought. It had been a long time since anything felt that easy. Since someone felt that easy.

Camille had this way about her: calm and bright all at once. Her presence sneaks up on you, softening all the sharp edges before you realize it's happening. Watching her move around that apartment, hearing their soft voices down the hall, seeing her carry an entire world on her shoulders and still sit beside me at the end of the night did something to me. And when she leaned into me, just barely, trusting me with that little bit of weight.

I wanted this. All of it. The spaghetti-stained tables, the bedtime routines, the cautious smiles. The weight of it hit me harder than I knew how to handle. In those little moments, it all clicked. My life had been running a little off-balance, and that one quiet moment had lined it all back up.

I leaned back against the couch, a slow grin tugging at my mouth. Damn, it felt good to feel this again.

For years, it had just been noise: work, training, the routine. Empty space filled with motion. But tonight felt different. The world was cracking open just a little, and I could finally see some light coming through.

I thought about texting her, thumb hovering over her name. Part of me wanted to tell her everything. How she made my night, that I couldn't stop replaying her smile. But it was late, and I didn't want to mess up the calm we'd found. I looked down at my phone, her name glowing on the screen. My thumb hovered, heart hammering. Nothing I typed felt right.

How do you tell someone you're falling for them when you still wake up with your chest tight and sweat soaking your shirt? How do you admit that your last marriage ended because you couldn't be the man she needed, and you're terrified this will end the same way?

So instead, I just sat there for a while. Still hearing her laugh, remembering the way her curls framed her face, feeling the warmth of her shoulder pressed against mine.

When I finally stretched out onto my bed, the apartment felt a little less empty than usual.

For what felt like the first time in a long time, I didn't fall asleep thinking about what I'd lost. I fell asleep thinking about her, her kids, and all the small, impossible ways she was starting to feel like something I might finally be ready for.

The next morning, the base looked the same as it always did. Gray buildings, uniformed figures moving with purpose, the low hum of radios. I should've been focused on my reports. Instead, I was replaying the sound of Zeke declaring me acceptable, the twins squealing over fox and bunny, and the way Camille's lips had felt against mine. The text I woke up to this morning:

Camille: *Thank you for coming. It felt good having you here and I think the kids really liked you.*

I couldn't stop grinning, which was both a problem and a dead giveaway.

"Alright, what's with you?" Nate's voice cut through as he dropped into the chair across from me, balancing his coffee like it was a trophy. "You've got the look."

I frowned. "What look?"

"The look of a man who either got promoted or got laid." He

leaned back, smirking. "And since I know your boss doesn't like you enough for the first one…"

I rolled my eyes, reaching for the stack of reports. "You're an idiot." Nate was technically my boss, although after years of serving together, he was more like my brother.

"That's not a no," he sing-songed, clearly delighted. "So, spill. How was dinner with the MILF?"

I gave him a warning look. "Don't call her that."

Nate held up his hands. "Fine, fine. Dinner with Camille. Details."

I hesitated, then sighed. "It was…good. Better than good. I think the kids liked me."

His eyebrows shot up. "All three? You got past the gatekeepers?"

"Apparently," I muttered, but I couldn't hide the smile tugging at my mouth.

Nate slapped the table, grinning. "There it is! Atta boy. So why do you look like you haven't slept?"

He wasn't wrong. I hadn't slept much. Not because of bad dreams this time, but because of good ones. The kind that kept me awake with want instead of fear. The kind that whispered maybe, just maybe, I was allowed to want this. I shrugged, trying to downplay it. "I'm just… thinking. Trying not to screw it up."

Nate sipped his coffee, eyes sharp for once. "You won't. You show up. You don't play games. That's more than half the battle." Then, with a grin, "Also, snacks. Kids are cheap dates."

I shook my head, laughing. "You're a real fountain of wisdom."

"Don't forget it." He stood, stretching. "Now get your head

out of la-la land and finish those reports. Or I'll tell the boys you're over here daydreaming and writing love letters." I groaned, but my grin stayed. Because he wasn't wrong. I was daydreaming.

The rest of the morning rush went by in a blur. I signed papers, fixed a mess someone else had caused, but it was all autopilot. My brain wasn't in the office; it was back in her apartment. I kept thinking about the way Zeke's face lit up when I said rockets were my specialty. The way the twins giggled. The way Camille leaned against me on the couch, hesitant but real, testing whether I'd hold steady. I wanted that again. All of it.

Then came the voice I was able to push off until now.

Was I ready for this? For three kids who weren't mine, but who could be in every way that mattered, if I stayed? For a woman whose past was heavier than she let on, but who still smiled at me like I was making it lighter? Could I be reliable enough, present enough, *good* enough for them? A part of me whispered *no*. That same part that had been whispering since the divorce, since the Corps, since the nights when I'd sat awake in my apartment staring at nothing. That part said I wasn't built for this. That sooner or later, I'd let her down.

I pinched the bridge of my nose and drew a slow breath through clenched teeth. The Marine Corps had trained me to handle chaos, but not this kind. This wasn't bullets or orders. This was bedtime tantrums, spaghetti wars, and the terrifying possibility of belonging again.

A family. A home.

I leaned back and stared at the ceiling until the tension behind my eyes eased just enough for another voice to break through, a gentler one. *You showed up. You stayed. You made them laugh. You made her smile.*

Sitting there in her space, surrounded by all that life, had felt like I'd come home.

But "home" was a word I'd learned not to trust. Home wasn't something I let myself imagine anymore. The Corps had been home once. Then the marriage…until it wasn't. Since then, it has just been me, the apartment, and the job. Quiet. Safe. Detached.

Until last night.

I rubbed a hand over my beard and exhaled hard. I wasn't used to hope anymore, but she made me feel it again. And I didn't hate it.

Under all the noise, that steady hum of excitement wouldn't quit.

Chapter Twenty Five

Camille

Dani had been at the house bright and early the day after dinner to catch up on the prior night's events. The house still smelled faintly of garlic from last night's spaghetti. The kids were camped out on the couch, cartoons flickering blue across their faces. I leaned against the counter, nursing a cup of coffee that had already gone lukewarm, caught somewhere between exhaustion and the afterglow of last night.

Dinner unfolded softer than I'd let myself hope. Hunter moved through the house with a quiet steadiness, filling the space without ever asking for it. He knelt beside Zeke, helping him piece together the little spaceship, laughter mingling with the twins' shrieks. Every so often, his eyes would find mine, a flicker of something gentle that left my cheeks flushed. Later, he rolled up his sleeves and started on the dishes while I wrangled pajamas and toothbrushes, no words needed. Just there, as if he'd always known how to fit into the edges of our evening.

My eyes drifted to the bouquet on the counter. That was him too, the small, deliberate gestures that said more than grand ones ever could. He didn't show up empty-handed, and it wasn't about impressing me. Every gift, every word, every quiet act felt intentional. Thoughtful. Like he'd been paying attention all along.

By the time my mom arrived for her usual Saturday visit, the story had already spilled out of me twice—to Dani, and to myself, replaying it in my head.

"You look good," Mom said, stepping through the door with her ever-present tote bag and a bakery box. "Did something good happen, or did you finally sleep a full night?"

I smiled into my coffee. "Not exactly sleep. Dinner went really well last night. The kids loved him. He even cleaned up while I got them ready for bed."

Dani, perched on the arm of the couch, nearly choked on her muffin. "Hold up. He cleaned? Like, voluntarily? You left that part out!"

"Yep," I said, grinning. "Didn't even have to ask."

She pointed her mug at me. "That's husband material, Cam."

"Daniela," Mom warned, though the edge of her mouth twitched.

"*What?* I'm serious. Men who do dishes are unicorns."

I rolled my eyes, fighting back a smile. "It's not like that. We're just… taking it slow."

Mom sat beside me, her smile softening. "That's good. Taking it slow is smart. But, honey…" She hesitated—the same pause she always took before saying something she wasn't sure I'd want to hear. "You said he was military, right?"

I recognized that tone, the one she used when she wanted to

shield me without pushing me away. She was always the first to nudge me out the door, whether it was brunch with Dani or a rare date night while she kept the kids. But I knew her worries about dating came from somewhere deep, carrying the weight of old hurts she never quite put down.

"Former Marine," I said quietly. "He got out a couple of years ago."

Her face softened, but the worry lingered there, the kind that had lived in the lines around her eyes for as long as I could remember.

"You know I respect that. But it's not easy, being with someone who's seen that kind of life. I just don't want you walking into something that could break your heart."

Dani leaned forward, always ready to defend me. "I think Hunter's different. He's not Cami's dad."

Mom exhaled slowly. "Different is good. I just want you to have fun, to get out of the house, to smile more. Just don't lose yourself in someone else's story."

Her face gentled, but the worry stayed, etched into the lines at the corners of her eyes. The kind that had settled there over the years. Her words weren't sharp, just heavy with old ache. I understood. She spoke from scars, not from judgment. Still, something in me bristled, a quiet urge to defend what I was starting to feel.

I reached for her shoulder, my fingers tracing the tension until it eased.

"I know, Mom," I murmured, hoping she could feel the truth in my touch as much as in my words. "I promise I'll be careful."

I'd be lying if I said I hadn't had my own concerns. I could see the subtle ways that the military left its mark on Hunter, and I'd spent enough time in school to know what trauma can do to a person; I wasn't naive. But Hunter hadn't given me any reasons to be concerned. If anything, he was the one with all of the reasons to run for the hills. I was the one who came with what felt like hundreds of pounds of baggage.

Mom sighed, but her eyes softened. "I'm glad, sweetheart. I really am. It just makes me nervous, that's all. You've been through so much. I don't want anyone undoing all the strength you've built."

"I know," I said quietly. "He's not perfect. But he shows up, makes me laugh. He actually cares. And that's… more than I've had in a long time."

Dani leaned back, crossing her arms with a satisfied smirk. "See? I like him already. Plus, he's a major upgrade from that guy—"

I groaned, cutting her off. "Oh my gosh, don't start."

"What?… I mean, it sets a high bar. Maybe it's time I rethink my own standards." A playful, yet honest tone slipped through. "Does he have any single Marine friends?"

Before I could respond, my phone buzzed against the table. Once. Twice.

Dani's brows lifted. "Oh, look who can't wait for his good-morning text."

I ignored her and picked up the phone, though the smile was already tugging at my mouth.

Hunter: *Good morning, Beautiful.*

Hunter: *Thank you for last night.*
I'm pretty sure I liked it just as
much as they did. Maybe more.

> **Me:** *You only say that because you got extra dessert.*

Hunter: *That helped. But that's not what I meant.*

> **Me:** *Oh?*

Hunter: *I meant being there with you and them.*

It just felt right, in that way you can't quite name but know all the same.

I tried to suppress the grin spreading across my face, but Dani leaned over my shoulder before I could turn the screen away.

"AW," she said, gasping dramatically. "He's *sweet*. Like, emotionally stable and everything."

"Dani," I hissed, laughing despite myself.

Mom pretended not to eavesdrop, but her voice carried amusement. "He said that?"

I bit my lip, typing before I could overthink it.

> **Me:** *You have a way of saying things that makes it hard to know what to text back.*

Hunter: *No response needed. Just know I meant it.*

Heat climbed up my neck. I took another sip of coffee just to hide it.

CHAPTER TWENTY FIVE

Me: *You did great with them. Zeke's already asked if you'd come back.*

Hunter: *Guess I made the cut, huh?*

Me: *Looks like it. My mom might be a tougher critic, though.*

When I set the phone down, Dani was grinning like she'd just witnessed a rom-com montage come to life.

"He really likes you," she said. "It's about time someone does."

Mom sighed, still cautious but gentler now. "I'm glad he makes you happy, sweetheart. Go out, have fun, laugh a little. You deserve that, no matter where this goes."

I nodded, smiling faintly. "I know. And I am having fun."

Dani smirked. "I'll bet."

"Dani!"

"What? It's a compliment." She winked.

I groaned. "Nope, we're not doing this again."

Mom chuckled softly. "Dani's not wrong. He sounds... good for you."

"Yeah," I said, unable to stop the smile tugging at my lips. "I think he is..."

Mom reached across the table, her hand warm over mine. "Just be careful with that big heart of yours. I know how you love. All in. No guardrails. That's a beautiful thing, but it's also what makes you vulnerable."

"I know," I whispered. "But maybe... It's okay to let someone in."

Her eyes glistened just enough to make me look away.

Dani broke the silence, nudging my shoulder. "And if he ever hurts you, I'll key his car."

I laughed, shaking my head. "I'll take the motorcycle," I said playfully.

Her grin widened. "Even better."

Mom sighed, but there was laughter in it now. "Lord help him if he crosses either of you."

I smiled into my coffee, warmth spreading through me. Between my mom's cautious love, Dani's reckless loyalty, and Hunter's quiet steadiness, I realized something I hadn't let myself feel in a long time.

I wasn't bracing for the next heartbreak anymore.

I was just… living.

And when my phone buzzed again on the table, I didn't even need to read it to know who it was.

Hunter: *I'll earn her approval too.*

I laughed, shaking my head as both women leaned closer to peek at the screen.

Mom smiled despite herself. "He might actually pull it off."

Chapter Twenty Six

Hunter

Nights at Camille's had a kind of noise that I was quickly becoming more familiar with. It wasn't the chaos of a squad room or a crowded bar, but the kind that came from life: kids laughing, toys clattering across the floor, the smell of dinner mixing with that vanilla candle she always lit. The twins climbed everything in sight, Zeke guarded his Lego fortress like it was top secret, and it all left me feeling at ease.

At first, I thought I was the outsider. Too big for their couch, too new in their space. But over time, I saw the way Zeke watched me, careful and quiet, waiting for proof that I was safe. Camille told me later he had seen too much too young, that he had learned what anger sounded like behind closed doors. After that, I noticed how he would step between us sometimes, small but like he could protect her if he had to. He was just a kid, but he carried that same kind of vigilance I knew too well. That instinct to guard the people you love, even when you don't have the words for it.

The night he climbed onto the couch and leaned against me changed everything. He didn't say a word, just rested his head against my arm and fell asleep. It was such a small thing, barely a touch, but it was the start of something I didn't want to mess up. I sat there afraid to move, afraid to lose that fragile trust.

It didn't take long for those small moments to turn into more. The line between her life and mine blurred until I couldn't tell where one ended and the other began.

Now, the late afternoon sun stretched long across the park, painting the grass gold and turning the air heavy with summer warmth. Cami sat cross-legged on a picnic blanket, trying to convince the twins to share their fruit snacks while Zeke showed me how fast he could kick a soccer ball.

"Watch this!" he shouted, his grin wide, the light catching in his hair. He took off across the field, legs pumping, determination written all over him. I couldn't help but laugh, calling out encouragement while pretending not to notice the way my chest ached watching him, because somewhere along the way, this kid had stopped being just hers and started letting me in.

I made a show of bracing for impact, even though the ball rolled to a stop halfway between us. "That's some serious power, buddy."

He laughed, a full laugh only kids can manage, and sprinted after the ball. I glanced back toward Cami, watching her tuck a stray curl behind her ear as she laughed at something Avery said. The sight got to me every damn time. She looked at peace. Soft. Unburdened.

Then her phone rang.

She glanced down, and her whole body changed. The laughter slipped from her face. Her shoulders went rigid. She picked up the phone as if it might bite her, the screen angled just enough that I caught the words: **Unknown Number.**

My pulse kicked up. "Everything okay?"

"Yeah," she said too quickly. "Probably spam."

The phone rang again before she could even lock the screen.

Her hands shook. She tried to hide it, pressing her palms together, but the fear flickered across her face before she could mask it.

"Cami," I said quietly, stepping closer, "Who is it?"

Her throat worked before she answered. "It's him."

I didn't speak for a second. I let the silence do the work. Let her breathe, let me think, let me plan. She tried to hide the screen behind her thumb, and I moved before I even decided to. My hand closed over her phone, and the vibrations stopped. The missed call glared up at me.

I didn't say anything at first. Just watched the phone buzz again in my hand.

"He shouldn't have this number," she whispered. "I changed it. Twice."

My jaw tightened. I reached for the phone. "Let me see it."

She hesitated, then placed the phone in my hand. The missed call notification still burned on the screen: **Unknown Number.**

The phone lit up again before I could think.

I didn't even ask. I swiped to answer, placing it on speaker.

"Yeah?" My voice was low and controlled. I kept it even, the kind of voice you use when everything inside is ready to snap, but you don't want the other person to know you're rattling.

Silence, then a man's smug, casual voice responded. "Who the hell is this?"

"You don't need to know who I am," I replied. "But you do need to stop calling."

"Where's Camille? Where are my kids?" he demanded. She flinched beside me, so I stepped away, taking the call off speaker, shielding her from the sound of his voice.

"They stopped being yours the day you signed over your rights," I said, stepping away from the kids so they couldn't hear. "You lost the right to call her. You lost the right to even say her name."

"You think you can tell me what to do?"

"I don't have to think." The heat in my chest rose, a dangerous pressure I knew too well. Combat taught me how to steady that heat, but it also taught me how fast it could turn into a fire I couldn't rein in. "I'm telling you right now. If you call her again, we're gonna have a problem."

He scoffed. "She got you playing bodyguard now? What are you going to do, call the cops? Cute."

"I don't need cops." My fingers tightened on the phone until my knuckles went pale. I leaned forward, letting the silence do half the work. "I can handle you myself. And I will."

He laughed, the sound like a gutter. "You can't keep me away. Camille's mine to call."

"Say her name again," I said, each word deliberate, "and I will make sure everything you care about goes up in smoke." No melodrama, no promises I could not keep. Just an edge sharp enough that it cut through his bravado.

He began to speak, and I spoke before he even had the chance to put together his thoughts. I spoke softer, closer to the wire. "Keep it up, and I promise I will find you."

There was a pause. Just breathing. Then that same mocking tone. "You don't even know who you're—"

Click. I hung up.

I stood there for a second, breathing too fast, my knuckles white around the phone. The urge to throw it, to break something, to *do* something burned under my skin.

"Hunter?"

Her voice was small behind me, careful.

I turned. She was watching me like she didn't quite recognize the man standing there. And she shouldn't have. That version of me, the one that spoke in threats and moved on instinct, was the one I'd left behind years ago. The one who solved everything with anger. In those moments, I reminded myself of the promise I made after service: to never let anger be the master of my actions again. All I could think about was protecting the woman I cared about and the kids that have quickly found their way into my heart.

I let out a rough breath and set the phone down on the blanket. "He's not going to call again." I said, but it came out too dark, too final.

She stepped forward, slowly, defusing the tension in the moment. "What did you say to him?"

"I told him to stop calling." I said. It wasn't a lie, but it wasn't the whole truth either.

Her eyes searched mine. I could see the worry there, a mix of gratitude and fear that gutted me. "Hunter..."

"I know," I cut in quietly. "I lost it." I dragged a hand down my face, the edge still humming under my skin. "I just—seeing that look on your face, I saw red."

Her eyes met mine, searching for more than an apology.

"Hunter, what's going on?" she asked, her voice barely above a whisper.

I hesitated for a moment, the rush of vulnerability unfamiliar but necessary. "It's not just about you," I admitted, swallowing hard. "It's about me too. I'm afraid of losing this… losing you. I've been in places where I had no control, and I can't stand the thought of not being able to protect you guys."

She closed the space between us, placing her hand against my chest. "You don't have to protect me, not like that."

"Yes, I do," I said, softer now.

The truth of it hit hard. The line between defending and destroying is thinner than most people realize. I'd spent years learning to stay on the right side of it, and tonight, I'd nearly crossed. Strength isn't fists, I reminded myself, but restraint. That promise echoed inside me, a quiet vow to protect without losing myself.

Her hand pressed a little harder over my heart. "It's okay."

I nodded, swallowing the lump in my throat. "I know."

She didn't answer, just stepped into me, wrapped her arms around my waist, and rested her forehead against my chest. I held her there, breathing her in, forcing my heartbeat to slow until the anger bled away.

And when the phone buzzed again, just a notification this time, not a call, I ignored it. I held her tighter. Because right now, walking away from my anger was the only kind of strength that mattered.

Cami stood there, arms wrapped around herself, staring at the ground.

"He hasn't called in months," she said softly. "I really thought—"

"He's testing you," I said. "Trying to see if he still gets a reaction." I touched her arm gently.

Her eyes lifted to mine, glassy with unshed tears. "I hate that he still has this kind of power over me."

I shook my head. "He doesn't. Fear's just muscle memory. But you've already done the hardest part; you got out. Now you stay out. And I'll help make damn sure he stays gone."

Her lower lip trembled, but she faced me with a determination I hadn't seen before. "Maybe it's time to change my number again and document these calls, Hunter. I need to be proactive too. If he thinks he can wear me down with fear, he's wrong. I can't let him win."

I nodded, admiring the resolve in her voice. "You don't have to fix it, Hunter," she added.

"I'm not trying to fix it," I said. "Just making sure the world knows it's not gonna break you."

Zeke came running over, holding a dandelion like it was a treasure. "Mommy, look!"

She knelt, wiping at her eyes quickly before smiling. "That's awesome, baby."

I watched her pull him into her arms, her laugh softer this time, shakier, but still there. The twins ran over too, squealing about snacks and juice boxes, and the world shifted back to normal, or at least the version of normal we've been building together.

But I couldn't shake the look on her face when that number flashed across her screen. I'd seen enough men like him to know they never stopped until someone made them.

And if it came to that, I damn well would.

Chapter Twenty Seven

Camille

By the time the kids were settled with their cartoons, the tension in my body felt like a second skin I couldn't peel off. Every time I looked at my phone, I half-expected it to light up again, with **Unknown Number** flashing across the screen.

Hunter noticed. Of course he did.

He crouched in front of me as I sat on the edge of the bed, his hand finding mine. His touch was gentle, grounding me in a way I hadn't realized I needed.

"What do you need? Just tell me. I hate seeing you like this." His voice was compassionate and soft. A tone I don't think he's ever used with me.

"I'm okay. It's okay." I said, trying to convince myself more than him.

"Go take a shower," he said softly.

"I'm fine," I lied, because that's what I always said when I didn't know how to untangle the mess in my head.

He raised a brow, that patient kind of look that didn't need words. "Cami." Just my name, but it carried a quiet authority that made it impossible to argue. "You've been holding your breath for hours. Go. Take a shower. It helps me when I can't shut my head off."

I hesitated, staring past him toward the hallway. "What about the kids?"

"I've got 'em." His voice was smooth, sure. "Go."

It didn't sound like a command. His tone was so gentle that it slipped past my usual walls. I nodded, slowly, feeling the ache in my chest loosen, just a little.

The bathroom filled with steam as I turned on the water. The first hit of warmth against my shoulders made me exhale for what felt like the first time all day. I braced my hands against the tile, closing my eyes, letting the sound of the water drown out the echo of my ex's voice in my head; that sharp tone, the control, the fear.

My mind drifted back to that afternoon in the park, when everything had spun out of control. Hunter was there; phone in hand, voice low but sharp enough to cut through every ounce of fear I'd been choking on.

He hadn't yelled. He hadn't postured. But there was something in his tone, that quiet steel, that made it clear he wasn't bluffing. It was the kind of voice that made men listen. The kind that said: *you don't get to touch what's mine.*

And the strangest part? I didn't flinch. I didn't feel the panic I used to whenever voices rose or tempers shifted. I felt… safe. Like someone was standing between me and the storm for once, and I could finally exhale.

It wasn't about control or ego; he wasn't trying to own me. He was protecting me. *Us.*

I'd never had that before.

And that version of Hunter— the one who could be calm one moment and terrifyingly certain the next—should've scared me. But it didn't. Because beneath the grit and the threat, there was heart. There was love.

Through the thin walls, I could still hear life happening. Hunter's low voice rumbling from the kitchen. Zeke's laughter was loud and unrestrained. The twins were squealing, probably arguing over who got the pink cup. It was a background noise that reminded me what peace actually sounded like.

When I finally stepped out, wrapped in one of my softest towels, the air carried a new smell. My stomach growled before my brain caught up.

I followed the scent down the hallway and froze at the doorway.

The table was set imperfectly. Two forks lay backward, and the napkins didn't match, but it was beautiful in the most ordinary way. Zeke was standing on a chair, helping Hunter fold the last napkin, and the twins were giggling in their high chairs, each clutching a french fry.

Hunter stood at the stove, sleeves pushed up, and hair messy. He glanced over his shoulder when he noticed me watching.

"Hey," he said softly, that slow, crooked grin forming. "You look better, Beautiful."

I smiled, still dazed. "You cooked?"

He gestured to the takeout containers on the counter. "Sort of. Ordered some of those truffle fries you like from Dukes. That counts as cooking, right?"

A laugh broke free before I could stop it. "You remembered?"

"Hard to forget," he said, opening a container and letting the steam rise between us. "You were so damn happy the first time I took you there. Figured their truffle fries might put that same smile on your face."

The words landed somewhere deep, warm, and unexpected. "They probably will," I said softly, smiling despite myself.

He chuckled, that low, easy sound that always managed to find its way into the cracks of my bad days. "Good."

Zeke spotted me and grinned. "Mom! Hunter let me help! I got to set the table!"

"I see that," I said, my throat tightening a little.

Hunter turned, plates in hand, and nodded toward a chair. "Come sit. Everything's ready."

We listened to every one of Zeke's stories, reveling in this moment. Hunter handed napkins to the twins without missing a beat, cut their food, and made sure I actually ate before I started cleaning up.

I sat there, just watching him. The way he moved around my kids as if he'd always been part of their orbit. The way he glanced at me every few minutes, checking to make sure I was still okay. There was no pity in his gaze, no tension, just a quiet steadiness.

When the chaos died down and the kids drifted off, Hunter helped me carry dishes to the sink. He rolled up his sleeves again, forearms slick with water and soap.

"You didn't have to do all this," I said softly, drying a plate beside him.

"I know." He smirked, not looking up. "I wanted to."

My chest tightened. I turned to say something, but he set the plate down and faced me instead.

"He's not going to hurt you again," he said, voice low,

deliberate.

His words didn't cut. They settled over me, calm and certain, a kind of safety I hadn't known I needed. A wall between me and the ghosts I kept running from.

I reached up, fingers brushing his jaw, rough with stubble. "Thank you," I murmured.

He shook his head slowly. "Don't thank me. Just… let me help carry it, okay?"

That settled deep in me. He wasn't just talking about the call or my ex. He meant all of it. The years spent holding everything together, pretending I was fine, never letting anyone see how heavy it really was.

I didn't argue. I just nodded.

Later, I curled up next to him on the couch. The TV was on low, some movie neither of us was watching. My head rested against his shoulder, his arm stretched along the back of the couch, fingertips tracing slow circles against my arm.

I still worried about being too much, about my chaos spilling into the lives of people I cared about. But when he shifted, tucking me closer like I belonged right there, the worry faded. It softened into something quieter.

"I'm sorry I didn't tell you everything." My voice was barely above a whisper as my hands rubbed them over my thighs. "About him." I hesitated, swallowing hard, the silence stretching between us as I struggled to find the right words. Hunter's expression shifted, his shoulders tensing just slightly, but he didn't say anything. He waited, unmoved and patient as always, letting me take my time.

"After he signed over his parental rights, I thought it was done. I really did." My voice cracked, and I forced a shaky breath. "But he started calling again. From different numbers.

Leaving messages, threats that he'd come back and take the kids. Sometimes, just breathing on the other end. And then one night, he showed up outside my mom's. Said he was there to take the kids, and either I went with him or he'd never see them again." I swallowed hard, heat rising behind my eyes. "That's when I got the restraining order."

Hunter's jaw worked, a muscle flickering near his temple. "When was that?"

"About a year ago." I looked down at my hands. "He left me alone for a while, but sometimes…he still calls." I exhaled, the air shaking out of me.

"I keep telling myself I'm past it, that I'm stronger now. But moments like today…" I trailed off, helpless.

Hunter shifted closer, the space between us shrinking. "Moments like that don't mean you're weak," he said softly. "They mean you survived something that shouldn't have happened. You don't have to worry about that anymore. Nothing will ever happen to you or the kids. I promise."

The pent-up emotions inside me let go. The guilt, the fear, the way I was always bracing for the worst. It all blurred as I leaned in, allowing his arms to envelop me in protection. For a long moment, we just breathed. His breath steady, mine uneven. The kids' voices floated from the bedroom, a fragile piece of normal in a night that felt anything but.

The adrenaline faded, leaving behind a hollow ache. Not fear now, but the kind that comes when you realize how close you came to losing the thin thread of peace you've built.

"Stay with me tonight?" The words came out small, as if I was asking for time I didn't quite believe I deserved.

Hunter's eyes flicked toward the kids. Zeke was already slumped against his blanket, the twins curled together like a pair of kittens. Then his gaze came back to me, unwavering. "Yeah," he said softly. "I'm not going anywhere."

I finally knew the words to put to this feeling: Trust. Safety. Because Hunter never made me feel like a burden. He made me feel *chosen,* and in that moment, I knew that love could feel like this. Unwavering, safe, and real.

Chapter Twenty Eight

Camille

I hadn't felt this nervous since our first date. It was silly, really. I was a grown woman, a mom of three, someone who had survived more than most. Still, standing in front of my crooked hallway mirror, smoothing my dress for the fifth time, I felt sixteen again.

Tonight, Hunter was taking me to dinner, the first time we'd be alone since everything with my ex. He kept showing up for me in quiet ways, consistent reminders that I was safe, that I mattered. He wasn't one for fancy places or big gestures, so I knew this was for me. And I needed tonight to be just that… a new memory. Something good to hold onto.

When his truck pulled up outside, I caught my breath. That massive truck filled the curb like it owned the street, headlights cutting through the dusk. He climbed out, dark jeans, fitted shirt, beard trimmed neatly. God help me, I almost forgot to breathe.

"Wow," I muttered to myself, grabbing my purse before I could chicken out.

He opened the passenger door for me, easy and unthinking, as if chivalry was just the way things were. When I slid into the cab, it smelled of leather and a scent that was only him, a trace of cypress and lime, clean and warm.

"Ready?" he asked, voice low, eyes catching mine for a second longer than necessary.

"Yeah," I lied. My stomach was still flipping somersaults.

The restaurant was somewhere in between, not fancy but not quite casual. Dim lights, brick walls, candles flickering on white tablecloths. The air was full of quiet voices and the clink of glasses, the smell of roasted garlic drifting from the kitchen. I felt out of place in my dress, but Hunter looked at me like I was the only thing that belonged.

He pulled my chair out and sat across from me. The conversation loosened as we waited, and he teased me for dipping bread into every sauce, and I teased him for the way he obsessed over tomatoes in his salad. At one point, I leaned forward, whispering as if it were a secret, "You know, it's a good thing you drove. Because if another man was that picky over his salad, I'd walk out."

He chuckled, shaking his head, that crooked grin spreading across his face. "Guess I'll have to make it up to you with dessert."

I was in the middle of telling him about how Zeke had decided to build a Lego "army base" in the middle of the hallway, complete with a blockade that nearly broke my toe, when I noticed it.

His knee bounced under the table, not just once or twice,

but steady, almost frantic, a rhythm only he seemed to hear. I hadn't started my internship yet, but I knew enough about anxiety to recognize it. His jaw tightened, eyes flicking to the window and back. Most people would've missed it. I almost did. But once I saw it, I couldn't stop seeing it. I trailed off mid-sentence, my fork clinking against the plate. He didn't even notice at first, lost in whatever storm was brewing in his head.

"Hunter," I said softly.

His gaze snapped back to me, too quick, like he'd been caught doing something he wasn't supposed to. "What?"

I tilted my head, keeping my voice gentle. "You okay?"

He gave me that easy grin, the one he used when he wanted to smooth things over. "Yeah… I'm good."

But his knee didn't stop.

I reached across the table, covering his restless thumbs with my own. The movement stilled him, his fingers pausing under my touch. He looked at me, eyes darting, then softening, as if he wasn't used to being seen. His grip tightened, just a little, a quiet signal that he was letting me in. Holding hands felt like a silent agreement that we were both in this together.

"You don't have to explain it away with me," I whispered.

For a beat, he just stared, silent, his chest rising and falling in a rhythm I could almost match my breathing to. Then he let out a long breath, the tension in his shoulders loosening just a little.

"You always know how to call me out," he said, a half-smile tugging at his mouth.

"Not call you out," I corrected. "See you."

The words hung there, heavier than the air between us.

His fingers turned, lacing through mine, holding on like he needed the reminder that I wasn't going anywhere. We sat like that for a long moment, neither of us touching our food. Just hands entwined, the quiet around us filled with clinking silverware and the low hum of strangers' conversations.

And then, almost shyly, he said, "It happens sometimes. I just… get anxious, you know? Crowds get to me sometimes. The noise. I guess I didn't expect it to be that busy. It's stupid." His voice softened, a vulnerability threading through. "I don't… I don't like to talk about it."

I squeezed his hand. "It's not stupid. But you don't have to talk if you don't want to. Just… let me sit with you in it."

His lips twitched like he wanted to argue, but instead, he nodded. He decided then that he wasn't hiding behind jokes or teasing. For once, he was letting me hold some of the weight. When the waitress came by with refills, we both pulled back, but the warmth of his hand lingered long after. His knee stayed still for the rest of the night.

And as I watched him bite into his pie with exaggerated seriousness just to make me laugh, I realized something: I wasn't the only one learning how to trust again.

Chapter Twenty Nine

Hunter

The first thing I noticed when she stepped into my apartment wasn't how out of place she looked, it was how everything in the room shifted around her. My place had always been simple: clean lines, quiet, untouched. But with her there, curls falling over her shoulder, the faint scent of rain clinging to her clothes, it suddenly felt lived in. Warmer.

She curled into the couch, blanket sliding down her shoulders, the lamplight catching the gold in her hair. She tried to look relaxed, but I could see the nerves in the way she tucked her hands into the blanket and laughed at nothing. The air between us felt charged.

She smiled down at her phone, trying to stifle a laugh. I didn't have to guess who it was. Her mom. The same woman who'd told her not to come home tonight. Camille turned the screen toward me, cheeks flushed.

Mom: *Don't rush home. The kids and I*

are having fun.

Camille buried her face against me, giggling into my shirt. "She's incorrigible."

I chuckled, pressing my lips to her hair. "Smart woman."

She swatted my chest lightly but didn't pull away. Instead, she leaned closer, her hand sliding across my ribs to rest over my heart.

Then more messages crossed the screen.

Mom: *I'm serious.*

Mom: *And no, I won't let Zeke eat cereal*
  for dinner, stop worrying.

Mom: *Have fun. XO.*

Camille groaned, burying her face in her hands.

I couldn't help it. I laughed. A real one, the kind that shook through my chest. "Sounds like she's your biggest wing man."

"She's embarrassing," she mumbled, though her shoulders shook with her own laugh.

"Embarrassing or not," I said, leaning a little closer, "she's right."

The rain kept tapping against the windows, filling the silence that grew between us. She shifted closer, her knee brushing mine, and I could feel her pulse in the air, the push and pull of wanting and holding back.

"This place feels like you," she said softly.

"Yeah?"

That's how the night began. Not with nerves or rushing, but

with laughter, trust, and the quiet certainty that something ordinary had turned extraordinary. Two glasses on the coffee table, a single sock left behind in our scramble, curled at the foot of the couch. A small sign that my apartment was ours, even if just for tonight.

Her eyes flicked up at me, wide, searching. And there it was again. The weight of all her hesitations, the careful walls she'd built. I felt it in the way her breath hitched, even as she leaned toward me.

So I didn't push. I just reached over, brushed a curl back from her cheek, and let my hand linger for a second longer than necessary. "No pressure, Camille. Not tonight. Not ever. "

Her lips parted, and she whispered, "Okay." A beat later, she looked at me, her brown eyes solemn. "What if…" I swallowed hard. "What if you don't like what you see?"

My brow furrowed. "What are you talking about?"

"My body." The words slipped out before she could stop them, quiet and raw. "The stretch marks. The stomach. The parts of me that don't look the way they used to."

My hands found her face, holding her firm but gentle as I led her to meet my eyes. "Camille, I like *you*. All of you. Every curve, every mark, every scar, because they're you. And I've never wanted anyone the way I want you."

"You're beautiful," I said quietly, the words confident and certain. "Not just when you try, not just when you hide in the right clothes. Always. And it drives me crazy that you can't see it."

She blinked fast, not knowing what to do with that. "You have to say that," she whispered. "You're supposed to say that."

I shook my head, a small grin tugging at my mouth. "Nope. If I were supposed to, I'd just nod when you talk down about yourself. But I'm not. Because it isn't true."

She groaned, covering her face with both hands. "You're so annoying."

"Yeah," I murmured, prying her hands away, brushing my beard against her knuckles before pressing a kiss there. "Annoying enough to keep reminding you until it finally sticks."

She laughed under her breath, quiet and shaky. And then, just when I thought the moment had settled, she whispered something that cracked me open. "You really don't give up, do you?"

I grinned, the corner of my mouth twitching because she didn't realize how right she was. "Not when it comes to you."

Her eyes lifted to mine, wide, questioning. So I went on, because she needed to hear it.

"You've got this habit of muttering under your breath when you think I'm not listening. Usually it's harmless — grocery lists, school stuff, to-dos. But sometimes, it's not."

"Not?" she echoed.

I exhaled slowly. "Sometimes it's little daggers. Things you say about yourself. Things that aren't true."

She didn't speak, and for a moment, the quiet between us pulsed with everything unspoken. I went on, my voice low. "You wrinkle your nose at your reflection. You mutter about not being enough. And every time, it's like watching someone kick a diamond into the dirt."

She tried to roll her eyes. "You make it sound so dramatic."

"It is dramatic," I said simply. "Because it's you."

That pulled a real laugh out of her, soft and wet at the edges from tears she didn't want to let fall.

"You really think that?" she whispered.

"I don't think it," I said, my thumb tracing her jaw. "I know it. And maybe that's why I tease you. Why I make you laugh. Because it's the only way I know how to drown out that voice in your head that won't shut up."

She pressed her forehead to my chest, her breath catching as a tear slid warm through my shirt. "You're too good at this," she said.

"Maybe," I murmured, my hand finding the back of her neck, thumb stroking her hairline. "But I mean it. And I'll keep telling you. I'll keep showing you, in every way I know, that you're more than enough. Even if you never fully believe it. Even if it takes the rest of my life."

She lifted her head then, and I saw it, that quiet breaking open behind her eyes. The walls she'd spent years building, softening under the weight of trust. "Why?"

I smiled, slow and lopsided. "Because I love you. Frustrations, doubts, stubborn walls, and all. Loving you isn't hard, Cami. It's the easiest thing I've ever done."

Her breath hitched, the air between us shifting, trembling, then settling as her shoulders relaxed and the tension eased out of her body. I could feel the shift. She leaned in a little more, close enough that her breath warmed my collarbone, and I felt my chest tighten.

Desire thrummed through me, slow and deliberate. Not hunger, not heat, but something deeper. I wanted to learn her by touch, to prove to her she was more than the lies in her head. She wasn't a dream. She was flesh and fire, solid and here.

I didn't push, didn't rush. I just sat there, my hand cradling her jaw, my thumb sweeping slow circles across her cheek. When she finally looked up, the uncertainty was gone. And when she kissed me slowly, searching, I knew this wasn't just another night.

Chapter Thirty

Camille

My breath caught, and for a second I thought about pulling back, about making some excuse to head home. But the truth was, I didn't want to. Not tonight.

"Hunter," I whispered, my voice barely carrying in the stillness. He hummed, low in his chest, waiting.

"I'm… nervous," I admitted, heat crawling up my neck.

His thumb brushed along my shoulder where the blanket had slipped, gentle, grounding. "Then we go slow. Or we don't at all. Whatever you want." He paused, meeting my eyes with care.

That was the moment something inside me broke wide open. The choice. The patience. No demands, no pressure. Just him, waiting for me.

I leaned up before I lost the courage, my lips brushing his, soft at first, testing, like dipping my toes into water I wasn't sure I was ready to dive into. A flicker of doubt stirred within me, but his gentle approach quelled the fear. He met me halfway, slow and careful, his mouth warm and steady against mine, as if reassuring me with every second. The kiss deepened little by little, each moment unraveling another layer of apprehension yet leaving room for those lingering uncertainties.

My fingers grazed his shirt, pulling him closer before I could stop myself. His hand slipped to the small of my back, anchoring me as his other hand skimmed up to cradle the back of my neck. Every touch was deliberate, patient, but charged in a way that left an ache at my core.

I'd forgotten how it felt to be kissed like this. Not rushed, not taken, but cherished. His lips traced the line of my jaw, down to the hollow of my throat, each kiss stealing another piece of the walls I'd built. I gasped, my body torn between nerves and craving.

"Tell me if it's too much," he murmured against my skin, voice rough.

I shook my head, curls spilling across the cushion. "Don't stop."

Clothes slipped away slowly, not with urgency but with reverence, each layer another secret shared. My skin burned under his hands, but it wasn't just heat; it was relief. For so long, I'd carried shame, fear, the memory of being touched without gentleness. And here, with him, I was relearning. In the brief silence between our whispers, we were creating a cocoon around us that sheltered our tender exchanges. Every laugh when our knees knocked clumsily, every whispered check-in, every kiss that stole my breath. It stitched something in me I didn't know was still frayed.

Every touch was slower than I expected, gentler than my fears told me it would be. Hunter wasn't rushing or trying to take anything from me; he was simply *there*, fully present, steady in a way that made my heart ache. The longer I let myself lean into him, the louder the noise in my head became. I'd told myself I wasn't enough. Those stretch marks, softness, and scars were barriers. But the way his hands lingered on me, memorizing, not judging me, unraveled those lies one by one.

"You're so fuckin' beautiful," he murmured against my skin, and the words cracked me wide open. No hesitation, no pity. Just the truth, spoken so simply, it made tears sting my eyes.

"Wait, not here." He said breathlessly. He picked me up, arms strong and sure, carrying me through his apartment. It was dark, barely lit by the light from the street lamps outside. As he lay me across his bed, my breath tangled. Anticipation bloomed. A slow, aching heat landed at my core. He moved between my legs, filling the space between us, his weight pressing into me until my pulse stuttered.

I hooked my legs around his hips, drawing him closer. My hands traced the hard curve of his arms, fingers slipping into his hair. I tugged, needing him, pulling his mouth back to mine. His lips were steady, patient, letting me set the pace. That patience undid me. I deepened the kiss, hunger rising, months of restraint dissolving between us. His tongue teased against mine, coaxing, until I melted beneath him.

"I've wanted this," he murmured against my lips, his breath hot.

"Then stop waiting," I whispered, tugging harder.

The rumble in his chest vibrated through me, heat surging as his hand slid slowly up my thigh, gripping my hip and pulling me closer, like he couldn't bear even an inch of distance.

"Fuck, Camille," he breathed, my name breaking on his tongue, the only word that mattered. A moan slipped out before I could stop it. His smile brushed my mouth as he kissed me harder.

The scrape of his beard against my skin as he kissed up my neck made me shiver. I arched into him, unguarded, wanting more. His hands mapped me, memorizing every line, every curve.

I moved on instinct, my body answering his. My fingers tangled in his hair, desperate for more, my body moving before my mind could catch up. Fear dissolved in his touch. His hand slid higher, tracing my hip, slipping beneath fabric, and I gasped, chest rising against his. It had been years since I felt free of fear and hesitation. All that mattered was him. "More." I breathed, my voice breaking on the plea.

He groaned, my name rough in his throat, his hand sliding higher, slipping beneath fabric. I gasped, chest rising against his.

When he looked at me, eyes burning, asking without words, I nodded, trembling. He pressed into me slowly, filling me, stretching me until I clung to him, overwhelmed. It was too much and somehow just right. His jaw clenched, a curse slipping from his lips as I arched beneath him, greedy for more.

"Fuck." he breathed, forehead pressed to mine. "You're perfect. Feels so damn good."

Our bodies moved together, instinctively, a rhythm that needed no words. Every thrust unraveled me, his touch grounding and consuming at once. His forehead pressed to mine as I clung to him, trembling. The rhythm built, relentless, until I couldn't hold back the sounds spilling from me, broken gasps, pleas, his name. My body trembled, strung tight, until it snapped, shattering around him and pulling him with me. He collapsed against me, still trembling, pressing a shaky kiss to my shoulder. My walls were gone, every barrier stripped away, but I didn't feel bare. I felt seen. Chosen.

This wasn't just fire, though it burned hot and wild. It was trust. It was a surrender. It was me letting every wall fall, letting him in, not out of weakness, but because I chose him.

The room was quiet, a hush that settled in late at night, broken only by the hum of cars outside and the slow tick of the clock. This was his world, his safe little corner, and tonight Hunter had brought me here.

The light from the outside threw a gentle glow across the room, catching the lines of his jaw, the curve of his mouth. The sheets were still warm and tangled, the air carrying that lazy stillness that always came after intimate moments like this.

Hunter lay beside me, his arm draped loosely over my waist, fingers absently tracing idle circles on my hip. My head rested against his chest, his heartbeat steady beneath my ear, grounding me in a way words never could. The faint scent of cypress and passion lingered in the space between us, familiar and comforting.

That's when I noticed it again. The tattoo across his chest. It had caught my eye earlier, when my hands had roamed across his skin, but the moment hadn't been right to ask. Now, with the rain quieting the world outside, I let my fingers drift up, tracing the dark ink just below his collarbone.

In clean, timeless script, it read "May you never lose your way."

Below the words, a small compass was etched between two sparrows in flight. It was an intentional design, its intricate lines weaving tales of direction and self-discovery.

He stilled under my touch. For a moment, I thought about pulling my hand away, but then his voice came, low and rough, vibrating through my cheek where it rested on his chest.

"Got that after my first deployment," he said. "I was eighteen, barely knew who I was. I guess it was supposed to be a reminder."

"A reminder of what?" I asked softly.

He exhaled, slow, steady. "To not lose myself. To remember my moral compass, no matter where I ended up. To find my way back."

The words sank deep. I let my fingers trace one of the sparrows, wings stretched mid-flight. "Did it work?"

His chest rose under my palm, a long pause filling the space before he answered. "Sometimes," he said. "Sometimes it's easy to forget what you're fighting for. Who you are. But I guess," he continued, and I mirrored his slow, steady breath, feeling his rhythm almost in sync with mine. His hand came up, threading gently into my hair, thumb brushing along the back of my neck. "I'm still finding my way."

I lifted my head, meeting his eyes. The look he gave me was unguarded in a way I'd rarely seen, open and quiet, honest. My thumb brushed the compass again, right over where his heart beat steadily beneath it.

"You found it," I whispered. "Your way back."

He studied me for a moment, then smiled, small and crooked. "Yeah," he murmured. "Maybe I did."

He leaned in and kissed me, slow and unhurried. It wasn't about heat or urgency, but about grounding, about presence. When he pulled back, I rested my cheek against his chest again, my fingers tracing the lines of ink over his skin. The compass, the sparrows, the words—they told his story. Each tattoo carries its own memory. The koi fish from his time in Hawaii, the "Semper Fidelis" on the back of his arm for the young marine fresh out of boot camp, and the sparrows, a quiet reminder to never lose himself.

"Hunter?" My voice cracked, fragile.

"Yeah?" His tone was rough, uncertain, but open.

The words slipped out, fragile as glass. "I love you." It felt like standing at the edge of a cliff, the ground uncertain beneath me. What if his silence lasted forever? What if I'd read it all wrong? The quiet stretched, my mind racing with the fear that saying it could mean losing him, but not saying it meant losing myself. My heart pounded in the hush.

The silence stretched, my chest tight, but then his hand cupped my cheek, tilting my face so I had to meet his eyes. "Say it again."

My breath hitched, but I didn't look away. "Well, techni-cally, you said it first. You said earlier, loving me was easy… I love you, Hunter."

It was like watching his koi fish come alive, colors shifting under water. I felt it in the way he kissed me, slow and certain, nothing held back. When he pulled away, his forehead rested against mine, his voice raw, every wall gone. "I love you too, Camille. Probably love you more."

Tears slipped free, but I laughed through them, burying my face in his chest. A giggle bubbled out, muffled against his skin, because the relief was overwhelming. His fingers threaded through my curls, his lips pressing against the top of my head, and I realized I was smiling so wide it almost hurt.

In his arms, I didn't feel like too much. I didn't feel broken. With him, I could set the weight down because I found what I'd believed was possible. Outside, the world remained as it was. But inside, I could feel him breathe, the air between us warm and still. And in that moment, I realized that maybe neither of us was lost anymore. We'd both just been finding our way home.

Chapter Thirty One

Hunter

Repeating her words. *I love you.*

She'd cried, laughed, buried her face in my chest like she couldn't believe it was real. And I'd held her, threading my fingers through her curls, breathing her in, whispering it again against her hair because once wasn't enough.

All I could think was, this woman had every reason not to say those words. In her words, she'd been bruised, abandoned, and left to raise three kids. She has carried scars no one should carry alone. And still, she chose to love me.

All my life, I'd been taught love was weakness. That showing it, saying it, meant you were soft, vulnerable, open to being broken. But in that moment, with her heart pressed against mine, I realized the truth: Loving her wasn't a weakness; it was the bravest thing I've ever done.

The drive back to her apartment that night was quiet, the kind of silence that held meaning rather than emptiness. She sat beside me, curled slightly toward the window, her fingers absently twisting the hem of her shirt. I didn't need her to say anything. I could feel it. The guilt. The tug of two worlds she was constantly balancing. One part of her wanted to stay, to let the night linger, to fall deeper into us. The other part was already back home, where three little hearts depended on her.

I tightened my grip on the wheel, not out of frustration, but to remind myself that this wasn't about what I wanted. It was about meeting her where she was. She'd already let me closer than I ever expected, already trusted me with parts of herself most people never saw. That mattered more than anything.

The truck rumbled beneath us, the glow of streetlights washing in and out like waves. I kept my eyes ahead, letting her have the quiet. She bit her lip, shoulders tense, the kind of small tell that said more than words could. almost reached for her hand to tell her she didn't have to explain, but I held back. Sometimes the quiet said it better.

When we pulled into her complex, she finally turned toward me. Her eyes were soft, almost apologetic, but I shook my head before she could speak. "You don't need to explain," I said quietly. My voice came out rough, but steady. "I get it. You're a mom first. That's who you are. And that's one of the things I love about you."

Her lips parted, wanting to argue, but then she stopped. I saw the tension in her shoulders ease, just slightly, like maybe she believed me.

I parked in the same spot as always, the truck idling low. She fiddled with her bag strap, reaching for the handle, but I caught her wrist. Not to stop her, just to anchor her for a moment. "Camille," I murmured, waiting for her eyes to meet mine. "Tonight was…" I trailed off, searching for words that always felt too big. "…real. And I'll take real over perfect any day."

Her throat worked as she swallowed, eyes glistening in the glow of the streetlamp. She leaned in, pressing a quick, soft kiss to my cheek before slipping out of the truck.

"Thank you…for understanding. I enjoyed tonight." She whispered.

"Anytime, Beautiful," I murmured back.

I watched her walk toward her building, her shoulders squaring as if she was pulling her armor back on. Just before she disappeared inside, she glanced back. The smallest smile tugged at her lips, and it was enough.

I let out a long breath, leaning back against the seat once she was gone. Part of me wanted to chase after her, to tell her she didn't have to run, that she could stay, and the world wouldn't fall apart. But I knew better. She wasn't running from me. She was running toward the people who needed her most.

And if I was going to be part of her world, I had to prove I could handle that.

As I started the truck again, the low, insistent rumble was a comforting backdrop to the whirlwind of thoughts racing through my mind. Her scent still clung to my skin, and the ghost of her kiss lingered on my cheek, a gentle reminder of the night we'd shared.

This evening had been more than just a moment; it was a pivotal shift in my world, one that left me both exhilarated and introspective. I realized that Camille trusted me enough to let me in, a type of trust I hadn't been certain I'd ever have with anyone again. It was as though the walls around my heart had been carefully dismantled, brick by brick, and in their place was new and uncharted but profoundly real.

Driving home, I knew I had to be patient, to prove that I could be part of the world that mattered most to her, the world where she was needed. And despite the uncertainty and the challenges ahead, the feeling that prevailed was worth waiting for, time and again.

Chapter Thirty Two

Camille

Two days later, the glow had started to fade, and in its place came nerves.

Not because Hunter had done anything wrong. He hadn't. He'd texted me, checked in, and made me laugh the way he always did. He'd been reassuring, consistent. Everything I said I wanted.

But that was the problem.

I was waiting for the crack.

History has taught me there was always one. The slow fade of texts. The excuses. The way interest turned into silence. I told myself not to compare, not to drag the ghosts of old relationships into this one, but it was hard to shake the memory of my ex walking out the door and never coming back. Or the others who'd sworn they could handle my life, only to realize it was heavier than they'd bargained for.

So even as I folded laundry, wrangled the twins, and helped Zeke build yet another rocket, the doubts spun in my head like a broken record. I tried to push the thoughts away. Focus on schoolwork. On the kids. On anything but the way my phone buzz made my stomach twist with both excitement and dread.

And when his name did pop up on the screen, I hesitated. Because part of me wanted to answer right away, to lean into the comfort of his voice. But another part wanted to wait just a minute, just long enough to prove to myself that I wasn't too eager. That I could play it cool.

It was ridiculous. I knew it was ridiculous. But trauma has a way of turning simple things, like texting a man who makes you laugh, into a minefield.

By bedtime that night, I was stretched thin, nerves buzzing under my skin. I kissed Zeke's curls, tucked the twins in, and lingered at their door as they drifted off. My heart ached with love for them—and fear. Because if Hunter became a fixture in their lives and then walked away, it wouldn't just be me who was shattered this time.

It would be them too.

Back in my room, I curled under the blanket, phone in hand. His last message blinked on the screen, simple and sweet:

Hunter: How's your night, beautiful?

My thumb hovered over the keyboard, nerves warring with giddiness and the desire to be honest with him: that my night was messy and loud, that I was scared, that I didn't know how to trust good things when they showed up.

But instead, I typed back: *Long day. Kids are finally down. How's yours?*

Simple. Safe.

His reply came a minute later.

Hunter: Quiet night. Boring without
  spaghetti wars.

> *Me:* Trust me, you'd be begging for
> boring after two full days of
> craziness.

Hunter: Nope. I'd trade boring for
  that any day.

My chest squeezed. It was banter, light and teasing, but I could feel the truth under it.

  The voices in my head were loud, but then another buzz pulled me back.

Hunter: What if I take you and the
  kids to the aquarium next weekend?
  My treat. They'd love it.

I froze. Aquarium. A real outing. I stared at the screen too long, chewing my nails. What if one tantrum too many sent him running? Had he realized this wasn't just a cute dinner in my kitchen or a low-stakes meeting at the park? This was the reality: straps and buckles, Goldfish crackers spilling from little fists, endless "are we there yet" before we even hit the highway.

> *Me:* That's… a lot. I don't know.

Hunter: Bad idea?

> *Me:* Maybe. It's not you. I just… I don't

want to scare you off.

Hunter: Beautiful. If I was going to run,
   I would've done it already.

                          Me: You don't get it. People say
                              that. And then they leave.

His reply came back almost instantly.

Hunter: I'm not those people.

I covered my mouth, heart thudding so hard it felt like it might wake the kids in the next room.

                              Me: I know you're not.

Hunter: Good. And I'll keep showing
   up until you believe me.

I sank deeper into the blanket, as tears pricked the back of my eyes. I stared at his words glowing on the screen, hope pulsed through me stronger than the fear.

                          Me: I look forward to it.
                    Me: And the Aquarium. The kids
                              would love that.

When I hit send, my chest fluttered with equal parts nerves and butterflies.

By the time Saturday rolled around, my nerves were stretched thin.

I'd agreed to the aquarium. I'd actually said yes. And for three days, my brain had been running in circles about it.

Not because I didn't want to go, I did. The thought of the kids pressing their little noses to the glass, wide-eyed at sharks and stingrays, made me giddy. The thought of Hunter being there beside us, seeing them like that, made warmth bloom in my chest.

But that warmth came with shadows.

What if it was too much? What if the noise, the effort required, the inevitable tantrum-in-public moment pushed him away? What if he looked at me differently afterward, saw me not as the woman who made him laugh over coffee, but as the single mom juggling three small humans who sometimes felt like too much even for me?

I kept telling myself not to spiral. Except spiraling was second nature by now.

"Mommy, do they have jellyfish at the aquarium?" Zeke asked, bouncing onto the couch while I wrangled the twins into matching outfits. His eyes were bright with excitement.

"Yep," I said, tugging Chloe's shirt over her head. "Big glowing ones."

"And sharks?" he pressed, eyes wide.

"Uh-huh. Sharks too."

"And sea turtles!" he added proudly, like he already had the tour guide script memorized.

I smiled at him, but inside my stomach twisted tighter. He was already excited. Already expecting something magical.

Which meant if things went wrong, if Hunter didn't stay, he'd be the one asking me why.

And I didn't have another explanation left in me.

The twins toddled over with their toys, clutching the fox and bunny in sticky fists. They squealed "fishy!" in chorus, like they somehow knew what the day had in store. I kissed their curls, breathing them in, letting their joy soften the edge of my nerves.

I wasn't sure how this day would go. I wasn't sure if I was making the right choice by letting him in this far.

Hunter: Don't worry about driving.
I'll pick you and the kids up.

I stared at the words, pulse thudding in my ears.

He wanted to pick us up. To see it all up close. The whole picture. Three car seats crammed in the back. A diaper bag stuffed with snacks and wipes. The double stroller that always seemed bulkier than it needed to be.

The circus. My circus.

Panic twisted in my stomach, leading to another line of doubts.

Me: Are you sure? We can meet you there. A trip out requires a lot.

Hunter: I know. And I want to.
Car seats, snack bags, the whole shebang. I'm good, Camille.

I bit my lip, fighting the sting in my eyes.

Because part of me still wanted to push him away, because it would hurt less if he bailed now than if he bailed later. While another part kept growing every time he showed up, steady and unshaken, wanted to believe him.

I tucked my phone into my pocket, exhaled, and whispered to myself: *Okay. Let him show you he means it.*

Zeke ran up, tugging at my sleeve, curls bouncing. "Can we go yet?"

"Not yet, baby," I said softly, glancing toward the window. My heart pounded, equal parts dread and butterflies.

By the time I wrangled shoes onto all three kids, packed the diaper bag with bottles, snacks, wipes, and emergency snacks (because there's always an emergency), I was already sweating. The stroller leaned against the wall, daring me to figure out how to get it down the steps with two toddlers on my hip.

That's when I heard the low rumble of a truck engine outside.

I peeked through the curtain and froze.

When he parked at the curb, the engine cut off with a growl, and the silence left behind seemed louder than before.

And all I could think was: *What the hell is he doing here with something that nice when I'm about to cram three car seats, two sticky toddlers, and a five-year-old into it.* I had driven in his truck before, but for some reason I'd overlooked just how pristine he keeps everything: his apartment, his clothes, his truck.

Instant anxiety shot through me.

He was out of the truck a second later, tall, broad-shouldered, beard catching the morning light.

He looked so calm. Meanwhile, I was on the other side of the door trying to remember if I'd packed enough diapers or if my shirt had toothpaste on it.

A knock. Then his voice, warm and breathy: "Camille?"

He greeted me with that crooked grin. Before I could second-guess myself, he leaned down and kissed me. It was soft, easy. Like he was coming home after a day of work. That triggered butterflies, nerves, relief, all tangled up.

Then he pulled back, nodding toward the pile by the door. "That the load out?"

I laughed nervously. "Yeah. Sorry. It's... a lot."

"Not a problem," he said, already scooping up the stroller effortlessly. He slung the diaper bag over his shoulder with his free hand, leaving me standing there blinking.

"Wait," I called, following him toward the truck. "Do you know what you're doing with those?"

But he was already opening the back door, placing each of the kids' car seats in the truck, without a second thought. I stopped short. "You... you know how to install those?"

He smirked over his shoulder. "Yeah. My buddy Logan's got a daughter. Made me practice until I could do it in my sleep."

I stared at him as he clicked the first seat into place, muscles flexing, movements confident.

In that moment, it hit me: he wasn't flinching, wasn't hesitating, he was making space in his shiny truck for my kids' car seats like it was the most natural thing in the world. He practiced so that he could do it right, which told me he might also be holding his own doubts close, fighting his own battles against long-held fears of his own inadequacies. Yet, he stood unwavering, and that vulnerability, whether voiced or unvoiced, mirrored my own, knitting our shared courage tightly together.

Within minutes, the twins were strapped in, happily squishing their toys against the car seat fabric, babbling to each other. Zeke climbed up into his booster, legs swinging, already peppering Hunter with questions.

And me? I stood there on the curb, a diaper bag still slung across my chest, watching Hunter tighten straps and double-check buckles with practiced hands.

"You don't have to—" I started, but my voice faltered.

He glanced up at me, his blue eyes unwavering. "I want to." That's simple. No fuss, no hesitation.

I slid into the passenger seat, heart racing, while he folded the stroller into the bed of the truck without a hitch. The second he climbed in beside me, the smell of his cologne mixed with the faint new-leather scent of the truck, and I felt my nerves spike all over again because here we were. Him behind the wheel. Me in the passenger seat. My kids in the back.

He glanced over before starting the engine, that grin tugging at his mouth. "Ready, Beautiful?"

"Do I have a choice?" I muttered, fiddling with the strap of the diaper bag.

He chuckled, leaned over, and kissed me quickly, right there with my kids squealing behind us. Just a gentle brush of his lips. "C'mon, it'll be fun," he said softly, before turning the key.

The truck rumbled to life. Zeke cheered. The twins squeaked their toys in unison, as if approving the plan.

And me? My heart pounded, my doubts hummed, but for the first time in a long time, I let myself sit back in the seat and hope.

Chapter Thirty Three

Hunter

The truck had never sounded this loud.

No, not the engine. The laughter. The chatter. The squeak of toys and the constant stream of questions from the backseat.

"Are we there yet?" Zeke asked for the third time, legs swinging against his booster seat.

"Buddy, we're not even close, I said, glancing at him in the rear-view mirror.

He grinned back at me, unbothered, then went right back to explaining which shark was the fastest swimmer.

Beside me, Camille sat with her diaper bag tucked at her feet, hands clasped tight in her lap. She kept sneaking glances at me, waiting for me to flinch, to roll my eyes, to sigh at the circus taking over my truck.

But the truth was, I kind of liked it.

The noise filled in parts of me that I hadn't realized were empty. It was messy, sure. Loud. Unpredictable. But it was *real*. And it was them. Her kids, her world, and somehow she'd continued to let me into it.

I caught her looking again, nervous, lips pressed tight.

"You okay?" I asked, keeping my tone light.

She gave a quick smile. "Yeah. Just… waiting for you to run off screaming."

I laughed, shaking my head. "Not a chance. I've been in combat zones quieter than this. I can handle a few squeaky toys."

That earned me a laugh, the kind that made her whole face light up.

I reached across the console and took her hand, my thumb tracing slow circles against her skin.

At a red light, I glanced at the bouquet of sunflowers she'd put in a cup holder between us, stems sticking out awkwardly. She'd insisted on bringing them along "so they wouldn't wilt," but I knew the truth. She just didn't want to let go of them yet.

This wasn't just a date. This wasn't just dinner and a kiss on the couch. This was me, behind the wheel, with three kids in the backseat, calling the shots. This was the kind of step you don't take unless you're serious.

And I was.

Scared? Sure. Overthinking every second? Absolutely. But serious all the same.

I tightened my grip on the wheel and told myself what I'd been telling her: I'd just keep showing up and doing my best.

I peeked in the rear-view mirror again, except this time I didn't just see kids.

I saw *her*.

Zeke had her curls, the same stubborn spring that refused to be tamed. His eyes were hers, too. I caught myself thinking he had her determination, the way he asked questions, and shared her genuine curiosity about the world.

The twins were even more dangerous for my heart. Those big brown eyes? Same as hers, wide and deep, full of kindness and innocence. Their little giggles echoed her laugh. Bright, infectious, the kind of sound that worked its way under your skin and stayed there.

It hit me then, these kids weren't just hers. They *were* her, in pieces. Living proof of her strength, her chaos, and her love.

And if I wanted her, it meant wanting all of them too. The realization was heavy. But it wasn't the kind of weight that pushed me down; it was the kind that made me think, *Yeah. I can carry this.*

The drive wasn't long, but it felt like a shift. Each mile put me deeper into her world. By the time the blue dome of the aquarium came into view, Zeke was practically bouncing out of his booster seat, yelling about jellyfish and turtles.

"Sharks first!" he demanded.

"No, fishy first!" Avery countered, smacking her toy against the car seat.

"Bunny!" Chloe shouted because, apparently, her stuffed bunny was now part of the tour.

Camille's laugh was soft, but her shoulders were still stiff, her hands twisting in her lap. Bracing for me to glance in the rear-view mirror, see the chaos in full force, and put the truck in reverse. I wish she could see the resolve in my mind.

I parked, cut the engine, and turned to look at her.

"You okay?" I asked quietly.

She gave me a smile that was more nervous than joyful. "They're... a lot."

"They're perfect," I said before I could stop myself.

Her eyes flicked to mine, wide and searching, like she was trying to decide if I really meant it. I held the gaze, because I did. Climbing out, I grabbed the stroller from the bed of the truck before she could, unfolding it in one practiced motion. She raised a brow.

"You sure you haven't done this before?"

I smirked. "Told you. My buddy has a daughter. He made me practice until I could do it blindfolded." That earned me a laugh that was genuine this time.

We got the twins strapped in, Zeke's hand snug in mine as we crossed the parking lot. Camille walked on the other side of him, glancing at me now and then like she still couldn't quite believe I was here. Carrying the bag. Pushing the stroller.

And maybe I couldn't quite believe it either. Because walking into an aquarium with three kids and the woman who'd slowly undone all my walls felt like uncharted territory. But it also felt right. Maybe I was exactly where I was supposed to be. The moment we stepped into the aquarium, the kids froze in their tracks. The glass tunnel stretched ahead, glowing blue, schools of silver fish darting past like a living current. Light rippled across the floor, painting their little sneakers in shades of ocean.

"Whoa," Zeke breathed, his hand tightening in mine. "It's like we're *underwater*."

Avery squealed, pointing both fists at the glass where a stingray slid past. Chloe gasped and pressed her bunny against the stroller tray, as if showing it the view too.

Beside me, Camille exhaled softly. Relief, maybe. Or nerves, loosening just a little.

"They like it," I murmured, leaning closer.

Her lips twitched. "That's an understatement."

I couldn't help smiling. Because watching them watch the fish was better than any exhibit. Zeke's eyes were wide, his mouth hanging open. The twins squealed with every new sound and color.

And Camille… the way she watched me like she was waiting for me to pull back, to sigh, to reveal that this was too much. But I didn't feel that way at all. I felt…like this was exactly where I was supposed to be.

We moved slowly, Zeke tugging me toward the shark tank like he was on a mission. "That one's a hammerhead! Did you know they can see almost all the way around their heads?"

I chuckled. "Guess I'd better be careful then. He'll see me coming before I even wave." Zeke laughed, delighted, and the sound hit me deeper than I expected.

The twins clapped at the jellyfish display, glowing pink and orange in the dark. Avery whispered, "Pretty," while Chloe hummed her nonsense tune, swaying in the stroller.

I bent down, pointing at the tank. "You're right, Avery. Pretty. Like your mom." Camille elbowed me, cheeks flushing, but I caught the small smile she tried to hide.

Halfway through, we stopped at the touch tank. Zeke rolled up his sleeves, eyes gleaming. "Can I? Please?"

"Go for it," I said, guiding his hand toward the stingray gliding lazily by. He squealed when it brushed against his fingers, turning to look at his mom with wild excitement.

"Mommy! It's slimy!" Camille laughed, and for once, the sound didn't have an edge of exhaustion. It was pure, unguarded joy. I glanced at her, catching that light in her face, and knew I'd fight like hell to keep being the reason she smiled like that.

By the time we made it to the sea turtle exhibit, Zeke was drooping against the glass, the twins babbling sleepily in the stroller. I pushed it while Camille walked beside me, close enough that her arm brushed mine now and then.

"You did good," she said softly, almost like she didn't mean for me to hear it.

I looked at her, steady. "We did good."

Her eyes flicked to mine, and for a second, the walls she carried cracked again. And in that tiny opening, I knew this was something worth staying for.

By the time we circled back to the entrance, the magic was fading fast. Zeke's steps dragged, his bottom lip sticking out as he whined, "My legs are too tired." The twins squirmed in the stroller, rubbing their eyes, one starting to fuss, the other repeating "fishy, fishy" like a broken record.

Camille's jaw tightened. I saw it in the way she adjusted the diaper bag higher on her shoulder, bracing herself. I knew that look, it was the one of someone already preparing to carry everyone else through the hard part.

"C'mere, buddy," I said, crouching in front of Zeke. "Want a lift?"

His eyes lit up. "On your shoulders?"

"On my shoulders."

In a second, he was grinning, arms wrapped around my head as I hoisted him up onto my shoulders. He giggled, legs swinging against my chest. "I'm taller than everyone!" he shouted, his voice echoing through the entrance.

Camille blinked, surprise flickering across her face before softening into something that made my chest tighten.

We made our way back to the truck with Zeke perched high

on my shoulder, directing us like a tiny general, the twins sat quietly in the stroller, and Camille walked close, eyes darting to me every few steps as though she couldn't quite believe what she was seeing.

At the truck, Zeke slid down, landing with a thud before proudly declaring, "Hunter carried me!" like it was the highlight of his day.

The twins were fussing by then, tired and cranky, but I leaned close to Camille as we buckled them in. "Everyone's secure," I murmured, trying to ease the tension I could still feel rolling off her.

Her lips twitched, exhaustion warring with a smile. "You didn't have to do that."

"Yeah," I said, brushing my hands off on my jeans. "But I wanted to."

For the briefest moment, her walls cracked wide enough for me to see the relief, the gratitude, and the tiny spark of hope she was still afraid to name.

And as I slid into the driver's seat with Zeke already munching his cookie and the twins drifting off in the back, I realized I'd do this again in a heartbeat.

Because maybe this wasn't just her life anymore. Maybe it could be ours.

Chapter Thirty Four

Camille

The truck rolled to a stop in front of my apartment. The twins were snoring softly in the back and Zeke laid slumped against his booster seat with cookie crumbs on his shirt. I reached across to grab Avery's bottle from the cup holder…only it slipped from my hand, rolling onto the floor mat and splattering milk across the spotless leather.

I froze. My breath caught in my throat. His *new* truck. His perfect, gleaming, not-a-scratch-on-it truck.

Heat rushed up my neck, panic clawing at my chest. This was it. The crack. The reason to sigh, to mutter something about carelessness, to remind me in some small way that this: me, my kids, my mess…was too much.

"I'm so sorry," I blurted, scrambling for wipes in the diaper bag. My hands shook as I dabbed at the mess, the sour smell already creeping into my nose. "I swear I usually…this doesn't…"

"Cami" His voice cut through calmly.

"I'll clean it, I swear. Just give me…" I was elbow-deep in the diaper bag, pulling out everything *but* what I needed. A pacifier, a toy car, a half-empty snack pouch—no wipes. With a sigh, I grabbed one of the extra shirts I'd packed for the twins and did my best to mop up the spill.

"Camille." I looked up, expecting the sigh, the edge, the disappointment. He came up beside me, plucked the shirt gently from my hand, and grinned. "Relax. It's just milk. My truck will live."

"But it's *so perfect*," I whispered, my voice cracking with how much more I meant than just the seat.

He tilted his head, eyes soft. "So are we. And I'm not gonna let a little spill ruin either."

The tightness coiled beneath my ribs softened, just a little, as he reached forward, flipped open his center console, and pulled out a pack of wipes without a second thought.

My eyes widened. "You… keep those in here?"

He shrugged, a crooked grin on his face as he knelt to swipe at the spill. "I figured there may come a time when we needed them."

We.

I stared at him, stunned. The easy way he said it. The way he wiped the leather without a flinch or a scowl. He didn't make me feel like I'd ruined something precious. He just wiped the spot once more, before tossing the wipe into the bag.

"At least it wasn't an apple pouch," he teased. "That would be a real tragedy."

A startled laugh burst out of me.

"See?" he said, flashing that crooked smile. "Still standing. No one's running."

And in that moment, milk splatters, cranky toddlers, and all...I believed him.

Once the mess was cleaned, I looked to the back seat. Zeke's head lolled to the side, asleep, cookie still clutched in his hand. The twins' breathing was soft and even, toys tucked against their cheeks. He lifted Zeke gently from the booster, the little boy murmuring but not waking, then nodded toward the stroller still folded in the bed.

"I'll carry him in," he said simply, as though it wasn't even a question. I swallowed hard, nodding.

Together, we moved up the steps. I carried Chloe and Avery, their warm little bodies limp with sleep, while Hunter balanced Zeke against his shoulder like he'd done it a thousand times. He carried the diaper bag, too. Of course he did.

As we reached the front down, I turned to him, my hands full of curls and sleepy sighs. "Thank you," I whispered.

He smiled, shifting Zeke slightly. "Always."

After the kids were tucked into their beds, Hunter lingered at the door. He leaned down, close enough that I caught the warmth of his cologne, and kissed me softly. My knees wobbled, my heart stumbling in my chest.

"Goodnight, Beautiful." he murmured, brushing a curl from my face.

And then he was gone, walking back to his truck like it was the easiest thing in the world to carry my chaos and still want more.

Later, when the kids were asleep and the house was still, I sat on the edge of my bed, fingers pressed to my lips where his kiss still lingered. He hadn't shown any sign of being overwhelmed or frustrated. Not at the aquarium, not at the spilled milk, not at the mess of bedtime and bags and bottles. He'd just stayed. And that scared me more than anything, because if he kept staying, I might actually start to believe he meant it.

And if I believed… there would be so much more to lose.

But even with that fear whispering in the dark, I couldn't stop the smile tugging at my mouth. Because it felt like maybe, just maybe, I wasn't carrying the weight alone anymore.

Steam curled around me as I stood under the shower, the water pounding against my shoulders, washing away the smell of sunscreen, spilled milk, and faint aquarium salt. But it didn't wash away the thoughts spinning in my head.

I closed my eyes, letting the heat soak into my tired muscles, but all I could see was him carrying Zeke on his shoulders, steadying the stroller with one hand, leaning down to kiss me at the door like it was the easiest thing in the world.

And the mess. The spilled milk in his spotless truck. The dread that had gripped me, certain he'd finally see me for what I was: messy, too much, not worth the hassle. But he didn't run. He grabbed wipes from his own center console, cracked a joke, and made me feel safe when I was seconds away from falling apart. I braced my hands against the cool tile, the water mixing with the sting in my eyes.

Why did it feel so impossible to believe someone might actually stay? Because history had already written its story for me. My dad had left when I was a little girl. Sometimes he'd call, sometimes he'd send a card, but he was never *there*. I grew up watching my mom hold everything together, and I swore I'd never repeat that cycle. But here I was, trying to do the same thing. I leaned my head against the wall, the water cascading down, whispering into the steam, "Men always leave." That was the story my life kept writing.

By the time I slipped into bed, hair damp, body heavy with exhaustion, my phone glowed on the nightstand. I picked it up, thumb hovering. My instinct was to say nothing, to let the silence keep me safe. But tonight felt different.

> **Me:** *Thank you. For today. For not making it feel like too much.*

The three dots appeared almost instantly, then stopped, then blinked again.

Hunter: *Thank you for letting me be there. I wouldn't trade it for anything.*

My chest tightened, tears blurring my vision.

Chapter Thirty Five

Hunter

The drive home should've been quiet. The twins had drifted off before we even made it back to their apartment, Zeke dozing off with his cookie still clutched in his hand. The night settled quietly around us, the steady hum of the truck the only sound as the red light spilled through the windshield, painting Cami in soft, borrowed color beside me.

But my head wasn't quiet.

It was buzzing. Loud. Alive. I was replaying every moment of the day.

Zeke squealed when I lifted him onto my shoulders. The twins' little fists pressed against the glass, babbling "fishy!" as jellyfish glowed above their heads. Camille's laugh was soft, cautious at first, but freer every time I cracked a joke to ease the tension. The way she looked at me when I handed her wipes from the console, struggling to believe I wasn't mad about spilled milk.

And that kiss at her door. Damn, that kiss.

It wasn't fireworks or desperation; it was *anchored.* The kind of kiss that doesn't fade when the night ends, that makes you think about mornings, and staying, and everything after. About all the things I swore I wasn't cut out for anymore. Because yeah, I'd done the car seats, I'd carried Zeke, I'd made her laugh. But there's a difference between surviving a day at the aquarium and surviving the long haul. Between being the fun guy with cookies and being the reliable man who shows up through tantrums, sickness, and exhaustion.

I gripped the wheel tighter, knuckles white.

A year ago, my marriage had ended because I couldn't be what my ex needed. I'd been too guarded, too scared from deployments, too… me. And now here I was, driving away from a woman who carried more weight than anyone I'd ever met—and asking myself if I could actually help carry it, or if I'd just add to it.

But the thing was… I couldn't walk away without trying.

Because Camille wasn't just another woman I'd met on a dating app. She was *it.*

The way she fought for her kids, the way she kept moving even when life knocked her down, the way she looked at me tonight, was equal parts terrified and hopeful.

And I did. I wasn't sure I deserved her. Hell, I wasn't sure I deserved the chance to be in her kids' lives either. But tonight, walking them to the door, holding her in my arms, I'd felt like an urge to fight for it, for them. For her. Even if it terrified me more than the silence waiting upstairs.

Chapter Thirty Six

Camille

I rode the high of our trip to the Aquarium for over a week. Recalling candid moments. Looking back at the pictures I took. Catching Hunter in sweet moments between him and the kids. That day played on repeat…until today.

The numbers on the screen blurred together until they may as well have been written in another language. The negative wasn't blinking at me yet, but it was close. Too close. Rent is due in a week. Groceries are half gone. Gas tank sitting at a quarter. And no child support in sight.

I refreshed my bank account again as if that would make money magically reappear. Nothing. The pit in my stomach deepened.

I pressed the heel of my hand to my forehead, the pressure doing nothing to ease the pounding behind my eyes. My ex hadn't sent support this month…again. I thought of the phone call earlier from his mother, her voice tight with practiced sympathy. *He's back in rehab, Camille. He got arrested for DUI last week. I'm sorry.*

Sorry. The word was useless. Sorry, I didn't put food in the fridge or keep the lights on. Sorry, I didn't explain to the twins why mommy had to work overtime again. It was situations like this that led me to block his number and not believe the times he'd tried to pop back in before.

I rubbed my face hard, trying to push back the sting of exhaustion. My textbooks sat open on the table, untouched. Assignments were due, the laundry basket overflowed, and I didn't have the energy to care. I was so tired that the exhaustion seeped into my bones. It whispered that I wasn't enough, and asked how many more spinning plates I could keep in the air before one came crashing down.

The twins shrieked from the other room, one stealing the other's toy, the sound jagged and piercing. I dropped my head into my hands. I couldn't even muster the energy to get up and intervene. Silent, heavy tears I hadn't meant to let fall, the kind that soaked into my hands before I could wipe them away.

That's when my phone lit up. *Hunter.*

I hesitated, swiping quickly at my cheeks before answering. "Hey."

"Hey, beautiful." His voice was warm, rich with the energy I couldn't seem to find for myself. I could hear movement in the background, probably him walking to his truck after work. "Just got off work. Been thinking about you all day. How's my girl?" My throat closed.

"Fine." I lied.

"I was thinking maybe we could take the kids to the park this weekend. I found this place that has a playground and a trail by the water. They'd love it."

His excitement bled through the line, a picture I could almost see. Him pushing the twins on the swings, Zeke racing down the slide, laughter threading through the air belonging only to us.

But right now, with the weight of bills pressing in, with the ghosts of men who had left my kids and me behind still whispering, I couldn't step into that dream. I couldn't risk letting him hear how broken I felt.

"That sounds nice," I whispered, my throat tight.

"You okay? You sound tired."

I turned away from the table, from the stack of unopened envelopes, from the bank account still glowing on my laptop screen. "Just a long day." My voice cracked just enough to betray me, exposing an unspoken yearning for refuge.

"You hungry? Nate told me about this place just off base that sounds amazing. I'm just getting off, I can bring it by for dinner or occupy the kids while you study." The safety Hunter offered was everything I craved, yet the fear of becoming a burden loomed large, making hope feel fragile.

"No." The word came out too sharp, so I softened it quickly. "I just… I've got schoolwork to finish. And the kids. " My voice cracked again. Damn it. I bit my lip hard, fighting it back.

Silence stretched. He didn't push, but I could feel him listening, the way he always did. Patient. Steady. The opposite of everything I'd ever known from a man.

"I'll let you go," I rushed out, panic bubbling with the tears I couldn't stop. "I'll call you later, okay?"

"Camille…" His voice caught, wanting to stop me, but I ended the call before I broke down completely.

I dropped the phone onto the couch, pressing the heels

of my hands into my eyes until all I saw were stars. The apartment was still quiet, but it felt louder now, the silence full of everything I couldn't say. I was drowning, and I didn't know how much longer I could hold it all together. Part of me hated myself for even letting him in when my life was this much of a mess.

I stayed there in the dim living room, whispering the same words I always did when it got this heavy: *Just keep going. They need you. Just keep going.*

Because what choice did I have?

Chapter Thirty Seven

Hunter

Camille's apartment door was unlocked when I got there. That alone set off all kinds of alarms. I knocked anyway, giving her the chance to tell me to leave if she wanted, but when no answer came, I pushed it open.

The living room was dim, lit only by the glow of a cartoon on the TV. Toys littered the floor. The twins had fallen asleep curled against each other on the couch, pacifiers half-slipping from their mouths. Zeke was slumped in the recliner with a blanket, his chest rising and falling in the slow rhythm of deep sleep.

And then I heard a soft, muffled sound. I followed the sound and found her in her room.

It was small, but it was her. The walls were crowded with snapshots. Her kids at the park, messy hair and toothy grins; a few of her and Dani mid-laugh; even a couple of faded Polaroids tacked up like tiny treasures. A stack of textbooks slumped against the nightstand, pages flagged with neon sticky notes. Tiny heaps of laundry dotted the floor, folded halfway or waiting to be.

Her bedspread was covered in faded flowers, the fabric soft from years of washing. On the dresser sat a vase with the first flowers I'd ever given her. Long dead now, petals brittle and curling, but she hadn't thrown them out. And next to them, still somewhat presentable, were the flowers I had given her when we went to the aquarium.

And then there was her.

She was curled up on the bed, knees drawn tight, her face buried in her hands. Shoulders trembling. Her phone lay face down beside her, screen still lit from the unanswered call I'd made on my way over.

"Cami," I said softly, leaning against the door frame.

She flinched, then looked up, eyes red-rimmed, cheeks wet. "Hunter... what are you doing here?"

"You didn't sound okay," I said simply. "So I came."

She shook her head, trying to swipe at the tears with the back of her sleeve. "You shouldn't see me like this."

I stepped closer, my voice low. "Why not?"

Her lips trembled, and then the words spilled out. "Because it's too much. The kids, school, work. Him." Her throat caught on that last word. "Their father hasn't even bothered this month. Not a dollar. Nothing. And I can't do it all, Hunter. I thought I could, but I can't."

My jaw clenched so hard it hurt. I didn't know every detail about their history, though she had been open and shared as much as I think she felt I wanted to know, and enough for me to hate the guy. From that day in the park, I'd known there was more to the story; more than just his absence that made her flinch at the sound of his name. But that hadn't been the time to ask, and maybe I wasn't ready to see the look in her eyes again if I did.

I still couldn't fathom how the hell any man could walk away from kids like hers. Kids who ran barefoot across the living room, giggling like sunshine, who clung to her like she was their whole world. Because she was.

And him? He wasn't even showing up.

The thought alone made me want to track down this man and make good on the promise I had made.

But that wasn't what she needed. Not tonight.

Instead, I decided to focus my energy differently. I sat down on the edge of the bed, careful, steady. "You don't have to do it all alone." Her eyes lifted, searching mine, wanting to believe me, but didn't know how. I forced my voice softer. "You're not failing. You're fighting. And I've seen a lot of fighters in my life, Beautiful. You're one of the strongest."

Her breath hitched, and then she leaned forward, burying her face into my chest. The sobs shook her body, cries muffled against me. I wrapped my arms around her, hand steady at her back, cradling her close.

And as I held her, breathing in the faint floral notes from her hair, the rage in me quieted. Beneath it lingered a trace of vanilla, warm and subtle, the kind that reminded me of comfort after long days. It wrapped around me, steady and grounding, softening the edges of the storm that always seemed to churn inside me. Because more than anything, I wanted her to feel safe. Wanted her to know that no matter how heavy the load felt, she didn't have to carry it by herself anymore.

We stayed that way until the tears slowed, until her breathing evened out. When she finally pulled back, her voice was a whisper. "I don't want to scare you off."

I brushed a curl from her damp cheek, my thumb lingering just a little too long. "You couldn't, even if you tried."

Her laugh came out soft and gentle as she buried her face in my chest again, giggling against me despite the tears.

"I shouldn't dump this on you," she whispered. "It's too much." She pulled back, wiping her face with the heel of her hand, eyes shining and raw.

"Camille," I said quietly, steady. "If you're carrying it alone, then it's already too much. Let me share some of it."

For a long moment, she stared at me, unsure if I meant it. Then, her lips trembled, and the words began to spill.

"He wasn't always like that. When we met, he was charming. Fun. But... he drank. More than I realized at first. And I was so young when I had Zeke, I just pushed myself to overlook it and try to make things work. But then he turned to abusing pills, and things just got worse." Her fingers twisted the blanket in her lap, the one covered in faded flowers. "By the time I was pregnant with the twins, I barely recognized him. The anger, the shouting...it became more than just words."

My chest tightened, heat crawling under my skin. I didn't need the details—I already hated the son of a bitch. The thought of anyone yelling at her, hurting her, using that same soft voice she saved for her kids made my fists curl.

"I stayed too long," she said, voice cracking. "I thought I could fix him, maybe if I just loved him enough, he'd stop. But he didn't. It just kept getting worse. And then one day..." She trailed off, tears filling her eyes again. "One day, I packed everything I could fit into the car, buckled the kids into their car seats, and I just... drove. I didn't even tell him where. My mom met me halfway and helped me start over here."

She broke then, covering her mouth with her hand, trying to push the sobs back down. "And I still feel guilty. Like I failed them. I should have known better, done better, protected them sooner."

I wanted to tell her she was wrong. That leaving took more courage than staying ever could. That guilt had no place on her shoulders. But the words stuck in my throat, tangled up with the anger burning low in my gut.

I couldn't stand the guy. He left bruises on her heart, made her question her own worth, and abandoned kids who deserved the damn world. Every mark he'd left on her lived under my skin now, turning my calm into something sharp. I didn't care what it cost me. I'd burn the world down before I let him hurt her, or them, again.

"I don't understand him," I said finally, my voice low, rougher than I meant. "I don't understand how anyone could walk away from you. From them."

Her eyes snapped up to mine, wide and glassy.

"You didn't fail them, Camille," I added, softer now. "You saved them. You saved yourself."

Her lip trembled, and before I could say more, she leaned into me again, burying her face into my chest. This time, it wasn't desperate; it was surrender.

I wrapped my arms around her tighter, steady, promising silently that I'd never be the man who left her to cry alone in a small room filled with dead flowers and unfinished laundry.

Because if I had anything to say about it, she would never carry that weight by herself again.

Chapter Thirty Eight

Camille

The silence pressed in once the lights were out, heavy enough that I could hear the uneven rhythm of my own breathing. Too much silence had never been kind to me because it left room for old memories, for the voices I tried to keep buried. So without thinking, I grabbed the remote from the nightstand and flicked the TV on. The soft glow filled the room, muted voices drifting from some late-night sitcom rerun. I didn't even care what show it was. I just needed the noise to keep me from drowning in the quiet. To keep my thoughts from drifting to the days I'd awoken with bruises, or crying kids that quickly triggered yelling.

Hunter didn't say anything. Didn't tease. Just adjusted on the bed, his weight shifting slightly as he leaned back against the headboard. I stayed curled under the blanket, eyes fixed on the screen, though I wasn't watching.

My body betrayed me before my brain could catch up. Slowly, passively, I let myself lean toward him, as if gravity had decided for me. My shoulder brushed his arm, tentative, testing. He didn't flinch. Didn't move away. Instead, he angled slightly, enough that his solid frame was there if I wanted it. A quiet offer. So I closed my eyes, breathing him in. His smell was fresh and grounding, the kind of scent that made the tightness in my chest loosen.

"You're alright," he murmured, voice low, steady. Not demanding. Not fixing. Just… there. "You don't have to hold it all together tonight. I've got you, Beautiful."

My throat burned, but no tears came. I was too tired, too wrung out to cry again. So I let myself sink into him, cheek resting lightly against his shoulder, the steady rhythm of his breathing pulling me in.

And then I noticed it. His heartbeat. It was steady, but intense. Each thud echoed against my ear, against my own uneven breaths. It wasn't just a heartbeat; it felt like the walls I had built around myself, the ones I thought were impenetrable, breaking down one by one. I tried not to think about how dangerous that was. How terrifying it felt to lean into someone after years of convincing myself I didn't need to. But right then, wrapped in his warmth, breathing in cypress and lime, I couldn't stop myself. His chest rose and fell beneath my cheek, anchoring me. His presence was unyielding and impossible to resist, and in his arms I felt safe.

I shifted slightly, allowing my fingers to brush against the fabric of his shirt. The urge to pull back, to apologize for needing too much, flickered through me. But before I could, his hand moved, resting lightly on the blanket near my side. Just close enough to remind me he wasn't going anywhere.

"You're alright." He murmured again, his voice low and certain.

My eyelids grew heavy, the soft flicker of the TV blurring

into nothing. My body was heavy now, exhaustion pulling me under, but I fought it, afraid this fragile peace might vanish if I closed my eyes. I felt his fingers brushing lightly against my curls. Slow. Gentle. Almost absent-minded, like he wasn't even aware of the comfort it gave me. He twisted a strand around his finger, then let it fall, only to smooth it back again. The simple rhythm was as grounding as his heartbeat beneath my ear.

Every time he touched my hair, the knot of tension in my chest unraveled a little more. My breath evened out, eyelids growing heavier, the world blurring at the edges. I should have pulled back. I should have said something to break the spell, reminded him, or maybe reminded myself that this was temporary, that he didn't owe me this kind of tenderness. But I didn't.

Instead, I let my cheek press deeper against his chest, a quiet giggle slipping out of me at the way he toyed with my curls.

He chuckled softly in return, the sound rumbling beneath me. "What's funny?" he murmured.

"Nothing," I whispered, words already thick with sleep. "Just... feels nice."

And with that, the last of my walls lowered. His hand kept combing gently through my curls, safe in the warmth of him. And that night I drifted off not in fear, not in loneliness, but with someone reminding me, simply by staying, that I wasn't too much.

CHAPTER THIRTY EIGHT

Chapter Thirty Nine

Hunter

Her breathing was paced now, warm puffs against my chest, the kind of rhythm you don't fake unless you're deep in sleep. I kept my hand moving gently through her curls, careful not to wake her, but maybe more careful not to let myself stop.

She looked so small like this. Not fragile, never that, but small in a way that made me want to protect her. And that scared the hell out of me because big emotions weren't my thing. They never had been. My dad had hammered it into me young: boys don't cry, men don't complain, feelings are weak. The Marines doubled down on that lesson, ten years of it. Of shutting it down, push it away, mission first. There was no room for softness in combat.

So I learned to live without it. Without letting anyone close enough to see me crack. Without sitting still long enough to feel anything deeper than adrenaline. But here I was with her asleep against me, curls tangled in my fingers, her weight tucked into my side. And I felt everything. I hated knowing what her ex had done to the girl I loved. She hadn't given me all the details, but she didn't have to. I thought back to the call back at the park, the entitlement in his tone. And I'd heard enough to know he didn't deserve her, didn't deserve the kids, didn't deserve a second thought. The part that gutted me most was that he'd walked away like staying was optional and showing up for his own kids was negotiable.

I couldn't understand that. Couldn't even wrap my head around it. Those three little ones... they were part of her. And anyone who couldn't see that as a gift? A man like that didn't deserve to breathe the same air as her.

My chest tightened. Anger simmered low, dangerous, the kind I'd only ever felt in combat. The instinct to track him down, make him feel every ounce of the pain he'd left behind, resurfaced sharp and hot in me. But then she shifted in her sleep, scooting closer, and it soothed me. My fist unclenched and returned to leaving lazy circles on her warm skin. This wasn't about him. This was about her. About being the man she needed now, not the one who'd already failed her.

I wasn't good at this part. Sitting with the heavy stuff, letting myself feel it. It made me itch, restless in my own skin. But when I looked down at her, the blanket tucked under her chin, the dried flowers I'd given her still sitting on her dresser like she couldn't bear to throw them away... I realized something.

I'd learn. For her, I'd figure out how to sit with all of it, the grief, the fear, the weight of everything she carried. Because she was worth it. She was worth breaking every rule I'd ever been taught about what it meant to be a man. Her curls tickled against my chin when she stirred, a soft sound escaping her, not quite a word. My arm tightened instinctively, pulling her closer.

With her this close, holding onto someone no longer felt like a weakness. It felt like the bravest damn thing I'd ever do.

The soft morning light slipped through the thin curtains, casting shadows across Camille's. Her head rested against my chest, curls splayed everywhere, warm breaths tickling my skin. I'd woken before her, but I didn't move. Not yet.

The night still sat heavy in me, the way the words had cracked something open deep inside that I didn't know I'd been holding shut. I'd said it back, meant it deeper than anything I'd spoken in years. I brushed my hand gently along her back, slow strokes over the curve of her shoulder. She stirred a little, sighing, before burrowing closer, not quite ready to let the world in. I could've stayed like that forever. But the thought of three kids barging in made me huff a laugh against her hair.

My thumb brushed across her shoulder where the blanket had slipped down. Her skin was warm, her body soft against mine. She shifted, eyelids fluttering, still fighting the pull of sleep.

"Morning," she whispered, voice rough, barely awake.

I smiled, brushing a curl from her face. "Morning."

"I better get going before the kids come in and see me," I murmured, my voice low, rough with sleep. Half teasing, half serious.

Her hand fisted in the fabric of my shirt, stopping me. She tilted her head up, her eyes heavy but sure. "Stay. They love you. They'll be happy to see you. They ask for you whenever you are not here." Her voice still thick with sleep.

The words hit deeper than I was ready for. They weren't casual, not for her. Those kids were her world; she protected them, saying that left me with a kind of aching gratitude I didn't have words for.

I kissed her hair, whispering against her curls, "I love you." Saying it felt easier this time, not like a leap off a cliff but like solid ground under my feet. She looked up at me, and I said it again, firmly: "I love you, Camille."

Her smile was tranquil, soft, the kind that could undo me in an instant.

The moment barely settled before I heard the patter of small feet down the hall. The door creaked open, and Zeke appeared first, his blanket trailing behind him, those guarded brown eyes scanning the room. The twins were right behind, giggling, one clutching a stuffed bunny by the ear.

I froze for half a second, waiting for the judgment, for the distance, for Zeke to tense the way he used to. But instead, he climbed onto the bed without a word, wedging himself between his mom and me like it was something he'd done hundreds of times before. His little head found her shoulder, but his small hand rested on my arm, testing, almost claiming. That small gesture was a wordless attempt at connection, a tiny hand showing so much courage. In that moment, I felt a shift; it underscored the trust that had been carefully built between us. I knew how much it took for him to reach out, and I silently vowed not to break that trust.

The twins scrambled up too, squealing, piling across Camille's legs. One plopped right onto my chest, grinning down at me like I was a jungle gym.

Camille laughed, her eyes crinkling as she tried to wrangle them. I couldn't help laughing too, even with a five-year-old elbow digging into my ribs.

The familiar scent of vanilla and lavender lingered around us, a comforting reminder of the warmth and safety of Camille's room. In the chaos of blankets and giggles, her laughter undercut by the gentle hum of the TV playing softly in the background, I felt a profound sense of completion, as if life had come full circle. The memories from the night before echoed softly in the air, anchoring us to this newfound peace.

And right there, in the chaos of blankets and giggles and sleepy hair sticking up in all directions, I realized this was it. This was what love looked like for me. Not mornings alone, not control, not perfection. But this, messy, loud, unconditional.

I tightened my arm around Camille, let the twins climb all over me. In that room, I didn't feel like an outsider in my own life. I felt like I belonged.

The weight of those words settled deep, heavier than any battlefield gear I'd ever carried. They love you, too. She wasn't just talking about herself anymore. She was talking about Zeke, about the twins, about all the trust I'd been trying to earn piece by piece.

I swallowed hard, tightening my arm around her. "I love you," she said. No hesitation at all. Just the truth. "More than I ever thought I could."

Her smile bloomed slow, shy, but steadily. A smile that rooted itself in your chest and refused to leave. She pressed a hand to my jaw, thumb brushing over my beard, memorizing every word, every look.

For years, I'd lived convinced that love wasn't meant for

me anymore, that too much had been broken, that too many ghosts lingered. But hearing her say *stay*, hearing her claim that her kids loved me too, affirmed that this wasn't temporary.

This was a life being built brick by brick.

I kissed her forehead, holding her closer. "I'm not going anywhere, Camille. Not from you. Not from them," telling her just as much as I was telling myself.

"Okay, okay!" I tried to sit up, but the toddler on my chest squealed, bouncing like she'd discovered her own personal trampoline. "You guys are ruthless."

"Again!" one of the twins demanded, giggling so hard she hiccuped.

I groaned dramatically. "What am I? Your jungle gym?"

"Yes!" Zeke piped up from the other side of the bed, not even looking up from the Lego figure he'd smuggled in with him.

Camille shot me a look through her laughter, the kind that said *welcome to my life*. And for some reason, instead of feeling out of place, I felt like I'd been invited in.

Chapter Forty

Camille

My textbooks lay scattered across the kitchen table, a single highlighter tracing neon across pages, the unfinished paper blinking from the laptop with expectation. Hunter hung out with us for a while longer that morning, before heading off to get himself ready for work. The coffee he'd made before he left now sat cold on the table. Fatigue hung in the air, a heavy fog that wouldn't lift. Responsibilities crowded in; deadlines loomed, the endless juggle of work and home, the nagging ache of feeling never quite enough. I felt hollowed out, bone-tired, with rare moments never refilling me completely. And then, when least expected, there was him.

My phone buzzed. No caption. No emoji. Just a link.

Hunter: "Beautiful Crazy" by Luke Combs.

I stared at the screen, chest tightening before I even pressed play. It was so him, sending a song instead of words, letting the music say what he never quite could. Somehow, that said more than any message ever would.

I tapped the link and let the first smooth notes fill the room. His voice wrapped around me, warm and sure, carrying a promise I could almost believe. I closed my eyes, pulled the blanket tighter, and let myself just be present for a while.

The lyrics washed over me, sudden and overwhelming.

"Beautiful, crazy. She can't help but amaze me."

The words landed deep. The song wasn't just about looks, it was about being seen, every flaw and edge, and still being chosen. The lines about waking up grateful just to have her there, about finding joy in a smile, felt like he was holding up a mirror I barely recognized.

"Yeah, she's crazy. But her crazy's beautiful to me."

I pictured him crouched on the floor, building Lego towers with Zeke as if nothing else mattered. Letting the twins climb onto his back, laughing as he dropped into push-ups until they shrieked with delight. Catching my eye across a crowded room, smiling as if I was the only one there.

I typed fast, fingers shaking:

Me: You can't just drop this on me with no context.

The reply came almost immediately, like he'd been waiting for it.

Hunter: Don't need context. Just listen.

So I did. Again.

Every lyric pulled me deeper, threading into places I

thought I'd hidden for good. Words about gratitude, about never taking her for granted, about being enough just as she was.

No one had said things like that to me in years. Not in a way that felt real. Not in a way that felt earned. My ex's words had always been sharp, critical, and draining, and by the end, I believed I was the problem, the reason he turned to drugs. The reason he became angry was that I finally left. There was this one night, I remembered sitting on the porch as he reminded me that I was too much and not enough all at once, as if the very fabric of who I was would never be right. Those words lingered as a constant reminder of why I felt undeserving of Hunter's love. Yet now, I could see his judgment wasn't a reflection of my worth. I was not too much or too little; I was simply more than he could handle. And here was Hunter, saying the exact opposite, without saying it at all.

Tears slipped down my cheeks as I curled into the corner of the couch, swiping them away with the back of my hand. The light from my phone blurred, and I pressed it to my chest, allowing it to anchor me. Blanket pulled up to my chin, soft threads twisting between my fingers, I tried to find some small comfort against the rush of feeling inside me.

I wanted to tell him what it meant to me, but the old ache in my chest took shape, whispering doubts spun from every past hurt, murmuring that I was never enough. Vulnerability felt dangerous, like asking more than I thought I had left to give. That small, stubborn hope pressed in, an urge to trust again. Maybe, with time, I could let him all the way in.

So instead I sent back the safest thing I could manage:

Me: I love you, Hunter.

Hunter: It's all true. I'm sure you're
overthinking that. And I love
you too.

That was all he wrote. And somehow, it was enough to undo me all over again.

Because I finally understood, this was how Hunter loved. Quiet, steady, without fanfare. He wouldn't flood me with declarations. He'd hand me a song and trust me to hear everything he couldn't say. Sometimes, in those rare moments when his guard slipped, I'd catch glimpses of Hunter's own fears and doubts. He never spoke of them directly, but there were nights when his eyes looked perilously tender, as if his heart bore silent scars he was still learning to heal. This unspoken vulnerability made the way he loved all the more profound and trustworthy.

And the wildest part? I did.

Chapter Forty One

Camille

H*unter:* Some of the guys from my unit and their families are getting together this weekend. You should come.

Just like that. No pressure, no expectations, at least not the kind he'd ever say out loud.

I stared at the message far too long, my thumb hovering over the keyboard.

> *Me:* That sounds… nice. But I don't know. I wouldn't want to intrude.

Hunter: You wouldn't be intruding. You'd be with me.

> *Me:* I'm not sure how I'll do with meeting friends. I'm kind of out of practice.

Hunter: Then we'll call it a practice run.

Hunter: No pressure, Cami. Just good
food, good company, and maybe a
bonfire if the weather holds.

Me: You make it sound easy.

Hunter: It is. You'll see.

He meant it. I could tell. But the truth was, nothing about this felt easy to me. After I set the phone down, my chest ached with that familiar tug-of-war between wanting more and being terrified of it.

That's when my mom came in, wiping her hands on a dish towel. She gave me a knowing look before I could even open my mouth. "Let me guess," she said. "Hunter invited you somewhere, and you're talking yourself out of it."

I blinked. "How do you always know?"

"Because I did the same thing for years," she said simply, sitting beside me. "You should go, Camille." Her tone was gentle, but it landed like a crack in the shield I'd been patching for years.

The day of the trip, I stood in front of my closet. Clothes spilled onto the bed. A variety of jeans, blouses, and dresses I hadn't touched in years. None of it felt right. Too tight. Too loose. Too "mom." Too much.

Dani had barged in with iced coffee and a mischievous grin,

immediately tossing half my pile onto the floor. "Not that. Not that. Oh, hell no. Camille, why do you still own this cardigan?"

"It's comfortable," I muttered, grabbing it protectively.

She plucked it out of my hands. "Comfortable is not the vibe. This is an overnight with Marine Ken Doll. You need cute, flirty, *but still you.*"

My mom poked her head in then, clearly amused by the chaos. "I'm with Daniela on this one."

I groaned, covering my face with both hands. "Can't I just wear leggings and call it a day?"

Dani and my mom answered in unison: "No."

By the time my bag was finally zipped, I felt wrung out from nerves alone. The kids were buzzing with energy, sensing something was different.

"Where you goin', Mommy?" Zeke asked, climbing into my lap as I double-checked the twins' bottles.

"Just having some mommy time for one night," I said softly, kissing the top of his curls. "Grammy's got you covered."

He squinted at me, suspicious. "Is Hunter going?"

Heat flooded my cheeks. "Yes."

"Good,," he said firmly, satisfied.

I laughed, hugging him tighter.

But later, when the house was still, and my mom shooed me off to bed, guilt crept in heavily. I have never spent a night away from them. Every part of me screamed that I should stay, that leaving them made me selfish.

And yet, underneath the guilt was excitement.

Later that evening, Hunter's truck pulled up to the curb. I spotted it from the window and felt my breath catch. He'd washed it, the exterior gleaming in the setting sun, and suddenly my nerves spiked all over again.

"You look hot," Dani whispered from behind me, giving my shoulders a squeeze.

He stepped out of the truck looking handsome in dark jeans and a fitted white shirt that clung to his broad shoulders, his beard trimmed neatly. He wore his signature Vans sneakers today in teal. ??He leaned against the door frame like he had all the time in the world, his grin easy, steady, the kind that made everything inside me feel steadier too.

Seeing him, I almost second-guessed my outfit. Mom jeans, of all things. But the way they hugged my curves gave me a hint of confidence. He always teased me, claiming my butt was his favorite thing about me, so I chose them for him. A little gift wrapped in denim. I'd paired them with an off-the-shoulder top, soft cotton brushing my skin, simple but feminine.

The way his gaze flicked down and then back up told me he noticed. Heat crept up my neck, and I bit back a smile.

"Hey, Beautiful," he said, leaning down to kiss me before I could lose my nerve. Quick, sure, warm. The kind of kiss that left me dizzy.

"Hey," I whispered back, clutching the strap of my bag.

For a beat, neither of us moved, just taking each other in. And then he reached for my bag without thought, like carrying my weight was never in question.

"Ready?"

"Define ready," I muttered, earning his laugh.

He glanced at Dani and my mom, both smirking behind me as co-conspirators. "Thank you for talking her into this."

"Oh, she owes us." Dani quipped.

"Big time," my mom added with a wink.

I groaned. "I hate you all."

As Hunter opened the passenger door and held it for me, butterflies fluttered in my stomach. Because even with the guilt, the nerves, the insecurities, and the endless doubts, I wanted to see his world.

I wanted *him*.

Chapter Forty Two

Hunter

The road stretched out ahead, headlights carving a tunnel through the dark. The hum of the truck was steady, the quiet between us broken only by the occasional shuffle as Camille shifted in her seat, tugging at the hem of her top in an attempt to make herself smaller.

I wanted to tell her she didn't need to. That she didn't need to change a single thing to fit into my world. But I knew her well enough by now to understand that silence wasn't indifference, it was nerves. She was probably overthinking everything. What my friends would think. What their wives would say. Whether she'd measure up.

She didn't see what I saw: a woman who held her whole world together with both hands and still found room for me in it.

I glanced at her, curls framing her face, lips pressed tight like she was holding back a storm.

"You okay?" I asked softly.

She gave me the world's smallest smile. "Define okay."

I chuckled, shaking my head. "Is that your response to everything today?"

Her laugh had a nervous edge to it.

The truth was, I was just as nervous as she was. Not about her, never about her, but about me. Because tonight she'd see me in a version of myself that was different than the man she'd been spending time with. Around my old unit, I defaulted to the easy mask: the Marine who laughed too loud, threw back beers, and dodged real talk. The man who kept things surface-level, because digging deeper meant facing what I'd buried.

But with her, I didn't want to be that guarded version anymore. I wanted her to see the real me, the one I wasn't sure I even knew how to show. Part of me worried I wouldn't measure up. Not just to her, but to the idea of who I was supposed to be. Could I balance the world I left behind, all the discipline and walls I'd built, with the warmth she offered so freely? The fear sat heavy, whispering that maybe I'd never quite fit in either place, that I'd end up letting her down in ways I couldn't even name.

To lighten the air, I grinned. "So… just a heads up. The guy hosting? His wife makes these insane brownies. But I call dibs on at least two."

She snorted, covering her mouth. "Oh, I'll fight you for them."

"There it is," I teased, pointing at her. "The competitive streak. You only hid it at mini golf."

Her laugh was easier this time, shoulders dropping as the tension bled away. And in that moment, with her laughter filling my truck, her hand brushing mine, the night unfolding ahead of us, I felt it again. That dangerous, thrilling thing I'd been trying not to name. Hope.

By the time we pulled into the driveway, laughter and music spilled out into the night. The house glowed with porch lights, silhouettes moving behind wide front windows.

Camille stiffened beside me, her hand twisting in her lap. I could almost feel her thoughts buzzing. I killed the engine and reached over, brushing my thumb across the back of her hand. "Hey."

She looked at me, wide-eyed.

"You don't have to prove anything to them," I said quietly. "You're with me. That's all that matters."

Her lips pressed tight, but her shoulders dropped a fraction. "You make it sound easy."

I grinned. "That's because it is."

Inside, the smell of barbecue hit me first, followed by the familiar sound of a couple of my old unit guys laughing too loudly, competing to tell the best story. For a second, I was back on base, surrounded by my brothers. Only this time, I wasn't alone.

"Bennett!"

Mike's voice cut across the room before I even saw him. He barreled through the crowd with a beer in hand and the same grin he always wore. He clapped me on the back hard enough to rattle my teeth. "You actually showed up!"

"Wouldn't miss it," I said, steadying myself. "Brought someone I want you to meet."

Camille hovered close, her curls catching the warm light, eyes wary but steady. I slipped an arm around her waist, drawing her in. "This is Camille."

Mike's grin widened. "Nice to finally meet the woman who tamed him." He said, slapping me on the back.

Her cheeks flushed, and I felt her stiffen, but I squeezed her side gently. "Ignore him," I murmured. "He thinks he's funny."

She glanced at me, lips twitching. "I've noticed you keep those kinds of friends."

"Occupational hazard." I teased.

One by one, the guys filtered over: Nick, with his dry humor and that knowing look that always felt like a quiet check-in; Logan, tall and solid, a little quieter now that life had slowed him down, his daughter Harper tucked against his shoulder.

Nick raised an eyebrow as he reached us. "Well, hell. Bennett's domesticated."

I rolled my eyes. "Nice to see you too."

Camille held out a hand. "Hi, I'm Camille."

Nick took it with a grin. "We've heard plenty. Glad to see you're real. We were starting to think he was lying."

Logan chuckled. "Yeah, man's been smiling at his phone like a teenager."

Camille laughed, the tension in her posture melting away as she glanced at me.

"Camille," Logan said, shifting Harper into her arms. "This is my daughter, Harper."

Harper blinked at Camille, then reached out to touch her necklace, fingers tracing the tiny pendant.

"Pretty," Harper said solemnly.

"Thank you," Camille whispered, her smile so soft it hurt to look at.

Logan's eyes met mine over their heads, a small grin tugging at his mouth.

"She's good with kids," he said later, low enough only I could hear.

"She's got three," I said. "Good ones. You should bring Harper by sometime. They'd love her."

Logan nodded. "Yeah, we can do that."

Across the room, Nick whistled. "Listen to you — already making play dates. Guess you're officially one of us now."

I smirked. "You're just jealous I get to sleep past six a.m."

Nick laughed. "Yeah, yeah. Give it time. You'll join the club soon enough."

We drifted toward the kitchen, the noise growing louder as beers were cracked open and stories got taller. It was comfortable...too comfortable, maybe.

I wasn't standing outside looking in. I was in it. Surrounded by laughter, music, people I trusted, and Camille right in the middle of it all. Glowing in a way that I couldn't stop watching.

Somewhere between Mike's bad jokes and Sarah's brownies (which I only got one of, because Camille beat me to seconds), I realized the truth.

This wasn't just about proving she fit into my world. It was about me realizing she had already been a part of it.

Later in the evening, as the room was buzzing with stories and laughter, I noticed Camille had wandered toward the kitchen, drawn into a conversation with one of the wives about school. She was smiling warmly, curls catching the light.

And that's when Sean slid in.

Sean, the kind of guy who thought charm was currency and

didn't notice when it ran out. He wasn't a bad man, just one who'd never learned the line between friendly and flirting.

He leaned in close to Camille, his hand braced casually on the counter near her hip. She laughed politely but in a careful way that told me she wasn't sure how to brush him.

Jealousy wasn't something I let myself feel often. In the military, it was pointless. But standing there, watching another man angle toward her, stirred something primal in me. The jealousy didn't feel ugly. It felt clarifying, because tonight, with her by my side, I wasn't guessing anymore. I knew I couldn't let anyone else have her.

She wasn't just a date I brought. She was *mine*.

Nick, standing next to me, caught my shift before I even moved. "Uh oh," he muttered, half amused. "Here we go."

I set my beer down slowly.

"Sean doesn't mean anything by it," Nick said.

"Doesn't have to," I replied.

Logan's brow lifted, a ghost of a smirk forming. "Man, I haven't seen that look on you before. You about to take him down or just glare him into submission?"

I ignored them both and crossed the room. My steps were easy, but my pulse wasn't.

Camille saw me coming, relief flickering in her eyes just before I reached her.

I slipped an arm around her waist, the move natural, unforced — like muscle memory I didn't know I had. "Careful, Sean," I said lightly, but there was steel beneath it. "You're talking to my girl."

Sean froze mid-laugh. "Hey, no offense, man. Just talking."

"Well, now you're done," I said easily, smiling like it was a joke. But I didn't move my arm.

Camille leaned back into me, allowing her body to be soft against mine while her hand found its place resting on my chest. Her cheeks flushed, but her eyes gleamed with something that looked an awful lot like trust.

I leaned down, murmuring just for her, "You look too damn good tonight to expect me not to notice when someone else does."

She nudged me with her elbow, whispering back, "Play nice, Marine."

"Always."

Sean laughed it off, moving on, but I didn't miss the look Logan shot me from across the room, both half-teasing and half approving.

Later, when the laughter died down and the kids were half-asleep on the couch, we all sat out on the deck. The night smelled of smoke, beer, and fresh California air.

Nick cracked open another bottle, leaning back in his chair. "You know," he said, nodding toward Camille inside, "You did good, Bennett."

Logan nodded. "Yeah. She fits."

I stared through the sliding glass door at her laughing softly with Sarah, her hands moving as she spoke, that light in her eyes I didn't think I'd ever get tired of seeing.

"She's it, boys." I said quietly.

Nick smirked. "Careful, man. That's how it starts. Next thing you know, you're buying a minivan."

I snorted. "Not a chance."

"Uh-huh," Logan said. "That's what Nick said too."

We all laughed, but then the quiet settled again, the kind that said more than words could.

"You good, brother?" Logan asked, finally.

"Yeah," I said, meaning it. "Better than I've been in a long time."

Nick nodded. "That's all that matters."

I leaned back, the hum of cicadas filling the silence, the glow of the house soft behind us.

For the first time in years, I didn't feel as though I was caught between two worlds; I felt whole.

And when Camille came outside, sliding her hand into mine, exactly where it belonged, I realized I didn't just want her in my world.

I wanted to build a new one with her. She'd been nervous walking in, I knew that, but she'd held her own. And I was proud to have her by my side.

The hotel was only a few minutes away. The room was simple. It held neutral walls, a king-sized bed, and a lonely desk tucked into a corner. Yet standing there with her bag on the chair and her curls spilling over her shoulders, she stood out. She lingered by the dresser, clearly unsure what to do with herself. I wanted to close the space between us, to kiss her until she forgot every doubt, but I also knew how fragile this was.

So I sat on the edge of the bed, leaning back on my palms. "You hungry? I swiped extra brownies. Might've hidden them in the truck."

That earned me a laugh, shaky but real. "I can't believe you stole the brownies and the plate."

"Yeah," I said, grinning. "Figured you'd want your usual late-night snack." Her eyes flicked to mine, and something in her face softened. She crossed the room slowly, then sat beside me. Close enough that her warmth brushed against me.

"You okay?" I asked, keeping my voice low.

She glanced at me, gave a tight little smile. "Yeah. I had fun. I enjoyed seeing that side of you. It's just hard to be away from the kids. And this just feels different, more at stake."

I reached over, brushing her hand with mine. "I'm glad you came." Her eyes softened, and she nodded, though I knew the battle inside her wasn't won that easily.

For a while, we just sat in silence. The hum of the AC, the muffled sound of a TV, since Cami could never fall asleep without it on subtly in the background. My pulse was steady, but heavy with restraint. Except I couldn't help but kiss her. And when I did, it wasn't about proving anything. It was slow, careful, like telling her with every brush of my lips: *You don't have to hide. Not from me.*

And with that, I let myself fall asleep listening to the peaceful rhythm of Camille's breathing against my chest. For a while, the warmth of her weight soothed the edges of my thoughts and anchored me.

But sleep has never been kind to me.

One minute, I was in a hotel bed with her curled against me, and the next I was back in Afghanistan.

The dream was sharper this time. Not flashes, but full color, full sound.

Sand in my mouth. The air was ripped apart by gunfire. My buddy's scream echoed as the ground exploded. I reached for him. Fingers brushing his sleeve. But then he was gone, swallowed in smoke and silence.

And then, silence turned into screaming. Mine.

"Hunter!"

Her voice cut through, jolting me upright. Reflexes ready to defend myself and my men. My chest heaved, lungs burning like I'd run miles. Sweat dripped down my temple, soaking the sheets. My hands trembled, fists knotted so tight the nails dug into my palms. And then I noticed that Camille was half-sitting, half-crawling back, curls piled on top of her head, eyes wide and glinting in the dim light. Fear flickered there, not of me, but for me.

I hated that I put it there.

"I'm sorry," I rasped, dragging a hand down my face. "I didn't mean to…"

"You were yelling," she whispered, still catching her breath. "You scared me."

Her voice cracked, and shame hit me like a punch. The last thing I wanted was for her to see this, the broken parts I kept buried.

"I'm sorry. It's just nightmares," I muttered, trying to pull back. "Doesn't matter."

But she shook her head, steadier than I expected. "Of course it matters. This is you. Talk to me."

I hesitated, jaw tight. I didn't want to name it. The word was a brand. PTSD. Letters stamped across me as proof that I was damaged.

Finally, I forced it out. "It's… PTSD. That's what they call it, anyway. I despise the label. Feels like it defines me, like I'm just a broken Marine with bad wiring."

Her hand reached for mine, hesitant but sure, fingers uncurling my fists one by one. "You're not broken," she said softly. "You're human. What does it look like for you? When it shows up?" The question gutted me because no one ever asked, not like that.

I swallowed hard. "Sometimes it's nightmares. Sometimes it's the noise of fireworks, a car backfiring. My chest locks up. Feels like I'm back there, waiting for the next blast. Other times…" I exhaled, shaking my head. "Other times it's just me. Staring at a wall at 3 a.m. because sleep feels like a trap."

Her thumb brushed my knuckles, grounding me. "You didn't have to hide that from me."

I met her eyes then. They were wide, worried, but steady, allowing me to believe her. She wasn't running. Not from the mess. Not from me, and for a long moment, silence hung between us. My breathing was still uneven, the ghost of sand and smoke clinging to me. I half-expected her to pull away, to shift to her side of the bed, deciding she didn't sign up for this.

Instead, she moved closer. Her hands were small and steady as they slid along mine, prying my fingers open gently. She pressed her palm flat against my chest, right over my heart. "You're here," she whispered. "Not there. Here. With me."

The words cut through the fog sharper than anything else. Her touch was grounding, warm, real.

I let out a shaky breath, my forehead dropping to hers. "I hate that you had to see that."

"I'd rather see it," she murmured, "than let you fight it alone. Plus, I've noticed things before, just never knew how bad it got, I guess."

I didn't know what to say. The shame was still there, crawling under my skin, but so was…relief.

She eased us back against the pillows, her body curling into mine, her arms wrapping around me like she could anchor me there. Her cheek rested against my shoulder, her breathing slow, deliberate. "If it happens again," she said softly, "wake me, please. Don't carry it by yourself."

They were words no one had ever said to me, and if they'd come from anyone else, I wouldn't have believed them. But the way she said it with confidence and empathy, I knew I could trust them.

I pressed a kiss to her hair, inhaling the faint scent of her shampoo, the warmth of her skin. "You don't know what you're signing up for," I whispered.

"Maybe not," she admitted. "But that doesn't change anything for me. I know what I want." Her certainty unraveled me. My hand slid into her curls, tilting her face up to mine. She was so close I could see the flecks of gold in her eyes, even in the dark.

"Camille…" My voice was hoarse. "You're the only thing that's felt real in a long time."

Her lips found mine, soft and lingering, not rushed or desperate, but gentle. It wasn't about forgetting the darkness. It was about us, about this moment, about choosing to be here. I kissed her back, slow at first, letting her fingers tangle in my hair. My body, still tense, softened under her touch. Every pull of her hand broke down more of my walls.

I shifted us gently, easing her onto her back, my forehead still pressed to hers. Her voice was steady as she said, "I love you, Hunter. Please don't treat me like I'm fragile." The words weren't just a plea. They were a claim of her own strength. Even as I wanted to protect her, her gaze told me she was just as strong as I was.

I kissed her again, deeper this time, breathing her in. My hands traced the lines of her body, slow and careful, memorizing the shape of her. She arched into me, a soft sigh escaping her lips.

"Beautiful," I breathed, my mouth trailing down her jaw to her throat. Her gasp sent a shiver through me.

My hand drifted lower, tracing her hip, slipping under the fabric touching the swell of her breast. Her breath caught, her body moving with mine. She cradled my face, her thumbs brushing my mouth as I moved.

"You're here." Her voice airy, the words catching on a soft gasp.

"I'm here." I echoed, my voice breaking, because it felt true in a way it hadn't in years.

We moved together like that, slow and deep, the room except for our breathing. When I finally eased into her, it was slow, steady. The sound left a fire in my lungs. She clutched my shoulders, nails pressing crescents into my skin. The stretch of her around me was almost unbearable, tight and hot, but I held back, giving her time, giving us time.

Her lips parted on a shaky breath. "Hunter..."

She kissed my mouth, my cheek, my throat, whispering "I love you" between each press of her lips. I found a rhythm, not rushed but deep and steady, each movement drawing another sound from her. Her legs tightened around me, holding me close, her soft cries finding their way through me, filling the quiet with something I didn't know I'd been missing.

"Look at me," I whispered.

Her eyes opened, wide and trusting, pupils dark. The connection knocked the breath from my lungs. This wasn't just her body. It was her, trusting me, choosing me.

With our bodies tangled, I remembered seeing her for the first time: the hidden confidence, a storm in her eyes. I knew then she was strong enough for both our demons. Camille broke the silence with a soft laugh, pressing her palms to my chest and rolling me onto my back.

Her hair fell around us, a dark curtain, as she moved over me, straddling my hips. My hands slid up her thighs, settling at her waist as I looked up at her, undone.

"Cami…" My voice cracked on her name.

She bent low, kissing me slowly and deeply, her body pressed close as she began to move. The pace was hers, gentle, rhythmic, unhurried. Every movement drew a breath from my lips.

She lifted her head, curls falling around her face, as I whispered, "I want you like this. I want to see you."

Her gaze never left mine as she moved, every rise and fall threaded with trust, every gasp a confession. I reached up, cradling her face, my thumb brushing the corner of her mouth as she trembled above me. "You're beautiful," I whispered, voice breaking. "Every fucking part of you."

Her release came first, shuddering through her, her cry caught in a kiss as I pulled her down against me. The feel of her unraveling pushed me over the edge, my own climax tearing free in a rough groan as I buried my face in her neck.

Afterward, she draped over me, cheek pressed to my chest, breath warm and steady. I wrapped my arms around her, holding her close, not wanting to let go.

"Still here," she whispered, the words humming into my skin.

"Still here." I echoed, my voice gravely.

I closed my eyes, letting her steady rhythm pull me back from the edge. My body, no longer tense from the nightmare. Her presence filled the cracks the memories had split open. And as sleep threatened again, I wasn't afraid of closing my eyes.

The first thing I noticed when I woke up was the quiet. It wasn't the suffocating kind that usually pressed in after nightmares, but a softer, calmer kind since Cami lay next to me. Her legs wrapped around mine, as the sunlight spilt weakly through the curtains, catching in her curls where they spilled across me. Her hand was still resting against my chest, right over my heart, like she'd left it there on purpose.

For a second, I didn't move. Didn't breathe. Just watched her, trying to memorize the way she looked in sleep. Peaceful. Strong even here, wrapped around me as if she were the one protecting *me*. Then the shame crept back in.

I'd woken her by yelling. Scared her. Dragged her into the hell I tried so damn hard to keep buried. And still she'd stayed. Grounded me. Told me not to carry it alone. The part of me that had lived by discipline and silence wanted to recoil, to put the walls back up before I gave away too much. But another part, the part that had kissed her forehead and listened to her whisper, she wanted to stay, wanted to hold on.

You said too much. You showed her the cracks. The ugly parts. She'll change her mind now.

But when she stirred and shifted closer, tucking herself tighter against me, the noise in my head went silent. Maybe she didn't see me as broken. Maybe she just saw… me.

I brushed a curl from her face, careful not to wake her, and let out a long, shaky breath.

I didn't know if I was good enough for her. For her kids.

For this kind of life. But last night, with her whispering me back into calm, I'd felt something I hadn't in years.

Like maybe I could be.

Chapter Forty Three

Camille

The ride back home was filled with less chatter than the drive out.

The radio hummed softly in the background, sunlight spilling through the windshield, catching on the edge of Hunter's beard. He looked steady behind the wheel, one hand resting casually at the bottom, the other on the console. Every so often, his fingers brushed mine, a silent check-in.

I kept glancing at him, trying to read him. Trying to put words to everything that had changed between us in just one night.

Because something *had* changed.

Last night hadn't just been about us crossing a line of intimacy. It was about the way he'd let me in, really in. I'd seen the nightmare claw him awake. I'd seen the shame in his eyes when he realized he'd scared me. I'd seen the vulnerability.

And he hadn't pushed me away afterward.

But now, doubt whispered all over again.

How did I not recognize it? What if he closes up again? What if you're not strong enough to handle the weight of his past on top of your own?

I traced circles on my jeans with my thumb, stealing a glance at him. He caught me looking and gave a crooked little smile, the kind that always felt like it cracked straight through my walls.

"You okay?" he asked, his voice low, steady.

I nodded too quickly. "Yeah. Just tired."

He didn't press, and part of me was grateful, part of me disappointed. I wanted to talk about it, and I wanted to tell him how much it meant that he trusted me with the parts he'd shoved down. I was also terrified. Of saying the wrong thing. Of making him regret opening up.

A bag of snacks Hunter had picked up for the kids sat piled in the backseat, a reminder of the world waiting for me at home. My chest tightened with guilt and relief all at once. I'd missed them. Every mile closer felt like a knot unraveling. But another knot had formed too, one tangled in Hunter's hand brushing mine, in his nightmares, in the way I'd felt safe in his arms even when he was shaking.

I watched him out of the corner of my eye, my chest tightening. To anyone else, I might have looked restless. But to me, it was more. It was the echo of battles I didn't fully understand but could feel in the way he carried himself. And the part that undid me most was that even through his quiet storms, he still looked at me like I was something worth pouring into.

I wasn't sure where this road was leading. I just knew I wasn't letting him walk it alone. And I could tell that he felt the same way for me.

By the time we pulled up, I was half buzzing with anxiety, half desperate to scoop my kids into my arms. My mom met us at the door, her smile wide, the twins already wriggling in her arms, Zeke darting out with a hundred questions. Any guilt I held melted away the second I kissed their cheeks, breathing them in like I'd been gone for a month instead of a night.

Hunter stayed just long enough to help carry my bag inside and give me one of his signature grounding smiles and a quick kiss before heading out. He didn't push. Just squeezed my hand and murmured, "Call me later," before disappearing out the door.

And then, of course, Dani showed up.

She didn't even knock, just breezed in like she always did, plopping onto the couch with her iced coffee. "Well? Spill it."

I groaned, flopping into the armchair. "Hi, Dani, how are you? Yes, I missed you too."

"Cut the polite crap," she said, grinning like a cat who already knew the answer. "Overnight trip. Hotel room. Tell. Me. Everything."

My mom chuckled from the kitchen. "I'll leave you two to it. Don't let her downplay it, Dani. She came back glowing."

"Mom!" My face burned.

Dani gasped dramatically. *"Glowing?!* Oh, honey, we're skipping straight to chapter twelve of your romance novel!"

I buried my face in a pillow. "It wasn't like that."

"Uh-huh," she said, dragging out the sound, her grin pure mischief. She took a long sip of iced coffee, eyes gleaming over the rim. "So you mean to tell me you went all that way, stayed overnight with a six-foot-something former Marine with that voice, and what—played Uno until bedtime?"

"Dani!"

She lifted one brow. "What? I'm asking the important questions."

I rolled my eyes, but she wasn't wrong. My reflection in her oversized sunglasses probably gave me away: my curls tousled, skin flushed, that stupid little smile I couldn't quite hide. A soft happiness that sneaks up on you after years of survival mode.

I hesitated, peeking out from behind the pillow. "Okay, first of all, you're impossible. Second, it wasn't… that kind of night."

Dani leaned forward, all faux innocence. "So… it *was* a night."

A laugh slipped out before I could stop it. "Yeah. It was a night."

That was all it took. She squealed, grabbing the throw blanket from the back of the couch and waving it like a victory flag. "I *knew* it."

"Okay, fine," I admitted, sitting up and hugging a pillow to my chest. "It was… amazing. But also terrifying. I kept thinking, *what if I don't fit? What if his friends look at me and see a mess?*"

Dani arched a brow. "Beautiful, smart, hilariously self-deprecating, you?"

"Messy, overthinking, single mom me," I corrected.

She smiled while rolling her eyes dramatically. "And?"

I gave Dani a rundown of the party. How Hunter never made me feel out of place. How he just kept a hand on the small of my back, a grounding reminder that he was there with me. The way I fit into his world, talking with the other wives and girlfriends and meeting his friends.

CHAPTER FORTY THREE

Dani's expression softened even more. "Cam…"

I shrugged, trying to keep my voice steady. "His friends were kind. Loud, but kind. They teased him like brothers do, but you could tell there was love behind it. And one of them, Logan, had his little girl there. She was this sweet, wild-haired kid who had me out there dancing with her."

Dani laughed. "Leave it to you to befriend kids at adult parties." She said teasingly.

I smiled at the memory. "You should've seen Hunter with her. I've obviously seen him with the kids, but it was different to see him with her. I could tell it was genuine. He knelt down, tied her shoe, and he even sat there sneaking her cookies. She calls him 'Uncle Hunt'. "

Dani fanned herself. "Oh, that's domestic fantasy fuel right there."

I laughed, but the sound wavered. "It was nice, though. Seeing him like that. He's always so… contained. But around them? He was loose. Happy. Confident. It was like seeing a version of him that belonged, and he still kept looking for me across the room — checking that I was okay."

Her eyes softened. "That's not casual, Cam."

"I know," I whispered.

Silence stretched between us for a beat, comfortable and heavy with meaning. I picked at a loose thread on the pillow, remembering the smell of the bonfire smoke, the way Hunter's laugh rumbled low in his chest, the teasing between him and his friends that spoke of years of history and loyalty.

"Okay, spill it!" Dani said suddenly, eyes glinting.

I blinked. "What?"

"Come on. That little pause in your voice? That's the sound of a woman who saw her man go caveman."

I bit my lip, smiling despite myself. "There was… this guy. Sean. One of Hunter's friends. Not a bad guy, just—"

"Flirty."

"Persistent," I corrected, though Dani's grin said she knew better. "He was talking to me in the kitchen, leaning a little too close, and before I could even figure out how to sidestep, Hunter was just *there*."

Dani's eyes widened. "Oh, there *there*?"

"Yeah," I said, heat crawling up my neck at the memory. "He just slid an arm around me, calm as ever, and said, 'Careful, Sean. You're talking to my girl.'"

Dani gasped, "*My girl?!* Oh, my. I need a moment. Do you realize how hot that is?" fanning herself dramatically.

"Dani!"

"Don't pretend you didn't like it."

I tried to fight a smile and failed. "Okay, maybe a little."

"Maybe? Cam, he basically claimed you in front of a room full of Marines, and you're telling me you didn't immediately combust?"

I laughed, face burning. "I might have short-circuited a little."

She smirked, clearly satisfied. "And did you make him pay for that later?"

I threw the pillow at her. "You're awful."

She dodged, giggling. "I'm invested! So what happened next?"

I sighed, softer now. "He leaned down, and he said it wasn't about jealousy. That I just looked too good for him not to notice when someone else did. And Dani, he meant it. There was this tone in his voice, like he was still half surprised I was even with him. It wasn't possessive. It was… protective. It made me feel safe. Like I could breathe again."

Dani's teasing melted into enthusiasm. "That's big, Cam. After everything you've been through… It's good to see you letting someone show up for you."

"Yeah," I whispered. "It is. He's different. He's not scared of the messy parts."

"Good," she said, smiling again. "Then maybe you can stop running from the good parts, too."

I thought about that—the quiet drive home, the way he'd brushed my hair behind my ear before kissing me goodnight, slow and steady like he was afraid to rush something sacred.

I looked at Dani, a small laugh breaking through. "You should've seen him at the end of the night. Standing there with his friends, beer in hand, it hit me that I wasn't seeing the careful, quiet version I usually get. This was his world, and he looked at home in it. But he still looked for me. Every time I moved across the room, his eyes would find mine, like he was checking in, making sure I was okay."

Dani smiled, soft but mischievous. "That's not just attraction, babe. That's a man choosing you, even when he doesn't have to."

"Yeah," I said, voice barely above a whisper. "And that's the part that scares me."

For a moment, my mind drifted back to that night, the part I hadn't told Dani about. The night I woke to Hunter thrashing beside me, his breath ragged, his eyes wild and far away. The way he'd snapped awake, gasping, and how fast he'd pulled back, murmuring *sorry* like it was a reflex. I hadn't pushed him. Just placed my hand on his arm, slow and steady, until he came back to me.

He never told me what the dream was. And I never asked.

It wasn't my story to demand.

Dani's voice broke through my thoughts. "You okay?"

"Yeah," I said quickly, forcing a smile. "Just thinking."

She tilted her head but didn't press. That was the thing about Dani, she could read me like a book but knew when to let a page stay unturned.

I exhaled, "You should've seen him at the end of the night," I said quietly. My thoughts drifted back to the barbecue. Hunter standing there with his friends, beer in hand, that low laugh of his, it hit me that I wasn't seeing the careful version I usually get. This was his world, and he looked at home in it. But he still looked for me. "Every time I moved across the room, his eyes would find mine. Like he was making sure I was okay."

Dani's smile turned soft. "That's not just attraction, babe. That's someone *choosing* you."

"Yeah," I said, voice barely above a whisper. "And that's the part that scares me the most."

"Why?"

"Because," I said slowly, "I want him to stay. I want to believe he will."

Dani was quiet for a long moment before bumping my shoulder. "You know what I think?"

"What?"

"I think he's got you by the heartstrings."

I groaned. "Don't say that."

"Too late. It's written all over your face."

She grinned again, playful. "So, was he at least good at Uno?"

I threw another pillow at her. "Get out!"

The pillow hit her square in the chest, and her laughter

filled the room — wild, bright, alive. And somewhere under it, mine joined hers.

It wasn't the brittle kind of laughter that used to break under its own weight. It was lighter. Freer.

And beneath all the teasing and fear and hope tangled inside me, I realized the truth.

Hunter Bennett had started to become the quiet in my chaos, and I didn't know if that terrified me more than it saved me.

Chapter Forty Four

Hunter

If someone had told me a year ago that this would be my life, I would've laughed them out of the room.

Laying on the floor surrounded by blocks and stuffed animals, Zeke narrating some elaborate battle plan with his toys, the twins squealing with delight every time I pretended to "lose" to them. Sitting at Camille's kitchen table, textbooks spread between us, quizzing her like some kind of fake professor while she rolled her eyes at me and tried not to smile. Me: carrying diaper bags and strollers without thinking twice, like it was second nature.

Yet here I was. And the craziest part? I liked it. It didn't feel like babysitting someone else's chaos. It felt like being part of it.

The kids had wormed their way into me faster than I expected. Zeke, with his endless questions, testing me on sharks and space like I should have a degree in both. The twins toddling after me with their curls bouncing, calling out "Hunty!" like I was their favorite discovery.

And Camille… She was the center of it all. Strong and stubborn, always pushing forward even when I could see the exhaustion in her eyes. She carried so much, but when she let me shoulder even a piece of it, I felt like maybe I was finally doing something right, and I hadn't felt that in a long time.

But there was still the other side I didn't let her see too often.

Instead, I tried to just be the guy who brought toys, fixed cabinets, and made her laugh. And every now and then, when she looked at me like she trusted me, as if she believed in me, and I felt the weight of it.

Because I didn't just want to be a visitor in her world.

So I decided to open up to her one night when she came by my apartment. I'd spent months dodging her questions about the Marine Corps. I'd joke, brush it off, change the subject. But tonight, the silence was too heavy.

"In the ten years I was in, I did four deployments to Afghanistan," I said finally, my voice rougher than I intended.

Her eyes softened, lips parting, but she didn't interrupt. That silence, her silence, wasn't judgment. It was space. And somehow that was worse.

"The last one…" My jaw clenched. "That one was bad."

She hesitated, then asked the question people dance around but always want to know. "Did you…?"

I let out a slow breath and stared at my hands. "Out there, you don't get a choice. It's them or you. They don't hesitate." My throat burned. "You just do what you have to do to get home." The words hung heavy, like smoke.

I left the couch, needing to move, needing to do something with the buzzing in my veins. From the back of the closet, I pulled the small box I hadn't touched in years. When I set it on the table, the weight of it thudded louder than it should've.

Inside were campaign ribbons, medals, and unit patches. Bits of metal that meant survival, though to me they looked like reminders of loss. "These don't mean much anymore," I muttered. "Medals and ribbons for different accomplishments or trainings. But all I see are the guys who didn't come home." I went through each one, answering the questions as she asked, and tried to let the appreciation and validation in her eyes sink in.

Her fingers hovered, careful, like the box held everything she'd been searching for. "Hunter…" Her voice trembled. "You made it home. You gave everything, and you're still here. That matters. I'm proud of you."

With those words, the carefully constructed walls I'd built began to come apart. Nobody's ever said that to me, not like that.

When she asked why I kept them in a box, I didn't have a real answer. Truth was, they reminded me of stuff I'd rather leave in the past. Yet seeing the way she looked at me, maybe I didn't have to keep hiding those parts anymore.

Days passed, but that night stayed with me.

The way she said she was proud of me.

The way her voice cracked like she meant it. Nobody had ever said it like that before. Not even me.

So when she texted one night saying she had something to show me, I didn't think much of it. Probably another excuse to see her, not that I needed one. Any reason to end my day in that small apartment of hers, surrounded by toys, the faint smell of lavender, and that quiet warmth she carried like a light, was enough.

But when I walked into her living room, I froze.

It was sitting on the coffee table.

A black frame with a glass front. Inside, every medal, every ribbon, every piece of that old life I'd shoved into a box years ago was laid out in careful rows. My unit patch near the top, a faded photo of my squad tucked in the corner.

Camille stood beside the couch, fingers worrying the hem of her shirt. "I made you something," she said quietly, nerves flickering behind her smile.

For a second, I couldn't move. My throat tightened, and the air felt heavy, thick. I crouched down, resting my elbows on my knees. The medals caught the light, all lined up like they belonged to someone who had his life together, someone proud of what he'd done. They didn't look like mine.

The faint hum in my ears was the same one that used to hit before a firefight, like the world had gone still, waiting to see what I'd do next.

"You did this?" I muttered, my voice rough.

"I didn't want them hidden," she said. "You gave so much of yourself. You shouldn't hide it. You should honor it. It felt like the least I could do."

That one hit deep. The kind of truth that burns on the way in.

I cleared my throat, trying to ground myself. "Camille...I kept these packed away for a reason," I said, nodding toward the frame. "They don't feel like accomplishments. They feel like... ghosts. Names I don't get to say out loud."

She stepped closer, voice warm, "They're proof you came home. That you fought your way back."

I let out a slow breath, rubbing the back of my neck. "Yeah. Sometimes that's the part that stings the most."

Her hand found mine then. They felt so small and warm in my grasp, but it was all it took for the noise in my head to quiet.

Her voice wavered. "I'm sorry…did I overstep?"

I looked up at her, the uncertainty showing in her eyes.

For a second, I didn't trust myself to speak. I just stood there, taking her in. The quiet doubt behind her question, the way her hands trembled ever so slightly.

Then I shook my head. "No. You didn't overstep."

She exhaled, a small, shaky breath that hit harder than I expected.

I stared at the frame again. At the medals, the photo, the dust of years between who I'd been and who I was now. Usually, it felt like looking at someone else's life, a different time, but now, it felt like it was mine.

"You didn't overstep," I said again, quieter now. "You gave me something I didn't think I'd get back."

Her eyes softened. She didn't fill the silence. She just stood there, letting me find my footing.

"Thank you," I said, and it came out rough, too small for what it meant. I shook my head, searching for words that didn't exist. "You don't know what that means to me, Cami. For the past year, I tried to forget that part of my life. Figured if I buried it deep enough, it couldn't reach me. But you…" I paused, swallowing hard. "You didn't try to fix it. You just saw it. You saw *me*. And you didn't flinch."

Her eyes glistened, and she smiled. "You deserve to be seen, Hunter."

The air between us shifted. For a heartbeat, everything felt still. Like the first breath after surfacing from deep water.

I stepped closer, brushing a curl from her cheek with my thumb. "You didn't have to do this," I murmured.

"I wanted to," she said. "You should be proud of who you are."

I nodded, jaw tight. "Yeah, maybe you're right."

She smiled again, and for a long moment, neither of us said anything. I just listened to the sounds of her apartment, all of it grounded me in a way nothing else could.

When I finally leaned in and pressed a kiss to her forehead, a thank-you I couldn't put into words.

Her hand squeezed mine gently, and I caught myself thinking how damn lucky I was that she saw something worth saving in a man who'd spent years running from himself.

This wasn't just a frame on a coffee table. It was proof that someone saw me, all of me, and stayed anyway.

That was the first time I didn't feel like a soldier just trying to survive.

Chapter Forty Five

Camille

Weeks later, the way he looked at the shadow box, like it was delicate and loaded, still held a hold on me. The way his voice cracked when he said thank you, like the words had been scraped raw from somewhere deep.

We came to a point where I thought maybe we had turned a corner. For a while, it even felt like we had. He lingered longer, opened up more, and there was an ease between us, the kind that comes after a storm when the air feels clean again, and the world softens around the edges. The kids adored him, my mom teased me about the way I smiled when his name came up, and at night, when the house went still, I let myself imagine a future that didn't end with someone walking away.

Life was still messy, with school deadlines scattered across the kitchen table, bills tucked into the drawer I tried not to open, and Zeke's boundless energy colliding with the twins' daily chaos. But it all felt lighter with Hunter around.

He was simply there. Bringing takeout when I was too tired to cook, taking the kids to the park on Saturday mornings so I could finish assignments, and fixing the loose hinge on the cabinet. The girls would squeal his name whenever his truck pulled up, curls bouncing as they ran to meet him, and even my mom couldn't help but say how natural he looked in the middle of it all, like he had always belonged there.

We fell into a rhythm I didn't expect. Piece by piece, wall by wall, I started to believe that maybe he wasn't going to leave, that maybe, for once, I was safe.

Some mornings, he would swing by before work, coffee in hand, with Zeke dragging him into elaborate games that involved roughhousing and at least three costume changes. The twins demanded "uppies" until he caved, curls bouncing as he lifted them high, their laughter spilling into every corner of the house.

Other nights, he showed up after bedtime, sinking onto the couch beside me while my textbooks lay open on the coffee table, ready to quiz me for class while pretending to be a strict professor until I was laughing too hard to study. Other times, we didn't need words at all. My leg flung over his thighs, his hand resting warm against my knee, both of us breathing in the home we had built.

Even the silence between us had started to feel easy, like the kind that doesn't need to be filled.

We've had quiet nights tangled together on the couch, talking about things I never thought I'd let myself say out loud again: hopes, fears, what the future could look like if neither of us ran.

This was him stepping into our world, piece by piece, without hesitation.

Even Dani noticed. "You're lighter," she said one afternoon, stealing food off my plate at the diner. I rolled my eyes, but she wasn't wrong. "It's still there," I admitted. "The stress, the chaos, but I don't feel alone in it anymore."

She grinned, smug. "That's what happens when you let a good man in. You stop carrying the whole damn world by yourself." I smiled into my soda, unwilling to say it out loud, but knowing she was right.

For a while, everything felt steady.

But as the summer crept closer, something in him began to shift.

It started so small I almost missed it. Hunter would drift off in the middle of a sentence, his gaze caught by movement outside the window. Not really *seeing*, just staring, like he was searching for something I couldn't. Something I couldn't reach. Sometimes he'd come back to me with that easy grin, the one that used to melt me, and for a heartbeat, I'd almost believe everything was fine. But then it would happen again. The quiet. The distance. The way his eyes seemed to live somewhere else.

I kept asking myself what changed that I wasn't aware of, if maybe I'd done something to push him back without realizing it.

I went through the mental checklist like I could logic my way out of heartbreak before it even arrived. My ex had stayed away, no more calls from blocked numbers, no more late-night threats that made my stomach twist. For once, life had felt still.

When Hunter was around, he *fit*. Not just with me, but with *us*. He blended in effortlessly, like he'd been written into our lives long before he showed up.

His friends became mine, and when I brought him to brunch with Dani, she grilled him relentlessly before giving me a look that said she'd approved. We even spent time with Nick and Logan and their kids. There had been one Saturday when we met at Logan's house by the beach. A glimpse into what *our* world could look like, all of it woven together. Hunter had leaned close to me that day, hand brushing mine, and said softly, "This is nice, isn't it?"

I'd nodded.

But now, it was like he'd forgotten.

My heart ached to reach out and erase the distance and find that spark we had before, the one that used to light up entire rooms. But fear pinned me in place. Every time I looked at him, I felt that old ache stirring. The one that whispered, *Don't hold too tight; people leave when you do.*

I watched the steam curl from my coffee, untouched and cooling between us, a quiet clock marking the space growing wider. When I asked what was wrong, he'd just smile in that small, polite kind of smile that never touched his eyes before changing the subject like it was nothing. But it wasn't nothing.

Every small gesture, every pause that stretched too long, every quiet that felt like goodbye. They piled up until the air between us felt heavy. The world kept moving, the kids kept laughing, the days kept passing, but I felt the ground shifting beneath us, subtle and slow.

I knew it wasn't just me overthinking. I felt it everywhere. In the restless edge of my dreams, in the way my chest tightened every time he left, in how my nerves seemed to hum louder when I was alone.

At night, I replayed every small moment: the phone calls

that ended sooner, the reasons he gave for leaving early, the way his hand barely lingered at the small of my back. Each detail pressed heavier on my chest, the voice in my head growing louder with every passing day.

The pressure built in my chest, a knot tightening in my throat. The world felt off-kilter, the mattress shifting beneath me, dropping me into that old, familiar ache of doubt. My therapist would call it my inner critic, the voice that makes me question everything I thought I knew.

The more I tried to push it away, the heavier it settled. Every silence became rejection, every sigh a show of disappointment, every glance at the door a reminder of time running out. I told myself he was tired, that life was heavy, that maybe he was carrying things he couldn't say yet. Maybe that was true. But deep down, fear twisted every answer into proof of what I'd always dreaded: people didn't stay. Not for me. Not for long.

And every time he pulled away, even just an inch, it felt like I was losing him piece by piece.

I hated how quickly the old wounds reopened, how easily the scars split apart. The guilt pressed in, too, because I knew he was fighting his own battles. I saw it in the restless tap of his knee, the way his thumbs worked against each other when he was anxious, the hollow in his eyes when he thought no one noticed.

But when the house settled at night and the kids were asleep, the weight crept back onto my shoulders, pressing down a little more each day. Lying there, staring at the ceiling, I wondered if I should start preparing for the day he just stopped coming back.

Chapter Forty Six

Hunter

Things with Camille had been going well.

The noise in my head went quiet when I was at her place—Zeke's laughter echoing down the hall, the twins' squeals mixing with the smell of her favorite candle and half-broken crayons scattered across the table. It was chaos, sure, but it was *good* chaos. Real. They made space for me without even trying, and before I knew it, I'd fallen into *our* life. Mornings half-awake, hair a mess, standing barefoot at her stove cooking eggs while she stole sips of my coffee when she thought I wasn't looking.

She'd even started riding with me more. Out there, on the road, it was just us. The wind, the hum of the engine, her arms around me. Every mile stripped something heavy off my chest. With her on the back of the bike, I didn't think about the past or the things I couldn't fix. I just *felt;* her laughter against my shoulder, the warmth of her hands, the quiet trust in the way she leaned into every turn.

One night, when we pulled back into the garage, I caught

her eyes in the mirror. Her helmet was off, hair wild, cheeks flushed from the ride. She looked alive in a way that made my throat tighten. I'd said the first thing that came to mind. "You did good, Beautiful." She pretended it didn't make her blush, but I saw the pink rise on her warm cheeks.

And right then, it hit me how damn easy it would be to give all of myself to her. To them.

How, without even trying, they'd made the world feel like something worth coming back to.

At least until fireworks went off early one night, a sharp pop that split the daze of summer.

The sound twisted, became the crack of a gunshot, gunpowder thick in the air, desert heat pressing close. My shoulders drew up, muscles tight, heart pounding against my ribs. My breath caught, shallow and sharp, pulling me backward. My ears rang, my jaw ached, and I stayed locked in that instant. Her living room faded, replaced by a memory I would have given anything to forget.

That whip-crack pulled me straight into desert nights. Every muscle braced for the next hit. Air thin, breath tight. Past and present tangled until I couldn't tell one from the other. In my head, I was back in the desert with dust in my eyes, ground shaking under my boots, screams in my ears.

I forced myself to look around, anchored to what was real. Zeke sprawled on the rug, twins clapping, laughter bouncing off the old couch. Camille, in a red dress, bent over her books, blue mug in hand. They were safe. I was here. My body didn't buy it.

That's the worst part, my own mind betraying me, ripping me out of safety, leaving me raw. PTSD doesn't wait. It kicks down the door, wrecks your peace, and drags you right to the edge, and it doesn't matter if you scream or not.

So I stepped back. Kissed her forehead, muttered about being tired, got out before the night could unravel. I didn't want her kids to see me fall apart, but she noticed. Eyes wide, searching. I wished I could explain how each blast yanked me out of the house and right back to the desert. Gunpowder in my nose, sweat and sand on my skin, body braced up and tight, every breath a fight. I couldn't stop it. Couldn't separate now from then. Just caught in the loop, hoping it would pass.

At first, I played the part. I smiled, brought cookies, wrestled with the kids, and stole kisses from Camille in the laundry room. On the surface, I looked steady. Underneath, I was unraveling. But I didn't want the kids to see me fall apart, didn't want Zeke to catch my hands shaking or the twins to see the panic in my eyes. So I stayed distant, told myself it was safer. Yet each time Camille looked at me, worry in her face, the guilt pressed in. I was breaking something good before it had a chance.

It's been this way since my second deployment. July creeps up, pressure builds. Fireworks, crowds, flags waving, and everyone celebrating while I brace for impact. The nights are worse. Dreams I can't wake from. Faces I can't forget. Then the days hit me with smaller things like a slammed door, a car backfiring, even a toy dropping, and suddenly I'm back there again.

She didn't know that part of me yet. Not really. The part that flinches at the wrong sound, that wakes up drenched in sweat, that stares at the ceiling trying to remember where I am. And I couldn't bring myself to tell her. How do you explain something like that to someone who finally made you feel normal again?

Truth is, I pulled away because I was scared. What if she saw the parts of me I tried to hide? What if her kids noticed me flinch when popcorn popped in the kitchen? I can't explain PTSD to a five-year-old. Hell, I can barely explain it to myself. Would letting her in show the cracks, or would that finally be real strength?

I hated the space between us. I noticed how her shoulders tightened when I left early, how her eyes lingered when my smile didn't quite land. She thought it was her, too much, too complicated. But she wasn't too much. She was everything. I was just afraid of breaking what we had.

Chapter Forty Seven

Camille

Eventually, Hunter distancing himself became enough that everything in my world tilted. And it came at the worst time, too, because my own life hadn't slowed down.

I was tired. Bone-deep tired. But his presence had made that weight feel lighter, manageable even. He'd been steady, grounding, the one bright thing at the end of long days.

He'd still show up, but he'd leave earlier. His texts came slower. His smile didn't quite reach his eyes. He was there, but I felt him slipping, like sand through my fingers. Was I too much? Was it the kids? Was it my ex bringing disruption? Or was it something else, something he wasn't telling me?

Instead of letting these thoughts consume me, I decided to take action. I reached out to Dani and set up a time to meet. Over lunch, I opened up to her about my fears and confusion, hoping her perspective might shed some light on the situation. I also booked an appointment with my therapist, realizing that I needed professional guidance to navigate my own emotional maze. These steps felt small but significant, a way to regain some sense of control in what felt like a spiraling situation.

The not-knowing was worse than anything.

I'd survived other exits. But with Hunter… I didn't want to just survive this.

I wanted to fight for it.

But how do you fight what you can't name?

The silence came slowly, like a door easing shut.

At first, it was just a longer pause before he replied. A text I'd send in the morning that he wouldn't answer until lunch. Then it became whole afternoons. I'd type something like *How's your day?* and watch the little "delivered" icon sit there, staring back at me. Hours passed before a reply, and sometimes, there wasn't one at all.

The phone calls dwindled, too.

Where he used to call me every night, sometimes twice in a day just to hear my voice, now it was every other night. Then every few days. When he did call, his voice sounded tired and distracted, as if he were talking through a fog.

I told myself not to overthink it. That he was busy. That work was heavy. That maybe he just needed space. But at two in the morning, when the twins were finally asleep, and Zeke was snoring down the hall, I'd sit with the glow of my phone in my hand, staring at a blank screen, wondering if I'd done something wrong.

Each unanswered text twisted the knife deeper. They pulled me back into old stories that I swore I'd stop telling myself that people always left, that I was easier to walk away from than to stay with. And still, every time his name lit up my phone, even after hours of silence, my heart jumped like it always had. Because even as I doubted, even as I hurt, I wanted to believe he wasn't like the others. I wanted to believe he'd come back. But by the end of the second week, the silence wasn't subtle anymore. It was obvious.

I'd send him pictures of the kids like Zeke showing off his block tower, the twins covered in applesauce, and where he used to respond in seconds with *look at them!* or a dozen laughing emojis, now it was hours. Sometimes, there was no reply at all.

The calls were worse.

I found myself clutching the phone at night, waiting for it to ring, replaying old conversations just to remind myself what his voice sounded like when he was present. But when it did ring, once, maybe twice a week, he sounded distant, his words clipped, laughter forced.

And still I clung to those scraps because between work at the doctor's office, rushing to pick up the kids, late-night studying for exams, and exhaustion pressing down on me like a weight, his presence had been my one soft place to land.

Now that softness was gone. The twins hadn't noticed yet; too little to understand. But Zeke did.

One night, while I was cleaning up toys, he looked up and asked, "Why doesn't Hunter come over as much?"

The question hit like a gut punch. I smiled too quickly, smoothing his curls. "He's just busy, baby."

But as Zeke nodded, already distracted by his toy car, I felt the lie settle heavy in my chest. Because I didn't know if Hunter was busy… or if he was leaving.

Chapter Forty Eight

Hunter

The Fourth of July came in full force.

Cami planned a small cookout at her mom's. Hot dogs, sparklers in the driveway, nothing wild. The night before, she texted to ask what kind of pie I liked, her messages scattered with emojis and that easy warmth she carried into every corner of her life. She sent a picture of Zeke, tiny flag in hand, grinning as if he'd already claimed the whole day for himself.

I wanted to say yes. Hell, I wanted to be there more than anything.

But when the day came, I couldn't do it.

I told her I wasn't feeling well, blamed it on a rough night, and said I'd try to catch up on sleep. The lie slipped out too easily, and that stung more than I wanted to admit. Her reply came after a pause I could almost feel, a gentle hesitation that pressed through the screen. *"It's okay, maybe next time."*

She didn't push, and that somehow cut deeper.

By dusk, the air outside had that heavy July heat that sticks to your skin. I sat on my couch with the TV on low, trying to pretend the silence didn't bother me. I thought about calling her, just to hear her laugh or the kids running in the background, but the guilt hit before I could reach for the phone.

Then a single firework went off outside.

Pop.

Too sharp. Too close.

And just like that, my chest tightened, breath caught halfway. A high-pitched ringing started in my ears, drowning out the world around me, growing louder with each heartbeat. My vision narrowed, colors blurring as if I was looking through a warped lens. My body moved before my brain caught up. I dropped low, shoulder against the wall, muscles locked and ready for impact. The sound cracked through me like a live wire.

Another pop. Then another.

The air thickened. The flash through the blinds hit the room in bursts of red and white, and suddenly, I wasn't in my apartment anymore. The floor wasn't carpet, it was dirt. The smell wasn't barbecue, it was smoke, fuel, sweat.

My hand twitched toward a weapon that wasn't there.

The old training kicked in fast—scan, cover, assess—but there was no threat, no orders, no team at my back. Just me. Alone. In a living room that didn't feel safe anymore.

I tried to breathe through it.

Four in. Six out.

But the noise outside wouldn't stop. Each one felt like it dug deeper, pulling pieces of the past I'd buried under miles of silence.

The convoy ambush.

The flash before the dust.

The sound of someone yelling for a medic, only to not hear an answer.

My throat burned. I could almost taste the metallic tang of the blood and the way your mouth goes dry when the adrenaline finally runs out.

People think PTSD is just fear. It's not. It's *memory*. It's your body remembering faster than your mind can forget, like a smoke alarm that blares for burnt toast as if the house were on fire. Just a hint of smoke triggers the siren, regardless of how real the threat is, and your body is trapped in that same loop, responding to echoes of danger long after the fire is out.

Another explosion—louder this time. My hands shook. My heartbeat felt like gunfire under my skin.

I hated that I couldn't control it. Hated that some cheap fireworks could pull me apart.

Then my phone buzzed.

A picture from Cami.

Zeke was holding a sparkler, grinning ear to ear. The twins were beside him, sticky with Popsicle stains, and she was smiling— she was smiling, that tired, beautiful smile that always made me feel like maybe I could stop running.

Camille: Wish you were here.

And it wrecked me.

Because I *did* wish I was there. I wanted to be in that driveway, laughing with them, holding her hand, not sitting in a dark apartment fighting ghosts that never learned to stay dead.

The fireworks didn't stop.

Pop!

Every echo rolled through me like aftershocks, too sharp, too close. The walls of my apartment felt smaller by the minute. Outside, I could hear a neighbor's carefree laughter, a reminder of celebrations that only deepened my sense of isolation. I needed noise, something I could *control*.

I grabbed my phone and opened the first playlist that came up. The speakers kicked in, bass rumbling through the floor, so loud it almost drowned out the sounds in my head. Almost.

It was country at first, something easy, but it wasn't cutting it. Too close to home. Too full of words that felt like things I'd lost. I switched it to rock, volume up until it rattled the windows. The guitar hit like a wall of sound, drowning out the phantom explosions outside, replacing one kind of chaos with another.

For a minute, it worked.

The vibration under my feet, heavy drums, voices rough and wordless, all of it kept me anchored in the present. Loud meant safe. Loud meant *now*.

I stripped my shirt off and walked straight to the shower, not caring that the lights were still off. The water came on hard and cold at first, then scalding, filling the room with steam that burned the air from my lungs. I braced both hands against the tile, head bowed under the spray.

It was the only thing that helped drown out the weight of it. The sound. The simplicity.

No sand. No smoke. No ghosts. Just the steady rhythm of water against skin, trying to wash away everything the night had brought back.

I stayed there until my fingers wrinkled and my head felt

hollow, until the heat had faded to lukewarm and I couldn't tell if I was shaking from the cold or from everything else.

When I finally turned the water off, the thoughts quickly returned.

The music was still blaring from the other room, but it sounded far away, muffled by the steam and the fog in my head. I dried off, walked barefoot across the floor, and grabbed my phone to shut it off.

That's when I saw her text.

Camille: Hope you're feeling better. The kids and I missed you tonight.

My throat tightened.

Even in a few words, she managed to bring a warmth to my world. Like light after dark.

I stared at the message for a long time, thumb hovering over the keyboard. The words lined up in my head, the truth right there: *I wanted to be there. I'm sorry I lied. I'm trying.*

But I couldn't type any of it. Not tonight.

Instead, I set the phone face down and sat on the edge of the bed, the music still humming low in the background.

My chest was heavy, my muscles buzzing with leftover adrenaline that had nowhere to go. The apartment felt too still again, too neat. Everything in its place except me.

I leaned forward, elbows on my knees, and just stared at the floor. The carpet blurred. The sound dulled. My head finally started to empty.

And that's when the switch flipped.

It's not something you notice happening. One moment you're wound tight, ready to jump at every sound, and the next… nothing. There's a quiet so deep it hums. Your body shuts down before your brain can argue, limbs weighted with wet sand, too heavy to lift, as if anchored to the earth. The shift is sudden and complete, leaving nothing but a hollow echo where tension used to reside.

So I let it.

I lay back on the bed, still half-damp, still in the same clothes I'd pulled on after the shower. The pillow was cold as I pressed it to my head, attempting to drown out the distant noise outside.

My heartbeat raced until even that faded into background noise.

The world didn't stop. It just dimmed, edges softening until everything felt far away.

And somewhere between the echo of fireworks and the hum of silence, I fell asleep.

When I woke, morning light cut across the floor in sharp stripes. My mouth was dry, head was pounding. The music must have stopped hours ago, since my phone now lay dead beside me.

But the weight hadn't gone anywhere. It sat low in me, dull and familiar, the kind of ache you don't walk off. Guilt. Shame. Both heavy as armor, I couldn't take off.

I'd lied to her. Lied about being fine. Lied about needing rest when the truth was worse. I couldn't even show up for fireworks and sparklers in a driveway. Couldn't stand the noise long enough to see the way her kids' faces lit up.

And that thought, that I'd failed her before it even mattered, cut deeper than I wanted to admit. If I couldn't handle that, how was I supposed to show up when things actually got hard? When they needed me?

I plugged my phone in and watched the screen flicker back to life. A missed FaceTime call from Camille and one text waited.

Camille: Zeke saved you a sparkler.

Something so small, so kind, and I didn't deserve any of it. She had no idea what last night had been for me. The panic. The noise. The part of me I'd thought I'd buried years ago was clawing its way back up.

She still saw me as the steady one. The safe one.

And maybe that's what hurt most, because I wanted to be. For her. For them.

But I wasn't there yet. Not even close.

Wanting to be enough didn't mean I was. And until I figured out how to quiet the war still living under my skin, distance felt like the only way to keep her safe—from me, from this, from everything I still hadn't learned how to fight.

Chapter Forty Nine

Camille

It had been a week since Hunter canceled on the Fourth of July. Those seven days also came with fewer texts and shorter calls. I tried to give him space, told myself he was busy, that maybe it was just stress. But space turned into silence, and silence felt too much like goodbye.

When he came by that evening, quiet as ever, I watched him move through the apartment like he was already half gone. I couldn't ignore it anymore. I knew what being half in looked like, felt like, and I didn't want that for any of them.

I held the towel in my hands, turning it over and over, the familiar action grounding me momentarily.

Breathing deeply, I said, "You've been… different lately." I placed the towel down deliberately, attempting to steady myself, while my heart pounded with each word.

My eyes flickered to Hunter's face, searching for a hint of reassurance, but finding the same guarded expression.

"And while I respect you might need space," I continued, my voice softening despite the tightness in my chest, "if there's something going on, I need to know. I need honesty, even if it's messy." I took a small step closer, vulnerability lacing my words. "I want us to be able to work through things together." I finished, the weight of my own fear pressing me to the edge, a silent plea in my gaze.

His shoulders stiffened, eyes glued to the book. "It's nothing."

"Hunter," I pressed, stepping closer. "Something's wrong. I can feel it. You don't talk to me the same. You're barely answering my messages—"

He snapped the book shut, not loud but sharp enough to make the twins startle. "I said it's nothing." His words stung, the edge in his voice so unlike the man who used to make me laugh until I couldn't breathe, who whispered comfort into my hair when the world felt too heavy.

My throat tightened. "I'm not trying to fight with you. I'm just... worried. About you. About us."

For the first time, he looked at me. His blue eyes weren't cold, but they were tired, bone-deep tired. "Cami, not everything needs to be talked about. Sometimes I just need space. I can't always play twenty questions."

The kids chattered in the background, their voices a blur. I stood in the living room, the ground unsteady beneath my feet. I'd promised myself I wouldn't beg anyone to stay, so I stood there, arms crossed, heart pounding in my ears. He'd never snapped at me before.

"I'm not asking for every detail," I said, voice barely above a whisper. "But I can't pretend I don't notice. You're pulling away, Hunter. And it hurts."

He rubbed a hand over his beard, sighing like the weight of the world was pressing down on him. "It's not about you."

I know that, but when you shut me out, when you don't answer, it feels like it is. It feels like you're already halfway gone, and I'm left guessing why," I said softly, trying to reach him through the wall he was building.

I took a small step closer, searching his eyes for something, anything, that would let me in. "Can't you see how much I'm trying here? Every unanswered text, every call that goes to voicemail, they feel like tiny rejections. I'm reaching out, hoping you'll reach back."

His jaw tightened. "Because talking about it doesn't fix it. Because dragging you into my shit doesn't help either. I don't want you or your kids seeing me like that."

His words landed sharply. "So you'd rather leave me in the dark? Pretend nothing's wrong until I finally give up?"

The twins let out a squeal as Zeke zoomed a car across the floor, crashing it into the coffee table with a triumphant "BOOM!" The sound made Hunter flinch, almost imperceptibly, but I caught it.

"See?" I whispered, stepping closer. "I notice, Hunter. I notice even when you don't say anything."

He looked at me then, eyes haunted, walls up so high I wasn't sure I'd ever scale them. "That's exactly why I'm trying to keep space. Because once you *really* see what it's like, you'll wish you hadn't."

The silence stretched, wide and impossible.

I wanted to tell him he was wrong. That I wouldn't run just because he'd finally shown me what I already knew was there beneath the surface. But the words never came. The anger did. The hurt. The fear of abandonment. It all hit first.

"If you want out, just say it."

Hunter's head snapped up, eyes flashing. "That's not what

I said."

"But that's what it feels like!" My voice cracked, louder than I intended. "You don't answer my texts, you barely call, you sit here like you'd rather be anywhere else. How am I supposed to believe you still want this?"

His jaw clenched, hands fisted against his knees. "Because I *do* want this. I want you. I want the kids. But I can't just…" He broke off, dragging a hand through his hair. "You don't get it."

"Then help me get it." I fired back, my chest heaving. "Stop shutting me out like I'm too fragile to handle the truth. I've been through hell, Hunter. I can take it. What I *can't* take is being kept in the dark until you walk away."

The kids' laughter softened into silence. Sensing the tension, Zeke looked up from his car, eyes wide. My stomach twisted, guilt slamming into me, but the words wouldn't stop.

I lowered my voice and took a step towards Hunter to close the distance. "You think hiding from me protects me? It doesn't. It just makes me feel like I'm not enough for you to trust. And sure, those may be my own insecurities, but I need to feel safe, I need you to communicate with me. I want to know you just like I let you know me, Hunter."

Hunter stood, restless, his fists opening and closing at his sides. He looked away, breath shaky. "You want the truth?" The words barely made it out.

He dragged a hand over his face, eyes tired. "My head's a mess. Most days, I wake up from dreams that feel too real. Sounds, smells, they pull me back to places I wish I could forget."

His voice broke, softer now. "Fireworks… they take me back. I was tired on the 4th of July, I was checked out… a mess." He shook his head, voice almost gone. "I hate feeling like this. It makes me feel weak." He looked at me, pain flickering in his eyes. "I'm scared that if you see it, you'll realize I'm not the one you want. That you and the kids are better off without me. There, I said it. Any other questions?"

His words landed hard, tears burning behind my eyes. For a heartbeat, neither of us moved aside from the kids who shifted nervously as the room buzzed with tension.

For the first time since meeting him, I didn't feel safe in his silence. I felt like we were standing on opposite sides of a chasm, both of us shouting into it, too scared to cross. The silence after his outburst stretched thin. My chest ached, eyes burning with tears I wouldn't let fall in front of the kids.

Hunter's face was hard, but behind it I saw the cracks: the fear, the shame, the storm he was trying to hold back. And then he moved, but not towards me. He grabbed his keys, jaw set, shoulders stiff, holding himself together by sheer force. For a brief second, his hand hovered over the door handle, a moment so suspended it felt like the world paused with him. He almost stepped forward, an inch that could have made everything crumble or come together, but his foot stayed planted, frozen between choices.

"Hunter…" My voice caught, broken.

He didn't meet my eyes, but I could still see the regret. "I can't do this right now. I'm sorry Cami."

I caught myself aching to go after Hunter, to grab his hand and make him stay, but the door slammed behind him, leaving the sound ricocheting through the apartment. I stood there frozen, arms wrapped around myself, listening to the echo of his absence. I forced myself to kneel, to gather my kids close, to steady my voice even though my chest felt like it was splintering.

"It's okay," I whispered, more to myself than to them. "It's okay." Quickly trying to redirect them.

But deep down, nothing felt okay. It felt like losing him, and the slam of the door rang in my ears long after he was gone. The kids clung to me, their little faces tight with worry they didn't have words for. Zeke asked in a small voice, "Is Hunter mad at you?"

My heart clenched. I smoothed his curls, forcing a smile I didn't feel. "No, baby. Grown-ups just… need breaks sometimes."

He seemed to accept that, though his eyes lingered on the door like he expected Hunter to walk back through it any second. The twins fussed, climbing into my lap, their weight anchoring me when I felt like I might float right out of my skin.

I held them, kissed their cheeks, and rocked them until their breathing slowed. On the outside, calm. Inside, breaking.

Later, after they were asleep, I stood alone in the living room, staring at the couch where he'd been just a few hours ago. The pillow still held the faintest indentation from his arm.

Part of me was furious, furious that he'd left, that he couldn't just stay and talk to me, furious that his silence always left me feeling like I wasn't enough. Furious that he did that in front of the kids. But beneath the anger was fear. Fear that this was it. That my kids would ask for him tomorrow, and I'd have no answer. That the little piece of hope I'd finally let myself hold onto was slipping through my fingers like all the times before.

I curled onto the couch, hugging a throw pillow tight, my

tears hot against the fabric. I'd promised myself I wouldn't beg anyone to stay. Not after my dad. And not after my kids' father. But Hunter wasn't them. He was different. He had been different. And that's what hurt the most. Because for the first time in years, I'd let myself believe.

Chapter Fifty

Hunter

The door slammed harder than I meant it to, the echo rattling through me like an aftershock.

I didn't stop walking. Down the steps, across the grass, and into the truck. My hands shook as I shoved the key into the ignition, but I couldn't sit still. I had to move. Had to get out before I said something worse, before I broke something I couldn't fix.

The engine roared to life, but I just sat there, gripping the wheel until my knuckles went white.

Her face wouldn't leave me. The hurt in her eyes when I snapped, when I told her the part I've buried from everyone, that my head's a minefield, that I'm terrified she'll see too much and decide I'm not worth it.

Because the truth is, I already believe it.

I told myself I stormed out to protect her. Protect the kids from seeing me lose it. But sitting there with the engine running, sweat slick on my palms, I knew the truth. I ran just like my old man said I would. I could still hear him, rough as gravel: "Stop crying, boy. Weakness gets you killed. No woman wants a man who can't control himself."

I'd spent my whole life proving him wrong, pushing harder, holding it together, locking it down. And yet here I was, thirty years old, a Marine, sitting in my truck shaking like the scared kid he always accused me of being.

And worse, I'd left her standing there with the kids, her eyes shining with tears I caused.

I hated myself for it.

I knew I should go back up, drop my pride, and tell her that I was scared, that the noise was getting louder, that I pulled away because I cared too damn much.

But instead, I shifted into drive. Because I didn't know if I could stand in front of her again without breaking. I didn't even have a destination. Just drove. Past the same streets, same gas station, world blurring into headlights and traffic lights, I barely noticed.

The truck felt too small, too loud, every beat of the engine echoing the pounding in my chest.

As I drove, I replayed the fight on a loop. Her voice breaking as she said, *"If you want out, just say it."* The way Zeke had looked up from the floor, confused, holding his toy tighter than he should be. The twins fussed, sensing tension but not understanding why.

And me, walking out.

My hands had been gripping the wheel so tight they ached. I hated myself for leaving, but the shame was heavier than the urge to turn back.

I ended up in an empty parking lot, the kind where no one asked questions. Killed the engine and sat in the dark until my phone buzzed once, her name lighting the screen.

I couldn't pick it up.

Instead, I dropped my head back against the seat, exhaling hard.

I thought about my dad, how he'd sneered at weakness, how he'd told me emotions made men soft. And I thought about Camille looking at me like my mess didn't scare her, like she wanted in, no matter what. Her eyes could cut through the fog and see the parts I tried to hide. That last look she gave me held no judgment and stuck with me. It made me think maybe I wasn't as broken as I felt. I wanted to hold onto that, let it anchor me. Those two voices pulled at me in opposite directions, leaving me stuck in between, paralyzed as I opened the text she'd sent.

Camille: Please be safe.

Not come back to me, not explain, just safe. Something in my chest cracked. I wanted to turn the key, drive back, and fall at her feet. The shame of it kept my hands frozen. So I sat in the dark, phone burning in my hand, wondering if this was the moment I finally ruined the best thing I'd ever had.

It should've been a relief, but all I could hear was the echo of every other time someone had decided I wasn't worth the fight.

I rubbed a hand over my beard, jaw tight. I could go back. Walk upstairs, tell her the truth, let her really see me. The nightmares. The shakes. The way every pop of fireworks sent me straight back overseas.

But what if she didn't like what she saw? What if Zeke stopped looking at me like I was his hero and started seeing me as another guy who couldn't hold it together? What if the twins stopped reaching for me, sensing the storm I tried to keep buried? What if she stopped looking at me like I was home and started looking at me like I was broken? The thought was unbearable.

So instead of turning back, I sat there telling myself distance was better. It was easier to believe she'd be fine without me and to think she deserved someone steadier, not a guy who flinched at shadows. No woman wants a man who can't hold himself together.

I had just sabotaged the one good thing I'd found by staying away and convincing myself she'd be better off if I let her go.

The next few days blurred into the same routine: work, gym, home. I avoided Camille's place entirely, convincing myself that distance was best. My phone buzzed more than once with her name lighting the screen, a reminder of the life I was missing. Zeke drew something for you. The twins learned a new word today. Little updates that tugged at me. Each one I read but left unanswered, all the replies that went unsent. I let the silence stretch, believing it was kinder somehow, that it kept me from saying the wrong thing.

I threw myself into work on base, clocking extra hours I didn't need. I pushed harder at the gym, letting the weights grind out what sleep couldn't. And at night, when I lay awake staring at the ceiling, I convinced myself this was temporary. That giving her space now would protect her from the worst of me later.

But the truth was, I missed them.

I missed Zeke's endless questions, the twins' squeals, the way Camille laughed when I teased her out of her own head.

I missed walking into her world and feeling like maybe, just maybe, I belonged there.

And the more I told myself I was protecting her, the more I knew I was lying. Because deep down, I knew this wasn't protection. It was fear, and it had me by the throat.

Chapter Fifty One

Camille

The thing about abandonment wounds is that withdrawal and silence hurt more than an argument ever could.

Days passed with no word from Hunter, and each hour without a text felt like a fresh reminder that I was too much and he'd gone, just like the others.

I tried to keep myself busy, but he lingered in everything. In the empty spot on the couch where he usually sat with Zeke, building Lego sets. In the swing at the park, where the twins looked forward, as if they expected him to push them higher. In the way my phone lit up at night with everyone and everything but him. I checked anyway, though, constantly.

A ridiculous part of me hoped I'd see his name, hear his voice, get some proof that I hadn't just imagined the love between us. But when I did hear from him, it was short. Flat. Messages anyone could have sent. *Busy. Talk later.*

But later never came.

I tried to keep up appearances for the kids. Smiled when

Zeke asked about him, kissed the twins' curls when they babbled "Hunty!" like he was still about to walk through the door. Yet when the house was quiet, I curled on the couch with my textbooks untouched, staring at the last picture I'd taken of him holding the twins. He hated pictures, but he never complained about the countless pictures I took when he was in the moment; those candid shots were the only thing I had to remind me that this was all real.

As I fell deeper into the pits, I started to second-guess it all. The last time he smiled at me. The kiss before he left. The way he'd picked up Zeke and swung him around like he wanted to belong here.

Had I read it wrong? Had I been stupid enough to believe someone like him could actually want someone like me with three kids, stretch marks, messy hair, and all?

The ache curled tight in my chest, familiar and bitter. I'd felt it before. Each loss in my life taught me to build walls higher, to guard my heart more fiercely. Yet, with Hunter, it cut deeper because I'd let him in, believing he wasn't like the other men in my life who tossed me aside the moment they determined I wasn't worth the effort it took to stay.

And now I wasn't sure if that belief made me brave… or just naive.

Chapter Fifty Two

Hunter

I hadn't planned on saying anything. Hell, I'd barely planned on leaving the apartment but I was stuck in my head.
My boots thudded against the hardwood as I dropped them by the door, jacket slung over the back of the chair.

The shadow box Camille had made me sat where it had for weeks, on the dresser in my bedroom. I'd look at it sometimes, just long enough to feel that familiar ache in my chest, then turn away.

I told myself I wasn't ready. That those medals, those ribbons, weren't about me. They were about the men who didn't make it home. But tonight, I stood there longer. The black frame caught the low light, the glass reflecting back my face. Her touch was all over it, the careful way she'd arranged the rows, the way she'd included that worn patch I thought was worthless, the photo of my unit tucked into the corner. She hadn't just made a display. She'd made a reminder, something she'd said I should be proud of, not ashamed.

Her voice echoed in my head: You shouldn't hide it. You should honor it.

But I wasn't ready for that. And after three nights of staring at the ceiling and two skipped texts I couldn't bring myself to answer.

I put my boots back on and ended up at Mike's place. Mike had been in my unit. We've seen the same sand, heard the same blasts, and carried the same ghosts. If there was anyone I could halfway talk to, it was him.

He shoved a beer into my hand the second I walked in. "You look like hell, man."

I snorted, collapsing onto his worn-out couch. "Thanks for the warm welcome."

"I doubt you're here for compliments, Bennett." He dropped into the recliner, studying me like I was a puzzle missing half its pieces. "So. What's eating you? Work? Nightmares? Or..." He paused, a smirk tugging at his mouth. "...woman trouble?"

I glared at him over the rim of the bottle. "Don't start."

"That's a yes," he said, grinning like he'd scored a point.

I scrubbed a hand over my face. "It's... complicated."

"Complicated how?"

I hesitated. Saying it out loud felt like ripping a scab. "She's good. Too good. And I'm... not."

Mike raised a brow. "Translation?"

"You know how it is, little stuff sets me off. Sometimes I pull away, sometimes I get pissed."

Mike leaned forward, resting his elbows on his knees. "Let me get this straight. You've got a woman who actually likes you. Hell, from what you've told me, loves you. And kids who look at you like you hung the damn moon, and you think the right move is to ghost them?"

I stiffened. "I'm protecting them."

He barked a laugh. "Bullshit. You're protecting yourself. Big difference." The words hit harder than I wanted to admit.

I sat back, staring at the beer bottle in my hands. My chest was tight, my throat burning with all the things I couldn't say.

Mike shook his head. "You survived ten years in the Marine Corps, Bennett. Four deployments to the middle of Afghanistan. But you're about to blow up the best thing you've got because you're scared she'll see you bleed. Newsflash: she already knows you bleed. And she's still there."

I didn't answer. Couldn't. Because the truth was, he wasn't wrong, even if I wished he was.

"She's not Kelsey."

Mike's tone was even, but there was weight behind it. "Never liked her for you, by the way. But I saw you with Camille. The night you brought her over. You weren't as rough that night."

"I know she's not like Kelsey," I said, my jaw tightening. "Not even close."

And damn, did I know it.

Cami was warm—bright in a way that didn't fade when things got hard. She showed up for people without needing a reason, without keeping score. Kelsey, my ex-wife... she'd been the opposite. Cold. Calculated. The kind of woman who turned love into leverage. I'd spent years walking on eggshells, trying to keep the peace. And when I came back and needed her to step up for me, she'd quickly forgotten it all.

Mike leaned back, his expression grim as he turned the bottle in his hands, watching the way the light caught the glass. "You know," he said after a long pause, "you're not the only one who tried to run."

I frowned, glancing at him. "What do you mean?"

"Sarah," he said. "When we first started dating, I damn near ruined it. Same crap you're pulling now. My fuse was short, and I thought the only way to keep her safe from me was to push her away."

I raised a brow. "You? Didn't see that coming. You two look solid."

He chuckled, humorless. "Now, yeah. Back then? I ghosted her for a week once, just a couple months in. Told myself I was sparing her the mess. Truth was, I was scared as hell. Scared she'd see me shaking in the middle of the night, scared she'd look at me differently." He shrugged. "Guess what? She already knew."

"Didn't mean it was easy," he went on. "I blew up at her once, snapped at the wrong moment. She almost left. And you know what changed it? I finally admitted I needed help. Not from some VA doc, not from a checklist. From her. From the people I wanted to build a life with." I stared at the bottle, his words hitting harder than I wanted to admit.

Mike's gaze sharpened. "So tell me, man. Do you want Camille and those kids in your life, or do you want to keep hiding until you're sitting alone in this dump with no one left to fight for?"

I swallowed hard, throat tight. The picture of her flashed in my head with her curls spilling over her shoulders, her laugh when Zeke told some ridiculous story, the twins climbing into my lap like I'd always been there. I wanted it badly. But wanting and thinking I deserved it? Two different fights. I shook my head, a bitter laugh. "You make it sound simple."

Mike's eyes narrowed. "It's not simple. But it's not impossible either."

"You don't get it," I muttered, jaw tight. "Sarah didn't have to watch you freeze up every time the world got loud. Never saw you bolt awake, drenched in sweat. The night of that party, I woke her up screaming in my sleep. She looked terrified. I should be the one making her feel safe. Instead, I was the reason she was scared. Camille's got three kids, Mike. She doesn't need another thing to take care of."

Mike leaned forward, elbows on his knees. "So what you're telling me is she already knows? She's already seen it, months ago, and was still there?"

I looked away, heat crawling up my neck. "Not all of it. If she did…" I trailed off, throat thick. "If she did, she'd realize I'm not what she needs."

"Bullshit," Mike shot back. "That woman looks at you with hearts in her eyes. Those kids? They already see you as family. You want to be the guy who teaches them men bail when things get hard?" That hit like a punch to the gut. Exactly what I swore I'd never be. Especially not after what they've all been through.

I clenched the bottle, voice rough. "Better I leave now than before they get too attached."

Mike stared at me like I'd grown another head. "That's not protecting them, Hunter. That's running. And we both know running never fixed a damn thing."

I rubbed my beard, fighting that familiar sting. I wanted to believe him, wanted to let myself think I could be what

Camille and those kids needed. But every bit of me felt it was a lie.

I set the bottle down, pushing up off the couch. "Thanks for the beer," I muttered. "But I should go." Mike started to argue, but Sarah stepped in from the kitchen, towel in hand, eyes sharp, reading the whole room in a heartbeat.

"Giving him the tough-love speech again?" she asked Mike, eyebrows up.

"He needs it," Mike said gruffly.

She crossed the room and handed me a folded card. "And he needs more than pride and beer." Her voice was softer, empathy lacing each word.

I frowned and took the card without thinking. Just a name, a number, and a clinic logo I didn't know.

"She works with veterans," Sarah said. "The real kind, not just numbers on a file. Mike won't say it, but he went to see her. More than once."

"Sarah…" Mike muttered, shifting in his chair, but she shot him a look that shut him up.

I blinked between them. "Mike, of all people, Mr. 'Suck it up, Marine', sitting in a therapist's office?"

Sarah's tone softened, her hand on my arm. "You don't have to carry it alone, Hunter. Pushing Camille away doesn't protect her. It just hurts both of you. If you want to fight for her and those kids, fight for yourself first."

The card felt heavy in my hand. I wanted to shove it in my pocket and forget it existed. I wanted to believe I could grit my way through like always. But the part that saw Camille's tears, Zeke's confused little face, the twins' wide eyes knew Sarah was right. And maybe grit wasn't enough anymore.

She leaned forward. "That's a good place to start."

Sitting there in that living room, I didn't feel picked apart. I felt like maybe someone was willing to help me dig out, not just cover it up.

Chapter Fifty Three

Camille

Life didn't slow down to give me room to feel Hunter's absence. Mornings were the same whirlwind, packing lunches, chasing Zeke to put his shoes on, juggling twin tantrums while trying to get out the door on time. At work, I smiled at patients, filed charts, answered phones, all while my mind replayed our fight like a broken record.

I told myself I was angry. If he wanted to pull away, fine, I'd survived people leaving before. My dad's absence. The day I realized the kids' father was lost to drugs. The heartbreak of realizing the man who came before him wasn't sticking around either. I'd survived all of that, raised three kids, and kept going.

But underneath, the anger melted into dread. Dread that this time I hadn't just been left behind, but that I'd pushed him there. I remembered the look in his eyes before he walked out. Tired. Haunted. Like he was carrying something I couldn't touch. I hated that he wouldn't let me in, but I hated more that maybe he truly believed he wasn't worth letting in.

I kept moving, kept checking things off the list. Because if I stopped, if I let myself breathe, the silence wrapped tighter around me. And at night, I'd catch myself remembering. Hunter leaning over my textbooks, making some dumb joke just to make me laugh. Him pushing the twins in their swings, Zeke squealing from his shoulders at the park. His truck pulled into the lot, the way my chest always lifted when I heard it.

But, there's only so much waiting a person can do.

After another long day of work and class, the kids running circles around me, I sat down at the table, phone in hand. The last message I'd sent him was two days old, still unanswered. Just a simple picture of the twins, hair wild, mouths sticky with peanut butter. Nothing complicated. Nothing demanding. And still, nothing back.

I stared at the blank screen until my chest hurt. Then I did something I hadn't let myself do in weeks. I put the phone down, flipped it face down on the table, and decided I was done waiting. Done refreshing, done hoping, done holding my breath for a man who clearly wasn't holding his for me.

It wasn't anger. It was a kind of exhaustion that settled deep, the kind that made my bones heavy. I'd begged people to stay before, and I couldn't do it again. I needed to choose what was right for the kids and me, to build a life that didn't hinge on someone else deciding if we were enough. So I folded laundry, packed lunches, and finished my reading for class. I tucked the kids in with extra kisses and let myself breathe without reaching for the phone.

I wanted the kids to see it was okay to ask for what we needed, to build resilience, but also to recognize the gentle strength of setting boundaries.

Chapter Fifty Four

Hunter

It took me longer than I'd like to admit to pull myself together. To hear Mike's words, to feel Sarah's hand press that card into mine, and to finally realize I couldn't keep hiding behind silence.

Typed out, 'I'm sorry. I want to talk.'

Deleted it. Tried again: 'I miss you. Let me see you.'

Still sounded weak. Deleted that too.

Instead I kept it simple.

No frills. Just straight.

Me: Can I come by?

Then I waited. And that was the worst part. The minutes stretched, my chest tight. Every time my phone buzzed, I snatched it up, only to see another notification, an email, a weather alert, anything but her.

But Camille didn't reply. Not that hour. Not that night.

I was the one staring at the silence, realizing what it felt like to be on the other side. And, it gutted me. And that's why the next day, I found myself near her apartment. I don't even remember turning down her street. I told myself I was just driving, trying to clear my head, but my hands had other plans, and before I knew it, I was creeping past her building, my heart pounding.

She was standing by the window, hair messy from a long day, holding one of the twins on her hip while Zeke zoomed around behind her with a toy plane. She wasn't looking for me; she didn't even know I was there, but the sight of her, of them, hit me harder than anything had in years.

They were all that I wanted. Everything I told myself I couldn't have. Right then, I knew I could keep running and keep screwing things up, or I could fight. For her. For them. For me.

My hands shook as I pulled the therapist's card from my pocket. The name and number stared back at me, heavier than a rifle in my hands. The voice on the other end was calm, professional. I almost hung up.

My throat locked, my chest screamed don't do it, but I forced the words out. "My name's Hunter. I, uh... I was given your number. I'm a veteran. I..." I swallowed hard. "I want to make an appointment."

To my shock, she said she had an opening that afternoon. No waiting list, which meant no excuses. For a second, I froze. I didn't trust it or myself. Didn't trust the idea that sitting in another office could do more than waste time. But then I glanced back at the window, at the life I wanted and was about to lose, and I turned the truck toward the clinic.

My palms were slick on the wheel, my chest tight with

nerves, but I wasn't running. I was driving straight into the fire. Because maybe, just maybe, it was the only way through.

The clinic was small, tucked between a laundromat and a pharmacy. Nothing fancy. The kind of place you could drive past a hundred times and never notice. I sat in the parking lot for a full ten minutes before I made myself get out. My chest felt tight, my legs heavy. Walking into combat felt easier than opening that glass door.

Inside, the air was too clean, too quiet. The receptionist smiled and asked me to sign in. My hand shook as I scribbled my name. By the time I sat in the therapist's office, I was already coiled tight, arms crossed, jaw locked. ??She was calm, older than the woman at the VA, softer voice, eyes that didn't dart to a clipboard every five seconds. Still, I didn't trust her.

"So, Hunter," she said, not pushing. "Tell me what brought you here today."

I shrugged, staring at the carpet. "I don't know. My buddy's wife gave me your card. Figured I'd… check a box."

Her lips curved, not unkind. "Okay. Then let's start with the box. What would you want it to say when you leave here?"

I didn't answer. My throat was too tight, but she didn't press; she just waited. And maybe that's why, after a long stretch of silence, I muttered, "I can't keep living like this."

Her nod was slow, like she'd been waiting for those words. "Like what?"

The words stuck in my chest, heavy. I wanted to swallow them down.

"Like I'm still there," I forced out. "Even when I'm not."

The admission sat between us, raw and jagged.

Chapter Fifty Five

Camille

The days blurred together, one long stretch of work, classes, and kids. On the outside, nothing had changed. I still woke up early to pack lunches, chased Zeke around with his shoes, and wrangled the twins through breakfast. At the doctor's office, I smiled through check-ins and answered calls, my mind split between tasks and the heaviness that lingered in the background.

I hated myself for missing him. Hated that even when I promised I was done, part of me still hoped. Still wanted the sound of his truck pulling into the lot, the kids shouting his name, the way my chest lifted just knowing he was near. Hunter wasn't supposed to be another chapter in the crappy part of my story. He was supposed to be the happy ending. But I knew it didn't work like that.

And it shows in the way I was unraveling.

Every laugh Zeke shouted across the room, every twin giggle, every little moment we'd once shared with Hunter twisted inside me. The kids asked less about him now, but that almost hurt more. It was like they were already learning how to stop expecting people to stay.

At night, after everyone was finally asleep, I'd sit in the quiet and feel the weight of it. The silence. The loss of something I'd started to believe might finally last. I hated myself for it, but I missed him.

I missed the stupid banter, the way his eyes would take on a new brightness when he looked at the kids, the steady presence that made my chaotic world feel just a little more balanced.

But I was done reaching out. Done sending texts that went unanswered. Done waiting for a knock at the door that never came.

I told myself this was survival. That I'd been here before, that I knew how to stitch myself back together.

Yet whenever I closed my eyes, I saw him sitting on the couch with Zeke talking about spaceships, pushing the twins on the swings, and leaning close to kiss me after he'd cornered me in the kitchen.

And the ache of losing that was worse than I wanted to admit.

Dani recognized the toll it took on me first.

She always did.

We were sitting in our usual booth at the diner, she sipping on iced coffee while I picked at fries I didn't really want. She leaned back, studying me like I was one of her patients.

"You're too quiet, Cam," she said finally.

"I'm tired," I answered, too quickly.

She rolled her eyes. "You've been tired since freshman year of college. This is different. Spill."

I sighed, staring at the fries. "Hunter and I… we're not talking much."

"Not talking much," she repeated flatly. "Or not talking at all?"

I didn't answer, and that was enough.

Her expression softened. "Oh, babe. What happened?"

I told her about the last few weeks—the silence, the distance, all the ways I kept trying to find fault in myself, as if that might explain why things were slipping.

Dani listened quietly, then sighed. "I know you're scared of chasing someone who doesn't want to be caught," she said, her voice soft but steady. "But you can't keep bleeding yourself dry waiting for scraps."

Later that night, almost as if Hunter had heard the chatter in my head, I noticed a missed call and voicemail from Hunter.

His voice had filled the room, rough and uncertain, carrying the weight of something he wasn't used to saying. "Hey, Camille. It's me. I… I've been working on some stuff. Real stuff. I'm sorry for the silence. I don't want to lose you. Or the kids. I know I don't deserve another chance, but I want to try. Please. Just… call me back."

By the end, my throat was tight, eyes stinging. His words lingered in the quiet, hope and hesitation tangled together, pressing against old wounds and stirring something I thought I'd buried. I closed my eyes and let his voice settle over me, pulling me back to the small, ordinary moments when his presence made the chaos feel less sharp.

I wanted to believe him. Part of me leapt at the sound of

his voice, at the word *try*. But another part reminded me of past broken promises, men who swore they wouldn't leave. And every time I ended up alone.

It was for that reason that I hadn't responded to the text he'd sent me the day before.

He didn't get to show up and make it better with one message. Not after disappearing, not after leaving me to pick up the pieces again. I couldn't let another person think they could walk in and out of my life whenever it suited them — knowing I'd always open the door. That's how it had always been before. Second chances that turned into third, fourth, and fifth ones. Apologies that came too late, words that meant nothing once the damage was done.

I couldn't do that again.

So I left his message unread. Not because I didn't care, if anything, because I cared too damn much. Because part of me still wanted to believe him, and I couldn't afford false hope.

Life didn't stop for heartbreak or hope; it just kept moving. And I sat there in the middle of it, torn between the ache of missing him and the fear of letting him close enough to hurt me again, but I couldn't call back because I wasn't sure if I had it in me to be the only one holding us together anymore. The kids needed me, school deadlines didn't wait, and patients at work didn't care if I was distracted. I moved through it all with a smile that didn't quite reach my eyes, saving the storm for the quiet moments after bedtime.

I told myself I should delete the voicemail, that leaving it there was just asking for more hurt. But whenever I picked up the phone, my finger hovered over the trash icon and froze.

Instead, I replayed it. Once, when the kids were napping. Once, when the house was quiet, and I couldn't sleep. Once, when the ache in my chest felt too heavy to carry alone. Each time, the same words pressed deeper: *"I don't want to lose you. Or the kids. I want to try."*

At night, I lie in bed and let myself imagine both paths.

One where I called him back, let him in again, risked it all only to have him walk away. And another where I stayed silent, closed the door, and taught myself once more how to carry the weight alone.

Neither felt safe.

But the one that terrified me most was the first.

I didn't know if I could survive watching him leave again.

Chapter Fifty Six

Hunter

I hadn't been back to upstate New York in almost two years. Not since I'd gotten out of the Corps. Not for birthdays, not for holidays. I didn't even run home after my divorce. I toughed it out, slept on a buddy's couch, let the silence gnaw at me until it dulled. After I got out, I sank into a hectic routine, piecing together a new life. Found a new place, settled into my new job, and meticulously polished every inch of my bike, all while pretending I had it under control.

Each new project was a way to silence the guilt of not visiting, of not picking up the phone to just say 'hi.' I told myself I'd make time, that I'd fly back soon, but months turned into years, and with each passing day, the thought of seeing her filled me with a mix of longing and anxiety. Excuses stacked up until I stopped trying to explain them, to others and to myself. So now, I ran back home, unsure what to do in the days after my call to Cami went unanswered after my third therapy session.

I was already sharing things I'd buried for years. The therapist wasn't like the ones at the VA. When I told her everything, she said, "Thank you for sharing that with me," and began helping me unravel the guilt, anger, and trauma of those experiences. I wasn't cured, not even close, but I wasn't drowning alone anymore. I wanted to get better. Not just to breathe, but to be a man who could stand in Camille's kitchen, lift her kids into his arms, and not feel like he was falling apart.

After my third session, I sat in the truck long after sunset, skipping through songs Camille used to tease me about. I felt lighter. I thought about her laugh, the kids' smiles, the way she looked at me that night before I left. I couldn't lose that. Not because of fear. Yet when I called her to tell her I'd been working on things, apologize for the walls, and let her know I couldn't lose here, my call went unanswered. I probably didn't deserve another shot, but my hands shook in an attempt not to run away, but towards her.

She hasn't called back, though. Probably decided I'd done too much damage at that point. So here I was at my mother's. Pulling into her driveway, duffle bag heavy on my shoulder, I felt small again, like a kid waiting outside the principal's office. The porch light blinked on, and there she was, my mom, framed in the doorway.

Her hands flew to her mouth. "Hunter." Just my name, but it broke something open inside me. She hurried down the steps and pulled me into a hug, fierce enough to steal my breath. The world outside faded, replaced by the memory of sun-drenched afternoons under the old oaks, the air thick with the promise of summer. Her arms, smaller than I remembered but steady, held me in place, and for a moment I was a kid again, safe and unburdened. Her perfume was the same, warm and floral, a scent that felt familiar. The soft texture of her sweater brushed against my cheek, just like when I'd leaned into her as a child, and it anchored me further in a moment I hadn't realized I missed so much.

"You finally made it," she said against my chest, pulling back to look me over. Her eyes swept my face, my beard, the tired lines around my eyes. "God, it's been too long." She shook her head, swatting my arm lightly. "You never make time. Always too busy. Too far. Too… something."

I tried for a grin, weak as hell. "I'm here now."

She studied me a beat longer, her eyes softening. "Yeah. You're here." She kissed my cheek, then motioned me inside.

The house smelled the same, lemon cleaner clinging to the air, fresh bread warmth drifting from the kitchen. Curtains, sun-bleached and fraying, fluttered in the breeze, painting shifting patterns across the floor. On the fridge, a faded photo of me, gap-toothed and grinning, hid among newer snapshots and a scatter of holiday magnets. My mom's love for small, seasonal touches was everywhere: a summer wreath on the door, sunflowers brightening the table. I stood there, duffle bag at my feet, oversized and out of place, a stranger in the place that used to be a sanctuary.

At first, she let me settle in, piling food onto my plate, asking about work, the truck, if California still felt foreign. She laughed at my half-answers, acting as if she didn't notice how I couldn't sit still. But by the second morning, she had me pinned at the kitchen table, coffee steaming between us, her eyes fixed on mine as if she could see every secret I'd tried to bury. My heart thudded hard, matching the weight of her stare. The air felt close, my breath shallow, as if the walls were inching in.

She set a mug of coffee in front of me at the kitchen table, then finally asked, "So. Why now?"

I froze, fingers curling around the mug. She didn't ask gently. She never did. With my mom, you didn't get coddled. You got the truth, straight and sharp.

"I just needed to… get out for a while," I said carefully.

Her brows lifted as she studied me. "Is it about a girl?" Her gaze was sharp, too knowing, pinning me across the table. "You didn't run home after your divorce," she added, letting the words hang between us like a truth neither of us wanted to face. Her eyes searched mine, waiting for the true answer. "So why now? Don't sit there and tell me it's just to see me. I know you, Hunter. You don't fly cross-country without a reason."

Her words cut because they were true. I dropped my gaze to the mug in my hands. "I screwed things up, Ma."

"With that girl?"

I didn't answer, which was all the answer she needed.

Her sigh was sharp. "Then fix it. Don't you dare sit here in my house, hiding, licking your wounds, and pretending that's easier. You chose her, Hunter. You don't get to run when it gets hard. You hear me?"

I nodded, throat tight. "Yeah." I let the silence fill in what I couldn't say. I'd never told her much about Camille or the kids. I kept most things to myself. She didn't know the ways the military had worn me down, or how my body sometimes ached in places I didn't talk about, or how my relationship felt like a secret I was still learning to trust.

I remembered taking Camille out on my bike for the first

time, the way she leaned into me, the way she looked so at peace sitting on the pier, curls blowing wild under the setting sun. Her laugh echoing in the hallway as she joked with Chloe, her voice a melody that chased off my doubts for a moment. Avery's sticky fingers grabbing my hand, anchoring me in the middle of the storm. Those small, ordinary moments became my quiet refuge. It wasn't that I didn't love Camille or want to share her with the world. I just knew some things were safer kept close.

She leaned back, arms folding. The softness from before shifted into steel. "You always did have a bad habit of running when things got too real."

I opened my mouth, but she cut me off. "Don't. Don't tell me it's different this time. You chose her, Hunter. I can see it all over your face. And now you're here because what, she scared you? She made you feel something you weren't ready for?"

Her words landed heavy, right where I didn't want them to.

"I'm not running," I muttered, but it sounded pathetic even to me.

Her eyes narrowed, sharp and knowing. "Don't lie to me. You're not eighteen anymore. You don't get to play boy and man at the same time. You either show up, or you don't. You chose her, Hunter," she pressed, voice softer now but no less firm. "Don't you dare run from someone you already chose. That's not how love works."

The truth of it burned because she was right, and with my mom, you don't ask questions and, you don't argue, you do what she says. And this time, as hard as the truth was, I knew she was right. She may have stood at only four-foot-eleven, but what she lacked in height she more than made up for in pure, loving intimidation. As I sat there, the weight of her words settled into my bones.

After dinner, I fell asleep in my old room, staring at the same ceiling fan that had seen me plot escapes and practice speeches and pray for things I didn't know how to name. My luggage slouched in the corner like a guilty dog. I didn't dream; I just sank.

By the third night, even the quiet was too loud. When Ben texted, *"Beers? Luke's in town too,"* I answered yes without thinking.

The bar hadn't changed since we were idiots with fake IDs. Neon signs buzzed in reddened corners. A snowmobile helmet hung above the dartboard like a trophy. The jukebox cycled through Springsteen, 90s country, and a random salsa track someone always played to mess with the locals.

Ben was already in the booth when I walked in, nursing a beer while enjoying his first moment of solitude in a week. He looked good in the way tired men look good: content, a little rumpled, a wedding band he twisted without noticing. "There he is," he said, standing to pull me into a shoulder-pound hug. "Thought you'd gone witness protection."

Luke slid in a minute later, haircut still sharp enough to measure angles, that watchful ease some of us never lost. He chin-jerked hello and took the outside seat, back to the wall, the way we all did without saying a word. It had been years since we'd all been together; the last time was my brother's wedding, five years back. Ben had a whole family now, a wife and five kids. Luke was still single, still living the bachelor life, still on active duty in the Corps. He left for boot camp just a year after me.

"Look what the cat dragged in," Luke said.

"Nice to see you too," I muttered, but my mouth quirked.

Ben poured me a beer and pushed it across the table. "We heard you're back for a minute. Figured that either means you're avoiding the law or a woman. Your face says woman."

Luke snorted. "If it were the law, he'd look happier." He turned to me. "You look like shit. Girl trouble?"

We traded the low-grade insults that meant I love you in our family. The pitcher sweated. The jukebox switched to an old country song I didn't know.

Ben's voice shifted, serious now. "You gonna tell us why you're really here? I know you. I've never seen you like this. You've been half alive for years, Hunter. Divorce, deployments, the military grinding you down. And now you're sitting here looking like someone ripped your heart out. That tells me you found something worth bleeding for."

His words echoed the fear that chased me: what if I'm not enough? I laid it out for them. Cami's smile that unhooked something in me, Zeke's side-eye and quiet courage, two little girls who thought my back was a jungle gym, the way my chest felt like it finally had instructions.

Then the fight. It started small, but underneath, I was wrestling with the fear of losing myself. I picked at the softest spots because I was scared of being asked to be the man I said I wanted to be. The worry that I'd fail them, that I'd come up short, wouldn't let go. Panic rippled through me, whispering that the easiest way to avoid more pain was to leave. So I ran, caught a plane, hoping space would quiet the ache sitting heavy inside me.

"So," Luke said, eyebrows up. "The great Hunter Bennett got himself tangled up in something real, huh? Never pictured you as the family type."

Ben listened with his whole face, the way dads do when they've learned how to shut up and actually hear. "You love her," he said. After slapping Luke in the back of the head like the older cousin he was.

I took a long drink. "Yeah."

Luke cocked his head. "And she loves you?"

Everything in me flashed to the way she'd looked at me when I held the twins, how her shoulders dropped when I walked through the door with a bag of groceries, the night she fell asleep on my chest, and I stayed awake counting her breaths. "Yeah," I said again, voice low.

"Then what the hell are you doing here?" Luke asked, not unkindly, just direct. "We both know fear's loud. Doesn't make it smart. And you running cross-country to 'get space'... .that's not tactical, man. That's just retreat."

Ben leaned in, elbows on the table. "I had five kids in eight years. I never felt ready. Still don't sometimes. But the trick is boring: you keep showing up. You say 'I screwed up' faster. You learn your tells, and you fix what you can fix. You don't disappear when you're scared."

I picked at the water ring my glass had left on the wood. "I didn't even come home after the divorce," I said, surprised by my own confession. "And I came now. I don't know what that says, but it doesn't feel good."

"It says you're not done running yet," Luke said. "But you could be. That part's a choice."

Silence shimmied in, not awkward, just present. On the

TV, a hockey game halfheartedly fought itself into overtime. A woman at the bar laughed too loudly at something no one else heard.

Ben cracked a smile. "Also, we gotta say this for the record: three kids? You sure you're not trying to get your ass kicked on purpose?"

I laughed, a genuine laugh. "You saying I can't hack it?"

"I'm saying you can," he answered. "But only if you want to."

Luke knocked his knuckles against mine, a soft, precise tap. "And if you don't go back and fix it, I'm flying out there, finding Cami, and telling her she can do better."

I shot him a look sharp enough to cut drywall. Ben barked a laugh. The tension bled out of my shoulders by degrees.

We talked until the jukebox gave up and the bartender stacked chairs on tables with that gentle finality of small towns closing for the night. On the walk to the parking lot, our breath made ghosts in the air. Gravel crunched. Somewhere two streets over, a dog barked once and decided against it.

"You gonna call her?" Ben asked, hands jammed into the pockets of his Carhartt.

I looked up at a sky punched full of cold stars. "Tomorrow," I said. "I'll book a flight in the morning."

Luke clapped my shoulder. "Good. And Hunt?"

"Yeah?"

"When you go back, don't show up with speeches. Show up with groceries and a plan."

"Bossy," I said.

"Effective," he corrected.

Back at the house, the porch light was still on, because my

mother never stopped believing I'd need it. I stood there for a long minute, the night pressing its chilled palm to my face. Inside, the clock in the hallway ticked steadily.

Back in my childhood room, I sat on the bed, pulled out my phone, and opened a browser.

One-way ticket back to California. The first flight I could get that wouldn't send Mom into a full interrogation about why I was leaving at three a.m.

I booked it. Waiting for the confirmation ding to cast an echo in the room.

From the hallway, I heard the soft creak of the floorboard that always betrayed anyone moving past the linen closet. Mom's small shadow paused in my doorway. "Booking a flight?" she asked, voice threaded with I-already-know.

"Yeah," I said.

"Good," she answered, warm and fierce. "Now get some sleep. Tomorrow you'll practice what you're going to say. And then you say less of it and do more."

"Yes, ma'am."

She smiled, the kind of smile that made men twice my size confess things. "There's my boy."

She padded away. I lay back on the bed and stared at the fan blades until they blurred.

I thought of the future I wanted, the one I'd been too scared to claim.

No more running.

Chapter Fifty Seven

Hunter

Three days after I landed, I was boarding another plane. But this time, I wasn't running. I was going home to deal with the mess I'd made.

When I walked through that door, I would do so with an open heart and a plan to show Camille and the kids that I was all in. Ready to face the hard parts, to show up, to love deeper. Determined to be there, not just in body but in spirit, building new memories that might one day heal the old ones.

Therapy helped me peel back the guilt, but it didn't erase the truth that I'd left her standing in that living room, and then I'd buried her in weeks of silence. If I wanted a shot at fixing it, a text wasn't going to cut it.

So I showed up.

She was just stepping out of the clinic, hair pulled back, bag slung over her shoulder, her whole body carrying the weight of exhaustion. My chest squeezed at the sight of her.

"Camille," I called softly.

She froze, eyes widening when she saw me by the truck.

The guarded look in her face told me I was the last person she expected, or wanted, to see here.

"I need to talk to you," I said, stepping closer.

Her lips pressed into a thin line. "I can't. I've got to pick up the kids."

"I already asked your mom," I said quickly. "She's got them for the evening."

Her brow furrowed, surprise flickering across her face. "You… you talked to my mom?"

I nodded, heart pounding. "I told her I screwed up and that I wanted to fix it. She said she'd keep them for as long as we needed."

For a moment, she just stood there, staring at me, the wall between us almost visible. Something flickered in her eyes, a mixture of hesitation, hope, and the hurt I had inflicted not so long ago. Doubt tugged at the edges of her expression, betraying the struggle within her. ??I shoved my hands into my pockets, fighting the urge to reach for her. "Please, Camille. Just let me take you somewhere. Just talk to me. If, after tonight, you still don't want this, I'll back off. But give me the chance to say the things I should've said weeks ago."

Her silence stretched, leaving my pulse drumming in my ears.

But I didn't move.

This time, I just waited.

Chapter Fifty Eight

Camille

For a moment, I thought I had misheard him. Did he say he'd actually gone to my mom and arranged for her to take the kids? It was such a Hunter thing to do. He was reckless, bold, and frustratingly thoughtful all at once.

The hollowness that lingered inside me was knotted with every quiet night between us. The unanswered texts. The way he'd stormed out and left me standing in the living room with three pairs of little eyes watching me break. Their confusion and worry mirrored what I felt inside, telling me, without words, that they sensed something was wrong. The twins continued their babbling of "Hunty," while Zeke grew quieter, his questions held tightly behind a brave face. It was like sharing my heartbreak each day, their innocent hopefulness wrapping around my own doubts, pulling them into our uncertainty.

The hurt was still raw, sharp enough to make me hold my ground as I crossed my arms, allowing my bag to slip down my shoulder. "You think one gesture makes up for weeks of nothing?"

His jaw worked, eyes locked on me, pleading. "No. I think showing up is the first step to proving I'm not running anymore." I hated how much those words cracked me open.

Silence stretched between us, heavy and alive. Cars passed on the street, the hum of life moving on, while we stood stuck in our own mess. Part of me wanted to say yes. To slide into the passenger seat and finally hear the explanation I'd been craving. The other part wanted to walk away, to protect myself before hope sank its claws in again. So I stood there, torn in two, staring at him, hoping the answer might write itself across his face.

And he didn't push.

He just waited.

The silence stretched so long I could hear my own heartbeat. He just stood there, steady, not pushing, not pleading… just waiting. And maybe that was what undid me. Because the Hunter who stormed out of my apartment, who shut me out with silence, would've already walked away. But the one in front of me now was still here, even when I hadn't given him anything back.

I let out a breath I didn't realize I'd been holding. "If I get in that truck, Hunter, this isn't just a ride. This isn't just a talk. You don't get to disappear on me again."

His eyes flickered, somewhere between pain and relief tangled together. "I know."

I studied him for another beat, my arms still crossed, bag strap digging into my shoulder. My gut twisted with every reason not to go: fear, pride, exhaustion. But underneath all that, the smallest spark of hope still flickered.

And against my better judgment, I leaned into it.

Slowly, I walked past him, opened the passenger door, and slid into the truck. The truck smelled like him, familiar and dangerous all at once.

He exhaled shakily, climbing in beside me. "Thank you," he said quietly, hands gripping the wheel like it was the only thing holding him there.

I wasn't ready to forgive, but I was ready to listen.

The hum of the truck filled the silence as we pulled away from the clinic parking lot. I stared out the window, arms wrapped around myself, fighting the urge to break the quiet first.

He gripped the wheel tighter than necessary, knuckles pale. Finally, he cleared his throat.

"I've been going to therapy," he said, voice low. "Two times a week."

I blinked, caught off guard. Of all the things I'd expected, that wasn't on the list.

"Why are you telling me that?" My voice was sharper than I intended.

"Because you deserve to know. I should've told you weeks ago instead of shutting you out. I thought I was protecting you and the kids from... me. From the parts I can't control."

I turned toward him, my heart pounding. "Do you really think silence protects anyone? Do you know how much it hurts to wonder if I did something wrong? To watch my kids wait for you?"

His face tightened, guilt flickering across his features. "I know. And I'm sorry. I was scared, Camille. Scared you'd see the nightmares, the panic, the way it still feels like I'm over there sometimes, and decide I wasn't worth the risk."

Beneath the frustration and hurt, I could hear the fear. The same fear that whispered in my own head: *too much, too broken, too complicated.*

We drove a few more blocks in silence, my eyes stinging. ??Finally, I whispered, "I never needed you to be some perfect version of yourself, Hunter. I just needed you to talk to me."

He glanced at me then, blue eyes raw, unguarded. "I'm trying. I don't want to lose you. I don't want to lose them. But I can't promise I won't struggle…"

A shaky laugh slipped out, tangled with relief and something close to grief. "You think I don't struggle? I've been raising three kids on my own, carrying more than I ever thought I could." My fingers drummed against the door handle, restless, the rhythm matching the mess inside me. ??Outside, headlights swept across the dashboard, shadows and light flickering over our faces. I watched them blur together, the way my feelings did.

"Struggle doesn't scare me. Lies do. Silence does." I glanced at Hunter, his eyes softening as he listened.

For a flicker of a second, his façade cracked, revealing a vulnerability that mirrored my own pain and loss. His breath was coming out unevenly, as if my words had hit him harder than expected. Seeing him react to my confession, his quiet struggle visible, I felt a flicker of connection. And for a moment, I let myself lean into that.

"Every twist, every hard day, it's taught me more than I ever wanted to know. But I'm still here. Still hoping." The rest I kept to myself, letting the quiet fill with everything I wasn't ready to say.

There was a shift between us. It was not fixed, not finished, but open. He nodded, gripping the wheel tighter. "Then let me prove I can do better. One day at a time."

The truck slowed as he pulled into a diner off the highway. A little place with neon lights buzzing in the window and cars lined up outside.

I arched my brow. "Here?"

He cut the engine, glancing at me like he was testing the waters. "I figured since food makes you happy… it might help my case."

I almost smiled despite myself. "Food fixes everything, huh?"

"Works with Zeke," he said, and there was that ghost of his old grin, the one that used to melt me before I remembered why I'd built walls in the first place.

For a moment, I hesitated. The smart move was to tell him to take me home, that this wasn't enough to erase the weeks of silence. But the truth was, I was starving: for food, yes, but also for this. For him trying. For something normal again.

So I followed him inside.

The diner smelled like greasy food and coffee. A waitress with tired eyes and a kind smile led us to a booth in the back. I slid into one side, bag at my side, while Hunter sat across from me, fidgeting with the menu.

We ordered quickly, and for a while, the silence was comfortable. Familiar in a way it hadn't been in weeks. When the food came, he pushed the ketchup toward me first. "See? Already doing better."

I rolled my eyes, but the corner of my mouth lifted. "Don't think ketchup earns you forgiveness."

"Noted." He dunked a fry into my ketchup, a smirk tugging at his lips. "Guess I'll have to try harder." And just like that, the tension loosened a notch.

I studied him as he ate, the way his shoulders still held tension, though not as tightly, and the way his eyes met mine. He wasn't fixed, not even close. But he was here. And maybe, for tonight, that was enough.

"Why do you always eat like it's your last meal?" I teased, raising a brow.

He grinned around a mouthful of fries. "Military habit. You gotta eat fast before you're out of time."

I laughed softly, the sound surprising me. It had been too long since I'd laughed around him without it catching on the sharp edge of hurt.

The laughter faded, though, replaced by the question I'd been carrying for weeks. "Why now, Hunter? Why come back after all…that?"

He set his burger down, wiped his hands on a napkin, and for once didn't look away. "Because I finally stopped lying to myself. I told myself I was protecting you, but really? I was protecting myself. From you seeing the worst of me. From you deciding I wasn't worth the fight."

I held his gaze, my chest tight. "You think silence made me feel like you were worth the fight?"

His eyes softened, regret spilling out of them. "No. But it made me realize how fast I was losing you. And I don't want to lose you. Or your kids. Therapy's helping, but… You help too. You make me want to be better. When I'm with you nond the kids, I feel like I'm actually living." I wanted to believe him. I wanted to believe this wasn't another chapter of abandonment.

I leaned back against the booth, biting my lip. "You can't disappear again, Hunter. I can survive a lot, but I won't survive letting my kids love you only to watch you leave."

He nodded slowly, the weight of my words sinking in. "I won't promise I'll never struggle. But I'll promise you won't go through it blind again. No more shutting you out."

We sat there in the warm hum of the diner, the clatter of plates and chatter of strangers filling the silence we couldn't. The ache in my chest wasn't gone, but it eased. And against my better judgment, I let myself hope again.

Chapter Fifty Nine

Camille

The diner lights faded into the distance as Hunter's truck rolled back toward town. I sat in the passenger seat, arms folded tight across my chest, still unsure if I'd made the right choice.

When he pulled into his complex, I hesitated. "Hunter…"

He cut the engine, turning toward me. "No pressure. If you want me to drive you home right now, I will. I just—" His voice broke a little. "I want you to see I'm not running this time."

Something in his tone soothed the parts of me threatening to fold.

I nodded slowly, unbuckled my seat belt, and followed him upstairs.

His apartment was still tidy, too tidy, like no one lived there. The couch cushions were square, the coffee table clear except for a few magazines and the remote. It didn't feel cozy or lived-in the way my cluttered, toy-filled apartment did.

Sinking into the edge of the couch, I fired off a quick check-in with my mom; her reply was almost a welcome distraction.

Mom: Kids are perfect. Zeke said he's
"in charge" until you get home.
Don't worry, I only let him make
minor executive decisions.

> **Me:** You're spoiling them. I'll be
> home soon.

Mom: Take your time, Camille. Hear
him out. And maybe remind him
my baby girl doesn't play around.
> **Me:** You're enjoying this too much.

Mom: Always. Now stop texting and
go figure out if this man is worth
my grandbabies' time.

I slipped the phone back into my bag, exhaling slowly. Leave it to her to cut right through me with a mix of love and sass. Hunter came out of the kitchen then, two glasses of water in his hands. He set one in front of me and sat across from me, elbows on his knees. "I know you don't trust me yet," he said quietly. "I don't blame you. But I'm here. And I'm not leaving until you've heard everything I should've said before."

I stared at the water glass, my reflection rippling on its surface. My guard was still up, my heart still sore. I let myself lean back against the couch and hear him out.

Chapter Sixty

Hunter

I set a glass of water down and took the next one across from her. My pulse was hammering as she sat back, arms crossed, eyes locked on me. They looked tough and wounded at the same time. Making me want to look away, but I held her gaze.

I'd rehearsed this a hundred times in my head. In the truck. In therapy. Even lying awake at night, staring at the ceiling, imagining how she'd look when I finally said the words. But standing here in front of her, all that I'd practiced scattered. So I started simple. "I was scared." Her brow lifted slightly, skeptical, but she didn't speak. So I pushed forward.

"I know, Beautiful… And I'm… I'm sorry."

I dragged a hand through my hair. "The nightmares, the triggers, the PTSD… it all makes me feel like I'm failing. Most days, I still feel stuck over there. Firecrackers, slammed doors, anything loud puts me right back in the middle of Afghanistan. I hate it. Hate the idea of our kids seeing me like that. And that is exactly what started happening. I started slipping." I said our kids without thinking. Her eyes softened, arms still crossed, but I could tell it landed. They felt like mine, even if not by blood.

"I'm serious about going back to therapy," I said. The words felt weird, but it was the truth. "Not the mandated stuff. Real therapy. Five sessions in. I'm not fixed, not even close. But I'm not trying to figure it out on my own. When I get triggered, like with sudden loud noises, I've started grounding myself. It's not automatic, not yet. But now I stop, look around, and it pulls me back. Small thing, but it means I'm working on it."

Camille's eyes flickered as I talked, but I couldn't read if it was relief or something else. She looked at me for a long moment, weighing every word, trying to decide if she could trust what she saw in my eyes. I caught a glimmer of hope in her face, a sign maybe I was finally getting through.

I swallowed hard, voice rough. "But sitting in that silence, knowing I'd lost you anyway? That was worse than any nightmare. I don't want to run anymore, Camille. Not from you. Not from them. Not from myself."

For once, I dropped the act. Let her see the fear, the shame, even a little hope. I just hoped it was enough.

The silence dragged out, my mind flashing back to therapy whether I wanted it to or not.

I hated therapy at first. Sitting in that quiet room, arms crossed, waiting for someone to poke at my head. The Marines taught me to lock it down. No weakness, no softness, no tears. My old man hammered that in even earlier. But therapy forced me to quit hiding behind silence.

In the first session, I barely said a word. Second, I let slip about the nightmares that left me waking up soaked in sweat, fists balled, sure I was back in Afghanistan. She didn't flinch or scribble notes like I was a case file. Just said, "That must be exhausting." And it was. More than combat, more than deployments. Carrying it every day, pretending it wasn't there, eating me alive.

By the third session, I admitted the truth I'd been swallowing for months: that I pulled away from Camille because I didn't think I deserved her. Every time the kids laughed or reached for me, it twisted something inside me, because I wanted it too much. I wanted them too much. The therapist nodded and said, "Wanting something doesn't make you broken. It makes you human." I didn't know what to do with that.

Now, sitting across from Camille, I realized this was the true test. Not therapy, not the worksheets or breathing tricks. But this, being honest, letting her see what I'd buried, fighting the urge to bolt when things got raw, that was the hard work. I wasn't sure I was strong enough, but I knew one thing: I wasn't going back to silence.

So I sat there, heart pounding, waiting for her to decide if I was worth it. Therapy isn't a quick fix. No magic words, no secret to erase the nightmares. But I'd been picking up tools, stuff I never thought I'd use. Grounding, for starters.

The therapist showed me how to pull myself back when my head started to spin. "Name five things you can see. Four things you can touch. Three you can hear. Two you can smell. One you can taste." At first, it sounded like kid stuff. But when fireworks went off down the block, and my chest clenched, I forced myself to try it. Truck. Streetlight. My boots. The scar on my hand. The moon. One by one, it brought me back to now, not stuck in the past.

Breathing too. Not the shallow kind I used to bark at recruits, but deep, steady breaths that actually unclenched my chest. It felt weak, like admitting I needed something so basic to survive. But it worked. Sometimes it was the only thing between me and snapping at someone who didn't deserve it.

And the guilt. I finally said it out loud. Told the therapist what I hadn't told anyone: I came home; others didn't. Some nights, I replayed orders I gave, wondering if I could've chosen differently, if someone's kid would have a dad now. She didn't say it wasn't my fault. Didn't pat my hand. Just told me, "You're carrying weight no one was meant to carry alone."

That broke me open. I'd carried it alone for years by hiding it under work, jokes, walls nobody could see through. Truth is, it made me short-tempered. The kind of man I swore I wouldn't be. I snapped at coworkers, ground my teeth when I should've stayed calm. Burying it was easier than admitting the cracks.

Therapy's teaching me to see it before I blow up. To say, I need five minutes. To walk out and breathe instead of losing it. It's not easy. Not perfect. But it's something.

Sitting across from Camille, I realized all that work I'd put in meant nothing if I didn't start here. She's the reason I want to fight for better. Not just to shut down the nightmares or guilt, but to stand in front of her and say, I'm trying. I'll keep trying. Because she and those kids deserve the best of me, not the shell I've been hiding in.

Chapter Sixty One

Camille

For a long moment, I couldn't speak.

His words filled the room, raw and jagged, and I just sat there staring at him. The man who had stormed out weeks ago, who had left me waiting in silence, was gone. In his place sat someone stripped bare, someone admitting fear, guilt, weakness. Someone I hadn't been sure existed beneath all his walls.

Part of me wanted to fold my arms tighter, to remind myself how many promises I'd heard before. My dad swore he'd be around, but then he vanished, again and again. The kids' father didn't necessarily walk out the door himself, but he did nothing to keep us there.

But then there was Hunter. Sitting in front of me now, his hands shaking just enough for me to notice, his voice low and uneven as he talked about nightmares and guilt he carried from a world I couldn't even imagine.

He wasn't hiding.

And for me, that mattered more than any perfect words ever could.

I thought about the tools he mentioned. They weren't just words; they were proof he was trying. Proof he was doing the work not just for himself, but for me, for my kids, for the little world we'd started to build together. And I couldn't ignore my own need for healing, the fears that kept me up at night. I had spent so long holding it together alone, afraid that if I let anyone in, I might lose control. My past, filled with broken promises and abandonment, was a shadow that lingered, whispering doubts about love and trust. I realized I needed to work on my own fears, find my own strength to believe in us again.

My throat tightened, tears stinging my eyes before I could blink them away. "Do you know what it means for me to hear you say that?" I whispered. "That you're actually trying? That you didn't just… give up?"

His eyes flicked up, blue and unguarded. "I want to be better. For you. For them. For me, too, I guess. But mostly for the life I don't want to lose."

The dam inside me cracked, just a little. Enough to let me breathe again. Enough to let a sliver of hope slide back in. I wiped at my eyes quickly, not wanting him to mistake tears for forgiveness. "I'm hurt. I still don't trust that you won't run again. But… I hear you, Hunter. And I can see you're not just saying all the right things. You're… showing me."

He nodded slowly, almost as if he'd been bracing for worse. I decided to let my guard slip, just enough to imagine how it might feel to trust him again.

The air between us was thick as his eyes searched mine, raw and unguarded, as if he was standing on the edge of a cliff waiting to see if I'd shove him off or pull him back. I could still feel the sting of the silence he'd left me with, the hollow ache of weeks of doubt, but I could also feel the shift in him. The truth in his voice. The pieces he'd finally let me see.

My chest rose and fell, unsteady. "You don't get to run again," I whispered, voice shaking. "If I let you back in, Hunter… this is it. No more leaving me standing alone in the dark."

He leaned forward, his voice just as rough. "I know, Camille. I'm not going anywhere ever again. I promise."

The space between us collapsed in a heartbeat. One second, I was still trying to hold myself back; the next, his hand was on my jaw, my fingers splayed out on his chest, and we were crashing into each other, like the fight and the fear had all boiled over into this one moment. Weeks of hurt, longing, and fear spilled out between us until I couldn't tell where one ended and the other began.

When we finally pulled apart, gasping, my forehead rested against his.

I closed my eyes, heart pounding. "You scare me, Hunter. Not because of your past… but because I think you might be the first man I actually believe will stay."

His thumb brushed my cheek, tender where the kiss had been rough. "Then let me prove I can be the man you deserve." The thought of letting him do just that was terrifying. But mainly because I knew he could if he truly wanted to.

The kiss left me breathless, my heart racing as if I'd just run a mile. His hands stayed on my face, gentle now, and for a moment I just let myself rest against him.

The raw intensity ebbed as he pulled back just enough to

study me, his thumb brushing away the tear I hadn't realized had slipped free.

Neither of us spoke. Words felt too fragile, too sharp, after everything. But his eyes told me more than any apology or promise could; that he was here, really here, not halfway gone anymore.

My guard was still there, my doubts still whispering. But in that moment, his arms were the safest place I'd been in weeks.

He kissed the top of my head, softer this time. "I don't deserve you," he murmured against my hair.

But he was wrong; perfection was never what I needed. I just needed something genuine. The quiet in the middle of the mess. It was trust, built slowly. It was the comfort of being seen and chosen, flaws and all. It was learning to forgive the past, letting hope take root where fear had once lived.

His hands framed my face, reverent this time, as if he was learning me all over again. The tension that had lived between us for weeks melted away. Our breaths mingled in the space between us. In that intimate moment, a faint trace of cypress from his shirt lingered in the air, pulling me deeper into the warmth between us. No words, just the soft rhythm of two people finally letting their guards fall.

His thumb traced the corner of my mouth, a gentle touch that said more than an apology ever could. I fell into it, into him, the weight of everything we'd been carrying finally easing.

He brushed a kiss across my jaw, down to the hollow of my throat, every movement careful, as if he was memorizing what it meant to be allowed this close again. I became acutely aware of my racing pulse that seemed to echo the tremor in his breath. The unspoken promise in the way his hands moved was deliberate, full of quiet awe. He pressed slow, lingering kisses down my chest, lips, and tongue mapping every inch, leaving a trail of fire in their wake before he settled between my thighs. The room felt charged, the quiet broken only by the quick, uneven cadence of our breathing. Every brush of his mouth, every warm exhale against my skin, made the air feel thick and electric, anticipation building until it almost ached. My body was hyper aware of everything: the slick heat where his hand slid against my body, the way our eyes met for a long heartbeat before he moved closer. Time seemed to stretch, each second heavy with want.

"Hunter," I whispered, my voice trembling with wanting, not uncertainty. It was permission, a plea for more. He looked up, and in that charged silence, everything else faded. All I could feel was the heat of his mouth, the hunger in his eyes, and the tension winding tight inside me, waiting to snap.

The feel of him at my core left a fire low and wild, need tightening in my belly. The heat of his mouth, the rough scrape of his beard teasing my most sensitive skin, sent shudders racing through me; my hips lifted, desperate for every stroke of his tongue.

The pleasure built, sharp and hot, until I had to bury my face in the blanket, embarrassed by the desperate sounds slipping out. Hunter gently pulled the blanket away as he tilted up my chin, grounding me. When our eyes met, I felt completely exposed, raw, and open.

"I want to see you," he murmured, voice thick and rough with desire, eyes dark and hungry as they roamed over me.

Before I knew it, I was on him, straddling his hips, my thighs bracketing his. There was only the warmth of his skin beneath my hands, the hard thud of his heart under my palm, the scent of him that was unmistakably his. The room was thick with heat and history; the old arguments, the silence, the distance all faded until only this moment remained.

Night air curled around us, cool against my overheated skin, making every touch feel sharper, every breath more urgent. In that moment, I realized how precious this was. All that existed was us, bodies pressed close, hearts pounding in sync, nothing held back.

As I rocked above him, arching to meet the rhythm we found together, his hands explored everywhere. His fingertips running down my spine, strong palms gripping my hips, pulling me closer with each thrust. His breath was hot against my skin, his voice rough with need, leaving every sound made in the air between us vibrating with tension.

"Damn, Beautiful. I love looking at you like this." His grip on my hips tightened, holding me firmly as we moved together, eyes locked, the world narrowing to the ache building between us.

He looked at me as if I hung the stars. Like I was the most beautiful thing in his world, and in that moment, I felt just that.

Everything built to a breaking point, and I came undone around him, our bodies moving together until there was nothing left but the sound of our breathing. I collapsed onto his chest, trying to find my breath, my body still trembling from release.

Later, when the room went still again, we stayed tangled together in the quiet. His arm draped over me, his breath tickling my neck. I traced idle patterns against his skin, taking in the feel of him.

He pressed a sleepy kiss to my shoulder, murmuring in a way I couldn't quite make out as I smiled into the darkness. The weight I'd been carrying didn't vanish, but it shifted, just enough for me to breathe again.

That night, I drifted to sleep with hope curled against my chest instead of fear. Still, as I faded, a question lingered, quiet and persistent. Could I risk it again? Could I allow myself to dream of a future where Hunter's promises became part of our life, building something lasting, something the kids could believe in, too?

A small image formed in my mind, a simple yet powerful wish: Saturday mornings filled with pancakes and laughter around the kitchen table, Hunter helping Zeke with his soccer practice, the girls clamoring for bedtime stories from both of us.

Could that dream become our reality, woven into the fabric of our lives, piece by fragile piece?

Chapter Sixty Two

Hunter

Traffic crawled, headlights blurring into the dusk as I made my way back to that small apartment that had become my home, with Camille and the kids, after another therapy session.

Months had slipped by. I could still feel the first click of the timer, the therapist's rooted gaze, the way her questions pressed against the places I wanted to keep hidden. Three sessions became six, then ten. Each time I walked through that door, it felt a little less like penance and a little more like searching for something I'd lost. Some days, I still bristled, arms crossed, words locked tight behind my teeth. But each session left its mark, softening the edges, letting a little more light in.

I started to notice the triggers before they swallowed me whole. I learned to breathe through the urge to snap. I learned to anchor myself in the present, instead of letting the past pull me under.

The nightmares still came, and the guilt still weighed on me, but it didn't crush me. And for the first time in a long time, I started to believe maybe I wasn't broken beyond repair.

With Camille and the kids, everything felt different when I was there. Really there. Not halfway, not slipping out the door at the first sign of my own shadows. I could sit cross-legged on the floor, helping Zeke stack Lego bricks, my mind staying here instead of drifting back to sand and gunfire. I could lift the twins when they squealed for me, just feeling their small arms around my neck, letting myself love them without questioning if I deserved it.

The therapist taught me grounding: those lists of sights, sounds, touches, smells. And at first, I thought it was a joke. But the night Zeke knocked over a glass that shattered against the floor, a sharp jolt ran through me: heartbeat thundering, skin prickling, chest tight. I caught myself counting—couch, window, Zeke's little hands, Camille's voice, the smell of dinner—and slowly, I came back. I didn't snap, didn't scare him. And later, when I knelt beside him to help clean up, I apologized, showing him that even grown-ups have hard days, and it was never his fault. That mattered.

In another session, I finally admitted what I'd carried for years: the guilt from my second deployment. Decisions I made in Afghanistan, although it wasn't my fault or my order, I could still recite the names of men who never made it home. I'd told myself their blood was on my hands, and I'd been punishing myself for it without any intention of pardoning myself.

The therapist didn't argue or try to take it away. She just asked, "What would you tell a fellow Marine carrying the same weight?" I told her I'd say: he did the best he could with what he had; he wasn't alone; he was still here, and that mattered. Then she asked why I couldn't give myself the same grace. That question echoed through every session.

I started tracking my stress the way I used to track supplies. I noticed the tightness in my jaw, the way my shoulders locked, the sharpness in my voice. Instead of swallowing it down until it boiled over, I learned to step away. A walk around the block before seeing Camille, or telling her I needed a few minutes to cool off, these became new rituals. It wasn't perfect. Some days, the old anger coiled inside me, ready to strike.

The biggest shift? I started to believe I could deserve happiness. Not because I'd "earned" it through pain, or because I was flawless now. But because I was showing up, even when it was hard. With Camille. With the kids. With myself. And slowly, that consistency started to stitch something new inside me.

When I tucked Zeke in at night, or felt the twins curl against me on the couch, or when Camille leaned into me after a long day, I didn't feel like an imposter. I felt like I belonged. For the first time since leaving the Corps, I could look in the mirror and see more than the broken pieces. I saw a man building a life he wanted to stay in.

Camille kept grinding. Work, school, motherhood, always juggling too much. I started stepping in where I could. Picking up groceries before she asked. Taking the kids to the park so she could study in peace. Sitting with her at the table late at night, quizzing her with flashcards until she leaned into me, half-asleep.

One night, after a long day, she slumped at the kitchen table, laptop open, eyes heavy. "I can't do this paper." I kissed her temple and slid a plate of food in front of her. "You can.

You've been doing it every day. Eat, then write. I'll keep the kids busy." Her tired smile said more than words. She noticed. It mattered. I didn't try to win her over with grand gestures. I leaned into the small things: a note in her bag before work, flowers on the counter just because, making her laugh when the day felt too heavy. It wasn't about one big moment. It was about showing up, again and again, in a hundred quiet ways.

For months, I'd lived waiting for the other shoe to drop, for her to wake up one day and realize she didn't need a man with scars and baggage. But therapy, and time, and showing up shifted something. The kids didn't flinch when I raised my voice to call them for dinner. They didn't tiptoe like they were waiting for me to leave. They ran into my arms without hesitation.

Camille leaned on me now, in small ways and big ones, trusting I'd help carry the weight. I found strength leaning on her, too. She reminded me that healing isn't something you do alone. With her, I felt braver facing my past, more hopeful about the future we were building. We found a balance, each of us reaching out when the other stumbled, building something steady, something genuine.

Chapter Sixty Three

Camille

I couldn't stop smiling as I listened to the kids race to the door, their voices overlapping in excited greetings when Hunter stepped inside. The familiar sound of their laughter mixed with his low chuckle filled the apartment, wrapping around me like sunlight.

I stood at the stove, stirring the pan of his favorite tacos, when I felt him come up behind me—his arms sliding around my waist, his warmth pressing against my back. He kissed my cheek, the kind of touch that still made my heart flutter no matter how ordinary the moment seemed.

I never expected to find myself here, in a place where my heart didn't feel like it was always about to combust. For so long, love felt like a trap, a promise people made, then left behind when my life got too heavy. I told myself I didn't need it. That I could raise my kids, build a life, and keep my walls high enough that no one could reach me, no one could hurt me again.

But Hunter proved me wrong.

He came into my life steadfast and patient. Never demanding, never rushing. Somehow, without even noticing, I started to let him in. Piece by piece. Moment by moment.

It wasn't easy. The hardest part wasn't loving him, it was believing I could be loved back. I carried so much hurt, so many old wounds, that I pushed people away before they could leave me. Like the night he called, wanting to talk, and I rushed him off the phone because I'd been crying over bills and broken promises. My instinct was always to retreat, to hide. But Hunter didn't let my walls scare him. He didn't chase or demand. He just kept showing up, steady, until I started to believe I was safe.

He saved me, not with grand gestures or movie moments, but in the quiet, ordinary ways that matter most. He saved me by getting down on the floor with Zeke, teaching him how to trust again. By letting the twins climb all over him, laughing as they turned his push-ups into a game. By looking at me in a way that made me believe I was still worth loving. By being there on days when I felt the stress swallow me whole, offering words of reassurance.

With him, I learned to be more than the mom who just kept things running. I became a better mother, but also a lighter one. A more joyful one. I laughed louder. Played longer. Let myself sink into the little things, bedtime stories, Lego castles, as if each moment was something to hold onto.

I'll never be untouched by pain. My scars ran deep, and some days the shadows still creep in. But Hunter showed me that scars don't make us unlovable. That love isn't about being perfect, it's about showing up, even when things are messy. In loving Hunter, I've learned to be gentle with myself, to remember it's okay not to have it all figured out. That kindness, even to myself, is part of healing.

And maybe that's what love really is. Not someone swooping in to fix the cracks, but someone holding your hand while you rebuild yourself. Someone reminding you, day after day, that you don't have to carry it all alone.

Hunter didn't just love me. He helped me remember how to love myself again. And that is how he saved me.

Epilogue

C*amille*

A Year And A Half Later

That's how long it had been since Hunter found his way back to us and chose to stay. Not perfectly, not without struggle, but he stayed. Therapy became part of his rhythm, as natural as brushing his teeth or heading off to work. He moved through our days with an ease that I'd never dared to hope for, softer with himself, more present with the kids and me, more than I ever imagined possible.

The kids adored him. Zeke bragged to his friends that he had "the coolest almost-dad." The twins clung to his legs when he came home, their curls bouncing as they squealed "Daddy!" as if the word had always belonged to him.

And me? I finally stopped waiting for the other shoe to drop. So when he told me he had a surprise and blindfolded me in the truck, I didn't panic. I laughed nervously, sure he was dragging me to some ridiculous adventure.

When we stopped, he helped me out, his hand warm on

372

the small of my back. "Okay," he whispered against my ear. "Open your eyes."

The blindfold slipped away, and I went still, breath caught. For a heartbeat, my mind flickered back to other surprises. Like the weekend he swept me away, only for us to end up stranded on the side of the road, laughter and frustration tangled together. My stomach tightened, anticipation and nerves twisting together in the quiet before me.

When I finally opened my eyes, a cozy white house waited in front of me. A clean porch wrapped in fairy lights and white siding with clean lines that gave the house a fresh, timeless charm. There were bright flowers in the flower beds, adding a pop of warmth against the black mulch. And off to the side, a swing set had already claimed its place in the yard.

My heart lodged in my throat. "Hunter..."

The front door opened, and Zeke bolted out with the twins trailing behind. "Surprise, Mommy!" he shouted, his grin so wide it nearly split his face.

The twins clapped, squealing. "House! House!" I turned back to Hunter, my vision blurring with tears. He pulled a small box from his pocket and sank to one knee, blue eyes locked on mine.

"Camille," he said, his voice rough but unwavering. "This isn't just a house. It's *our* home. A place for you, and me, and the kids, for us. I don't just want to love you. I want to build a life with you. Forever."

My hand pressed to my mouth, tears spilling hot and fast. For a moment, I could only stare. The man I once thought would leave, the man who almost did, the man who fought his way back, kneeling in front of me, offering the life I never let myself believe I could have. "I love you more than anything. I can't promise I'll always get it right, but I promise I'll always try my best."

He paused, taking a deep, shaky breath. "Marry me, Beautiful?"

"Yes," I choked out, my voice breaking. "Yes, Hunter."

The kids cheered, louder than before, as he slipped the ring onto my shaking hand. He stood and kissed me. Laughter and tears tangled between us, while small arms wrapped around our legs, pulling us into a hug that was chaotic and perfect all at once.

The kids wiggled out of our hug before I'd even caught my breath. Zeke darted straight through the front door, shouting, "This is my room! This is my room!" Chloe and Avery chased after him, squealing with each echo their tiny feet made against the hardwood floors.

Hunter grinned, slipping his arm around my waist. "Want to see what they're screaming about?" As he pulled me along after them.

Inside, the house carried the faint scent of fresh paint and pine. Sunlight spilled through wide windows, pooling across floors that seemed to shine just for us. My throat tightened. This wasn't just walls and a roof; it was so much more.

Zeke discovered a room with a rocket-ship comforter on the bed and let out a whoop of victory.

"You already decorated?" I asked, stunned.

Hunter scratched the back of his neck, sheepishly. "Just a start. I wanted them to feel like it was theirs from the moment they walked in." He pointed to a blue rocket lamp in Zeke's room that lit up the corner, and to the twins' room, where he'd put up a mural of a magical forest with friendly animals to keep them company at night.

Then he walked to a cozy little room off the living room. A tall bookshelf lined one wall, crammed with books, framed pictures of the kids, Hunter, and me—our family in snapshots. A small potted plant sat in the corner by the window, sunlight catching the leaves. In the center, a sturdy oak desk waited, already set with a new lamp, a stack of notebooks, and my favorite mug.

"So you've got a space to work now," Hunter said from the doorway, nodding toward the desk. "Figured you could study without having to move your books off the dinner table every night."

My throat tightened as I turned to him, emotion catching somewhere between gratitude and disbelief. It wasn't just a room. It was a piece of calm he'd built just for me.

We walked through the other rooms before turning back to the living room. And there hanging in the hall was the shadow box I put together for him so long ago, right where his eyes would land every time he walked to our room. The medals gleamed softly in the lamplight, the patch looked proud instead of forgotten, and the photo caught me the same way it had the first time. Rows of faces, some living, some not, all part of him.

I turned to him, my chest tightening. He was leaning against the door frame, arms crossed, watching me notice. No words, no explanation, just that doting look. Something cracked in me. Not sadness, not even pride. Something deeper.

"You hung it up," I whispered, almost to myself.

"Yeah," he said, voice low. His hand brushed over his beard, casual, like it wasn't a big deal. But his eyes told the truth, it was. "Figured it's time."

I crossed the space to him, laying my palm against his chest, feeling the echoing beat of his heart beneath. "I'm proud of you."

For a long time, he just looked at me. Then his arms slid around my waist, pulling me close until my forehead rested against his. His voice was quiet, but certain. "Me too."

Our last stop was the kitchen. It was spacious, with fresh marble counters; I could actually imagine spreading textbooks and meal prep across without bumping elbows. A bouquet of flowers sat on the island, a handwritten note propped against the vase: *Welcome home.*

My hands shook as I touched it. "Hunter…"

He stepped behind me, wrapping his arms around my shoulders, his chin brushing my hair. "I don't want this to be just my place or your place. I want this to be ours: the kids', yours, mine. A true home. No more temporary. No more waiting for the rug to be pulled out."

I turned in his arms, tears slipping free, and kissed him again. This kiss was softer, steadier, gratitude woven through every breath.

From the living room, Zeke yelled, "Mom! This TV is so big!" followed by twin laughter. We both burst out laughing, the kind of laughter that cracked open years of holding on too tight.

And in that moment, surrounded by squeals and scattered toys, I knew this was more than a proposal. For the first time in my life, I wasn't afraid of being left behind. This was the beginning of forever.

♡♡♡

Exactly a year after Hunter proposed in front of our first home, we stood in the middle of a small outdoor venue, just down the street from the mini golf place where our story had first begun.

No big guest list, no grand decorations, just us, a handful of friends and family, Dani ran around like the best maid of honor, making sure everything was perfect, and our three little whirlwinds stole the spotlight the entire time. Hunter's parents came too. Over the last two years, I've gotten to know them more. Sometimes they came to visit, and at other times we took the kids to New York and got to see the world he'd grown up in. His mom eagerly documented every moment, her presence adding warmth and familiarity to the day.

The twins were supposed to walk down the grassy aisle tossing flower petals, the quintessential flower girl duo. But, instead, they dumped the basket on the ground at the very beginning and spent the rest of the walk chasing each other, curls bouncing, dresses grass-stained before we even said, "I do."

Zeke, the proud ring bearer, took his job *very* seriously. So seriously, in fact, that he marched straight past Hunter and tried to hand the box to the officiant. The whole crowd laughed, and my mom had to gently redirect him back.

For a moment, I thought the chaos might ruin it. But then I caught Hunter's eyes. Those deep grey blue eyes, shining with an affection I'd never seen him let show in front of anyone. He slipped his hands into mine, squeezing gently, and the world shrank down to just us. "I didn't think I'd ever deserve this," he whispered, so low I barely caught it.

"You do," I whispered back, voice trembling. "You always did."

The words of the ceremony blurred, no matter how hard I tried to hold onto them. What stayed with me was Hunter's vow: raw, honest, promising not perfection but presence. And my own, promising not just to love him, but to keep choosing him, even on the hard days.

When the officiant finally said we could kiss, the kids squealed louder than the handful of friends and family clapping. Zeke fist-pumped like he'd won a championship game, and the twins tried to climb Hunter's legs mid-kiss.

Afterward, we danced around tables spread out beneath the trees, kids running wild while we cut into a cake that leaned a little to the left, Dani's doing, after she left it in her car too long. Hunter fed me a bite, I smeared frosting into his beard, and the kids screamed with laughter until my cheeks ached from smiling.

It wasn't the wedding little girl's dream about. It was better. Because it was real. Because it was us.

And then, our song played.

"I met you in the dark; you lit me up. You made me feel as though I was enough."

The first chords of Say You Won't Let Go by James Arthur spilled from a tiny speaker, and my heart caught. I'd sent him that song all that time ago, a few days after the night he showed up at my work and came clean.

I had been at my most vulnerable, and he'd offered reassurance I didn't even know I needed. That song had become ours. A reminder that we'd fight for each other and never let go. Because it reminded me of the exact moment I stopped running and started letting myself hope.

He pulled me up, right there on the grass, laughter still buzzing around us. His hand at my waist, his other lifting mine, clumsy but firm all the same. We swayed beneath the trees, kids chasing each other in circles around our legs, family snapping pictures, cake plates abandoned on the blankets. His forehead rested against mine, his lips brushing my temple as he whispered, "I love you."

I once thought love meant survival, holding it all together, never leaning, never letting anyone close enough to leave. But with Hunter, I learned differently. Love was showing up. Love was letting myself laugh again, play again, dance barefoot on the grass with the man who saved me from my own walls.

Looking at him with our kids clinging to his legs and our family cheering us on, I knew: he wasn't just part of my story.

He was home.

Hunter

A year after the wedding, after vows interrupted by giggling twins, after being convinced by Camille to dance to more songs than we agreed upon, after Zeke proudly declared himself "the best ring man in history", our family grew again.

Hendrix.

Our baby boy.

The pregnancy wasn't easy on her, and it wasn't easy on me either. Though I'd never admit that out loud at the time. Nights blurred together, broken by worry and the sound of her shifting restlessly in bed. Some nights I sat by the window, staring out into the quiet dark while she finally dozed, my chest tight with thoughts I couldn't shake. What if her body couldn't carry him to full term? What if something went wrong, and I couldn't do a damn thing to stop it? I'd been trained to handle chaos, to keep my composure when the world fell apart. But watching her carry our son—this was a different kind of battlefield. One I couldn't control.

I'll never forget one morning at the doctor's office. The room smelled too sharp, antiseptic, and bleach, all clinical brightness. She lay on the crinkling exam paper, eyes tired but hopeful, while I sat uselessly in one of those plastic chairs. My knees bounced, hands clenched, pretending I wasn't terrified. Time moved wrong in that room. The seconds stretched until my lungs ached with the wait. And then, just when my chest felt like it might cave, she stilled and whispered, "I felt him." A flutter, barely there, but enough to cut through the fear. Relief swept me like a tide, grounding me in the truth: he was fighting to be here, and so were we.

Through the months that followed, I did the only thing I knew to do: just show up. When the morning sickness left her pale, I rubbed her back. When contractions came early and scared us both, I held her hand tighter, telling her she wasn't alone. When she swayed under the weight of exhaustion, I planted myself at her side and refused to move. I didn't have magic words or promises I couldn't keep, but I could give her a presence that was solid and sure.

When Hendrix came screaming into the world after 24 hours of labor and an emergency C-section, I broke. Shoulders shaking, tears hot down my face, I held him close and kissed the light curls on his head. I'd thought I'd held everything in life there was to hold rifles, gear, grief, but nothing compared to the weight of my son in my arms.

"He's perfect," I whispered, my throat raw. And he was.

Perfect and loud and alive, more than I dared to hope for on those nights by the window.

Then Zeke climbed up onto the hospital chair, chest puffed like a little soldier, declaring, "That's my brother." My heart cracked wide open all over again. The twins squealed from their perch at the end of the bed, chanting "Baby! Baby!" like the universe had handed them a new adventure.

I looked at Camille then, her body limp with exhaustion, but her eyes shining, tears slipping free. For years, she'd carried her world alone, shouldering pain and responsibility no one should bear on their own. And now, here we were. Loud, messy, all of us together. Not surviving. Living.

I pressed my lips to Hendrix's head again and looked at the chaos around me.

The grinning kids, the crying baby, the exhausted but radiant woman who'd given me it all. This was it. This was home. Not perfect, not neat. But genuine. Messy and loud and full of love. A place I would fight for, stay for, build for. A place where I finally belonged.

Camille

Life didn't get easier. It just got fuller.

Hendrix's cries filled the nights, the twins' personalities continued to blossom, and Zeke's chatter remained endless. Our home was loud, messy, chaotic. There were days when dishes piled high, homework clashed with diaper changes, and sleep felt like a rumor.

But I never carried it alone.

Hunter was there, steady, present, consistent. Therapy had given him tools, but love gave him purpose. I remember one specific lesson he shared with me from his sessions: the 'grounding technique.' Whenever anxiety crept in, he would focus on his five senses, naming things he could see, touch, hear, smell, and taste. This simple exercise helped anchor him to the moment. Every time he grounded himself through a moment of panic, every time he bent down to meet Hendrix's curious eyes, every time he showed the kids something new. And every time I fell asleep on his chest, his hands tangled in my curls, I saw the proof of what it meant to keep choosing each other.

We weren't perfect, but we were real. And that was more than enough.

One evening, I stood on the back patio watching Hunter with the kids. Zeke was showing him his newest soccer trick, while Avery and Chloe ran around in circles, and Hendrix sat on his shoulder. He caught my eye and smiled, soft and sure, the kind of smile that said *home*.

I thought about the weight we've carried. The love we've found. The second chances, the healing, the nights we thought we'd lost each other. And I knew that whatever came next, whatever chaos, whatever storms, we'd face it together. Because this wasn't just survival anymore.

This was family.

This was love.

This was ours.

About the Author

Salisa K. Garrand is a California girl now soaking up the Florida sunshine. She's a mom of four amazing kids and is married to a Marine Corps veteran, who always keeps her laughing.

By day, she empowers and helps others heal as a Licensed Mental Health Therapist specializing in trauma and maternal mental health, with a passion for researching mental health in BIPOC communities.

Salisa has had her face buried in books since childhood: first obsessing over vampires and werewolves (*Team Jacob, obviously*), and now falling head over heels for romance and fantasy books. Writing a book has been her dream since she was a teen, and *The Weight We Carry* is proof that some dreams are worth holding onto.

When she's not writing or chasing her kids, you can find her sipping iced coffee, daydreaming about fictional love stories, and probably reading "just one more chapter."

You can connect with me on:

🔗 http://www.tiktok.com/@sgarrand_author

Also by Salisa K. Garrand

The Love After All Series

A heartfelt, emotionally rich romance series about healing, found family, and the courage to love again — with playful banter, deep connection, and just the right amount of spice sprinkled in.

In the *Love After All* series, love doesn't arrive neatly packaged. It shows up in the chaos, the laughter, and the quiet moments that make your heart ache in the best way.

Each standalone novel follows characters learning that second chances aren't given; they're built through honesty, vulnerability, and the unexpected joy of finding someone who feels like home.

Want to see more of Dani? Follow to see her story come to life in Book Two of the *Love After All Series*

Available April 28th - Preorder available now.

Turn the page to learn more!

The Love We Found

The Love We Found is a heartfelt, grumpy-sunshine, age-gap, romance about loss, laughter, and the courage to love again.

Daniela "Dani" never meant to fall for anyone.

She's spent her life building walls out of ambition and wit, determined to prove she can stand on her own. But when her best friend's wedding introduces her to a guarded former Marine and his six-year-old daughter, who steals her heart, her carefully planned world begins to unravel.

Logan stopped believing in love the day his wife died.

Older, quieter, and still haunted by the ghosts of what he's lost, he's not looking for anything beyond work and raising his daughter. But when Dani steps in to help while he's away, the lines start to blur. Late-night texts turn into something deeper, and *just helping out* starts to feel like home.

But love isn't simple for two people who've both learned how to survive alone.

When fear, distance, and old wounds threaten to pull them apart, they'll have to decide: keep hiding from the past, or finally step into the love they've found together.